Books by Holly Chamberlin

LIVING SINGLE

THE SUMMER OF US

BABYLAND

BACK IN THE GAME

THE FRIENDS WE KEEP

TUSCAN HOLIDAY

ONE WEEK IN DECEMBER

THE FAMILY BEACH HOUSE

SUMMER FRIENDS

LAST SUMMER

THE SUMMER EVERYTHING CHANGED

THE BEACH QUILT

SUMMER WITH MY SISTERS

SEASHELL SEASON

THE SEASON OF US

HOME FOR THE SUMMER

HOME FOR CHRISTMAS

THE SUMMER NANNY

A WEDDING ON THE BEACH

Published by Kensington Publishing Corporation

Summer with

My Sisters

Holly
Chamberlin

KENSINGTON PUBLISHING CORP.
http://www.kensingtonbooks.com

KENSINGTON BOOKS are published by

Kensington Publishing Corp.
119 West 40th Street
New York, NY 10018

All Kensington Titles, Imprints, and Distributed Lines are available at special quantity discounts for bulk purchases for sales promotions, premiums, fund-raising, and educational or institutional use. Special book excerpts or customized printings can also be created to fit specific needs. For details, write or phone the office of the Kensington special sales manager: Kensington Publishing Corp., 119 West 40th Street, New York, NY 10018, attn: Special Sales Department, Phone: 1-800-221-2647.

Kensington and the K logo Reg. U.S. Pat. & TM Off.

ISBN-13: 978-1-4967-2067-2
ISBN-10: 1-4967-2067-9
First Trade Paperback Printing: July 2015
First Mass Market Printing: June 2019

ISBN-13: 978-0-7582-7539-4 (ebook)
ISBN-10: 0-7582-7539-0 (ebook)

10 9 8 7 6 5 4 3 2 1

Printed in the United States of America

Acknowledgments

Once again I thank John Scognamiglio for his encouragement, intelligence, and good humor. I would also like to acknowledge the amazing work done by the Preble Street community with and on behalf of homeless and hungry teens and adults in Portland, Maine. And cheers to Bunny and Dottie, who were courageous enough to find new love together after loss.

That it will never come again
Is what makes life so sweet.

—Emily Dickinson

Chapter 1

Poppy Higgins hung the last of her tops and blouses in the large chestnut armoire that had once contained her mother's clothes and firmly closed the door of the beautiful old piece of furniture. She wasn't at all sure she belonged in this room, what had once been her parents' master suite, but here she was, stowing away her clothes in the armoire and laying out her makeup and moisturizers in their bathroom.

This was the thing. Poppy had decided that there was probably no way she could pull off a role of authority in the house on Willow Way if she continued to sleep in her girl-hood bedroom, the place where she had mooned over air-brushed boy bands and cried in frustration when her parents wouldn't let her see a movie all of her friends were allowed to see and dreamed childish dreams of a secret benefactor suddenly leaving her billions of dollars to spend in any way she liked. No, if she was going to succeed (or, at least make a stab) at being her sisters' guardian now that both of her parents were gone, she would need all the psychological props she could find, and installing herself in the master suite seemed like as good a prop as any.

Not everyone agreed with her. Sixteen-year-old Daisy wasn't happy about it; then again, she hadn't been happy about anything lately and Poppy really couldn't blame her. Violet had said nothing about the move, but anyone who knew Violet at all knew that she probably had a strong opinion about the matter. Violet was preternaturally mature, almost oddly so. Maybe *mature* wasn't the right word; maybe simply *odd* would do. She was as far from the average thirteen-year-old girl (if such a thing existed) as you could imagine, more interested in esoteric subjects like astrology than in pop culture, often shockingly blunt and straightforward in her speech, and possessed a highly developed and always on-target intuition about people and their motives.

Now, looking at the king-sized bed in which Annabelle and Oliver Higgins had spent so many nights of their married lives, Poppy wondered. Could you invade a person's private space even when they were dead? Was she indeed trespassing or being disrespectful? Maybe, but she was determined to stick it out in the suite, at least for a week or two. After all, she was supposed to be the adult in the house now, the one who acted with firmness and a sense of being in the right. A person who made a considered decision and stuck to it. The thought was terrifying.

Twenty-five-year-old Poppy had been back home—or, what had once been home—in Yorktide since the sudden death of her father in February and the completely shocking discovery, when his old friend and solicitor Frederica Ross, aka Freddie, had read his will to the family, that he had named Poppy legal guardian of her two younger sisters. He had requested she not move them to Boston, where she had been living for the past several years, but that she return to the house on Willow Way so that Daisy and Violet could finish high school and middle school without being wrenched from the community in which they had been a part for all of their lives.

It made sense, of course. Her father had known that Poppy had no deep roots in Boston. She had moved to the city after graduation from college more in the hopes of stumbling across something "interesting" than because she had a definite plan for her future. Still, not long before Annabelle Higgins died of lung cancer three years earlier, she had strongly encouraged her oldest daughter to return to Boston when she, Annabelle, was gone; she had urged her not to give up her quest for a meaningful life, not to feel that she need move back to Maine to be with her father and younger sisters. So Poppy *had* gone back to Boston shortly after her mother's funeral, but three years later she still had not found anything "interesting" to do with her life. Her job as a freelance writer for a few online "cultural" magazines was unfulfilling in the extreme; how often could you write creatively about a new beer-and-bacon joint or a pop-up dance club or discuss whether socks worn with sandals was actually "a thing"? The only reason she kept at it was to pay the bills. Unlike her highly motivated and focused parents, Poppy feared she was sadly directionless and quite possibly lazy.

Well, you could be directionless and lazy anywhere, so why not in Yorktide? Leaving her on-again, currently off-again boyfriend Ian had caused Poppy no regret. Ian could be a lot of fun, but not much more than that. The only thing—the only person—who she would miss—who she did miss—was Allie Swift, the woman who owned the beautiful old mansion in which Poppy rented a spacious and sunny top-floor apartment. Though Allie was forty and had seen an awful lot more of life than Poppy had, they had formed a true friendship and Allie had promised Poppy a place to stay when—if—she returned to Boston when her sisters were finally on their own.

Poppy placed the palm of her hand against the smooth, polished wood of the armoire and fought a fresh wave of sorrow. Soon after Annabelle's passing her clothes had been given to charity; Freddie, the aforementioned Higgins' family lawyer, and her partner, Sheila Simon, had orchestrated that for the sisters. First, though, each girl had chosen one or two of their mother's items as keepsakes. For Poppy, this was the slim gold bangle she wore on her right wrist and a black velvet shawl, fringed with jet beads. She remembered her mother wearing the shawl to formal occasions at Adams College, where she was a professor of American history, and to the ceremonial dinners her husband, Oliver, was compelled to attend, many of them in his honor. "You look like a princess," Poppy remembered telling her mother once. "Thank you," Annabelle had replied. "But remember, it's better to be queen."

Now her father's clothing had to be dealt with, and Poppy had decided she would see to the task herself. She was afraid she had already relied too heavily on Freddie and Sheila, who, as friends first of Oliver's father, Henry, and then of Oliver himself, were the obvious choice of shoulders upon which to lean. Still, she had been back at the Higgins house for almost four months now and had still failed to take the first step in sorting her father's beautifully tailored shirts and his bespoke suits. Oliver Higgins had been a brilliant intellectual on the international stage of political theory and economic practice, but he had also been a bit of a dandy. Alongside his beautiful wife, they had made a stunning couple, the kind of pair that turned heads and effortlessly drew people into the circle of their formidable personalities.

Annabelle Higgins's clothing might have gone to the local charity shop, but her jewelry (except for the bangle

Poppy wore) was locked in a safe in the master bathroom. Along with the pearls Annabelle had inherited from her grandmother, her diamond and platinum wedding set, and a hefty collection of Bakelite pieces from the nineteen thirties and forties, was Oliver Higgins's wedding ring. His watch, a Breitling, had been there, too, until a few days earlier Poppy had decided that she would wear it in much the same spirit she wore her mother's bracelet, as a physical reminder of the two most important people in her life. A local jeweler had removed a few of the links from the watch for a better fit and though Poppy felt a bit conspicuous wearing such an expensive piece, she was glad to have this bit of her father so close.

Poppy turned from the armoire and her eye caught her parents' official wedding portrait next to a spray of dried hydrangea, her mother's favorite flower, on the dresser against the wall opposite the bed. Annabelle and Oliver had been anything but run-of-the-mill types and had eschewed the popular bride and groom styles of the mid-eighties. (Hideous, in Poppy's opinion. Puffy sleeves? Really?) Her mother had worn a tailored white pantsuit; her father, a simple navy suit with a white shirt and no tie. His wildly wavy hair had already started to whiten though he was only in his early thirties at the time. It gave him a look of distinction and elegance.

Poppy looked more closely at the photograph. There really was a striking resemblance between Annabelle and her oldest daughter; everyone had remarked on it. Like her mother, Poppy was tall and slim, and her features were near perfectly symmetrical. Her eyes were as vividly green as Annabelle's and her hair as glossy a chestnut brown. Her complexion, like her mother's, was clear and pale. Daisy, on the other hand, took after Oliver Higgins, although not in the elegance department, as she would be the first to admit. But she had his darker skin tone, his infectious, lopsided smile, and his medium, slightly stocky build. Violet, Poppy thought, was a charming combination of both parents.

What would her own wedding day be like? Poppy wondered now, looking away from the photograph. No father to walk her down the aisle. No mother to help her plan the festivities. Maybe she would elope. It might be unbearably depressing to get through the occasion without her parents. Assuming she ever decided to get married, which meant falling in love with someone and so far, *that* hadn't happened. Sometimes it bothered her that in her twenty-five years no one had ever captured her heart or inspired her devotion. Sure, she had dated and had even been with one guy for about six months before things just fizzled. Maybe the fault was hers. She knew that she wasn't cold or unsentimental. She cried at the drop of a hat and all it took was a chubby-cheeked baby or a fuzzy kitten to cause her to ooh and aah. But for some reason when it came to romance, her heart, her inmost and truest self, just hadn't been brought to life.

How had Annabelle and Oliver done it? she wondered. They had been so deeply in love with one another. How had they found that sort of bliss? Sometimes Poppy wondered if her parents' perfect romantic union had tainted her own romantic career; maybe somehow it had caused her to despair of ever finding her own soul mate. But maybe that was just silly.

Bellisima. That was one of the affectionate names her father had called her mother and his favorite poem was Edgar Allan Poe's "Annabel Lee." In fact, he had had a few lines of the poem inscribed on his wife's headstone.

> *And neither the angels in heaven above*
> *Nor the demons down under the sea,*
> *Can ever dissever my soul from the soul*
> *Of the beautiful Annabel Lee.*

A grand gesture if ever there was one, though the lines had always disturbed Poppy. Maybe it was the word *dissever*. It gave her the creeps, and that was probably what the poet had intended. Doomed love. Love cut short.

Or, love eternal, Poppy thought now as she left the master suite and went downstairs to start dinner. And this was also something new. For the past few years she had been catching meals when she could, hardly ever cooking (boiling water for pasta didn't really count), and rarely spending more than twenty dollars at a time in the grocery store. Now, she was responsible for putting at least two meals on the table each day for three people and that took planning and time and energy. And money. Who knew the basics like milk and butter and eggs cost so much! Luckily, Annabelle and Oliver Higgins had left their children well provided for, with a mortgage fully paid and a portfolio of sound investments.

Things, Poppy thought as she entered the spacious, thoroughly modernized kitchen, could be much worse. She hoped that being back home with her sisters might help assuage some of the guilt she felt for having left them after Mom's death; that would be a very good thing. Though how she was going to form a definite plan for a productive and meaningful life in the future by playing parent to two strong-willed teenage girls was anyone's guess!

Chapter 2

Daisy was lying on her bed, staring at the ceiling on which her mother had pasted glow-in-the-dark stars so many years ago. They had lost some of their phosphorescence with the passing of time and Daisy occasionally thought that she should take them down, but the time never seemed right. She was afraid that once the stars were gone she would miss them too much. Replacing them with new stars wouldn't bring the old ones back. Gone meant gone.

Like her mother was gone. And now, like her father. Nothing stayed the same. The only thing you could count on was change and the unexpected. Like how just the day before Daisy had caught her older sister, Poppy, wearing their father's watch.

"That's Dad's," she had cried. "You have no right to be wearing it."

"Why not?" Poppy had asked, looking down at the large round face of the man's watch on her left wrist.

"Because you weren't here. I was the one who stayed with him after Mom died. I was the one who saw what it did to him. You were the one who left us."

Her sister had blanched. "Mom told me before she died that I should get on with my life when she was gone," Poppy said, her voice trembling with emotion. "I asked her if she wanted me to stay here with you and Dad and Violet and she said no."

Later, Daisy had felt bad about what she had said, but the pain of her father's death due to a sudden and massive heart attack at the age of just sixty was all too fresh and it wouldn't allow her to apologize to her sister. She just couldn't help but see Poppy's moving into their parents' bedroom and her adopting their father's watch as her own as an act of—an act of usurpation. Granted, Dad had appointed Poppy legal guardian over her sisters, but that didn't give her the right to co-opt Oliver Higgins. Daisy, as her father's favorite daughter (she knew this in her heart), was determined to be the keeper of his flame.

It was funny, she thought. If it were Violet who was wearing their father's watch, she wouldn't be half as annoyed, probably not annoyed at all. Toward her quirky younger sister Daisy felt nothing but straightforward and uncomplicated affection. Toward Poppy . . . Well, once they had been very close, but that was a long time ago, before Poppy had gone to college, before she had left them and moved to Boston. By the time she had moved back to Yorktide four months earlier, Daisy felt that Poppy had become almost a total stranger. She wouldn't be surprised if Poppy felt the same way about her. Anyway, nothing was as it should be now, so Daisy supposed she would have to get used to chaos. What she wouldn't give for a boring, routine-filled life that was guaranteed never to change!

She sat up on the edge of her bed, feet dangling. She had such clear and vivid memories of her father sitting just where she was now, singing her to sleep when she was little.

Daisy, Daisy, give me your answer do
I'm half crazy all for the love of you
It won't be a stylish marriage
I can't afford a carriage
But you'll look sweet upon the seat
Of a bicycle built for two

Interesting, Daisy thought now, that she was never good on a bicycle. Never good at any sport, really. Poor coordination compounded by lack of interest. She would rather be reading or doing a crossword puzzle or playing her clarinet with her best friend, Joel, or volunteering at the Pine Hill Residence for the Elderly than getting sweaty running around chasing a ball. Much like her father. It was he who had instilled in her a passion for crosswords and he who more than anyone encouraged her dream of becoming a doctor. Not that her mother hadn't been supportive, but it was Oliver Higgins who had given her a copy of the *Physicians' Desk Reference,* and a copy of a work by the ancient Greek physician and philosopher Galen titled *On the Diagnosis and Cure of the Soul's Passion,* a very early attempt at psychotherapy. For Daisy's birthday in April—two months after Oliver's death—Freddie had passed on the present he had purchased for his middle daughter some time earlier, a book of high quality reproductions of Leonardo da Vinci's anatomical drawings. The Galen and the Leonardo were two of Daisy's most valued possessions. Other sixteen-year-old girls—most of them, maybe—might be into taking endless selfies and following their favorite pop stars and models on Instagram, but not Daisy. It was with some pride that she considered herself a nerd.

Daisy turned to look at the sampler that hung over her dresser, next to a poster of the cast of *Game of Thrones.* (In

Daisy's opinion, the show was beyond awesome.) Ages ago her mother had painstakingly embroidered lines from William Wordsworth's poem entitled "To the Daisy." (Daisy couldn't imagine ever having the patience to make all those neat tiny stitches. Unless she decided to become a surgeon.)

> *Thou liv'st with less ambitious aim,*
> *Yet hast not gone without thy fame;*
> *Thou art indeed by many a claim*
> *The Poet's darling.*
> . . .
> *He needs but look about, and there*
> *Thou art!—a friend at hand, to scare*
> *His melancholy.*

She had mixed feelings about Mr. Wordsworth's sentiment, at least, in relation to herself. Less ambitious aim? Wasn't wanting to be a doctor a very ambitious aim? As for darling, well, she certainly didn't feel like anyone's darling, not now that her father was gone. And frankly, she didn't understand how anyone, not even a poet, could get so worked up over a silly flower! Well, there *was* her younger sister . . . Violet could get pretty obsessed about flowers and herbs and all the good things they could do for people. And all the bad things, too, Daisy supposed. Poisons and all that. Even more so than their mother, Violet was interested in the legends and lore associated with plants, not only in the care and feeding of the green world. As for Daisy, neither flora nor fauna interested her half as much as did human beings in the here and now.

And in the great beyond? Daisy got up from the bed and began to pace, something she did when she felt frustrated. She just didn't know about the great beyond. She would like to think that her parents were—well, that they were *some-where, somehow,* but she had no real faith that they were anything but gone.

Her eye caught the sampler again as she continued to tramp. Her name didn't really fit her at all, she thought. If her mother had been able to glimpse the sixteen-year-old in the baby she would have been better off calling her second daughter Cabbage or Pine Cone, something plain and prickly. Pineapple? Dangerous on the outside, sweet on the inside. Daisy smiled in spite of herself. And she realized that it was almost time for dinner and that she was seriously hungry. There probably wasn't any pineapple in the kitchen, but there had to be something edible—if Poppy had remembered to go to the grocery store. Most times Poppy acted so . . . so tyrannical! Trying to change the way Oliver and Daisy and Violet had been doing things for the past three years, pretending to know better. But she routinely messed things up, like forgetting to turn on the dishwasher after she loaded it and then blaming Daisy for not turning it on when she realized that it wasn't on and . . .

No, Poppy was no parental figure, that was for sure. And though it was probably unfair to expect her to be one, Daisy wasn't ready to be very sympathetic toward her sister. It wasn't Daisy's fault that Oliver Higgins had died or that he had requested (demanded?) that Poppy come home to the house on Willow Way. No, Daisy thought, coming to a halt and crossing her arms across her chest. None of it was her fault.

But then whose fault was it?

Chapter 3

"What do you think, Grimace?"

The large black and white Maine coon cat Violet had addressed stared unblinking at her from his seat at the exact center of her bed. Not long after Annabelle Higgins's death a neighbor's cat had given birth to a litter of eight and, thinking to raise the spirits of the youngest Higgins sister, the neighbor, a Mrs. Greene, had offered Violet her pick of the kittens. Violet had chosen Grimace; his name had come into her head only moments later.

Grimace was no Grumpy Cat; he had the usual "smile" of the average feline. But the name seemed to fit him. Either that or he had grown to fulfill the promise it suggested of an often ill-tempered animal who cared for only his own comfort, sometimes even at the expense of his devoted human caretaker. Grimace thought nothing of swatting Violet's face to wake her in the morning, or of screaming directly into her ear as she sat at her desk doing her homework because he wanted an after-dinner snack, or of chewing on her toes for no apparent reason at all, and none of this bothered Violet in the least. She loved Grimace. She needed him, especially now.

"Well?" Violet prompted. "What do you think of this scarf with this skirt?"

Grimace finally deigned to reply by getting to his feet, arching his back in an extreme stretch, turning his tail to her, and resettling in a heap.

"I thought so," Violet said to the back of her cat's head. She draped the silk paisley scarf over her desk chair and hung the long striped skirt in the closet.

Violet Higgins loved her home and she especially loved her room, which she thought of as a sort of grotto. She had painted the walls (with help from her father) sea-glass green, and the wide baseboards ocean blue. The ceiling was a slightly lighter blue than the baseboards and across it in billowy drapes she (again, with her father's help) had hung gauzy strips of pale pink and coral material. The room felt cool and soft and peaceful. A haven when the startling fact of her being an orphan flared into consciousness, which it might do at any time.

In addition to the bed, desk and chair, and comfortably saggy armchair, the room contained an old wooden dresser her mother had painted white. (Grimace was systematically removing the paint with his claws.) On top of the dresser sat a small bowl Violet had made at pottery camp the previous summer; in the bowl was a heap of quartz crystals. Beside the bowl lived a chunk of raw amethyst and one of rose quartz. Hanging from the bed's four posts were strings of beads—sponge coral, labradorite, aventurine, and carnelian. Because she was a Pisces, Violet kept a large, rough-cut aquamarine, one of the stones closely associated with the sun sign, on the small table beside her bed. It gave her a great sense of peace, as did the painting of a bunch of violets that hung over the dresser. Her mother had commissioned the painting from a local artist for her daughter's first birthday.

Over the years Annabelle had collected other images of violets—at flea markets and yard sales, at galleries and shops—and they had all found a special place in Violet's room, as had her mother's favorite gardening hat, which Violet had chosen to keep when most of Annabelle's clothing had gone to the charity shop. The floppy straw sun hat was perched on top of the bookcase her father had built for her. (He had built one for Poppy and Daisy, too.) Next to the hat Violet had stacked several different decks of tarot cards, but not the famous Rider-Waite deck, which she found extremely scary and negative. In the bookcase there was a copy of the *I Ching* her parents had given her for her eleventh birthday, and a copy of a beginner's guide to the Kabbalah. Next to that was a copy of the Egyptian *Book of the Dead,* her first online purchase made shortly after Christmas with a gift card the family's friends Freddie and Sheila had given her. Over the past two years Violet had collected no fewer than six books on astrology and its practical applications. In the back of each book she kept notes about the people close to her and how they did or did not or only sometimes "fit" the descriptions of their sun and moon signs. (She was saving up her money to have her own chart done someday by a real professional.)

On the shelf below these books were arranged some of her all-time favorite works of fiction: the trilogy by Philip Pullman called *His Dark Materials,* all of the Harry Potter titles, her mother's childhood copy of *The Secret Garden,* a copy of the original, uncensored fairytales by the brothers Grimm, and a collection of folktales from the British Isles. On the wall over her bed Violet had hung a Native American dream catcher. Next to it was a Celtic-style cross, made of iron. Her father had found it for her on a business trip to Dublin.

There was no mirror in Violet's bedroom. She didn't need to be reminded of her image; she knew it well enough. Though Violet put very little stock in appearance as a matter of achievement (a person's aura was far more interesting and telling than how tall or short he was), she knew from the way so many people stared at her that she stood out in some way she couldn't yet define. She was tall, like Poppy, and graceful in her movements. Unlike both of her older sisters she wore her hair very short, in a pixie cut. She had heard her features described as elfin. Her eyes were very blue and very large, much like her father's had been. She liked to wear all sorts of natural stones, choosing them according to her mood. This day she wore a string of lapis lazuli beads around her neck and a chunky turquoise and silver ring on the middle finger of her right hand. She mostly dressed in stuff she found in local thrift and antique shops. She did not wear jeans or sneakers.

Violet peered out of her bedroom window and noted by the quality of the light that it was almost six thirty and that meant dinnertime. Good. She was hungry. She hoped that Poppy wasn't attempting to cook something difficult; it would only make her frustrated. Poppy wasn't very good in the kitchen, but Violet sincerely appreciated her sister's efforts.

Grimace grumbled and Violet went over to the bed to stroke his muscular back. "Lay her i' the earth," she whispered as the cat's grumble became a loud purr. "And from her fair and unpolluted flesh, may violets spring!"

That was from Shakespeare's *Hamlet*. Violet had been leafing through Daisy's copy of the play one evening when she came across those lines and she had immediately thought of her mother. The cancer that had taken a year to kill Annabelle had not been kind; it had left her body ravaged. But her spirit! Her spirit had remained fair and unpolluted until—and beyond—the very end. It was awfully ironic that Annabelle Higgins should die of lung cancer when she had never smoked a cigarette in her life. It only proved what Violet had already sensed, that life and death and whatever came after it were great mysteries, to be treated with respect and also with awe.

Her parents had believed that, too. While neither had been religious, meaning they hadn't professed a particular faith, they had believed in the *possibility* of the unknown, of a spirit world of unfathomable beauty and meaning. Violet remembered her father saying, "Why should there be a life after death as we know it? And why shouldn't there be?" Violet believed—no, she *knew*—that there was more to life than what anyone could witness with the five senses. She felt this knowledge as surely as she felt hot under the summer sun and cold in the winter nights.

She thought now of the words inscribed on her father's headstone in the Yorktide Memorial Cemetery. "I go to seek a Great Perhaps." —François Rabelais. (Violet didn't really know much about him.) For her own headstone Violet thought she would rewrite the quote to be: "I go to seek a Great Certainty." Not that she was planning on dying any time soon. Not that she thought a lot about death. Only the usual amount. Only what could be expected of a sensitive thirteen-year-old girl who had lost both parents in the space of three years. And Violet knew that she was sensitive, and also, probably, what some people called "a sensitive." An old soul. It was just who she was.

There came a knock on the door and Grimace, who in

spite of his contented purring had been staring at it intently for some minutes, as if anticipating some approaching activity, let out a low growl.

"Violet?"

Violet opened the door to her oldest sister.

"Dinner's ready," Poppy said.

Daisy came out of her room across the hall. "Finally! What are we having?" she asked.

"Chicken."

"That doesn't tell us much," Daisy pointed out. "What kind of chicken?"

"Well, a dead one, of course," Violet said.

Her sisters looked at her. Daisy was grinning. Poppy looked appalled.

"What?" Violet asked. And then she, accompanied by Grimace, ran ahead of them down the stairs to the kitchen.

Chapter 4

Evie Jones wondered what people saw when they looked at her. She had never been so self-conscious as she had been these last few weeks. She was about five feet five inches, which she guessed was about medium height. Her eyes were brown fringed by long, thick lashes. Her hair had once been blond, but by the time she turned twelve it had darkened to a sort of honey tone. So far, so normal. But her hair was badly in need of a trim; the ends were all split and dry. She hadn't been able to take a proper shower since passing through that campground three days back and she was highly conscious of the stain on the left sleeve of her pink hoodie. She had lost weight in the past weeks and had had to turn down the waist of her jeans so they would stay on her hips. She could feel a pimple coming out on her chin; she hadn't remembered to bring any astringent with her when she left. There had been too many other more important things to remember.

But maybe people didn't even really *see* people like her—a fairly nondescript, slightly messy teenager. Maybe she was truly anonymous to the world. But she didn't think she was that lucky and so she prayed that her appearance wouldn't prevent her from being hired somewhere, anywhere. She would wait tables. She would clean toilets. She would walk dogs though dogs frightened her a little. She would babysit, if anyone were crazy enough to hire someone like her—no references, no friends, no family—to watch over their child.

Someone carrying a false ID card. She had gotten it from a senior at the last school she had attended. It had cost her so much money, almost all she had saved from her allowance (which had been severely reduced months before), but she had decided it was necessary. Her heart had been racing madly while she waited behind the 7-Eleven for Jason Ames to find her when he had finished his work. His sly grin when he finally handed the card to her had made her stomach heave.

Now Evie touched the pocket of her backpack where the card was stowed. She hoped it looked real. This was the first time she would have to use it (maybe) since leaving her aunt and uncle's house in Vermont in the dead of night a few weeks earlier. She had no fear that when she was reported missing Jason Ames had told anyone that he had made her a false ID; it would only get him in trouble. Plus, she hadn't said a word to Jason about her plans. For all he knew she wanted the ID—complete with a phony name—so that she could get into that eighteen-and-over dance club in town.

Evie stopped before a sign set back from the sidewalk, at the base of which was a ring of petunia plants. *Yorktide, Maine. Incorporated 1678.* She had determined on Yorktide as a destination because once, many years ago, she and her parents had visited for a three-day weekend. They had gone to the beach, eaten ice cream cones (her mother loved salted caramel ice cream), browsed in the craft shops after a dinner of lobster rolls and French fries and coleslaw, visited the

Yorktide Historical Society's museum, and had even gone into Ogunquit to see a musical at the playhouse, though Evie couldn't remember what it was. Something about pirates? She did remember her mother being so very happy, looking so lovely in her colorful sundresses and chunky turquoise jewelry, her eyes shining with pleasure. Her father, too, she remembered as happy and handsome, but she tried to block him out of the pictures in her head. She thought that if she tried hard enough she might be able to rewrite her past, cast it with only good people like her mother. *Just Mom and me . . .*

It might have been smarter to go somewhere she had never been, somewhere no one would ever think to look for her, but the whole idea of running away was so startlingly new and odd and yet frighteningly appealing that Evie's mind had felt all addled and revved up. She had no previous experience with any sort of deception, unless lying about the condition of your increasingly dirty home and your increasingly sick father counted as deception and not necessary self-protection. . . .

Evie walked on along the main street until she saw a notice in the window of a place called The Clamshell; there was an opening for a counter person to take orders and work the cash register. It didn't sound that hard and maybe she would be allowed some food as part of the job. She pushed open the glass door to the little restaurant and went inside.

The place was empty but for a young woman sweeping the floor and a gray-haired man behind the counter, tapping at a handheld calculator. He looked up from his work and smiled. "Sorry, we're not open for lunch yet," he said.

"Oh, no, I . . ." Evie gestured behind her. "I saw the notice in the window. For a job."

The man put down the calculator and came around the

counter. "Do you have any experience working in a restaurant?" he asked. "I'm Billy Woolrich, the owner."

Evie swallowed hard. "No," she admitted. "But I'm a good worker and I learn fast. And I . . . I really need a job."

"Badly enough to take cash?" he asked after a moment.

Evie nodded. Cash would be perfect. . . . It hadn't occurred to her before this moment that she had no way to cash a check. She wondered what else she had failed to realize.

"Well," Mr. Woolrich said then, "maybe I'm just a foolish old man, but you have a nice face. All right, I'll give you a chance."

Relief flooded Evie and she struggled not to burst into tears. "Oh, thank you!" she said after a moment. "Thank you very much."

Mr. Woolrich retrieved a clipboard, on which was clamped a piece of paper and a pen, from the order counter. "Here," he said, handing it to her. "Just fill out this form and I'll give you a schedule."

Name. Evie Jones. Age. Eighteen. Phone number. She wrote it down, though the battery of her cell phone was almost dead and she had forgotten to take its charger with her the night she had run away. Address.

There, Evie stopped cold.

"All done?" Mr. Woolrich asked.

"Um, almost. I . . . I haven't found a place to live yet. I just got in to town today and . . ." *Oh, please don't let him throw me out!*

Mr. Woolrich frowned. "Oh."

"Maybe you could recommend . . ." Evie couldn't go on. She knew that it was all over before it had begun, a chance at a fresh start.

And then Mr. Woolrich smiled. "As a matter of fact," he said, "I know a guy who needs a house sitter for the summer.

The one he had lined up bailed on him at the last minute. And, he owes me a favor." He reached over the counter and retrieved a pad of paper and a pen. "Here," he said, scribbling on the pad. "That's his name and address. I'll call and tell him you're on your way over. Take a left at the corner of Center Street, and then a right at Nubble Lane. His place is the last one on the road. Can't miss it. It's enormous and it's got a big tower, like a lighthouse almost."

"Thank you so much, Mr. Woolrich," Evie said, taking the piece of paper with a trembling hand. "You won't regret hiring me, I promise."

"Call me Billy, please. And we'll see you at eight sharp tomorrow morning."

"One more thing. Does the man have a last name?" Evie thought she might sound rude calling him by his first name when she had never met him.

Billy Woolrich laughed. "Nope. Just Nico."

Evie practically ran out of the shop, so eager was she to get to this Nico person's house, so eager to learn if she would have a roof over her head that night. So eager and yet so frightened of his answer to her request. If this man did let her stay she would be able to take a shower and if he had a pair of really sharp scissors somewhere in the kitchen she might be able to trim her hair though she had never done it before. In the old days her mother had cut it for her; she remembered so distinctly the sound of the scissors slicing through the hair with a clean, satisfying crunch. She remembered the pair of scissors itself; the handles were inlaid with mother-of-pearl. It had belonged to her grandmother. Evie wondered where the scissors were now. She didn't remember seeing them after her mother died. And now, with the house gone . . .

This had to be it. The last house on the road. And Mr. Woolrich was right. Billy, rather. It was huge and the tower did sort of make the house look like a lighthouse. Evie took a deep breath and rang the doorbell. Maybe, just maybe, everything would work out.

Chapter 5

Poppy was sitting on a stool at the kitchen island with her laptop opened in front of her. She was trying to focus on the checking account statement Freddie had asked her to review, but her mind kept slipping off to scattered memories of the final weeks of her mother's illness. Time didn't seem to lessen the random emergence of these memories. In fact, since her father's passing, thoughts of her mother's last days had been present almost constantly.

It probably didn't help that she was wearing Annabelle's bracelet. Sometimes it seemed to act as too strong a reminder of all that Poppy had lost. Her best friend. That was no understatement. Poppy had always been terribly close to her mother; after all, she had had Annabelle Higgins all to herself for nine years before Daisy came along. If Poppy believed such a thing was possible—and she didn't—she would say that she was her mother's favorite. Daisy clearly was the apple of Oliver's eye (they were so much alike) and Violet . . . Well, Violet was such a mystery! Poppy had only a vague idea of the nature of her little sister's emotional attachments. While she was very affectionate with her cat, she seemed to need no physical contact with humans at all, not even the occasional hug. But had she always been that way? Admittedly, Poppy's memories of Violet as a small child were dim.

Even before Annabelle had taken ill, Poppy had talked to her mom on the phone or via Skype at least twice a week and sometimes more. When she became sick those calls became even more important to Poppy, though it had deeply saddened her to watch her once beautiful mother grow so haggard and so thin, to see her once smooth and glowing skin become dull and blotchy, her gorgeous thick hair become sparse and lank. Watching her mother on the computer screen in those final weeks was oddly like looking into her own possible future. Who was to say that she, too, wouldn't get sick and die while only in her fifties, at the height of her career, leaving behind three young children and an adoring husband?

With a sigh Poppy closed her laptop. When these moods came upon her—nostalgia tinged with melancholy and regret—there was no use in pretending usefulness. Freddie and the checking account could wait.

At the end, when Annabelle had been moved to the hospice, she had been too weak to hold the phone (and she no longer wanted to bother with a computer). Oliver had held his cell phone to his wife's ear so she could hear their oldest daughter's voice. . . .

Poppy got up from the stool and stalked over to the sink, where she poured a glass of cold water. When it was empty she held the glass to her forehead and took a few deep breaths. This was one of the bad things about remembering. It could make you feel physically unwell. Poppy put the glass into the dishwasher—a bit of tidying neither of her sisters seemed to have adopted—and looked across the room at the fridge. Like the fridges in most homes it was decorated with colorful magnets holding photos in place. The photo on the top right . . . It had been taken at the party the history department at Adams College had held on the publication of Annabelle's book. Violet, only a baby, had been left home with a sitter, but Poppy and Daisy had been there along, of course, with Oliver. In the picture Annabelle was holding a copy of the book in one hand and a glass of champagne in the other. She was laughing. Such a happy moment.

Poppy looked away from the fridge. She kept a copy of her mother's best-selling book by the bed—*They Also Serve: A History of the Role of American Women in Wartime, Volume One: From the Revolutionary War to WWI*. All three of the Higgins sisters had read the book; Annabelle's writing style was far more accessible to a general audience than Oliver's. Then again, Oliver hadn't written for the masses (that was his term) but for an elite group of intellectuals. His wife's book had received attention throughout the popular media; even *People* magazine had reviewed and recommended it.

Annabelle had been working on the second volume when she died. Her notes—some handwritten in lined spiral notebooks, others stored in computer files—were treasured items in the Higgins house. Poppy knew that she wasn't the one to complete her mother's work, but she thought that someday she might seek out a young scholar to finish the second volume. In that way, her mother's voice would live on.

Still, it was just too bad that she didn't have an academic bone in her body. As graduation from Adams College loomed, Poppy had briefly contemplated continuing her formal education, but there was no area of study that fascinated her enough to make her want to spend her life writing and reading, studying and lecturing. In fact, the decision to move to Boston had been born out of mild desperation—what do I do with my life now? When the far-reaching future seemed too vast to imagine, deal with the immediate future. So Poppy had.

The transition had been facilitated by the fact that her parents had plenty of friends and colleagues in the Boston area. Annabelle's former college roommate, Louise, lived in Lexington. Louise's best friend, a woman named Barbara, owned and ran a PR agency whose clients were mostly on-line publications. A word from Louise had gotten Poppy an interview with Barbara, and ultimately, her first freelance assignment. One of Oliver's brightest former students was at Harvard studying law. He kept in regular touch with his favorite professor and when Oliver told him that his daughter needed a place to live in Boston, he put Poppy in touch with Allie Swift, a family acquaintance, who owned a beautiful old mansion on Marlborough Street in the Back Bay. Poppy took a lease on the top floor apartment; Allie occupied the rest of the house.

It had all been so easy and her new job and new apartment and the new people she was meeting had kept her busy enough for the moment. There was Ian Maxwell, for one, a fellow writer for what used to be called alternative media, back in the old days. Ian knew lots of people who played in popular local bands and had been able to get Poppy into sold-out gigs and wild after-parties at the current hotspots. Poppy didn't do drugs, didn't smoke, and she drank sparingly, but she did love a good party.

And then there had been Ian's friend Nate, who worked at a hip, high-end clothing shop on Newbury Street and was generous about sharing his discounts with her. Nate said he liked to see her wearing the crop tops and the miniskirts and the skinny, coated jeans. He said she looked like a model. (He wasn't the first person to have told her that.) Sometimes he took pictures of her wearing the clothing and posted them on his Instagram account. Ian had assured her there was nothing illegal about Nate's getting her the clothes on the cheap. But one afternoon she visited the store wearing pieces from its latest collection and the owner had given her a very suspicious and searching look. After that, Poppy began to feel uncomfortable about the arrangement and put an end to it. Not long after, Nate had been fired and Ian lost track of him.

It had been a carefree and in some ways a hedonistic few years with little responsibility other than to herself. Certainly handling her personal finances had been far less complicated than trying to handle the finances of the Higgins estate! Thank God for Freddie. *Right*, Poppy thought, glancing at the laptop. *The checking account. It couldn't be put off forever*.

But it could wait a few more minutes. What, Poppy wondered, if she *hadn't* moved to Boston after graduation? What if she had stayed in Yorktide at least for a year or two? She might have made her mother's last months easier. She might have been at her mother's bedside in the hospice when she passed, instead of stuck in northbound traffic on Route 1 during Annabelle's final moments, desperately pleading with a God she wasn't sure she believed in to keep her mother alive for a few more hours. She might have made a difference for her father, too. If she had been home to help him cope after Annabelle's death, he might not have had a heart attack at all.

Poppy sighed. "What-ifs" were pointless, but sometimes they were unavoidable. Everyone knew that children often felt responsible for their parents' divorce, no matter the assurances that they were not to blame. But Poppy wondered if it was normal for a child, even as in her own case, an adult child, to feel responsible for a parent's death. Certainly it was normal to feel guilty for bad behavior or missed opportunities or unkind thoughts. . . .

Her cell phone rang and Poppy saw that it was her old friend Julie Fisk, now Mayer. She let the call—the second one from Julie in as many days—go to voice mail. She and Julie had been inseparable through grammar and middle school, and had only begun to grow apart in junior year of high school when Julie started dating Mack Mayer, the man who would become her husband the summer after graduation. The idea of getting married at the age of eighteen and passing on the option of college had been almost incomprehensible to Poppy. She had been invited to the wedding and though it was a genuinely happy occasion for Julie, Mack, and their families, Poppy remembered feeling ever so slightly superior to the proceedings. A whole world was out there waiting to be experienced and here was Julie, giving it all up for marriage to a guy who had been her one and only boyfriend, giving it all up for what promised to be what Poppy saw as an insular sort of life on Mack's family's farm.

Now, seven years later, Julie was eager to catch up with her old friend and Poppy felt bad about those old critical and immature thoughts about Julie's choices. She, Poppy, had gone on to college and then to live in Boston—but what did she have to show for her efforts at experiencing the wider world? A career that was merely a way to pass the time. No steady relationship. A lot of designer clothes she no longer had any place or any desire to wear. No real sense of what she wanted to do with her one and only life. What she did have to show—and it had nothing to do with her own choices—was the legal guardianship of two minors.

One of those minors came into the kitchen now, wearing a string of intensely green peridot beads around her neck and a blue caftan-like garment in a very wrinkly, crinkly cotton.

"What was your major in college?" Violet asked without preamble.

"Media studies," Poppy replied. "It's what used to be called communications. Why?"

"I'm thinking about my future. Was it worth it?"

"What, college? Of course it was. And I don't mean just for the parties."

"I'm not so sure I'll go to college," Violet said. "I'm considering teaching myself. That way I'll be able to concentrate on learning what I want to learn."

Poppy was taken aback. "But you have to go to college, Violet."

"Why?"

"Because you just have to," Poppy said, aware that it wasn't much of an argument. "Mom and Dad would be horrified if you didn't." *There*, she thought. *That's better*.

"I don't think they would be horrified at all," Violet said quite calmly. "I think they would totally support my decision. In fact, I know they would."

"Violet, don't be silly. How can you *know* what they would think? They're—"

Poppy felt a wave of helplessness. The truth was that she couldn't force her sister to do anything. Even though she was responsible for Violet's welfare, she didn't have the moral force that a parent had to compel her sister to do something that was in her best interests.

"They're dead," Violet said flatly. "Anyway, I haven't made a final decision yet. What's for dinner?"

"What?" Poppy looked at the oven as if that appliance held the answer. "Oh. I don't know. I haven't thought about it yet."

"It's almost six o'clock."

"Is it? I'll call out for pizza."

"We need to eat more vegetables."

"I'll make a salad."

Violet opened the fridge. "We have no lettuce or tomatoes. Or cucumbers. There's a tub of olives, but they look kind of dried out."

Poppy gripped what was left of her patience with both proverbial hands. "Then we'll have to go without vegetables tonight, Violet. I'm sorry. I'll go to the store tomorrow."

Violet closed the door of the fridge and turned to her sister. "I'll go with you if you want. We're out of laundry detergent and kitty litter, too, so there'll be a lot to carry."

Poppy let go of the negative emotions that had begun to sprout in her heart. She really did love this slightly startling young girl she hardly knew. "Thanks, Violet," she said. "That would be nice."

Chapter 6

Daisy was wandering around the sunroom in the big old house on Willow Way. Her parents had bought the house back when Annabelle had been awarded the teaching position at Adams College, just before Poppy was born. Oliver's career was already well established and since he could work from anywhere, they had pulled up stakes and made the journey from Massachusetts to Maine.

Built in 1912 by an architect known as a maverick (there was documentation of this in the Higginses' study), the house had been called an architectural mishmash, a hodgepodge of styles, a dwelling of considerable charm, and an utter disaster. Whatever other people—some of them professional critics—chose to call it, everyone in the Higgins family loved its gables and eaves, its mix of stone and brick, its round and oval and square-shaped windows, and that was all that mattered.

Interestingly, the interior of the house was pretty simple, given the impression the exterior made on viewers. On the first floor there was a well-equipped kitchen large enough for an island with seating and a table where the family could eat dinner together. The living room was spacious and featured a massive stone fireplace. The table in the dining room could easily seat twelve people with room enough around the table for servants (if there were such people around) to pass easily behind the chairs. The study was the smallest room on the first floor, not counting a bathroom with a shower but no tub for bathing. Upstairs there were five bedrooms: the master bedroom, one each for the three sisters, and a guest room. A bathroom in the hall featured a whirlpool tub (Daisy had been very fond of that as a little girl). The bathroom attached to the master bedroom had a sort of antechamber large enough for a chaise, a tall cabinet for medicines and toiletries, and a safe in which the family's important papers and jewelry were stored.

Most everyone agreed that the house's best feature by far was the sunroom. The ceiling—soaring almost fifteen feet above the floor—was constructed of large glass panels framed in ironwork and reminiscent of Victorian conservatories. The walls, too, were largely glass, tall, broad panes interspersed by narrow panels of wood. The floor was laid with whitish stone tile the architect had purchased in Italy. Against the largest bit of wood paneled wall there stood a wood-burning stove that came in very handy during those long gray Maine winters. Naturally, plants of all varieties stood on tall stands or hunkered hugely around the room.

At one end of the sunroom sat a rectangular wrought iron table, just large enough for a family of five to enjoy having coffee there together, something the Higgins had done often. There was a bamboo couch with cushions upholstered in a cabbage rose print, and two armchairs, upholstered in a soothing mauve, were drawn up close to the stove. Three rocking chairs were grouped around a stand of ferns.

Against the only wall that was not almost entirely glass there stood a towering bookcase, filled with an assortment of works on art and politics and history. Hardcover copies of the four books Oliver Higgins had written and copies of the magazines and journals in which he had published scholarly articles occupied one entire shelf. And there were volumes upon volumes of crossword puzzle books, as well as stacks of conservation boxes in which Daisy's father had kept crosswords he had collected from better newspapers. Occasionally, Oliver had been asked to set a crossword puzzle himself; the pay was always terrible, but he accepted for the fun of it. Daisy's all-time favorite crossword was one her dad had written when she was in second grade; it was based on the theme of Greek mythology, with all those crazy gods and weird monsters. She had known all about Medusa and Hermes and the Cyclops before any of the other kids in her class had.

On impulse, Daisy opened one of the conservation boxes. Oliver Higgins was always challenging himself, always trying and most often succeeding in beating his last best time. His handwriting, so familiar to Daisy, caused tears to come to her eyes and she put the lid back on the box.

There were some relics of her father's life she was better able to accept without breaking down. For example, she kept the dictionary he had liked best in her room now, as she did her father's famous winter scarf, the one he had worn every year for as long as Daisy could remember. Heavy maroon silk on one side, the softest gray cashmere on the other. It still smelled of his favorite cologne. The scarf now resided in the bottom drawer of her dresser, safe from Poppy, who kept making noises about disposing of Oliver Higgins's clothing. Not that Poppy would clear out his wardrobe without first asking her sisters to choose a keepsake, but Daisy was taking no chances. Whether she would ever actually wear the scarf, well . . .

Though the plants that filled the sunroom had been her

mother's responsibility—for the past three years they had been cared for by Violet—for Daisy, the room had always felt like her father's place exclusively. From the first it had been his favorite room in the house and after her mother's death he had spent more and more time there, even sleeping some nights on the couch. It was there that he listened to his prized recordings of classical music (he particularly favored Mozart) on old vinyl records and worked on his articles and presentations.

It was in the sunroom that he had died.

There's a daisy: I would give you some violets, but they withered all when my father died. . . .

Daisy rubbed at her eyes. Those stupid lines kept popping into her head, try as she might to forget them. Her English class had studied *Hamlet* that spring, reading scenes aloud and then discussing them, and when one of her classmates, playing Ophelia, spoke those words about the character's father, Polonius, Daisy had started to cry. It had been so embarrassing though no one had laughed and her teacher, Mr. Robbins, had helped her to the guidance counselor's office where she spent the rest of the class period recovering. Not entirely recovering. She doubted that would ever happen. The problem was that there were so many reminders of her father—and her mother—in everyday life, not only here in the house but everywhere. She couldn't walk down the dairy aisle in the supermarket without remembering how much her mother loved chocolate chip mint ice cream. She couldn't drive past the miniature golf course in Wells without remembering all the summer evenings she and her father and Violet had gone there for a fiercely competitive game. She couldn't pass a newspaper machine without remembering that her parents had had a subscription to the local paper, the *Portland Press Herald,* the *New York Times,* and the *Wall Street Journal.* (The subscriptions were still active, as if none of the sisters could bear to cancel them, though most days the papers went unread.) And if the reminders would always be present, everywhere you looked, the question became: How did you stop them from making you *feel*? How did you learn to ignore them?

Daisy walked over to a framed photo of her parents that had been taken in Paris; they had spent a few days in the City of Lights for their fifteenth anniversary. Annabelle was wearing a genuine Hermès scarf around her shoulders. Oliver, his arm around his wife's waist, looked dashing in one of his custom blazers. That they were very much devoted to one another no one had ever doubted.

With a sigh, Daisy turned away from the photo. It had occurred to her before now that her father might have died of a broken heart. He had been so in love with his wife; perhaps he simply hadn't been able to go on without her. And because Daisy had been closer to her father than her sisters were—she was sure of that; it was important to her to remember that—a part of her felt rejected and betrayed by his death. She hated feeling that way and she would never admit it to anyone. Her father hadn't *asked* to die. Still, it was hard to feel at peace since he had gone. Instead, she felt constantly . . . agitated. Look at her now, wandering aimlessly. And she knew she was fighting Poppy more than she needed to, and over small things that didn't merit the angry energy.

"We don't refrigerate the butter," Daisy had announced that morning when Poppy was cleaning up after breakfast.

"Since when?" Poppy had asked.

"Since, like, forever. You've been back home for months and you didn't notice?"

Poppy had just shrugged. "Guess not. Well, now we're going to refrigerate the butter."

"Why do you always have to change things?" Daisy had demanded, tears threatening.

"Why do you always have to argue with everything I say?"

"You don't have to stay here, you know. If you hate it so much."

"If I don't stay here, you and Violet would have to go into the foster care system. Is that what you want?"

"Is that a threat?"

Poppy had sighed. "Please, Daisy, stop fighting me. And I don't hate it here. It's just . . . Never mind. Here, look, I'm leaving the butter out."

It had all been ridiculous, but little things meant a lot and establishing and maintaining an environment of constancy mattered to Daisy. It should matter to her older sister, too. It should.

Daisy flopped into one of the rocking chairs. The problem was that she wasn't very good at hiding her feelings. Lately, she had seen Joel, her best friend, looking at her with concern when he thought she was unaware. Poor Joel. She didn't mean to worry him. She was so lucky to have him in her life. Joel was a year ahead of her in school and when he graduated the following June he hoped to go to the University of Maine in Portland to study music. Joel was a gifted clarinet, saxophone, and flute player; interestingly, he was the first and only person in his extended family to have shown any musical talent at all. "I'm a mystery," he joked. "A mystery wrapped in a riddle." Daisy, who wasn't at all bad on the clarinet and otherwise loved being a member of the jazz band, always felt so awed when Joel played a solo that she wondered how she had ever been allowed to play alongside him. And, though this had nothing to do with anything, Joel was seriously good-looking. He was tall but not too tall and his eyes were big and brown with lashes Daisy would have killed to have herself, and his hair was . . . It was fabulous, dark with a natural wave. Add to that the fact that he was super generous to the people he cared for and that made Joel the perfect guy. Unfortunately, Daisy was in love with him. Unfortunately, because Joel was gay.

Which was something else to feel sad about—not his being gay, but his not being interested in her as a girl-friend—when her mood took a nosedive. But what was she supposed to do about feeling sad? You couldn't just will emotions away the way you could sometimes will away thoughts and whoever said that you could was lying. You just had to let feelings run their course and hope that some-day they would tire themselves out entirely.

Daisy's cell phone rang and she dug in the pocket of her jeans to retrieve it. It was Joel.

"I am *so* glad you called," she said before he could say hello.

"Why's that?" Joel asked.

"Because I'm sitting here brooding. Do you want to go do something? I have to get out of this house."

Chapter 7

"Now, this won't hurt a bit. See?"

Carefully, Violet removed a dead leaf from one of the rosebushes with the secateurs her mother had given her right before she died. She was wearing the big floppy sun hat that had belonged to her mother and thick gardening gloves. Annabelle had worn knee pads when toiling in the dirt, but Violet, being young and supple, didn't need them.

Grimace was stretched out at full length in the sun a yard or two away from the rosebushes, managing to look four or five feet long, like a thick, furry, black and white snake. Not that there was such a thing, but Violet liked to imagine there might be. Imagining things was so easy.

Like imagining what it would be like if she were able to perform miracles. What if she had been able to lay her hands on her sick parents and give them back the gift of good health? What if she could learn how to *will* people to be well? Not just the people she loved, like her sisters, but all people.

Violet sat back on her heels and studied the rosebush before her. To become a healer or a wise woman, a white witch, whatever you wanted it call it, Violet thought that you probably didn't need a regular college education (though Poppy seemed to doubt this), but you would need an education in things like vision quests and the power of ritual song and dance and the various sorts of prayer spiritual people had perfected over the centuries. You would need to know the history of herbal remedies and bodywork practices and the healing power of gemstones and how the chakras worked. You would also need to know how the body was put together and for that maybe you did need a formal class in advanced biology or something like that. Violet made a mental note to investigate this.

Whatever sort of study it entailed, Violet was excited about the life that lay before her, working to help people be healthy and happy. She knew there were probably plenty of tricksters out there, but she wasn't one of them. She knew without a doubt that she had what her father used to call "a line to the spiritual world" and she was determined to use it to bring happiness to others. Just because her own life had been pretty sad in the past few years didn't mean that other people's lives should be sad, too. She truly believed this.

"You believe in me, don't you, Grimace?" she asked her feline friend.

Grimace yawned hugely, turning his face into that of a long, furry black and white demon (they might exist!), ears back, eyes slit, teeth bared. "I knew you did," Violet told him.

"Hi!" It was Poppy, coming around the side of the house.

Violet got to her feet and waved. She hardly knew her oldest sister, but she had no problem in accepting Poppy as her legal guardian. She didn't expect Poppy to replace her mother or her father. She didn't think Poppy *wanted* to replace them. Daisy, though, was having a hard time dealing with the fact of Poppy's being back home—let alone of her having moved into their parents' bedroom and wearing their father's watch. It was too bad. Violet didn't like to see the people she loved stressed and unhappy, and not just because it made her stressed and unhappy, too.

"What are you doing?" Poppy asked.

"I'm tending these rosebushes. It can be hard to grow roses here in Maine. It's so cold for so long. Mom found these types that seem to be okay though. See," Violet said, pointing with her secateurs, "that one is an old-fashioned shrub rose. That one next to it is an English rose. It's more delicate than the shrub rose, but it's doing all right so far. We should get flowers in full bloom between mid-June and early July."

"Wow. I guess I never paid much attention to what grows out here and when things bloom. Did Mom teach you everything you know about gardening?" Poppy asked.

"Some of it," Violet said. "But I've been learning a lot on my own."

"And doing a really good job by the looks of it."

Violet smiled. "Thanks."

"Look," Poppy said, "I was thinking. Do you want to have a friend for a sleepover? We could have a fire in the fire pit and make s'mores. Rent a movie. Maybe even make pizza from scratch. I think I could handle that. And if I can't we'll call out."

"No thank you," Violet said quickly. Poppy's offer had surprised her, not that she had ever thought her sister ungenerous. But the idea of having someone over to the house to spend the night with her in her private space had never once occurred to her. In fact, it sounded kind of horrible, though she knew it was a popular thing for girls her age to do.

"Well, you know you can invite your friends here any time, right?"

"Yes," Violet said. "I know that I can. But I don't have any friends."

Poppy laughed. "Violet, you must have a friend or two."

"There's Sheila."

"You really consider Sheila your friend?" Poppy asked, frowning as if the idea truly puzzled her.

"Yes," Violet said. "And she considers me her friend, too." She was sure of it, and just as sure that the idea of a sleepover hadn't appealed to the thirteen-year-old Sheila, either.

"But Sheila's in her late seventies," Poppy said.

"I know."

"How much can you possibly have in common?"

Violet didn't know how to reply. It wasn't so much that she and Sheila shared hobbies and stuff, it was just that . . . It was just that it was easy for them to hang out together.

"Didn't Mom and Dad . . ." Poppy didn't finish her question.

"Didn't they what?"

Poppy shrugged. "I don't know, didn't they encourage you to make friends at school? Or at soccer practice or something?"

"No, why should they have?" *Mom and Dad knew who I was,* Violet added silently. *They let me be me.*

"But aren't you . . . Don't you get lonely?"

Violet considered. "Sometimes I feel a bit lonely, but it passes pretty quickly. Anyway, I'm not lonely for a friend."

"Then what do you feel lonely for?" Poppy asked gently.

For what used to be, Violet thought. "Nothing," she said. "It's nothing to worry about." She looked up at the sky. "It's almost one o'clock. Time for Grimace's lunch."

"Can you really tell the time just by looking at the sky?"

"Pretty much. It's not hard."

Poppy laughed. "For some people, maybe. As for me, I'll stick to my watch. Well, to Dad's watch now."

Violet and Poppy, herded closely by Grimace, walked toward the house. And as they went Violet wondered what she might do for Poppy and for Daisy, in terms of helping them to heal and be happy. Both of her sisters had done so much for her since their mother had died, sometimes sacrificing their own happiness for hers. Like Poppy's coming back to live in Yorktide. And like Daisy's habit of checking in on Violet before she herself went to bed. She would just nudge the door to Violet's room open and peek quickly inside, but Violet had come to count on that small gesture of comfort. She hadn't told Daisy how she felt about her visits; she had a strong feeling that Daisy, who didn't like attention drawn to her, would be embarrassed.

Poppy reached the back door first and held it open for Grimace to race through and for Violet to follow at a more normal pace. "Thanks," Violet said.

"What would you like for lunch? I could make you that tuna salad you like so much." Poppy smiled. "At least, I could try."

Yes, Violet thought. *I owe my sisters so much. At the very least I can spare them any of my sadder thoughts.* "Sure," she said. "That would be awesome."

Chapter 8

Freddie had invited the Higgins girls to an opening reception at the Winslett Gallery in the neighboring town of Ogunquit, where Sheila was showing some of her photographs, specifically black and white portraits of rundown barns, ruined outbuildings, sagging staircases, and dilapidated farmhouses.

"I like that all of the images are of things falling apart," Violet said. She was wearing a filmy white cotton dress that came to her ankles and a sparkly pink druzy pendant around her neck. Daisy thought she looked as if she had stepped out of the pages of a fairy story. Daisy herself was wearing jeans and a slightly too small T-shirt under a plaid blouse. The only remotely fancy thing she had to wear was the navy dress she had worn to her father's funeral, now stuffed in the back of her closet. She had vowed never to wear it again, but for some reason she hadn't been able to throw it away.

"I find beauty in the decrepit or the nearly so," Sheila explained to the girls.

Freddie laughed. "That's why she's with me."

"You weren't always decrepit, darling," Sheila replied. "But I tolerated you until you became interesting."

Violet nodded. "I agree with Sheila. I think newness and perfection are boring. Decay is poignant. That's why fall is my favorite time of the year."

"Beauty is in the eye of the beholder, right?" Daisy noted. "One person's perfection is another person's dilapidation. If that's even a word. I'll have to look it up when I get home."

"Have you always been into photography, Sheila?" Violet asked. "I mean, since way back when you were young?"

"Only since I retired. A late-life, golden years hobby, you might say."

Freddie nodded over Sheila's shoulder. "A hobby that's just netted you some cash. The gallery owner just put a sold sticker underneath one of your sagging edifices."

"Finally, appreciation comes knocking at my door!"

"I wonder who bought it. Can you find out?" Daisy asked.

"Certainly. Though I'm not sure I'll ever know where and how the owner will display it. That's frustrating. What if my beautiful work of art gets stuck on the inside of a bathroom door?"

"At least the owner will see it every day," Violet pointed out.

"Oh, lovely," Freddie said under her breath. "Here comes Georgette Lacey."

Daisy frowned. "Who?"

"The woman who owns that awful estate development on Baybridge Island," Sheila explained. "I'm sure you've heard of her. Your parents certainly knew all about her." Sheila lowered her voice to a whisper. "They couldn't stand her."

"My dears!" Georgette Lacey was extremely thin with a head of light blond hair so uniformly cut and colored Daisy thought it might be a wig. That, or a snap-on plastic hair helmet. She had definitely had plastic surgery; the skin on her face was so taut and strained it looked painful. She was wearing a bizarre pajama-like outfit in a wildly colored paisley print and a necklace of wooden beads that was so big and chunky Daisy was sure it would cause her to fall on her face before the night was over.

"I can hardly believe it's you!" the woman cried, crossing her hands against her chest and addressing the ceiling rather than Daisy and her party. "The poor orphaned children, or two of them at least. I was away all winter in Florida. I only just got back two weeks ago and I heard the bad news about Oliver. I've been meaning to send a card, but oh, there's been so much to do what with getting settled in and my winter tenants left the place in such a state and I just had to rush down to New York to attend the debut performance of a new opera at the Met and . . ."

"Yes, well, we're sorry for all that," Freddie said, putting her right hand on Daisy's back and her left on Violet's, and not too gently propelling them all away from the chattering woman and her unwanted attentions. "What an idiot," she murmured when they were out of earshot.

Sheila frowned. "Why is it that people so often make another person's tragedy—or happiness, for that matter—all about them?"

"I totally see why Mom and Dad didn't like her," Daisy said. "She's a caricature."

"She's scary," Violet said. "Her aura is all wrong."

That wasn't the only thing about her that was all wrong, Daisy thought. The woman was a phony through and through. It was easy to distinguish the genuinely sympathetic people from those who offered condolences just because they wanted to be a part of local news, from those who wanted a little claim to fame, like Georgette Lacey so obviously had. "Guess who I ran into the other evening?" Daisy imagined her telling her neighbors. "Those poor pathetic Higgins girls! *I* thought they looked just devastated."

Daisy sighed. She so wanted things to be normal again; she so wanted people to treat her as they had before she became the girl with no parents.

"They're passing around bacon-wrapped shrimp," Violet said. "Yum."

"Grab me one?" Daisy smiled as she watched her sister make off after the waiter. Violet might be into alternative healing, astrology, and the mystical power of stones, but she was as big a carnivore as the average American teenager.

Chapter 9

Poppy examined the photograph on the wall before her. "Crumbling Barn II." She liked Sheila's work, but at the moment she felt she could use a good dose of bright flowers and iridescent rainbows and sparkling waves. Color. Movement. Life. No more reminders of death, of things coming to an end.

Already Poppy had seen no fewer than five people not so discreetly nodding in her direction and whispering meaningfully to their companions. She had caught the eye of one woman she vaguely recognized and the woman had abruptly turned her back. Really, Poppy thought, some people acted as if death itself were contagious, as if mere eye contact with a grieving daughter would bring destruction on their own home. *It's going to happen to you, too,* Poppy said to the woman's back. *You can't avoid it by turning away.*

She sighed. Sometimes she felt annoyed by life in a small town and now was one of those times. Boston was not the biggest city, but it certainly afforded a strong degree of anonymity if you wanted it. And then she saw him and realized that at that particular moment anonymity wasn't very appealing.

Jon Gascoyne. She didn't think she had ever noticed how really handsome he was, in a model sort of way, except for the rough-around-the-edge touches—sun-etched lines at the corner of his eyes, windburned cheeks, and his hands . . . As he approached her she noticed that his hands were definitely not the delicate hands of a man who made a living posing in outrageously expensive clothing. At another time, Poppy thought, she might have been interested in him. But not now. Not when things were so up in the air.

"Hello," he said, extending his hand. "I don't think we've ever actually met, though of course I know who you are."

"No. I mean, you're right. We haven't officially met before. Poppy Higgins."

"Jon Gascoyne."

"Of the market and the restaurant," Poppy said, releasing his hand.

"And the lobster boat."

Poppy smiled. "I'm of Willow Way. That's about all."

"That's plenty. You have a beautiful house."

"Thank you. My parents loved it at first sight. Except for expanding the garden they didn't change a thing."

"I was terribly sorry to learn of your father's passing," Jon said. "He was a great man."

He looks me straight in the eye, Poppy noted. *He's not afraid.* "Yes," she said over a catch in her throat. "He was."

"My parents and I were at the funeral. It was pretty impressive. I'd never seen so many people turn out for a memorial."

"Almost six hundred," Poppy said. "The minister said we were breaking fire code, but no one had the heart to turn people away. And we got cards and notes from hundreds more who weren't able to be there."

Jon smiled kindly. "I hope that was some consolation. Knowing how much your father was loved and respected."

Poppy lowered her eyes, unable for a moment to bear the kindness. "Yes," she said. "It was some consolation."

"I took one of your mother's courses when I was at Adams, you know. She was a wonderful teacher, so entertaining. She always had time for her students, even after official office hours."

Poppy looked up again and smiled. "Thank you, again. I never took any of my mom's courses. We both felt that it wouldn't be right, that the other students might think she was favoring me. But I did go to hear her speak on special occasions."

"Me, too. I remember this one talk she gave, right after her book came out I think. It was a mob scene. You'd think she was a rock star."

Poppy laughed. "I was there! My whole family was, even Violet and she was just a baby."

"Speaking of your family, I see that your sisters are here, along with Freddie and Sheila. I bet they've been a help to you. Freddie and Sheila, I mean."

"Yes. I don't think that I could have . . ." Poppy found her voice too wobbly to go on.

"You've been living away, haven't you?" Jon asked.

A tactful question, Poppy thought. "Yes," she said, her voice restored. "In Boston. But I'm back now. Well, obviously."

"How long are you planning to stay in Yorktide?"

"Oh, not long at all. Well, that's not true. At least five years, until my youngest sister turns eighteen. I'm my sisters' legal guardian, you see. It was my father's idea."

"That must be challenging."

"Yes," Poppy admitted. "It can be. But it won't be forever. I'll go back to Boston when Violet is legally an adult and settled in college." *Assuming,* Poppy thought, *I can convince her to go to college.*

Jon smiled. "No chance that Yorktide will weave its charming spell over you and entice you to stay?"

"No chance at all. It's a lovely town for sure, but it's not for me in the end." *At least,* she thought, *I can't see it as the place for me. But I don't know much of anything for sure these days.*

"Well, at least we'll have you as part of our little community for a few years."

Poppy smiled even though she was slightly alarmed by this notion. She didn't want to "be had" by Yorktide or by anyone in it for that matter. But then . . . Well, it might be nice to feel tethered to a place and a person as long as you were also doing something that *mattered* with your life. . . .

"What about you?" she asked Jon then. "I mean, have you ever considered living somewhere else? I'm sorry. That's a personal question, isn't it?"

"No worries. And it's no secret that I'm in Yorktide for good. My family is here, my work is here. Everything I love, in fact. I've got no reason to leave."

"What about travel?" Poppy smiled. "Don't you ever dream about escaping to some exotic location?"

"Exotic? Not sure exotic locations are for me! But there'll be time for travel when I've really established myself and put away enough money. Until then, I watch the Travel Channel."

"I'm afraid I've hardly been anywhere," Poppy admitted. "My father traveled all over the world for so many years of my life I think I took against it somehow. I came to associate travel with missing him."

"There's always the future," Jon pointed out. "Should you change your mind."

The future, Poppy thought. *That mysterious, undecided thing!* "Yes," she said. "I don't think I could forgive myself if I never got to Paris."

"For me, it would be England. I'm a huge fan of British mysteries. There, I've confessed my secret addiction. Nothing more exotic for me than fields of grazing cows and windswept moors."

Poppy laughed. "Not such a bad addiction, I think. Oh, here come my sisters. And Freddie and Sheila."

"Beautiful photographs, Sheila," Jon said when the others had joined them. "Have you seen the crumbling barn behind my parents' house?"

Poppy almost laughed at the look of jubilation on Sheila's face. "No! I must stop by and have a look! If I may, that is."

"Anytime," Jon assured her.

"I'm Daisy. I'm a friend of your cousin Joel."

"Of course." Jon smiled. "He talks about you often. I thought he might be here tonight."

"He wanted to come," Daisy explained, "but he was asked to sub for a sax player in a band with a gig at a place just down the street."

"Will he get paid, I wonder," Freddie said darkly.

"The life of a professional musician is a tough one, but Joel's got the drive." Jon smiled. "He's especially impressive given the fact that no one else in our family has ever gone off to do something so out of the ordinary."

"I'm Violet," Violet announced suddenly. "The youngest Higgins."

Jon bowed slightly to her. "But certainly not the least important."

Violet smiled, and Poppy thought she saw a slight flush to her sister's cheeks. *Well,* Poppy thought. *He is awfully good-looking.*

"Are you a Virgo?" Violet asked Jon.

"Uh, yes," he said. "I mean, I think I am. My birthday is September nineteenth."

Violet nodded. "I thought so."

Jon shot Poppy a look of inquiry. "My sister," she said, "has a talent for such things."

Freddie checked her watch and announced that the opening would soon be over. "I suggest we go someplace to grab a bite. Won't you join us, Jon?"

Poppy was mildly alarmed by this suggestion. Since coming home to Yorktide her social life had been restricted to spending time with Freddie and Sheila, old friends who made no special demands for bright or interesting conversation, people in front of whom she wasn't embarrassed to cry, not that she had allowed herself much of that. She wasn't sure she was equal to more of the company of a virtual stranger—even a nice, interesting one like Jon Gascoyne— at least not at the moment. She was lucky.

"I'd like to join you," he said, "but I can't. It's already past my bedtime and the lobsters wait for no man."

Jon said farewell and went off.

"I've got a hankering for a crab roll," Sheila announced. "What say we go into Perkins Cove and grab a table on the patio at Barnacle Billy's?"

"Can we, Poppy?" Violet asked.

Poppy nodded. "Sure," she said. Honestly, she was tired and wouldn't have minded heading straight home. But she thought that the least she could do for her sisters was to give them a real night out.

"I am so getting fries," Daisy said, leading the way out to the parking lot.

Chapter 10

Evie opened the door to the pantry and surveyed the contents neatly displayed on the shelves. In the typed letter Nico had left her, crammed with instructions for her stay, he had told her that she could use whatever she wanted from the pantry, as long as she replaced anything she finished. Evie frowned. She supposed that was nice of Nico, but honestly, there was nothing in the pantry that appealed to her, not even when she felt really hungry. Dried seaweed? Water chestnuts? She didn't even know what they were. Glass jars of various colored beans. How did you cook beans, anyway? Evie closed the pantry door and wandered over to the window, which faced the small shady yard behind the house.

In his long letter of instructions Nico had also bragged that the house had a "spectacular" view of the water and Evie had imagined sunning herself on a large deck a stone's throw from the Atlantic. In reality, the only way you could see the water—glimpse it, really—was if you climbed the impossibly steep flight of stairs to a narrow tower extending skyward from the second floor of the house, eventually reaching the glassed-in apex from which, on a very clear day and if you squinted as hard as you could, you might just make out a tiny thread of something silvery blue and sparkly. Even this tiny little view added thousands of dollars to the worth of the house, Nico had written, as if it was something she needed to know. After two sweaty trips to the top of the tower, Evie had decided that she could do without a water view just fine.

Evie left the kitchen and went into the living room. There were two exhibit catalogues on the coffee table, both featuring Nico's work. Evie picked one up and opened it at random. "Assemblage," she read. "Mixed media." Mixed, she thought, was right. According to the catalogue, Nico's work included materials as diverse as nuts and bolts, sand, lengths of string, bits of newspaper, old typewriter keys, seeds, and bicycle gears. Frankly, Evie thought his work was hideous, but she figured someone must like it, if his house was anything to go by. The master bedroom was bigger than her old living room and kitchen combined. Not that she liked to think about the old house in Vermont or anything much from those days—before. Before her father had killed her mother and lost his mind along with his job and their house and everything else that mattered.

Evie placed the catalogue back on the coffee table. She had never known an artist before and never been in an artist's home so she hadn't known what exactly to expect. Weird uncomfortable furniture in the shape of body parts? Lava lamps? Art materials scattered everywhere? But maybe all that stuff was kept in a studio somewhere. Certainly the last thing that had come to mind was in fact what she had found—nothing. Rather, normalcy. It was the most boringly basic home she had ever been inside, and there wasn't one of his works to be found. (For that, she was grateful.)

A basic, three-cushion couch in a dull green print. Standard, square end tables. A rectangular coffee table, matching the end tables. Two tightly upholstered, high-backed arm-chairs in the same print as the couch. The framed pictures on the walls—a meadow dotted with flowers; a mountaintop covered in snow—looked as if they came out of a catalogue used by the designers who decorated doctors' and dentists' waiting rooms. The area rug was a sort of grayish green. Maybe, she thought, the enormous disconnect between Nico's art and the décor he had chosen for his home was intentional, a deliberate statement only another artist would understand. These things were beyond her, though her mother probably would have understood. She had owned a really cool shop back in Vermont, a "curated shop," her mother had called it. Once a year she had traveled to New York to meet with importers of beautiful fabrics from India, silver jewelry from Thailand, gold jewelry from Israel and Turkey, ceramics from Italy and Portugal, intricately carved woodwork from Indonesia. Evelyn had been so smart about so many things, and so open to new experiences. While still in college she had traveled to Vietnam and China all on her own; shortly after graduation, before she had met the man who would be her husband, she had hiked through the British Isles with a girl she had met on the plane.

It was this image of her mother as a courageous, creative, and intrepid person that had gotten Evie through some of the more difficult moments of life alone on the road. Like the night it had started to rain really hard and she had no choice but to crawl under a picnic table in the local park, terrified of being raped by the gang of drunken teenage boys she had seen earlier that evening. Like the night she had taken what shelter she could in a heavily wooded area and had sat up until dawn, listening to the awful screeching of owls and the unfamiliar sounds of nocturnal animals in the undergrowth. True, there had been a few moments when she had encountered kindness—like the time that truck driver had approached her in the little store at a gas station and given her ten dollars. "I can't take this," Evie had said, assuming he wanted something in return. "I have two girls about your age," the man had replied. "I can't imagine how I would feel if they were on the road." The man had turned away then, not before saying, "I've seen it all too many times before." And in those moments, too, Evie thought of her mother and believed that she was watching out for her.

Absentmindedly, Evie ran a finger along the back of one of the armchairs. If only she could lie low until she turned eighteen and could be legally declared an adult, she would be all right, no longer in need of a stranger's kindness. What "all right" meant exactly, she didn't really know. She hadn't finished high school, she had no real job skills other than taking orders and working a cash register, she had no money to speak of. . . . But she would think of all that later; like Scarlett O'Hara, the heroine of her favorite book, she would set her face forward. "After all . . . Tomorrow is another day," Scarlett had said. "It has to be," Evie added to Nico's living room.

Evie wandered into the hall between the living room and dining room and scanned the titles of the books on two small shelves. There was nothing much of interest to Evie—a biography of Andy Warhol, a history of the art colonies in Ogunquit, a paperback crime novel by a popular writer— and nothing in any language other than English. Evie was good with languages; she had been studying French in school since she was nine and had taught herself enough Spanish and Italian to hold a decent conversation, which she had often done with the Spanish teacher and a neighbor who was a native of Milan. She was looking forward to learning German in college. Well, she thought, turning away from the shelves. It was her own fault for forgetting to bring any books with her the night she had left her aunt and uncle's house. She had tried to prepare, to consider what she might need for the journey, to figure out how much she could carry, but in the end she had made a lot of mistakes. Like not bringing extra batteries for the flashlight she had taken from her uncle's workshop in the garage. Like not bringing a roll of toilet paper. At least she had found a pair of good sharp scissors in Nico's kitchen and had managed to trim her hair without drastic mishaps.

With a sigh, Evie turned away from the bookshelves and trudged up to her bedroom. At least, she thought, she hadn't forgotten to bring Ben. She had had the little plush bear for as long as she could remember; he was in almost every picture taken of her as a toddler. His fur had once been the color of heavy cream, but now it was a light brown and he was missing one button eye. Evie could easily have replaced the eye, but she loved Ben the way he was. Where was he, anyway? She thought she had left him on the dresser, propped against her backpack. But Ben wasn't on the dresser. Evie felt the panic rise fast in her. She threw back the covers on the bed. He wasn't there. She dropped to the floor and checked under the bed. No. *Please, oh, please,* Evie prayed. *Let him be here!* Evie climbed to her feet. There, on the armchair in the corner, where she had tossed her hoodie . . . Evie yanked the hoodie aside and there he was. Ben.

The sense of relief she felt was massive. She just couldn't stand to lose anything or anyone else. There was a limit to the pain a person could bear, she knew that there was, and she didn't want her courage or her sanity to be tested further. Clutching Ben tightly to her chest, she crawled into bed, ears pricked for the sound of an intruder.

Chapter 11

The garden was brimming with the most beautiful green and white flowers in the most fantastical shapes she had ever seen. Some were as tiny as blueberries. Others were as large as pumpkins. Fuzzy black-and-yellow bees hung heavily in the air, buzzing mildly, as if exhausted from the making of honey. From somewhere unseen came the sound of water trickling over stones. Violet felt dizzy with the sweet, spicy, and slightly rancid smell of fecund life.

She bent down and picked a flower with a profusion of mottled green and white petals in the shape of a pinwheel. She thought that she had never seen anything so lovely. She stood up to see her mother walking toward her. Annabelle was smiling. She was wearing a bright white hospital gown that came to her knees. Her feet were bare. Violet held the flower out to her mother. Annabelle stuffed it into her mouth, chewed vigorously, and swallowed.

"No!" Violet shrieked. "It's poisonous!" But her mother was already shriveling to dust before her eyes.

"Annabelle! Annabelle, where are you?" It was her father, his voice drowning out the buzzing of the bees and the trickling of the water.

She was frantic with guilt. She hadn't meant to kill her mother. She had only wanted her to have the pretty flower. She grabbed the flimsy hospital gown from the ground and began to run, pursued now by heavy footsteps. "Annabelle!" Her father's voice had become a throaty roar, like that of an angry animal. There, ahead . . . She ran toward the stone well. She could hide the telltale gown there. She looked over her shoulder, her father's footsteps thundering in her ear though she couldn't yet see him, then turned back and raised the bunched gown over the black hole of the well when up from the depths shot a demon, a beast snarling and red, with burning eyes and as he grabbed for her with shimmering claws—

Violet woke, gasping. Grimace was pawing her face and meowing demandingly. "Demons down under the sea," she whispered. Grimace removed his paw from her cheek and stared down at her. "Yes," she told him. "I know it's breakfast time."

Chapter 12

"What did you think of our Jon Gascoyne?"

"Our?" Poppy asked. She was with Freddie in her home on Howard Lane; more specifically, they were in the study, a room that looked like it had been plucked from a novel by Agatha Christie—high-backed leather armchairs, walls lined with bookshelves that reached to the ceiling, a massive stone fireplace, a mahogany desk fit for a famously brilliant detective. Poppy thought she wouldn't be surprised if one day Hercule Poirot himself minced into the room. *Jon would like this room,* she thought now. *With his addiction to British mysteries. Our Jon Gascoyne.*

"By which I mean Yorktide's," Freddie explained. "A true son of the land. And of the sea, I suppose."

"Oh. I thought he was very nice. I somehow can't see him as a lobsterman, though."

"Why not?"

Poppy shrugged. "I guess I'm guilty of stereotyping. I didn't expect a guy who makes a living hauling lobster pots out of the ocean to be at an art exhibit."

"You should be ashamed," Freddie said mildly. "Where did you get such prejudices?"

"Sorry. It was stupid. Anyway, he's very good-looking. Not that I'm in the market for a boyfriend."

"Not that he would choose you. Necessarily."

"I know that! I'm not entirely vain," Poppy protested.

"Well, a young woman with your looks almost has to be vain. The world won't let her be otherwise, I'm afraid."

"And look where my appearance has gotten me. Nowhere in particular."

"Good," Freddie said firmly. "Looks should be irrelevant. In a perfect world they would be."

Poppy couldn't argue that. Ever since she was small people had openly stared at her, whether she was on her own or with her parents. Total strangers had come right up to her and said things like, "You're gorgeous, do you know that?" She had always found the attention a bit puzzling as well as a bit annoying. Really, what did you say to questions like that? "Yes, I know I'm gorgeous." Then you sounded as if you were stuck-up. "Oh, no I'm not." Then you might be accused of false modesty.

There had been that man at the mall in Kittery. He had approached her as she was coming out of the Coach shop with some girlfriends (a mom of one friend had driven them as they were all only fifteen). He had politely introduced himself as a scout for a major New York–based modeling agency and handed Poppy his card. Her friends had squealed in excitement. Poppy stuck the card in her back pocket and forgot about it for three days until her mother unearthed it as she was putting a load of laundry in the washing machine. Her father had checked out the man's credentials (they were all mildly curious) and had found that he was indeed a legitimate scout. Still, Annabelle and Oliver had adamantly refused to let their daughter pursue a career in modeling. Poppy didn't care. At that point in her life she had never paid much attention to fashion and found the idea of modeling boring. Besides, the thought of having to leave her close-knit family was a bit terrifying.

And now . . . Now that close-knit family had been partly but irreparably unraveled . . .

"Why didn't you sue for legal guardianship of Daisy and Violet?" Poppy asked Freddie. "Why didn't Dad choose you? He'd known you forever and you *are* the family lawyer."

"If I had wanted children I would have had my own," Freddie said firmly. "Besides, I'm almost eighty years old. I'm far too tired to raise teenagers, even ones as lovely and interesting as your sisters."

"You forgot headstrong and difficult."

"Be that as it may, Oliver would never have burdened me—sorry to be blunt—with the care and feeding of his children."

Poppy smiled feebly. "You make them sound like pets. Cats and dogs."

"Cats, dogs, and human young ones need to be watered, sheltered, and fed. I see little difference. Cats and dogs and babies don't go on expensive spring breaks and they don't demand exorbitantly priced weddings. Not that all human children behave badly. You never did, from what I could tell."

Unless you count running off to Boston after Mom died. Abandoning my father and sisters, Poppy thought. What she said was: "There never seemed to be any reason to act badly."

"It was a happy home," Freddie stated.

"It was."

"It can be again, you know. Not in the same way, of course."

"And it's up to me to make us a happy family again."
Poppy wasn't sure if she meant that as a question or a statement of fact.

"Not only you," Freddie argued. "Daisy and Violet will also have to choose to make an effort. But yes, you are in the position of guiding spirit."

"Whether I'm up to the challenge or not."

"Exactly. But I think that you *are* up to the challenge, Poppy. The problem is you don't yet believe that. Now, enough talk. I've got to keep this old body moving. Use it or lose it. Do you want to walk down to the marshes with me or do you have somewhere you need to be? It's high tide and you know how beautiful the marsh is at high tide."

"Nowhere to be," Poppy said. "Unless I'm forgetting something. Like paying the electric bill or—"

Freddie took hold of her elbow. "Then come on."

Chapter 13

Evie glanced over her right shoulder and then her left. The convenience store was almost empty of customers; it wasn't yet noon when there would likely begin a rush of people wanting sodas and chips to go with the expensive sandwiches they had bought next door at the high-end takeout and café. Good. Hardly any people meant there was hardly anyone to catch her in the act of shoplifting. As if it mattered.

Slowly, Evie walked down the aisle of personal hygiene products, picking up a bottle of shampoo and a bar of soap here and there and pretending to read the ingredients. She hadn't shoplifted often, only twice before, and both times she had been desperate—the first time for sanitary pads and the second for water. And both times she had been sick with anxiety.

Today, though, Evie was feeling reckless. It had happened before since leaving her aunt and uncle's house, this temptation to throw all caution to the wind, to put herself in the path of exposure. So what if she got caught and sent to foster care or even to jail? How much worse could that be than the life she was living now, always looking over her shoulder for the police, always afraid at night, haunted by memories? Always alone. If nothing could bring her mother back then nothing really mattered. In these moments of recklessness she felt that she had been so stupid to run away from her aunt and uncle's home. She felt that she deserved to be punished for having acted so idiotically. She felt that she deserved to be caught.

Evie stopped before the shelves of toothpaste. With a final quick and furtive glance toward the front of the store where the cashier was stationed, Evie extended her hand toward the shelf at the height of her thigh. And then she stumbled.

"Oh, I'm sorry!" a girl was saying to her. "I wasn't paying attention."

"It's okay," Evie said quickly. Had the girl seen her hand reaching for the tube of toothpaste? But even if she had, how would she know that Evie was going to steal it? Still, her heart refused to calm to its normal beat.

"I'm always bumping into things," the girl went on. "And people. Bad coordination. It's why I'm awful at sports."

"Oh."

"Well," the girl said, turning away, "bye. Sorry again."

For a moment Evie stood frozen to the spot, her hands dangling at her side. And then she walked hurriedly to the door. The encounter, unsettling as it was, had served to deter her from shoplifting and for that, she was thankful. What would her mother have thought about her daughter being a thief? Surely Evelyn had experienced plenty of minor hardships while she was trekking through the Far East and the highlands of Scotland. And Evie was certain that her mother never would have resorted to stealing. Evie would simply make do without toothpaste for a day or two until she next got paid. Or maybe Nico had left a stray tube in the cabinet under the bathroom sink. She could replace it before he got back at the end of the summer.

None of the store's employees stopped Evie as she left the convenience store, though she half expected someone to have suspected her criminal intentions from the look of guilt that was probably all over her face. Once out on the sidewalk she put a hand to her heart and willed herself to calm down. And then she saw the girl who had bumped into her standing across the street. She was with another girl with very short hair and wearing a billowy mint-green dress; the second girl was chewing vigorously and holding a small bright yellow paper bag into which the older one now reached. Candy. Evie recognized the bag. The girls must have been to the homemade candy shop on the corner; they were sharing what they had bought.

Evie looked away, and with a powerful loneliness dogging her every step, she walked back to Nico's house at the end of Nubble Lane.

Chapter 14

"Are you ready? I don't want to be late to the vet."

Poppy looked up from the copy of *Coastal Home* magazine she was idly browsing. Her youngest sister was standing in a shaft of sunlight coming through the kitchen's skylight. A chunk of crystal quartz on a chain around her neck blared brilliantly. "What do you mean?" she asked.

Violet pointed to the purple plastic animal carrier sitting near her feet. "Grimace has an appointment at the vet this morning. His left ear, remember? It's been bothering him."

As if to prove the point, Grimace let out a dreadful yowl from behind the bars of his prison.

"But I made an appointment at the spa in Ogunquit for a hot-stone massage," Poppy said. "In half an hour."

"But I told you about Grimace's appointment days ago."

Had she? Violet never lied, but Poppy had no recollection of hearing this bit of news. "Can you reschedule Grimace's appointment?" she asked.

Violet stared solemnly at her. "I've got him emotionally prepared for the trip. It wouldn't be fair to change things now."

Poppy sighed. "Okay," she said. "Sorry. Just let me grab my keys."

Really, she thought as they left the house, her sister carrying the loudly protesting cat in his carrier. *How can you be so selfish? Does a hot-stone massage really trump the health of your little sister's beloved pet, the kitty that had helped her survive those first horrible weeks and months after Mom's death?*

"How much is this visit going to cost?" Poppy asked as Violet loaded the carrier in the back seat and got into the front passenger seat.

"I have no idea," Violet said over Grimace's screams. "The bill will come to you."

Julie had called Poppy three times now, inviting her to stop by and see the kids and the farm and catch up on old times. Poppy figured her old friend would continue to pester her with calls until she gave in and paid a visit to Fisk Farm; Julie had always been a persistent sort. Besides, she didn't really know what was holding her back from seeing her friend. True, they had taken very different paths after high school; Julie hadn't gone to college and she was married with two children. And maybe that was it, Poppy thought. Maybe she was afraid they would have no common ground. It would still feel like a loss if they faced each other across an abyss, realizing they had absolutely nothing to talk about anymore. And Poppy had had enough of loss.

Poppy pulled up the dirt drive and parked in front of the old farmhouse Julie called home. The house had been in Mack's family for generations and though it clearly needed some repair—a new paint job, for one—it looked sound enough and it certainly had charm. The front porch was right out of a home decorating editorial—white wicker rocking chairs, hanging flowering plants, a brightly colored flag proclaiming "Welcome," a child's tricycle. The front door was painted bright red and there was a gleaming brass knocker in the shape of a rooster. Set as it was on several acres of cultivated farmland and backed by fields of wildflowers, Poppy thought the scene before her was as near to idyllic as you might get on this earth.

Two children came running around the side of the house, laughing and chasing after a beat-up soccer ball. Julie's son and daughter. Virginia, she thought, would be about eight and Michael about five. Poppy thought again of her own "child"—Violet. She had apologized again to her sister and had gone into the treatment room with Violet and Grimace, though the ferocity with which the cat was clawing at the bars of his carrier had frightened her. (To her great surprise, he was as calm as a Buddha once released.) Really, she had to keep in mind that even though Violet could seem preternaturally mature and self-sufficient, she was only thirteen. She would have to pay closer attention to her youngest sister. After all, her mother had asked her only weeks before she died to look out for Daisy and Violet. *If only she had known what that would entail,* Poppy thought. *If only she had known that Dad would be with us for only another three years.*

Poppy got out of the car just as her old friend was emerging from the house, a smile on her face. Julie was a good deal shorter than Poppy (most women were), and looked to be about seven or eight months pregnant. Her hair, a natural peachy color, was pulled back in a messy ponytail and there was a smudge of what looked like jam on her cheek.

Poppy smiled. "Putting up preserves?"

Julie automatically wiped both cheeks with a small towel that hung over her shoulder. "More like peanut butter and jelly for lunch. My kids are addicted to it."

Poppy gave her old friend a hug. "It's good to see you, Julie," she said. "Number three! When are you due?"

"End of August, if this one can be patient. The way it dances around . . . Come inside. I'll make us some tea, unless you'd prefer coffee. Virginia! Tell your brother we'll be in the kitchen."

Poppy watched as Julie's daughter signed to her brother. Michael had been born deaf; Poppy didn't know exactly what had caused his deafness and she had always felt it wasn't her place to ask Julie for details. As long as Michael was happy and healthy . . . Poppy saw him nod and then give the ball a kick that sent it flying through the air.

"Michael's got quite a kick for a little guy," she said, following Julie through a spotlessly clean and impossibly neat living room and into the kitchen. The room was charming: dish towels printed with images of chickens and roosters were placed neatly over the handle of the oven door and on the lip of the sink; several gleaming copper pots hung on a rack to the right of the oven; a bright red enamel kettle was boiling away on the stove; an old scrubbed milk can stood in one corner, from which erupted a spray of dried Bells of Ireland.

"Where did you learn to be such a good housekeeper?" Poppy asked. "And interior decorator. If we were ever taught housekeeping in school I must have been sick that day."

Julie laughed. "My mother. Where else?"

"I guess I don't remember my mother doing all that much around the house," Poppy said, taking a seat at the round wooden table. "She spent a lot of time working in the garden, but otherwise we had a housekeeper. Do you remember her? Mrs. Olds also made a lot of our meals. With both of my parents always working so much and my father on the road so often it made sense. Of course, I never paid any attention to what Mrs. Olds was doing and now I regret it. I'm having to learn everything about keeping a house and a family in good working order all at once."

"It's not rocket science, Poppy," Julie said. "Mostly it's common sense and organization."

"I'm finding that out," Poppy admitted. She thought again of Violet and vowed to buy one of those large whiteboards and install it prominently in the kitchen. She would make it a habit to write down every appointment and event her sisters mentioned and to check the board regularly.

Julie brought the tea and a tin of homemade chocolate chip cookies to the table and sat down across from Poppy.

"So, what is it exactly you do in Boston?" she asked. "Or, I guess, did, unless you're working from home?"

"No, I'm taking a hiatus from work." As succinctly as she could Poppy explained the sort of writing and reporting she had done for the online magazines.

"It sounds so exciting," Julie said.

Poppy laughed. "Not exactly cutting-edge stuff, believe me." In fact, Poppy thought, Julie's cheese-making was far more exotic than what she had been doing for the past few years. "Mostly it's sitting at a computer for so many hours a day you almost forget how to talk to a person face-to-face."

"That *doesn't* sound very exciting, you're right. I'll stick to my curds and whey."

Poppy laughed. "What are they, exactly? Other than what Little Miss Muffet was eating when the spider came along."

Julie explained. "But enough about dairy products," she said then, "tell me more about you. Are you seeing anyone special?"

"No." Poppy shrugged. "Unlucky in love, I guess." *If never having been in love at all was unlucky,* she thought. Maybe it was a sign that she was somehow emotionally deficient. That was a startling thought.

"Maybe you'll meet someone here in Yorktide," Julie suggested.

"You've always been such an optimist! There can't be many single, eligible men in this little town."

Julie grinned. "All it takes is one."

"That's true, but meeting someone is the last thing on my mind. Honestly, I'm feeling a bit overwhelmed by—by life."

"You've been put in a tough position for sure. You know if there's anything I can do to help, I will."

Poppy was genuinely touched by her old friend's offer of support. "For one," she said, "you could give me the recipe for these cookies. Better yet, you could make me a batch. If you have time, I mean. I haven't attempted to bake anything since I last made brownies with my mother and that was from a mix."

"Gladly. In the meantime I want you to have these." Julie went to the fridge and retrieved a round of goat cheese and a wedge of what she described as an alpine type cheese made from cow's milk. "Fisk Farm's finest. Wow. Try saying that three times in a row."

Poppy smiled. "Thank you, Julie. What do I owe you?"

"Nothing," Julie assured her. "Just promise you won't be a stranger."

Poppy promised, said good-bye, and got behind the wheel of the car that had once been her father's. What choice did she have but to promise? she thought as she drove off. Even if she wanted to disappear into a life of solitude, she doubted it would be possible in a town like Yorktide, where everybody knew everybody and gossip was often more reliable than the newspaper. And maybe—just maybe—that would turn out to be a good thing.

Chapter 15

"He did have a flair for the dramatic, your father. Rabelais, no less."

Violet and Sheila were visiting the Higgins family plot in Yorktide Memorial Cemetery. Someday, Violet thought, she would be buried there, alongside her parents. She knew for sure that she didn't want to be cremated. She thought being buried was nicer, with a carpet of green grass over your head and pretty flowers sprouting from your body, like in those lines in *Hamlet*. She wasn't sure what her sisters thought about such things. She strongly suspected they wouldn't be comfortable talking about them.

Sheila placed the bouquets of wildflowers she and Violet had picked earlier on each of the graves.

"Do you believe in life after death?" Violet asked.

Sheila raised an eyebrow. "What a question! I wasn't sure anyone wondered about such things anymore. But yes, I don't see why not. Just don't ask me what it might be like. I don't know how anyone can presume to know such a thing, or even to hazard a guess."

"I think it must be very interesting, whatever it's like.

Life after death. Interesting and beautiful, like a spectacular garden." *But not like that garden in my dream,* Violet thought. The one in which she had killed her mother.

"I certainly hope so," Sheila replied.

"Though I doubt it'll be like those stories about heaven my mother told me she was taught when she was little. People meeting up again with long-dead relatives and friends, like at a big party."

"How confusing!" Sheila cried. "I always wondered how you would work things out, meeting former husbands and their new wives or the weird kid in high school who followed you around, desperately wanting to be your friend. Let's face it, there are some people you just don't want to meet again, here or there!"

"Oh, I'm sure. I believe in angels, too, but I don't think they have wings and wear flowing robes. I think they're more—presences."

Sheila looked carefully at Violet. "I didn't know young girls thought much about . . . presences."

"I do."

"Do you feel your parents' presences? That's hard to say, *parents' presences.*"

"Oh, yes," Violet said. "Of course I do. For a while after Mom died I actually saw her around the house. But it's been kind of a long time since that's happened. I guess she's moved on. That's the phrase people use—*moved on.*"

"My dear, I never knew you were so—"

"So what?" Violet asked.

"So attuned. Have you also seen your father?"

"No. It's been four months since he died, so I don't think I'll ever be seeing him. But I know he's around, or that part of him is."

"I understand," Sheila said. "When our cat Jack died— remember him?—I heard him for almost a year afterward. I swear he was still in the house. I'd hear the particular sound of his jumping from the bed and landing on the bare wood floor. I'd hear his unique way of meowing. Ma-Mow! Ma-Mow! Freddie thought I was losing my mind, I'm afraid. There's not an imaginative bone in that woman's body."

Violet nodded. "Freddie is very earthbound. You have to be earthbound to be a lawyer, I guess. She must be the practical one in your house."

"I can be practical, too," Sheila pointed out. "Don't forget, I was a very effective administrative assistant for many years. But when I don't have to be—earthbound—I'm glad. I know you understand."

Violet remembered how Poppy had sounded dubious when she told her that Sheila was her friend. As if two people so far apart in age couldn't understand each other. Couldn't count on each other. She looked up at Sheila. "You are my friend, aren't you?" she asked.

"What a question! Of course I am."

"And I'm your friend?"

Sheila smiled. "Violet, never doubt it for a moment. You're stuck with me through thick or thin."

"Good," Violet said. And she slipped her hand into Sheila's, aware that it was the first time she had initiated physical contact with another person since her father had died.

Chapter 16

Daisy climbed out of what had once been her father's car, murmured a hurried thank-you to Poppy, and jogged up the graveled path to the doors of Pine Hill Residence for the Elderly. Three people were coming out of the building as she dashed up the front stairs, a man, a woman, and a girl about Daisy's age. They had probably just paid a visit to an aged relative, Daisy thought. And the girl looked vaguely familiar . . .

Ah. She knew what it was. The girl looked a bit like the one Daisy had bumped into in the convenience store the other day, the one wearing the pink hoodie, the one who had seemed nervous or on edge. Well, Daisy supposed that having a stranger almost send you crashing into a shelf of toothpaste could unsettle anyone. She really wished she weren't so prone to stumbling! Poppy and Violet were both so graceful in their movements. *I'm the oddball sister,* she thought. *The ugly duckling among the swans.*

Daisy waved to the security guard by the front door and signed in at the volunteer station. Then she took the stairs to the second floor, where her favorite residents had a small apartment—one bedroom, one bathroom (complete with several safety bars), an open-plan living/dining area, and a kitchenette. Muriella and Bertie Wilkin had been married for sixty-three years; they were now in their late eighties. Daisy found Muriella sitting comfortably in an armchair, leafing through a magazine about quilting. (Arthritis had forced her to give up her favorite hobby, but she still kept up with the quilting community.) Muriella smiled when she saw Daisy. Though she had told Daisy she had once been five foot seven inches tall it was hard to imagine, seeing her now. Her shoulders were sadly bent and her neck was set forward, giving her, in her own words, "the look of a curious turtle." But Muriella's eyes were still bright and she was proud to tell anyone who cared to know that all of her teeth were the originals.

"How are you today, Mrs. Wilkin?" Daisy asked, kissing the woman on the cheek and taking a seat in the other armchair facing her.

"Just fine. And how are you? Enjoying the summer when you're not kindly paying a visit to my old bones?"

Daisy laughed. "I'm trying to. What would you like to do today? We could go sit on the back porch, but I have to warn you, it's pretty humid out there."

Muriella pretended to shudder. "The humidity always did wreak havoc with my hair. No, let's stay here."

"Where's Mr. Wilkin?" Daisy asked.

"In the lounge down the hall, playing checkers with that cheat, whatever his name is. I always forget."

Daisy laughed. "Does he—whoever he is—really cheat at checkers? I didn't know that was possible."

"Tom must—that's his name, Tom—because Bertie loses a dollar to him every time they play and let me tell you, Bertie never lost a legitimate game of checkers in his life."

"Do you want to report Tom to the staff?" Daisy asked. She wasn't quite sure how she felt about turning in a senior citizen, but the Wilkins were on a very fixed budget. A dollar here and there could really add up.

Muriella laughed. "Oh, no, that's the last thing I want to do. Bertie loves complaining about Tom and his underhanded ways. If Tom was made to be law-abiding, Bertie would be very annoyed indeed."

"Okay," Daisy said. "I'll keep my mouth shut." And then she got up from the chair and began to pace around the room.

"You've been thinking," Muriella noted. "Would you like to tell me what about?"

"Yes," Daisy said. "I would. The other day I read an article online about couples who have been married for fifty, even sixty or seventy years, dying on the same day or just about. They just can't live without each other. It's like they became one person somewhere along the line." Daisy came to a sudden halt and whirled to face Mrs. Wilkin. "Oh, I'm so sorry," she cried. "I shouldn't be talking about dying. I *told* myself not to and then I totally forgot!!"

Muriella laughed. "Why shouldn't you talk about dying? I *do* know that I'm going to die, and quite possibly some time very soon."

Daisy hurried over to Mrs. Wilkin and put a hand on her arm. "But I shouldn't be reminding you of it."

"Mortality, my child, is not something I'm likely to forget for more than a moment at a time."

"I guess," Daisy said, and sank back into her chair. "So . . . do you think that you and Mr. Wilkin will die one soon after the other?"

Muriella shrugged. "Impossible to say. But for myself, I suspect that if my beloved passes before I do, I won't much want to stay around. Not that I would take any measures to end my life. My religion forbids it and since it won't be long before I meet my Maker I don't want to start sinning now."

"No, of course not," Daisy said. "You know, Mrs. Wilkin, I really believe that my father died of a broken heart. I think he died because my mother had died. Not right away. He had my sisters and me to take care of. But I think that after a few years without my mother he just couldn't go on any longer."

Muriella leaned forward in her chair. "I do hope you don't spend too much time dwelling on such things," she said. "You're too young to be morbid."

"Oh, I don't think I'm being morbid," Daisy said quickly. "I mean, I hate the fact that my father is gone, but it is kind of wonderful to think that people can love each other so much they can't live without each other. That they're together again, forever."

"And there," Muriella said, sitting back, "you veer a little too close to the morbidly romantic, my child. Suicide pacts and whatnot. Romeo and Juliet. Better to look at those widows and widowers who were able to live on and rebuild a life while honoring the spouse's memory."

"Yes," Daisy said. She wasn't sure she agreed with Mrs. Wilkin, but she didn't want her friend to be worrying about her any more than she might already be. "I suppose you're right."

"Now, I think you need some cheering up. What do you say we go down to the café for an ice cream?"

Daisy smiled. "I'm supposed to be the one cheering *you* up."

"A relationship works both ways, my dear. And one is happiest when one feels needed."

"That's true," Daisy agreed. *And it made me so happy to take care of Dad. . . .* "How are your children?" Daisy asked as she offered a hand to Mrs. Wilkin and helped her out of her armchair.

"Causing their parents chest pains." Mrs. Wilkin peered up at Daisy. "You would think that after sixty or so years

Bertie and I would be free of worry about our children. But sometimes, it doesn't work that way."

As Daisy and Mrs. Wilkin headed for the elevator, Daisy wondered if Poppy would ever be free of worry about her sisters, now that she had taken on the responsibilities of a parent. *Poor Poppy,* she thought. *What did she do to deserve this?*

Chapter 17

"Start, you stupid thing!"

Poppy was on the front lawn battling with an old lawn mower she had found in the garage. For the past ten minutes—it had seemed like a century—she had been pulling on the starter cord to no avail.

"Need help with that?" a voice called.

Poppy straightened up and pushed her hair out of her eyes. It was Jon Gascoyne, sitting behind the wheel of his truck at the foot of the drive. "Do you have an axe with you?" she called back, wiping the back of her hand across her sweaty forehead.

"Uh, no. Why?"

"Because I want to smash this thing to bits. I just can't get it to start."

Jon smiled, climbed out of his truck, and loped up to join her. "There's probably no need for drastic measures. And why are you doing the mowing? I thought you had a landscaping service."

"We do. But I was feeling ambitious earlier and thought I'd drag out this old mower and get some exercise. . . ."

Jon twisted the cap off the gas tank and peered inside. When he looked up at her he seemed to be resisting a smile. "You do realize you need to fill the tank with gas? It's as dry as a bone."

"Oh," Poppy said. "Well, that was pretty silly of me, not to check the gas tank."

"Not everybody can be a mechanic," Jon said, wiping his hands on his jeans.

Poppy smiled. "You're being kind. From now on I think I'll leave the landscaping to the professionals. Look, do you want to come in for some lemonade? It's not homemade, but it's pretty decent. My mother used to make lemonade from scratch, but . . ." *But what,* Poppy asked herself. *Why can't I squeeze lemons just as well as Mom did?*

"Sure. Thanks. I've never been inside this house before," Jon told her as he followed her inside and through to the kitchen. "I've always wondered about it. The exterior is so unusual—I think your house is the only one in the county with good old-fashioned gables!—I figured the interior must be as well."

"Well, would you like a quick tour?" Poppy asked.

"That'd be great," he said enthusiastically.

So Poppy led him through the first floor, from the kitchen back to the living room, through the dining room, and into the study that had been her mother's favorite room in the house. "Upstairs," she explained, "are the bedrooms, nothing too special. The sunroom is really the showpiece of the house. Through here."

A moment later they stood side by side in the sunroom. Poppy watched as Jon noted the profusion of books, the green plants with their pink and purple flowers, the two massive jade plants, the comfortable couch and chairs, the collection of perfectly white seashells on a low wooden table. "I can see why it's considered the showpiece," he said, smiling at her. "It feels like an oasis of calm and beauty. I have a romantic side, you see."

"This is where my father died," Poppy blurted. "I'm sorry. I don't know why I had to tell you that."

"It's okay. It must still be so fresh. The memories. The feelings."

"Freddie found him. Daisy was home at the time, but she was in the kitchen. She could have been the one. . . ."

"But she wasn't."

Poppy silently scolded herself for sounding so maudlin. She didn't want Jon—well, she didn't want anyone—to think she was mired in sorrow and incapable of meeting the challenges of the new role she had been given. "Well," she said briskly, "let me get you that lemonade."

They went back to the kitchen, where Poppy retrieved the carton of lemonade from the fridge, added ice cubes to two tall glasses, and poured.

"Thanks," Jon said, as she handed him a glass. "I met your father once, you know, a long time ago."

"Really? I didn't know that."

"It was back when I was in college," Jon explained. "I knew who he was, of course. My economics professor had mentioned him several times and I knew that he was married to Professor Higgins. And, I'd seen him on campus—and on TV for that matter—so when I spotted him in town one afternoon I recognized him immediately."

Poppy smiled. "He *was* kind of distinctive, with that wild white hair. Kind of a cross between the actor who played Inspector Morse and Einstein."

"John Thaw. One of my favorites. Anyway, your father was kind to a gushing fan. He invited me to have coffee with him. He listened to my half-formed ideas without laughing.

He answered my fumbling questions in a way that made me feel I was almost an equal. A few days later there was a signed copy of his latest book on our front step. I still have it."

"But did you ever read it?" Poppy teased.

"Twice. And to be honest, I feel I've barely skimmed the surface of his arguments. He was a formidable thinker, your father."

"A genius, some said. Did you ever read my mother's book?" Poppy asked.

"Of course! Much more accessible for a layman."

"I feel I know parts of it by heart," Poppy told him. "We've all read it, even Violet. And we have all of my mother's notes. She was writing a second volume when she died. I keep thinking that someday I'll find someone who wants to finish the book. It would be a sort of tribute to her."

"That sounds like an excellent idea." Jon looked at his cell phone. "Two o'clock already. I'd better be off. Thanks for the lemonade, Poppy. And the tour."

"And thanks for diagnosing the problem with the mower."

Poppy walked him to the door and watched as Jon got into his truck and drove away. She wished he had been able to stay for a while longer. He was so nice. He was so kind. She wished . . .

Poppy shook her head, went back inside the house, and closed the door behind her.

Chapter 18

"Everything okay, Evie? Settling in all right?"

Evie smiled at her boss. "Everything's fine, Billy. Thanks."

"Good. You let me know if there's something I forgot to explain. The old brain isn't what it used to be."

Billy Woolrich wandered over to the large chalkboard on which the daily specials were listed (simple things, including a non-seafood sandwich and a soup) and Evie, on her fifteen-minute break, continued her inventory of the paper napkin supply. She was very aware of how lucky she had been to find a job working for such a nice boss. She had been so nervous the day she had applied for the job that she hadn't really paid much attention to what he looked like. Billy Woolrich was very tall, several inches over six feet, Evie guessed. She thought he must once have been very handsome. Even now, with his wavy gray hair and large brown eyes he was attractive. Not to Evie, of course—he was old enough to be her grandfather!—but she imagined that lots of adult women would like him in that way. Her mother might even have thought he was a good-looking man. But none of that mattered because Mr. Woolrich wore a wedding ring. His wife was probably as nice as he was.

"We're short a fry cook this afternoon," Billy suddenly announced, sticking his cell phone back into his shirt pocket. "Just got a call from Tommy. Says he's down with a stomach flu. Hope he didn't pick up something here!"

"Maybe Mrs. Woolrich could help out," Evie suggested. "Just for the day."

"Oh, no," he said, with a small smile. "I've been on my own now for almost eight years, ever since Susan passed away. Can't say I've gotten used to it, not really. I keep expecting Susan to come through the door and tell me dinner's ready or the washing machine's on the fritz again."

Evie felt her heart constrict. "I'm so sorry, Billy," she said. "I didn't know. I never would have . . . You . . . you must have loved her very much."

"More than a man can say. Sometimes I think it should have been me, but God's will be done." Billy turned away. "I'll be in the storeroom if you need me."

God's will be done. Evie had heard those words so many times since the car accident that had destroyed her family and she still couldn't see the sense in them. What sort of God willed destruction and sorrow? Whoever he was, he wasn't the sort of God Evie wanted to believe in.

A family of three came into the restaurant then. They were laughing and Evie watched as the father leaned over and kissed the mother's cheek. Evie turned away. She didn't want to remember her parents being happy together because it made it so much harder to maintain her anger against her father, the man her mother had loved, the man who had once been so good to his family. It was better—easier—to erase the memories of the happy years and of all the good things her father had done for them—like take Evie and her mother to a tree farm each Christmas season to choose the perfect tree, and grill hamburgers in the backyard on even the coldest of winter days, and fix anything in the house that was broken, and chase away the occasional bat that got into the house through the attic—and to see him only for what he had become. The man who had killed her mother. The man who had lost his job and the family's home because of addiction. The man who had abandoned his daughter.

The man who, like Billy, might still be mourning his wife.

Evie shook her head, as if to clear away that last thought. She went back to her place behind the order counter, thanking the girl who had taken over during her break.

Chapter 19

Peeling carrots. An oddly satisfying employment, Poppy thought, watching the pile of orange strips grow. She had decided to make her mother's famous carrot-raisin salad for dinner. The recipe was very simple, but Poppy had shied away from attempting the dish. The few times she had tried her hand at one of the old family favorites both of her sisters had barely touched their food. Maybe it was because she had badly over-salted. Maybe it was because memories could take an appetite away. Well, she would give it one more go and if the carrot raisin salad wasn't a hit with Daisy and Violet, she would try to feed them dishes with no associations good or bad. But what?

Poppy began to cut the pile of peeled carrots in chunks; they, in turn, would be shredded in the food processor, and the rest of the ingredients mixed in later. The task was simple enough to allow her mind to dwell on more important matters, like the fact that it had only occurred to her that morning as she was taking her birth control pill that while she had been focusing on things like buying health insurance (with Freddie's help) and budgeting for daily and monthly expenses (ditto) and making sure that her sisters were eating properly (she had caught Daisy drinking soda for breakfast the other day; since when did Daisy drink soda?) she had entirely ignored the potentially explosive subject of their sexual lives.

Speak of the Devil, Poppy thought, as Daisy came loping into the kitchen and grabbed a chunk of carrot from under Poppy's knife.

"Daisy, I need to ask you something."

"Okay," her sister responded around a mouthful of carrot. "Ow. I bit my tongue."

"Will you be honest with me? It's important."

Daisy shrugged. "I guess."

"Are you having sex with anyone?" Poppy asked.

"What!" Daisy cried, her hand halfway to snatching another piece of carrot from the cutting board. "No way. I don't even have a boyfriend, you know that."

"Girls in high school have sex with people who are not their boyfriends. Hookups, I think they're called, or they used to be."

"Well, I'm not one of them," Daisy said emphatically. "I think hookups are pathetic. What ever happened to self-esteem?"

Poppy felt relieved, but also realized that she wasn't really surprised. Daisy might be prickly and perverse at times, but she had always been levelheaded. "Good," she said. "So, you know all about sex, right? I mean, did Mom talk to you?"

"Of course she did," Daisy responded. "Jeez, Poppy, I'm sixteen. I've known all about sex for years."

"Well, that doesn't mean you don't have any questions. Do you?"

"And you're the expert?" Daisy laughed.

"No, but I've had sex and—"

Daisy put her hands over her ears. "Stop right there! I don't want to hear any details. And no, I don't have any questions."

"I wasn't going to give you any details," Poppy assured her, "and okay. But if you *do* someday have a question you know you should come to me. And when you need to get birth control—"

"Poppy!"

Poppy sighed. "I just want you to know you can count on me."

"Look, I won't be needing birth control any time soon, okay? I'm not planning on messing up my life. Really."

"Good. I mean, not that sex is wrong or bad. You know that, right?"

"Yes, Poppy," Daisy said, rolling her eyes skyward. "I know that. Thanks."

"You're welcome. I think. Look, what does Violet know about the birds and the bees?"

"I'm not sure," Daisy admitted. "I don't think Mom talked to her about sex. Violet was only nine when Mom died. And as for Dad . . . But I know she had a sex ed class in school. So did I. So did you."

"Hmm. But that doesn't mean she knows everything. Or that she knows enough to keep her safe." Poppy sighed. "I guess I'd better talk to her."

"None of this is easy for you, is it?" Daisy asked suddenly.

Poppy smiled ruefully. "No. It isn't. I feel like a pretender to the throne. Like a fake. Who am I to be counseling my sisters about life?"

"You're the one Dad put in charge."

Lucky me, Poppy thought. What she said was: "And how do you think I'm doing so far?"

It took Daisy a long moment to answer and when she did,

she didn't quite meet her sister's eyes. "Okay," she said. "I think you're doing fine."

Poppy didn't believe her for one second—Daisy had always been a terrible liar—but she said, "Thanks. Dinner at six thirty."

Daisy turned to go and then looked back. "Is that Mom's carrot-raisin salad you're making?" she asked.

"Yes," Poppy said.

Daisy nodded. "Good. Just watch the salt, okay?"

Chapter 20

"May I come in?"

Violet was polishing a chunk of some purple and white stone Daisy had never seen before. "Sure," she said.

Daisy stepped inside her sister's bedroom and as always, was struck by how vastly different it was from her own. The walls in Daisy's room were white. There were no floaty scarves or bowls of crystals. There were no books more esoteric than the King James Bible. The contrast always made Daisy wonder how she and Violet could be related and have such different tastes and interests. And then, of course, there was Grimace, who was draped across the back of an old armchair that used to live in the study. The chair had seen better days, and not only because Grimace used it as a scratching post, but for some reason Daisy couldn't fathom her sister was attached to it.

"I'm giving you a heads-up," Daisy said. "Poppy is probably going to ask you about sex."

"What do you mean?"

"Like, what you know and do you have any questions."

"I know all I need or want to know right now," Violet stated firmly.

"Yeah, but she's still probably going to want to talk to you."

Violet shrugged. "That's her job now, watching over us."

Like a hovering buzzard, Daisy thought. But that was unkind. "Are you doing okay?" she asked, sitting on the edge of her sister's bed. "Like, in general, you know . . ."

"Do you mean am I handling the fact of Dad's death in a healthy way?"

Daisy felt a bit embarrassed. Violet never seemed to shy away from or dance around the difficult subjects, the way Daisy often did. "Yeah," she said. "That's what I mean."

Violet nodded and sat in the old armchair. Grimace grunted. "I think that I am," she said. "I'm sad. I miss him, and Mom. But I'm not afraid. So many people are afraid of death, but I'm not. And I've got a home. I love it here. I really do. And Grimace. And you and Poppy and Freddie and Sheila. So, I'm okay."

For a moment Daisy wondered if her sister was protesting a bit too much. But that wasn't Violet. She didn't lie or hide things. "Don't you miss not having any friends your own age?" she asked suddenly. "Sorry, but I've wondered about that." And sometimes, she had worried.

Violet smiled. "How can you miss what you've never had?"

"Yeah, but . . . Don't you ever look at other girls around town or at the beach or in school and think it might be fun to hang out with them and talk about your teachers and cute boys and what bands are cool and just—stuff?"

"No," Violet said simply. "Don't *you* miss not having girlfriends? What happened to that girl you used to hang out with, the one you went to Girl Scouts with for a while?"

"Marla? She and her family moved away, like, four or five years ago. Anyway, I've got Joel." Daisy didn't want to think about what might happen to their friendship when Joel got a serious boyfriend, and he was far more likely to get one before she did—if she ever did.

"So, you're okay, too?" her sister asked. "About Dad?"

Daisy smiled sadly. "Not really. I keep thinking that, I don't know, that I could have saved him somehow. Don't ask me what I might have done! But I was in the house with him when . . ."

Violet got up from the armchair—Grimace grunted—and came over to put a slim hand on Daisy's arm. Daisy was startled. Her younger sister rarely touched another living creature but for Grimace. It hadn't always been that way. "It was his time," Violet said. "It was meant to happen the way it did."

Daisy wasn't sure she could believe that, but if it helped Violet to think so then she wouldn't argue. "Yes," she said. "I guess so. Hey, do you remember when Dad would go away on business, how he would always bring back something for each of us, even if it was just a pen from the hotel where he stayed?"

Violet smiled and sat down next to Daisy. "Once he brought me his name tag from a conference in London."

"I think that was the time he brought me a bag of peanuts from the plane! I loved getting those little gifts. It was so funny and so like Dad."

"I know. I wonder if Poppy kept anything Dad gave her."

Daisy shrugged. "I don't think Poppy's sentimental." *In spite,* she thought, *of her wearing Dad's watch and Mom's bracelet. In spite of her moving into Mom and Dad's room. Maybe I'm misjudging her.*

"We don't really know her at all," Violet pointed out. "I

mean, she's a Capricorn, but I don't see her as a self-assured go-getter. A lot of Capricorns are that way, though."

"They are? Anyway, you're right," Daisy said, "we don't really know her. I used to think that I knew her. When I was growing up. Before you were born, even. I adored her. I followed her everywhere. Isn't that weird?" *My beautiful older sister . . .*

"It's not weird."

Daisy shrugged again. She was sure of one thing. Her younger sister didn't *adore* her. Or Poppy. Really, she knew very little about what Violet felt for the people in her life. She was certain that Violet liked her, and Poppy, but did she actually *love* her sisters? Did she love anyone, now that her parents were gone? Because she *had* to have loved her parents. It was normal to love your parents. Besides, *everyone* had loved Annabelle and Oliver Higgins.

"Remember," Daisy said then, "how when Dad would come home from his business trips, Mom would say, 'Hail, the conquering hero!'"

Violet shook her head. "I don't remember that."

"Really? It always made Dad laugh. The last thing I am or want to be, he would say, is a conqueror. Too much work."

"Do you think Dad was a hero, though?"

"Yes," Daisy said promptly. "I do."

"So do I. Mom was a hero, too."

Suddenly, Daisy felt a surge of great big love for her little sister. How much harder for Violet it all must be, losing Annabelle and Oliver, at so young an age. How brave she was. Children could be heroic, too. Violet always seemed so calm and insightful, but that didn't mean she wasn't feeling all the emotions Daisy was feeling—sorrow, fear, loss. She was just better at handling those emotions.

"Poppy might be our legal guardian," Daisy said now, "but I hope you know you can count on me, as well."

Violet answered quite solemnly. "Yes," she said. "I know. And . . ."

"And what?" Daisy asked gently. It was unusual for Violet to hesitate when speaking. Most often she was pretty emphatic, sometimes disturbingly so.

Violet got off the bed and walked over to pet Grimace on his perch. "And it means a lot to me. I want you to know that."

Daisy looked at her sister, whose back was to her. Suddenly, she seemed so frail and vulnerable. "I do know that," she said over the catch in her throat. "And I won't ever forget it."

Chapter 21

"So, sign here and initial there," Freddie instructed. "Once they cash your check you'll be the proud owner of a life insurance policy."

Poppy smiled. "I never thought that at the age of twenty-five I'd be worth so much money to anybody."

"You wouldn't have been, not if your father was alive. Now, let's go to the kitchen for some tea."

When the two women had settled in the kitchen's breakfast nook with cups of tea and a plate of petit fours, Freddie's favorite pastry, Freddie looked closely at Poppy. "You look as if you haven't been sleeping well," she said. "What's wrong?"

Poppy laughed. "Everything."

"Be more specific, dear. And less dramatic."

"All right. It's just that it's been a horrible week. I forgot that Violet had a dentist appointment. Seems there's a financial penalty for missing an appointment. I keep meaning to buy one of those whiteboards, specifically so I can keep better track of things like that. But I keep forgetting to buy one!"

"Violet could have reminded you," Freddie pointed out. "She's probably thrilled that you forgot. She may be special, but she is still a kid."

The thought hadn't occurred to Poppy that Violet might have reminded her the way she had reminded her about Grimace's appointment with the vet. "Well," she said, "be that as it may, then I left the laundry in the machine for two days before I remembered it was there. Everything smelled of mildew. I had to wash it all again and then clean the machine with bleach. I can't believe I was so stupid."

"You're not the first person to be thwarted by laundry," Freddie said, taking a petit four from the flower-patterned plate between them. "And you won't be the last."

"It's not only the laundry," Poppy went on, determined to convince Freddie of her ineptitude. "I had a fairly disastrous chat with Daisy about sex. Turned out I was worrying about nothing. And last night I burned the rice. The pot is still soaking, but I suspect it's a lost cause. And it's too bad because it's one of the good pots Mom got at her wedding shower. All those years and it was just fine—until I got my hands on it."

"A pot can be replaced. And I never knew your mother to have an emotional attachment to her kitchen tools."

Poppy sighed. "That's not the point, Freddie. The point is that I don't know what I'm doing. I don't know how to run a household. I don't know how to be a parent." *God,* she thought, *I don't even know how to be an adult.* "I've never had to take care of anybody but myself, and I had help with that. Mom, Dad, the housekeeper we had for all those years, my teachers. I've never even had a pet I had to be responsible for. For that matter, I've never even had a plant of my own!"

"Poppy, no one knows how to get things properly done until they do. And they know only after they've made a thousand and one mistakes." Freddie leaned across the table and put a hand on Poppy's. "Look, here's one of my favorite quotes. I repeat it to myself every night. When I remember. 'Finish each day and be done with it. You have done what you could.' "

"Who said that?"

"Ralph Waldo Emerson." Freddie took her hand from Poppy's and sat back. "And it makes a good deal of sense."

"Unless you know that you could have done more. Or done it better."

Freddie sighed. "I see you're determined to be miserable."

"Why did my father make me legal guardian?"

"You've asked me that before. Who else would he have chosen? Neither of your parents had siblings, so no aunts and uncles, and certainly no long-lost relatives that I ever knew of. And don't make me repeat why I wasn't a candidate. Besides, he always had great faith in your abilities."

"I wish he hadn't. I wish he'd considered me an idiot."

"Then what would have happened to your sisters?" Freddie argued. "They would have been sent into the foster care system. They might have been sent to different homes. Violet would have had to give up Grimace. Would you have wanted that?"

"No. No, of course not. It's a horrible thought." *And Mom and Dad would have been so disappointed in me. . . .*

"Then let's move on. There's something else I want to talk to you about. There's a town meeting next week and I think it would be a good idea if you attended. As a representative of the Higgins family."

"Oh," Poppy said, with absolutely no enthusiasm. "What do you mean by representative? Please don't tell me I have to take on some formal role?"

"Of course not. What I mean is that by your presence you demonstrate that the Higgins family of Willow Way cares about Yorktide."

"What goes on at a town meeting exactly?" Poppy asked, not at all reassured by Freddie's words.

"Talk—debate, really—about matters that affect the town. Anything from local conservation issues to development issues. This meeting's agenda happens to include the case of one Will Mantel. He owns a large tract of wooded property on the outskirts of town and is requesting a permit to build a cell phone tower on a hill."

"And?" Poppy asked. "What's the big deal with that?"

"The big deal is that cell phone towers are hideously ugly and his neighbors oppose having an eyesore looming over them."

"Oh. That's a point. Who goes to these meetings?"

"Any year-round resident is welcome, though there are some who are expected to attend, the old families, the ones who have been here for generations. And the members of the Board of Selectmen, of course. They run it all."

Poppy sighed. "Honestly, Freddie, I have no interest in development issues, and definitely no interest in cell phone towers." Conservation, she thought, was another matter, but you didn't have to go to a town meeting to support the cause.

"It's not really about your personal interests. Being part of a community means making an effort."

Did it? Poppy wondered. Living in a city it was easier to, well, to be unconcerned, not entirely, but largely. It was easier in some ways to be lazy about your neighbors, whom you might hardly ever see, and even about your neighborhood, which you might likely leave every morning for your job in another neighborhood entirely.

"But you did say I don't have a formal obligation to York-tide. I mean, aside from paying taxes and not breaking any laws. I don't have an official role in the town, so no one can expect me to"—she had been about to say "to care"—"to get involved."

Freddie laughed. "People can expect all sorts of things from other people, reasonable or not. The point is that your parents were always informed about community affairs and more often than not, they got involved."

"But I'm not my parents," Poppy pointed out. "And I don't want to be. Oh, that sounds childish. You know what I mean."

Freddie put her hand on Poppy's arm. "Try not to always say no, Poppy. Try saying yes once in a while. Throw open a door every now and then."

"I'll think about it," Poppy said, aware that she was probably lying. "The meeting, I mean."

"Good. I'll be there, by the way. It's not like there won't be a friendly face. Jon Gascoyne will be there, too, if he's true to form. Following in his father's footsteps."

"What do you mean?" Poppy asked.

"Albert Gascoyne is a good old-fashioned pillar of the community. Without, I might add, the creepy dark side that so many of them seem to have, at least in books and on TV. I don't think he's ever missed a town meeting since he started going when he was in his teens. And he gives gener-ously to the food bank in Oceanside and to our own here in Yorktide. Sad to say, but even in our relatively affluent parts there are those who would go hungry if it weren't for people taking an interest in their welfare."

"I had no idea," Poppy admitted. "About Mr. Gascoyne or about the food banks."

"There's a lot you don't know yet about Yorktide and its inhabitants. A town meeting is a good way to start."

Poppy laughed. "Freddie, you're the most persistent person I know."

Freddie raised an eyebrow. "Sheila," she said, "would say I'm the most annoying."

Chapter 22

"I'll grab us seats at that picnic table. You go in and order."

"Right." Daisy left Joel and went into The Clamshell, already crowded though it wasn't quite noon. She got on the line to order. A few moments later she was facing the girl behind the order counter—a girl, she realized, she had already met.

"Hi," Daisy said with a smile. "Remember me? I'm the one who almost knocked you into the toothpaste at the convenience store last week."

"Oh," the girl said. "Hi." She didn't return Daisy's smile and she didn't quite meet Daisy's eye.

"I didn't know you worked here. The Clamshell has the best fried clams in town. I'm Daisy, by the way."

The girl didn't reply immediately and for a moment Daisy wondered if she had said or done something wrong or stupid. Could the girl really be angry with her for being clumsy?

"I'm Evie." The words came out as if reluctantly and the girl—Evie—looked down at her order pad. "What would you like?" she asked.

Daisy ordered and moved aside to wait for the food. And she noted that the girl—Evie—acted much the same way with the next customer in line, and with the one after that. Not rude, but definitely not friendly. Almost as if she didn't want anyone to really notice her. Almost . . . furtive.

Well, that was awkward, Daisy thought, when her order came up and she made her way out of the restaurant to where Joel waited for her. Maybe the girl behind the counter— Evie—was just one of those ridiculously shy people who wound up further isolating themselves by making the people around them feel uncomfortable. Whatever the case, Daisy wasn't going to dwell on it.

"Do you know the girl who works behind the counter here?" she asked as she took a seat across from Joel at the redwood picnic table. "The kind of medium-height one with long, light brown hair?"

So much for not dwelling, Daisy thought.

Joel shrugged and reached for a french fry. "No, should I?"

"No. It's just that there's something . . . something secretive about her. I don't know what it is. I mean, we've hardly said ten words to each other so I don't know what I'm basing this feeling on."

"Feminine intuition, probably."

"You're not making fun of me I hope."

"Not at all," Joel protested. "You know I have great respect for all the stuff women do and feel that most men can't seem to get their heads around."

"I know. You're not one of those dense men. Most times."

"Thanks. I think. Hey, did you see that bit on the local news last night about the annual Gay Pride celebrations in Portland next weekend?"

Daisy, mouth full of clams, shook her head.

"We were eating dinner, me and my parents, and watching TV." Joel half laughed. "The bit was only about a minute or so, really just a listing of events, the parade and parties and all that. But when it was over, I swear they looked at me like . . . I don't know, almost like they were afraid."

"Afraid!" Daisy exclaimed.

"I don't mean afraid like you're afraid of a guy with a gun. It's just that sometimes my parents look at me as if they expect my head to pop off or something. I think they expect me to be weird. I don't think they understand that being gay is just that—being gay, no big deal. Not strange or alien. Sometimes I'm tempted to do something outrageous, just to make them happy. Just to fulfill their expectations."

"But what if it made them mad instead?" Daisy asked, eyeing the two remaining fried clams in the cardboard tray.

"It wouldn't," Joel said with conviction. "Not if it wasn't something really terrible. My parents are good people, just . . . puzzled sometimes."

"You're not angry at them for being puzzled by you?" Daisy asked. She thought that she herself might be, if she were in Joel's situation.

"No. I find it sort of funny." Joel sighed dramatically. "What I *don't* find funny is my sorry lack of a love life."

"That guy who works at the ice-cream shop in Perkins Cove is gay. Not the old one, the young one."

"So? Just because we're both gay is no guarantee we'd like each other. Besides, he's got blond hair. I'm not a big fan of blond guys."

Daisy frowned. "Sorry. But there are other gay guys around. You're bound to click with someone."

"There are *hundreds* of gay guys around, especially in summer. Maybe thousands. It's not that."

"Then what is it?" Daisy asked. "You're handsome and smart and talented. Why don't you just ask someone out?"

"Why don't *you*? You're pretty and smart and talented."

Daisy laughed. "Yeah, right. Who would go out with me?"

"Lots of guys. Maybe not most of the guys at our school—they're so provincial!—but once you get to college you'll be fine."

"I doubt it! Anyway, there's no one around now who I like. In that way, I mean, so it doesn't matter if everyone at school is provincial."

Joel sighed. "Why don't we agree to drop this subject of dating until one of us gets totally swept off our feet? Okay? Otherwise it's just way too stressful."

"Deal. Are you going to eat those clams or . . ."

"Go ahead. I'm watching my figure."

"What!" Daisy cried. "You're fine the way you are!"

"It's a joke, Daisy," Joel explained, with wide eyes, as if he were talking to a child.

"Right."

When they had finished lunch, Joel carried their tray to the trash can, dumped the contents inside, and stacked the tray on top. Daisy followed, glancing through the big front windows of The Clamshell on their way to the parking lot. That girl who worked behind the counter. Evie. Maybe she needed help of some sort; maybe she wasn't shy at all but scared; maybe fear was making her seem secretive . . .

"Uh, Daisy?"

She looked for Joel, only to find him several feet behind her. "What?" she said.

"You walked past the car."

Daisy laughed and walked back to Joel's old black Volvo. "Daydreaming I guess."

Chapter 23

Evie was curled up in the bed in Nico's guestroom, Ben under her arm and a packet of chocolate chip cookies she had splurged on within easy reach. She had a pretty good idea that Nico wouldn't be happy to learn that she was eating in bed so she was very careful about crumbs and made it a strict point to wash the sheets once a week. (There was a machine in the master bathroom.)

"Ben," Evie said, reaching for another cookie. "Today was not a very good day." There had been this one awful customer who had come in just when they opened at eleven to serve the early lunch crowd. His hair was all greasy and his T-shirt rode up over his big belly. He had started to complain about having to wait for his order almost as soon as Evie had put it in to the kitchen. She had tried to assure him that his food would be coming soon, but he had persisted in complaining and berating the "idiot kids" in the kitchen. His verbal abuse had almost driven Evie to tears. Finally, Billy had come out front and with one menacing look had silenced the troublemaker. "I believe," Billy had said to the

man, "that you owe this young lady an apology." The man
had reddened and muttered "Sorry" in Evie's direction. Upsetting stuff like that didn't happen often at The Clamshell,
but when it did, Evie felt her aloneness and her vulnerability
fiercely.

But then that girl, Daisy, had come in, right before noon.
The girl who had bumped into her in the convenience store.
There was something about her Evie liked; she seemed like
an open and friendly person. But Evie had to be so careful.
So much was at stake. And a real friendship wasn't something Evie thought possible now. Not until . . . Not until
things changed.

Kate Willow. She had been her last real friend. Evie had
no idea what had been going on in Kate's life since she had
been sent away. . . . And yet, if it hadn't been for Kate and
her parents, Evie didn't know how she would have survived
those first weeks after the accident. Like, for example, the
day of the funeral. Evie's father was still in the hospital, still
in danger of losing a leg, so Evie had gone to the funeral
with Kate and her parents, sitting between Mr. and Mrs. Willow at the church and holding Mrs. Willow's hand at the
cemetery. Kate, she remembered, had lent her a sweater as it
had been an unusually chilly day and Evie had arrived to
stay at the Willows' house with only one hastily packed suit-
case.

The Willows had been so good to Evie in the weeks following Evelyn's funeral, too, taking her to visit her father in
the hospital (though she hated going; the place frightened
her and she had nothing to say to her father) and making
sure her clothes were clean for school. Mrs. Willow made
her favorite meals and Mr. Willow took the girls to a crafts
fair one afternoon. Both of Kate's parents helped Evie with
her homework. And even though she missed her mother ter-

ribly, though she missed her room and all of her things, Evie had started to think that she could stay with Kate's family forever. Nothing more would have to change. She wouldn't have to go back to live with her father. Maybe one day Mr. and Mrs. Willow would even adopt her.

Evie had been with Kate's family for about six weeks when one afternoon she overheard her friend talking to her mother.

"She's my friend and all," Kate had said, "but it's not like we can have a sleepover for the rest of our lives. I want my room back all to myself. She's so sad all the time. It's like I don't know what to say to her anymore."

Mrs. Willow had murmured something Evie couldn't entirely catch, probably something meant to reassure her daughter that before long Evie would be back where she belonged. "Just try to be patient, Kate, okay? She's been through something really traumatic." That much Evie had heard.

Then her father had been sent home from the rehab facility where he had been sent upon release from the hospital and after a few days during which a visiting nurse and a social worker helped settle him in and make a few adjustments to render the house more accessible for a man in a wheelchair, Evie, too, was sent home. She met the visiting nurse. She met the social worker. She met the physical therapist. The house—what had once been her home—felt as if it were being invaded by strangers, and there was nothing she could do about it. But it wasn't all bad. When those other people were there, Evie didn't have to be alone with her father. She didn't have to try and talk to him. And he didn't have to try and talk to her.

After a while the professionals stopped coming by. Dan was improving nicely, they said. Physically, he was on the mend. He would be able to go back to the law firm before long. But not one of them had been able to see that emotionally, Dan was not improving at all. He was deteriorating.

As for Evie, it was so hard to walk through the rooms her mother had once walked through and to know she would never return to them. It had been so hard to see the crystal vase her mother had loved and the curtains she had chosen so carefully and the beautiful little oil painting one of her friends had given her and to know that Evelyn would never be able to appreciate or find pleasure in them again.

About a month after he had been sent home Evie's father had made it known he didn't have the energy to go through her mother's clothing and personal items, so Evie had asked two neighbors who had offered to help. The afternoon before Mrs. Mallory and Mrs. Tribble were scheduled to come over, Evie had gone into her parents' bedroom, hoping to find a few things of her mother's she could keep, but after only a few minutes she had felt overwhelmed by sadness and had raced back into her own bedroom, slamming the door behind her. She had managed to take only her mother's gold locket in the shape of a heart with a tiny diamond on the cover. Inside was a photo of her father and one of her. She considered throwing the photo of her father in the trash and decided not to.

During that awful time she had been so torn between wanting and needing her father's love and comfort and hating him for what had happened to her mother. And then there was his foreignness. This man with the wheelchair and then the walker and then the cane, who was he? This man who never smiled and who could barely meet her eye when he spoke to her, was this her father? This man who barely managed to heat a frozen meal each night for their dinner, was *this* Dan?

Things began to fall apart slowly at first, then more rapidly. Evie grew embarrassed by her father's decline. There was his appearance, for one. He grew so thin; he wasn't eating and he was taking all those stupid pills. He shaved, but he never seemed to get all the stubble. He wore the same shirt three days in a row. His shoes were never shined. He couldn't keep up with the house and yard work. Evie did her best, but her mother had always done the laundry and cleaned the kitchen and the bathrooms and Evie just didn't know how. They had a housekeeper for a few months—Evie supposed her father had hired her, but maybe a social worker had taken care of it—but she had abruptly quit. Evie remembered the woman taking her hand on her last day, telling her to take care, looking at her so intently it had made Evie uncomfortable, like the housekeeper knew a dreadful secret about what was in store for Evie and her father, a secret she was forced to keep to herself.

And then there had come the day when her father had not gone in to work. He had not even gotten out of bed except to use the bathroom. It was the same the next day and the day after that. After an entire week of this nightmare of uncertainty, during which Evie felt constantly sick to her stomach, she had finally confronted her father.

"Why aren't you at the office?" she asked, standing in the doorway of the bedroom he had once shared with her mother.

He was sitting on the edge of the bed, his hands folded between his knees. He was wearing a pair of stained sweatpants and a T-shirt that had once been white. "I lost my job," he said.

Lost it. Like he had put it down and forgotten where he had put it. Like it had fallen out of his pocket. Evie felt faint. She put a hand on the doorframe to steady herself.

"You were fired."

"Essentially, yes."

"You were taking those pills at the office."

"No. I—"

"Are you looking for another job?" she demanded, the shock passing, being replaced by anger. "How will we get money?" *Who will hire him now? Who will trust him to be their lawyer?*

Her father put his head down and did not reply.

"I hate you!" she cried and ran off to her own room. She took her mother's locket from her jewelry box, opened it, removed the photo of her father, and threw it in the trash.

He hadn't come after her. He hadn't bothered to argue with her, to comfort her, to reason with her. He had lost himself, too.

After that, Evie began to withdraw from everybody, even Kate. She buried herself more deeply in her schoolwork. She searched every inch of the house for loose change. She went through her father's pockets when he was asleep—which was most times—looking for a stray dollar bill. Whatever she found she stashed under her mattress. She knew things couldn't go on like this forever and she wanted to be prepared. She hunted out a small photo of her mother and put it in the heart-shaped locket, across from the picture of herself.

And then, the day came when her father told her that he had lost the house, too. "I have nothing," he said. His wife, his job, his house . . . and now, his daughter. He sent her away to live with relatives, her Aunt Joanne and Uncle Ron and their kids, people she had seen only once in her life and barely remembered (there had been some falling-out among the adults and then a halfhearted reconciliation, followed by a lapse into indifference), and while her aunt and uncle were nice enough her cousins hadn't known what to do with this sad stranger now installed in their home. Alexa, who was a year older than Evie, was openly resentful of her presence. Craig, who was a year younger, mostly ignored her.

She would never forget the moment when her cousin Alexa told her that her father was sometimes homeless. Living on the streets, she had said. "What did you think would happen to him when you lost the house and he sent you to live with us? That he'd get some nice apartment and a new job and make back all the money he lost and then send for you?"

That was exactly what Evie had thought. Or, had hoped for, in spite of her hatred for her father. She had hoped that somehow, miraculously, they could start over together. Things wouldn't be the same as they had been before the accident. But maybe they could be . . . okay.

Evie stuffed the last chocolate chip cookie into her mouth and put the empty packet on the bedside table. She tried not to dwell on the past—staying alive and safe was work enough—but sometimes the past just wouldn't be ignored.

It was close to ten o'clock and Evie suddenly felt exhausted. She got out of bed and set about her nightly routine. She didn't know why Nico didn't have an alarm system. It seemed ridiculous for someone who lived alone in such a large house, even if the house wasn't exactly located in a high crime area. There was always the possibility of a dishonest person passing through town . . . *Like me*, Evie thought. *I don't want to be dishonest, but I have to be. Life has made me dishonest.*

First, she made it a point to double check that all doors and windows in the house were locked, and all blinds and curtains closed. Then she pushed a heavy wooden chest against the front door as another precaution. (Luckily, the back door, accessible from the kitchen, was dead-bolted from the inside.) Finally, before going up to the bedroom

Nico had told her she could use, she made certain that the light in the hallway leading to the staircase was turned on. Once back in the bedroom, she wedged a chair under the doorknob as the final bit of makeshift security and hugged Ben to her chest. Still, there was no guarantee of a sound sleep and sweet dreams.

Chapter 24

Freddie and Sheila lived in a charming post-and-beam house they had designed and built (with some professional help of course) back in the mid-eighties. It was a two-story structure with an enclosed porch on one side of the house and an open deck on the other. During the colder months the women ignored those areas in favor of the cozy central living area, complete with wood-burning stove, overstuffed couches, high-backed armchairs, and thick woolen rugs with patterns of maroon and gold and green. The two bedrooms were on the second floor; Poppy had seen the master bedroom only once, many years earlier, when Sheila was down with a nasty flu. Poppy had accompanied her mother to the house with a vat of homemade chicken soup and they had waved to the invalid from the door of her bedroom. Freddie hadn't allowed them to get any closer.

"Hand me that vase, will you?" Sheila asked. "The yellow ceramic one on the second shelf."

Poppy did. She and her sisters were at 14 Howard Lane for dinner, and while Daisy and Violet helped (or hindered) Freddie in the kitchen, Poppy was helping Sheila set the table in the section of the living space that served as a dining area. Poppy had always loved coming to this house. The feeling it projected was one of true peace and stability, and that, Poppy thought, was largely due to the lifetime's accumulation of mementos of important events and souvenirs of travel and works of art carefully collected and photographs of people long gone but still loved. It always fascinated Poppy to see how the homes of two people who had lived together in harmony for many years—fifty-three, in Freddie and Sheila's case—seemed to reflect the tastes and preferences of one many-sided person, a style that seemed to have grown naturally, organically over time, not a style imposed by one or the other person with a small, out-of-place piece that was a reluctant nod to the annoying whim of the other. She supposed her parents' house appeared to others like Freddie and Sheila's did to her, but as it was also her childhood home, she was too emotionally tied to every little bit of it to see anything at a critical, assessing distance.

"I do love a dinner party," Sheila said, making a final adjustment to the purple irises she had arranged in the yellow vase. "I even enjoy the cleaning-up process. I even enjoy ironing all the linen napkins!"

Sheila was wearing a smartly tailored taupe linen pantsuit with navy espadrilles. Around her neck were multiple strands of highly polished silver beads. On her wrist were matching silver cuffs. On the ring finger of her left hand was a chunky gold band that Freddie had given her many anniversaries ago.

Poppy smiled. "Sheila, you're the only one I know who can wear a suit at any time of the day or night, on any occasion, and make it look appropriate."

"You can take the girl out of the city," Sheila said.

"Don't you ever regret leaving New York? I mean, it's pretty much the opposite of Yorktide."

"Not for a very long time," Sheila admitted. "New York, after all, is just a place. To be sure, a wonderful place. But Freddie is a person. And I've always found that a person ranks much higher with me than a spot on a map."

Poppy sighed. "I wonder," she said, "if I'll ever love someone enough to make a sacrifice like that." Love someone at *all,* really. Oh, once she had been infatuated with a guy, back in high school. What was his name? And she had had her share of crushes; she recalled with some embarrassment how she had almost made a fool of herself over her French professor at Adams. (It was only after her mother, the man's colleague, had told her about his devotion to his wife that Poppy's ardor had waned.) And after college, there had been a few halfhearted relationships. But never *love.* Suddenly, Poppy wondered if she had been lazy in that aspect of her life, too. Had she neglected to develop her emotional life as she had neglected to develop a career? Or was cowardice at fault? Did she lack the *courage* to love?

"I don't see it as a sacrifice," Sheila was saying, and it took Poppy a moment to refocus on the conversation. "Oh, I did at one point, a few years into the relationship when Freddie and I were going through a rough patch. Self-pity took over I'm afraid. 'Look at all I've done for you, I've given up my home, et cetera, et cetera, and what have I gotten in return?' But I got past that fit of immaturity, I'm glad to say."

Poppy smiled. "Then I wonder if I'll ever be so mature."

Sheila excused herself to see if Freddie needed help in the kitchen and Poppy finished setting the table. As she straightened silverware and refolded a napkin, she wondered what her parents might have sacrificed for each other over the course of their marriage. She had never been aware of any sense of discontent on the part of either of them. But then again, no one outside a relationship really knew what went on inside it. And Oliver and Annabelle had made it a point never to argue in front of their children, even about small things. Of course there must have been disagreements, but none that Poppy could call to mind ever knowing about. And for that, she was grateful.

"Time to eat," Daisy announced, leading the rest of the group to the table.

"A nice, clichéd summer meal," Freddie said, as they took their seats. "Lobsters, corn on the cob, coleslaw, salad, and strawberry shortcake for dessert. Sheila made the short-cake from scratch."

"And I'll whip the cream by hand," Sheila added. "None of that artificial stuff from a can."

"I actually like that stuff," Daisy admitted, putting an ear of corn on her plate. "Dad used to like it, too. You know, sometimes I wonder if Dad would have preferred one of us die instead of Mom."

"Daisy!" Poppy cried. "That's an awful thing to say!"

Freddie agreed with her. "For God's sake, Daisy, don't be melodramatic," she scolded. "The man had a bad heart. Biology. Science. Genetics. His father had a bad heart, too. Henry died when Oliver was only twenty-six. Nothing to do with romantic notions."

Poppy looked at Violet. Daisy's blurted comment didn't seem to have disturbed her; she was aggressively cracking a lobster claw, a frown of concentration on her face.

"I wonder," Daisy said now, "what Mom would have done if she had had boys. I mean, you can't very well name a boy Rose or Lily, can you?"

My sister, Poppy thought, *is determined to be perverse tonight.*

Sheila laughed. "Not if you don't want them to be cruelly teased, taunted, and beaten you don't."

"Oh, she probably would have gone with something like

Sage," Poppy suggested, wondering why she was contributing to such a silly discussion. "That's not really a gender-specific name is it?"

"Thyme," Violet said, looking up from her mostly destroyed lobster body. "Tarragon."

Freddie shook her head. "I think your father would have had something to say about his son being named after anything in the plant kingdom!"

"Dad would have done anything Mom told him to do," Daisy argued. "He *did* do everything she told him to do. Because he wanted to. Not because he was afraid of her. He loved her. Well, we all know that."

"Not to change the subject," Freddie said then, in her forceful and authoritative attorney tone. "But, I'm changing the subject. I hope you girls are keeping up with your reading this summer. One doesn't want the brain to turn to mush."

"I've got my crosswords," Daisy said. "And I'm reading *War and Peace*. At least, I'm trying to. And I practice my clarinet every day. Well, every other day."

"I practice my flute," Violet announced. "And I'm reading the Arthurian legends for the first time. And I'm thinking about learning how to knit. Or maybe do macramé, like people did in the seventies. I saw something about it on the Internet. But I don't know if Grimace will let me alone. All that string."

"And what about you, Poppy?" Freddie asked. "Have you been challenging yourself intellectually?"

For a moment Poppy felt as if she were back in fourth grade, pinned under the eye of a particularly strict teacher. "Uh, no," she said. "Not really. Sorry."

"Don't apologize to me. It's your own self you're hurting. You know, having finished your formal education doesn't mean one is allowed to let the brain atrophy. Why don't you take the opportunity of being on hiatus from work to read one of your father's books?"

Poppy laughed. "I'm afraid I'm too dumb to read Dad's work!" And the trouble was, she half believed that. Sometimes she wondered how a daughter of two such prominent people as Annabelle and Oliver Higgins could feel so lacking in skill and talent. Maybe, she thought, it was *because* they were so prominent that she felt so insignificant.

Freddie harrumphed. "No," she said, "you most certainly are *not* too dumb. But you will need to apply yourself if you're to follow his arguments. Your father was a rigorous thinker and he challenged his readers. The payoff, of course, is worth the effort."

"That reminds me," Poppy said suddenly. "I got something from Adams College today. An invitation to take Dad's place on the committee that awards the scholarship in Mom's name."

"How wonderful," Sheila said.

"Not really. How can I possibly accept? I'm totally out of my depth in the academic world."

"You won't be making decisions on your own," Freddie pointed out. "You'll be part of a committee. You can learn from the more senior members."

"Who probably all have a PhD. Won't they resent my being there? I'm just Oliver Higgins's pretty daughter. I have no credentials."

Freddie sighed. "How do you think you earn credentials? By showing up. By listening and asking questions."

"But you're Dad's literary executor," Poppy argued. "You have more right than I do to determine who deserves a scholarship in Mom's name."

"Poppy, one thing has nothing to do with the other. Anyway, I strongly advise you to accept the invitation."

"Go ahead, Poppy." Daisy grinned. "The worst that could happen is you totally embarrass yourself and will never be able to hold your head up in Yorktide again."

"Adams College isn't in Yorktide," Violet pointed out, before Poppy could retort. "It's in South Berwick."

Sheila rose from the table. "If everyone is finished, I think I'll bring out the dessert."

Poppy rose with her. "Good idea," she said. "I'll help you clear. And no more talk about the scholarship committee, please."

Chapter 25

About some things Violet Higgins felt very certain. About others, she felt less certain, like, for example, her current state of mind.

The dream, that awful dream that took place in a fantastical garden, had returned twice in the past ten days. In the third version, which had taken place the night before, her parents' roles had been reversed. It was her father that Violet accidentally killed with a poison flower, and her mother who pursued her to the well. The demon was the same horrible character he had been in the first two versions of the nightmare.

Violet sat in the old armchair she had rescued from being thrown out and realized that even though she was in the haven that was her room, at that moment it didn't feel like the safe and calming place she had created it to be. That was weird and upsetting, as was the fact that she had lied to Daisy when she had told her that she was not scared of death. Well, at one time she *hadn't* been, but lately . . . Lately, the thought of Death with a capital letter seemed horrifying. Lately, a feeling of generalized apprehension seemed to creep over her at the most unlikely moments, not always but often, like when she was watering the rosebushes or reading from one of her favorite novels. Why should such usually pleasant activities suddenly cause—or be invaded by?—apprehension? Too often she found herself expecting something bad to happen, someone else to die, some unnamed tragedy to occur. Too often she felt *vulnerable,* and that was something she had never felt before. Never.

So the question was: Why was she suddenly not okay? Maybe, Violet thought now, she was suffering from delayed post-traumatic stress disorder. But she hadn't even been with her father when he died and wasn't PTSD caused by something horrible you had witnessed or experienced first-hand? True, she had been with her mother when *she* died, but her passing had been peaceful, and Dad and Daisy had been there, too.

Or maybe, Violet wondered, the cause of her distress was hormonal, all due to the phases of the moon and Diana, the goddess of nature and fertility and childbirth. She was still developing both physically and emotionally; her period still wasn't regular. Maybe this—this disturbance—she felt was normal, but the trouble was that Violet wasn't in the habit of sharing her fears and worries. She didn't really know how it was done.

Violet glanced over at her bookcase, crammed with books she had been collecting since she had first learned to read at five years of age. Several of her books on astrology stated that a career in the field of medicine was a good choice for someone who was born under the sun sign of Pisces, so her own decision (if it could be called that and not a calling) to become a holistic healer someday made perfect sense. But now Violet wondered. Shouldn't a good healer be able to heal herself first? If you were sick or troubled, how could you possibly make someone else well?

The night before, as Violet lay awake after the awful dream, the idea of going to a psychic had occurred to her. A good psychic might provide some useful insight into what was happening inside her, but getting to one wouldn't be easy to manage. First, and most importantly, she didn't *know* a genuine psychic and she didn't know anyone who did. Surely word of mouth was very important in these matters. But even if she did manage to get the name of someone reputable there was the problem of getting there and back and of paying for her services. An even bigger problem was that Violet wasn't sure Poppy would allow her to see a psychic; she wasn't a believer as far as Violet could tell and she suspected that because her older sister was taking her role as guardian so seriously she might insist that Violet see a psychologist or a counselor instead and that was *not* what Violet wanted at all. It was not what she needed. She knew that.

For the first time since Poppy had come home to live with them on Willow Way Violet felt a tiny thread of resentment toward her sister. Her parents would have let her go to a psychic, she was sure of it. Her parents *got* her.

But maybe she shouldn't assume that Poppy would object. . . . Violet hated to think or act unfairly and she suspected that she was guilty of unfairness now. She truly believed that Poppy and Daisy were there for her. The problem was that try as she might she couldn't imagine turning to them for help or understanding. And the biggest problem with that was *why* she couldn't imagine it, when imagining was usually so easy for her.

"I'm all confused," Violet told Grimace, who had just woken from one of his many daily naps and was stretching magnificently. "I don't like being confused."

In response, Grimace leaped off the bed and clear across the room to land in Violet's lap.

Chapter 26

A woman stood at the edge of the cliff overlooking the sea. She was wearing a long black dress with a cinched waist, tight sleeves, and full skirts. It was a dark, overcast day and the waves were crashing against the rocky shore. Poppy wondered if the woman was one of the Civil War heroines her mother had written about so feelingly. One of those kind and beautiful and brave women. Except that women in the nineteenth century usually didn't wear their hair down in public, did they? So maybe . . . Yes, of course, Poppy saw it now! The woman was her mother, it was Annabelle! And suddenly she was going over the cliff, her long dark skirts billowing around her, her arms outspread as if she would fly, her long dark hair spread out against the moody gray sky. . . . An awful cry of anguish rose from Poppy's lips as she rushed toward the cliff's edge. She would go after the woman. Her mother. She would save her, bring her back. It was only a mistake, her going over the cliff, only a misstep. It hadn't been meant to happen. Poppy spread out her arms in imitation of the woman, her mother, and then gentle but strong hands were gripping her waist. An angel from heaven above, she thought, come to help carry her over. She turned her head to see this angel, but it was Jon Gascoyne and he was holding her back, he wasn't helping her at all! She plucked at his hands around her waist. "Let me go!" she cried. "I have to go after her! I have to!"

Poppy woke in a cold sweat. A dream. Of course. Just a dream, but an awful one. She shivered and pulled the damp sheet up around her neck. Her mother's book was beside her in the bed; she had been reading from it before falling asleep. With a trembling hand she opened it to the photo on the inside of the back cover. Annabelle Higgins, alive and vibrantly beautiful. Even a professional photographic portrait, which so often could fail to capture the real nature of the sitter, couldn't mask her mother's lively spirit.

Like death could.

Poppy had been dragging all day, and not even three cups of coffee had helped wake her fully. She had been unable to get back to sleep after that nightmare. The image of her mother falling through the air like a dark angel dogged her every step, from the time she took the garbage to the curb for the weekly morning pickup to the time she started the preparations for dinner. Why hadn't she recognized her mother sooner? If she had, she might have reached her before . . . And for the life of her she couldn't figure out why Jon Gascoyne had been involved, why, indeed, he had come to her rescue. She barely knew him, after all. Maybe it had something to do with the fact that he had been her mother's student once upon a time. Not that that was much of a connection.

At least she had managed to be productive in one small way. She had gone to the OfficeMax in Kittery for a whiteboard and markers. The purchase made her feel a bit like a throwback. Most people these days seemed to keep track of their schedules on an electronic device. But electronic devices could be ignored and they were often temperamental. What was the worst thing that could happen to a whiteboard? It fell off its hooks?

"What's that for?" Daisy had asked when Poppy had finished nailing the whiteboard to the wall next to the fridge.

"It's so that I don't forget another doctor's appointment or whatever else it is I'm supposed to be remembering. We'll all write down our weekly schedule and that way we'll all know what everyone else is doing and when."

"Sounds like a police state to me," Daisy had muttered.

Damned if I do and damned if I don't, Poppy had thought, watching her sister tramp out of the kitchen.

There was still some time before dinner would be ready (she had put a casserole in the oven to bake, the lazy cook's dream concoction), and she decided to call Allie Swift. They hadn't talked in over a week and a text here and there didn't really count for much.

"Is this a bad time?" she asked when Allie answered the phone, sounding a bit breathless.

"Not at all. I'm just in from my yoga class—what a workout!—and I'm pouring a chilled glass of wine as I speak."

"Oh. Good."

"Such enthusiasm!" Allie laughed. "What's going on?"

Poppy sighed. "Nothing. And that's the problem. What's the *point* of my life, Allie? What am I here for?"

"Whoa, not even some meaningless chitchat? Why all the existential angst? And maybe you need a glass of wine, too."

"Because I feel so useless," Poppy told her, knowing that she probably sounded like a whiny teen but unable to help herself.

"Poppy," Allie said sharply, "you're not contemplating doing something drastic, are you?"

"You mean, am I suicidal? No, absolutely not! I'm not even close to despair. I just wish I could be certain that I'll—I'll leave a legacy. A good one, I mean. Like my mother did. And my father. You know, when each of them died, we got hundreds of cards and notes from colleagues and former students and even people who had read their books but never met them. Literally hundreds. It was extraordinary. I guess I want that kind of recognition for myself. But only if I've really earned it. And that's the problem: How am I to earn it? Where do I start?"

"If I might quote Soren Kierkegaard," Allie replied, "'Life can only be understood backward; but it must be lived forward.'"

Poppy laughed humorlessly. "Good ol' Kierkegaard."

"You'll find out someday if your choices and decisions were right," Allie assured her. "But you've got to make them first."

"But how!"

"You're going to have to trust your instincts, take a leap of faith," Allie said patiently. "There's no other way, Poppy. We're all in the same situation. None of us knows what's going to happen tomorrow or even in the next twenty minutes. We're all pretty much stumbling around blindly, if not always then most of the time."

"That's not a very comforting thought."

"Sorry. I meant you to realize that you're not alone. Look, are you sure you're all right?"

"Yes, absolutely," Poppy said firmly. "It's just been a tough day. I slept badly last night."

"Well, get to bed early tonight. Doctor Allie's orders."

"I will," Poppy said. "And thanks."

Daisy and Violet appeared in the door to the kitchen as Poppy put her cell phone on the counter. "We're starved," Daisy announced. "Is dinner ready?"

Poppy sighed. "Five minutes."

"It smells delicious," Violet said.

At least, Poppy thought, *I've mastered the art of the casserole.*

Chapter 27

Daisy pushed the vacuum cleaner across the living room floor. For the life of her she couldn't remember the last time anyone had used the room. It had seen a lot of life in the old days, back when both of her parents were alive. Annabelle and Oliver Higgins were naturally gregarious people and had been known for their frequent parties. How many times had Daisy come downstairs on a Sunday morning to find one or more of her parents' friends or colleagues asleep on the couch here in the living room, and also often in the study and sunroom?

We should shut this room up, she thought now, turning the vacuum cleaner off and winding the cord around the handle. It would be one less room to clean. Daisy wasn't sure why her father had fired their housekeeper not long after her mother had died. It meant that she and her dad were left to keep the house clean and in order; Violet was too young to be expected to pitch in, though she did keep her own room clean. Maybe he just hadn't been able to bear a relative stranger puttering around the house that his wife had loved so much; maybe the presence of Mrs. Olds felt like a violation, even though the family had known her for years. Daisy had never asked her father and now she would never know the answer to her question.

"Rats!" Daisy retrieved the figurine she had accidentally knocked to the carpet with the dust cloth. It was Columbine, one of the commedia dell'arte figurines her mother had collected. Poppy loved the figurines; what would she have said if Columbine had broken? Daisy decided she would talk to her sister about hiring a new housekeeper. They had the money to hire someone, maybe even a team of people, to come in at least once a week. It was silly to think that a bunch of kids—and that's what they were—could keep a huge house clean and in working order. Besides, housekeeping was boring.

Daisy gave the mantel of the magnificent stone fireplace a quick pass with the dust cloth, careful not to disturb the framed photograph of her father taken by one of his colleagues at a conference in Geneva about a year ago. (Though he had cut back on the number of public appearances he made since his wife's death, there were those occasional conferences he felt compelled to attend.) He was impeccably dressed beneath his head of wild white hair, wearing a tiepin that had once belonged to his father, Henry. That tiepin was another item Daisy had chosen to treasure after Oliver's death, along with his scarf and favorite dictionary. She didn't think that Poppy knew she had taken it from the safe. If she did know, she hadn't mentioned it. Poppy still hadn't gotten around to clearing out Dad's things and Daisy was in no rush to remind her.

Housework abandoned for the moment, Daisy flopped onto the couch. She remembered so clearly the day her father had died. He had been very upset that morning about not being able to find a particular photo of her mother, an old one taken before they had married. Daisy had assured him that the photo would turn up, but her attempt at consolation had fallen on deaf ears. And then, the letter had come, the letter relating devastating news about a respected colleague, a man with whom her father had gone to school. Dr. Morris, who had once been accused of plagiarism (her father had been a staunch supporter of his innocence, and indeed, he had been proved not guilty), had now been fired from his university for sexually harassing several students.

Not that Daisy had known what the letter contained. She had simply given it to her father in the sunroom and gone off. But what if she *hadn't* given her father that letter, what if she had read it first—not that she was in the habit of reading her father's correspondence—but what if she *had,* just that once? She might have broken the news to him another time, when he wasn't already so upset. She had left him alone while she started dinner (a cold salad and pasta with sauce from a jar) and then Freddie had come by the house and gone into the sunroom to see Oliver and then . . . And then Freddie had come back into the kitchen where Daisy was setting the table and the look on her face was enough to tell Daisy that the very worst thing that could happen had happened.

Daisy had only discovered the contents of that fatal letter (that's how she thought of it) when she finally had the nerve to go into the sunroom, after the paramedics had removed her father's body. It was lying open on the floor by his chair.

The doorbell rang and Daisy gratefully abandoned her housekeeping chores—and her memories—to answer it. Joel stood on the doorstep.

"You look glum," he said immediately. "Thinking about your dad?"

Daisy nodded and stepped outside to join him, closing the door behind her. It was the first time she had been out in the fresh air that day.

"Come on, I've got just the thing to cheer you up."

Joel grabbed her hand and pulled her after him out of the house and down to where his car was parked in the drive.

"Where are we going?" Daisy cried.

"To Ogunquit beach," Joel said, opening the passenger side door for her. "There's a kite-flying festival today. Kites always make people happy. Even grumpy-pants people like you."

Daisy smiled. "Will you buy me an ice-cream cone, too?" she asked.

Joel heaved a dramatic sigh and slid behind the wheel. "If it'll make you happy, I'll buy you two ice-cream cones."

Chapter 28

Evie, sitting on the edge of her bed after a long day at The Clamshell, removed the heart-shaped locket from around her neck and opened it. She studied the pictures inside at least once a day, comparing her mother's face to her own. They were so similar. The crooked smile. The slim nose. Even the same hairline. Still, there was no denying that she had inherited her father's eyes, wide set and slightly almond-shaped. No matter how hard Evie tried to reject or dismiss him, her father would always be a part of her. All she had to do was to look in the mirror.

With a sigh, Evie fastened the locket around her neck again and slipped it under her shirt the way she always did. When people saw a locket they automatically asked whose picture was inside and Evie didn't want to share her mother with anyone. She could lie, of course, say there were no pictures inside, but she was already lying about so many things . . .

Like the fact that she was an "unaccompanied teen." She couldn't remember where she had heard that term; probably, she thought, on TV or online. Either way, that's what she was officially, an unaccompanied teen. The term was broad enough she supposed to encompass teenagers whose lives had been badly disturbed in all sorts of ways, resulting in their being on their own and without a safe home. Teens whose parents were in jail. Teens who had run away from abuse. Teens whose parents or guardians had kicked them out for getting in trouble at school or with the police. Teens who had been dumped on distant relatives who didn't want them, like she had been.

Her aunt and uncle hadn't said as much and really, they had been nice enough to her, but from the moment Evie had set foot in their house she had felt more unwanted than she had ever felt before, haunted by a sense of dislocation, of shifting ground. People needed stability, a place to call their own. Even animals built burrows and birds built nests and each defended those homes against invaders, intruders, beings who didn't belong. Evie hadn't felt like an intruder when she had been living with Kate, not at first anyway. But she had known Kate and her parents for a long time and besides, Evie figured she had probably been in shock for the first weeks or maybe even months after her mother was killed and her father so badly hurt. Not able to fully realize her situation. Not able to comprehend that her life would never be normal again.

She would never forget the moment when her path became clear. She had been living with her aunt and uncle for about two months when her cousin Alexa had announced one night at dinner that the annual father-daughter dance for juniors was in two weeks and that she didn't want to go. Her uncle had asked why not and Alexa had replied that she thought the whole idea "boring and old-fashioned." If Uncle Ron was hurt by his daughter's decision he hadn't let it show; if Aunt Joanne was aware of her daughter's insensitivity, given Evie's situation, she hadn't said. But Alexa's dismissive attitude toward the event cut Evie to the core. At least her cousin *had* a father to take as her date to the dance. When Evie became a junior, whom would she be able to take? She supposed that other girls without a father asked another significant male adult to go; she supposed she could ask Uncle Ron. But it wasn't the same, not at all! And at that moment, over a meal of roast chicken and baked potatoes, Evie's decision was made. She would leave this house as soon as she possibly could. She simply didn't belong in the normal world.

The memory of that awful dinner still in her mind, Evie went into the bathroom that was hers to use. Suddenly, another memory confronted her. She saw herself as a little girl, watching her father shave before her parents' bathroom mirror. She remembered the routine. The way he splashed water over his face. The way he applied the creamy white foam. She heard the scratch of the razor as it passed over his cheeks. The whole thing had fascinated her, such an exotic ritual that belonged only to men, like Daddy. She remembered how her father would put a dollop of shaving cream on her nose and how she would squeal with laughter.

Evie shook her head. She hadn't thought about those times she had spent alone with her father in what seemed like an eternity. Watching him shave; spending long Saturday afternoons at the zoo while her mother was at her shop; sharing a bowl of popcorn while watching her favorite Disney movies, time and time again. She didn't want to think about those moments now. They might lead to her wondering where he was and what he was feeling. They might lead her to wondering if he was thinking of her.

Quickly, Evie brushed her teeth and turned off the bathroom light. But the images of her once-beloved father followed her in the dark.

Chapter 29

"Oh my God!"

Poppy opened the front door of the house on Willow Way to find her friend Allie Swift, Luis Vuitton travel bags in hand, standing on the porch.

"Is that a hello?" Allie asked.

"Yes, yes, it is. Come in!"

Allie was petite, barely five foot two inches tall, with short spiky hair dyed platinum, large chunky glasses, and an inevitable assortment of unique jewelry she collected from emerging designers, some of who were now well-known.

"I can't believe you're here!" Poppy said, leading her friend down the hall to the kitchen.

"I can easily book into a hotel if it's inconvenient for me to stay with you all."

"Not at all! Do you see the size of this place? But why didn't you tell me you were coming?"

Allie dropped her bags just inside the kitchen door. "I should have," she said, "but I guess I thought I'd take advantage of the element of surprise. Now that I'm here, you can't put me off."

"Why would I put you off?" Poppy asked.

"Poppy, do you remember our conversation the other day? You called me to bemoan the meaninglessness of your life."

Poppy felt a flush of embarrassment. "But I told you I was just in a mood. I'd had a bad dream the night before."

"That's called putting me off. I was worried about you. I didn't—I don't—believe that you're perfectly fine and thriving in your new role as mater of the Higgins clan. So I took it upon myself to butt in and offer my friendship at close quarters."

Poppy smiled. "And I'm so glad you did butt in, Allie, really. I'm so happy you're here."

"Good. Now, where's my room and where's the wine? And oh, my, God who is that?"

Poppy turned to see Grimace sitting in the exact middle of the kitchen table. He hadn't been there a moment ago. "That's Violet's cat," she explained. "His name is Grimace."

"I can see why. He's glowering, which is not exactly the same as grimacing, but . . ."

"He's actually quite friendly," Poppy said, "once you get to know him. Well, not exactly friendly, but he tolerates people pretty well."

"If you say so . . ."

Poppy grabbed Allie's travel bags. "Come on, let's get you settled. Dinner's at six thirty and you'll finally get to meet my sisters."

"And what will they think of me, I wonder," Allie said, following Poppy out of the kitchen.

"What was Poppy like in Boston?"

The Higgins girls and Allie were at the kitchen table, having a meal that Allie had largely prepared—classic

French-inspired meatloaf, roasted red potatoes with rose-mary, string beans, and biscuits (Allie had whipped those up from scratch). Daisy and Violet were regarding Allie as if she were some sort of celebrity. Poppy had noted that people often did, though she wasn't quite sure why. Maybe it was Allie's culinary skills. Violet would probably say it was her aura.

"Daisy," Poppy said, "what sort of question is that?"

"A perfectly normal one," her sister replied. "I have no idea what you did with your free time when you lived in Boston. I mean, who did you hang out with? Where did you go at night? Were you wild and crazy?"

"You could have asked me any of those questions."

Daisy grinned. "But you might not have answered."

Allie cleared her throat. "Well," she said, "Poppy was a model tenant. She always paid the rent on time and never threw loud parties. And she left the apartment spic and span and as neat as a pin when she left to move back here."

"Oh," Daisy said. "That's all?"

"I'm sorry to disappoint you," Poppy said. "I know you were hoping that for the past few years I'd been living a life of shameful debauchery."

"Have you really been to Stonehenge?" Violet asked Allie. "And to Newgrange?"

"Yes," Allie said. "I really have been. And you really do feel connected to the past in places like that. To the people who built them and worshipped there, or whatever it was they did, exactly. At least, I felt connected."

"I can't wait to go to Stonehenge and Newgrange and all the other ancient sites we know about!" Violet said excit-edly. "Maybe I'll even locate a lost site myself someday!"

Daisy reached for another biscuit. "I can't wait to go to California," she said. "It's pathetic. I haven't been any-where!"

"Don't exaggerate, Daisy. Dad and Mom took us plenty of places. New York. Boston. Colonial Williamsburg. Quebec."

"All on the East Coast," Daisy pointed out. "I want to go west."

"I'm sure you'll have plenty of opportunities to travel," Allie assured her.

"This is excellent, Poppy," Violet said, reaching for her third slice of meatloaf.

Poppy smiled. "Thanks, but I can't really take the credit. Allie did most of the work. Like, ninety-nine percent of it."

"Make sure you give Poppy the recipe," Daisy said. "Her repertoire is kind of limited."

"Bigger than yours!"

"I can make mac 'n' cheese from a box," Daisy explained to Allie. "And when Dad . . . When I was doing a lot of the cooking around here I did mostly cold stuff, like salads."

"Putting a meal on the table is an act of love," Allie said. "It doesn't matter what the meal consists of."

Violet shook her head. "Unless it's a beefsteak mushroom. That's a type of morel. They're poisonous."

"Violet knows about these things," Poppy told Allie.

"Ah, I see."

"Not that I would ever poison someone," Violet explained. "'Do no harm' is my motto."

"Easier said than done. What if you think you're doing no harm but you actually are?" Daisy asked. "What if you really believed the mushrooms you put in the pasta were harmless but they wound up killing your dinner guest?"

Poppy sighed. "Daisy, do you always have to be so . . . so . . ."

"Yes," Daisy said with a grin. "I do."

* * *

Later that night, after dinner, Poppy and Allie were alone in the sunroom, drinking wine and occasionally munching on the box of excellent chocolates Allie had brought as a hostess gift. She had also brought with her two bottles of expensive champagne and a silk scarf for Poppy from the latest major exhibit at the Museum of Fine Arts in Boston.

"Your sisters are lovely," Allie said, from the depths of the chair into which she had sunk. "So smart, too."

Poppy laughed. "I think Daisy would argue that she's decidedly unlovely. And I might agree with her. But Violet is truly a flower child. If I didn't know better I'd say that my parents found her nestled under a rosebush in the garden, left there by sprites."

"She does have an otherworldly quality about her."

"Do you think I should be worried? Do you think she's . . ."

"Normal?" Allie said. "Yes, I think she's perfectly normal, but then again I've only just met her. And I'm not her sister."

"I might be her sister, but I hardly know her at all. She was only just nine when I moved to Boston. And when I was in college . . ." Poppy shrugged. "What with keeping my grades up and maintaining a social life and working part-time at the dress shop in town, I never paid much attention to her. Is that horrible?"

Allie shook her head. "No, of course not. And now you have the opportunity to make up for those lost years, so to speak."

"True. Still, I wish the opportunity hadn't arisen in the way it did."

"I know. I *am* sorry. But so far you seem to be handling your new role with calm and dignity and grace."

Poppy laughed. "Oh, Allie, what a liar you are!"

Allie shrugged "I thought I'd give it a try. A little flattery can be helpful."

There followed a moment of comfortable silence. It was one of the things Poppy treasured about her friendship with Allie, their being so comfortable with one another.

"The poppy is the flower of 'forgetful ease,'" Poppy said after a time. "I think that phrase is from a poem, but I can't quite remember which one. It's the flower of 'blissful slumber.' That's also probably from a poem buried deep in my memory. The poppy is an opiate. A balm for the soul."

"And you're telling me this because . . ."

Poppy shrugged. "Just thinking aloud."

"'Hail, lovely blossom! . . . Soul-soothing plant!' *That's* from Charlotte Smith's poem entitled 'Ode to the Poppy.'"

"Impressive. See, the point I'm making is that the poppy is a drug. And that's the way I feel sometimes. Often. Let's be real, ever since I graduated from college. Drugged. Like I'm sleeping my way through my life. I need to wake up, Allie, before it's too late. But I have no idea how to wake up."

"All journeys start with one step."

Poppy frowned. "What if you don't know in which direction to walk?"

"I know," Allie said, leaning forward, elbows on her knees. "You could start a blog. You could create a persona, like Ree Drummond did with The Pioneer Woman. All the elements are in place to attract people to your story. Illustrious parents, both gone before their time, three daughters orphaned, oldest girl called upon to sacrifice, or let's say *postpone,* the life she'd been building in Boston to come home to care for her sisters. You could document your struggles, celebrate the triumphs, make light of the failures, share the surprises both good and bad. The exercise might help you to see your way forward."

"No," Poppy said emphatically. "I can't exploit my parents' death. Anyway, I wasn't exactly building anything in Boston. Except a friendship with you."

"Thanks, and I'm not suggesting you exploit your tragic loss and you know it. I'm just suggesting that you be creative about the situation in which you find yourself. Turn it into something—something really worthwhile. Possibility exists everywhere. You just have to be creative enough to find it."

"What if it turns out I don't have a creative bone in my body?" Poppy asked grimly.

"What if it turns out you do? Banish pessimism, Poppy!"

"Pessimistic Poppy. Catchy, no?"

"No."

Poppy sighed and reached for another chocolate. "You know," she said, "not too long before my mother died I was complaining about my directionless life in much the same way I'm complaining to you. And she told me not to compare myself with her or my father. To anyone. But it's so hard not to. It's so hard not to look around and see all these people doing wonderful and important things and feel—inadequate. I used to think I was just one of those later bloomers, and it didn't bother me too much. But now, with *both* Mom and Dad gone, well, everything seems more important, so much more urgent."

"Poppy, none of us can entirely avoid comparing ourselves to others. How else would we estimate our place and our value in society? But at your age comparison is unfair. You're untried as of yet. Largely untested. Give yourself time. Someday you just might achieve heights only dreamed of by your parents."

Poppy yawned. "That might be true," she said, "but right now I think that all I'm up to achieving is bed."

Allie looked at her watch. "Yikes, how did it get so late? I'm too old for late nights."

"Allie! You're only forty!"

"And? The beauty of being an adult, as you should know by now, is the freedom to go to bed as early as you want."

"And to spoil your appetite with cookies before dinner," Poppy added, turning off the lamp by her chair.

"That, too."

Chapter 30

Daisy stood outside The Clamshell. She was nervous. She had been thinking about what she was about to do for a while now. She didn't have her sister Violet's skills at discerning unspoken truths, but she just knew that something was troubling that girl Evie. And she thought that maybe she could help her in some way. If that was evidence of an overblown ego or of massive self-importance, so be it. Her curiosity was aroused and had to be satisfied.

But what possible excuse could she give for wanting to get to know Evie? She had thought and thought about it and finally, an idea had struck her, a decidedly weak idea, but it was better than none. A more creative person might be able to come up with a better plan for how she could go about befriending a virtual stranger, but Daisy was reluctant to involve anyone else in her—her scheme. Reluctant and a bit embarrassed. Anyone with a finely tuned sense of right behavior might think she was butting in where she wasn't meant to be. Daisy had been accused of that before, like the time she had gone up to a woman in the Kittery outlets mall. The woman was dabbing her red and swollen eyes and sniffing loudly. "Are you okay?" Daisy asked. "Are you hurt? Can I do something?" The woman had summarily told Daisy to "mind her damned business" and stalked off. Only later did it occur to Daisy that the woman might only have been suffering from allergies.

You think I would have learned my lesson, Daisy thought. *But I'm doomed to be a Good Samaritan.*

Without further hesitation, Daisy opened the door to The Clamshell and took her place in line behind a couple in matching Kelly green pants and bright yellow polo shirts. When the cheerfully dressed couple had placed their order and moved aside to wait for it, Daisy stood face-to-face with Evie.

"It's me again," she said.

"You must really like the fried clams," Evie replied with an awkward smile.

"I'm addicted to them." *Just do it,* Daisy told herself. "Look," she said, "I was kind of wondering if you wanted to hang out sometime. I know this sounds kind of pathetic, but I really don't have any girlfriends—I have two sisters, but they don't count—and I love my best friend, but he's a guy, so . . ." Daisy shrugged and was very glad she wasn't prone to blushing because she knew that her plan—such as it was—had failed. The look on Evie's face was one of—well, it was one of downright suspicion, maybe mixed with a little fear, the kind you felt when you met someone who was clearly deranged.

"I don't really have much time," Evie said, looking down at the order pad on the counter before her. "I'm working a double shift today."

"Oh," Daisy said. "Right. Well, maybe some other day."

"Yeah. Maybe." Evie looked up again, but her eyes wouldn't quite meet Daisy's. "So, do you want to place an order?"

Daisy didn't feel at all hungry, but she thought that not to order something might make Evie think she was even more deranged than she already suspected. "Uh, sure," she said. "The fried clams. And an order of fries."

She stepped aside to let the person behind her order, and when her meal was ready she took the tray from the server behind the counter with Evie and left the restaurant quickly. Oh, well, she thought, settling at one of the picnic tables outside. Nothing ventured, nothing gained. Still, she did feel like a bit of an idiot. Who in her right mind went up to a virtual stranger and confessed that she was lonely for a friend? Okay, it had been a ruse to cover the fact of her curiosity about Evie. Still, what would Poppy say if she knew? What would Joel say? Violet would probably want to cure her of her pathetic-ness (Daisy knew that wasn't a word, but she liked it) with some herb or stone.

Well, it didn't matter what anyone thought of her behavior because nobody was going to find out about her failed attempt to—to what? To rescue someone. Like she had failed to rescue that woman in the mall.

Like she had failed to rescue her father.

Chapter 31

"It's very pretty, as cemeteries go."

Poppy nodded. "Yes, and very old. Some graves date back to the seventeenth century."

"Lots of babies and children, I suppose." Allie shuddered. "I'm so glad to be living in the twenty-first century, though we certainly have our problems."

"Yes. It was my father's decision to have the lines from the Edgar Allan Poe poem put on my mother's stone, you know. She just wanted her dates and something like 'loving wife and mother.'"

"Really? Do you suppose she'd be mad?"

Poppy smiled. "I don't think my parents were ever mad at each other, for anything. And if they were they must have gotten over it pretty quickly because I never witnessed a fight, not even a squabble."

"Hard act to follow."

"Hmm."

"What about the Rabelias quote on your father's stone?" Allie asked.

"He left instructions about that in his will."

"So much easier to be cremated. No pressure to choose memorable final words."

And what would my final message be, Poppy wondered. At that moment she had absolutely no idea.

"Do you come here often?" Allie asked.

"Not really. I can think about my parents just as easily from home." Poppy smiled. "Cemetery visits are more Violet's thing. As far as I know Daisy hasn't been here since my father's funeral, and before that, my mother's."

"Well, I must say I've never been a huge fan of cemeteries, aside from their possible historical and aesthetic interest."

Poppy looked down at her parents' graves and fought a familiar wave of sadness. Sometimes it was so hard to believe that the two most vibrant people she had ever known were still and under the earth. No more fascinating talk. No more bell-like laughter. No more smiles.

"I want my mother to look down at me," she said quietly after a moment, "assuming she's somewhere above me, of course; why do human beings always think of the afterlife as in the sky? Anyway, I want her to be proud of how I'm helping my sisters. But I can't help but feel—I can't help but *know*—that she isn't proud. That she's disappointed in the way I'm handling this responsibility. Dad, too."

Allie gave a mirthless laugh. "We're always trying to please our parents, even when they're gone. Even when we didn't like them when they were here."

"Did you not like your parents?" Poppy asked. "You've never really talked much about them."

Allie laughed. "What do you think? They basically sold me into marriage when I was twenty-one. Well, that was the sort of people they were. I don't think they had a warm feeling between them. And I was completely in their thrall."

"Completely? I find that hard to believe, knowing you. You always seem so in charge."

"I was very different then," Allie said, her voice taking on a more serious note. "A child, really. My marriage was Prince Charles and Princess Diana all over again, a suave man and a naive girl. A man who was in love with another woman, and three is most definitely a crowd. Luckily I worked up the gumption—what a funny word that is! It always makes me think of barbershop poles and penny candy shops! Anyway, I finally worked up the gumption to leave after two years. To say my dear spouse was relieved would be an understatement. To be fair, I think he was as unhappy in the marriage as I was. Barely a year later he married his true love and I have to admit they make a charming pair."

Poppy found the whole thing pretty appalling, but was always reluctant to join in criticism of someone else's parents. "Well, your parents couldn't have been *all* bad," she said, aware it was a lame remark.

Allie looked up at her. "Oh?"

"Sorry."

After a long beat of silence, Poppy ventured another question. "When did they die, anyway? You never told me."

Allie frowned. "Confession time. They didn't. They're still alive. Well, as far as I know. I cut ties with them years ago. I'm not entirely sure they've noticed. They've still got my brother—I'm assuming. He's a good doobie, a chip off the old block of granite. The parents arranged his marriage, too, but he proved far more willing than I was to play the game. She's an heiress, by the way. Of course. Oh, and did I mention that after my divorce I was cut out of my parents' will? Good thing my beloved cheating husband settled a few million on me. And that I evinced a talent for investment."

"I'm so sorry, Allie. I'm always going on about how great my parents were, how happy we all were. I shouldn't have . . ."

"Hey, don't apologize for loving your mother and father! Frankly, it's nice to know that happy families do actually exist."

"Or did."

Allie took Poppy's arm. "You and your sisters are still in the here and now. Don't forget that. The Higgins family is changed, not gone."

"I'm not sure I believe that," Poppy admitted. "I'm pretty sure Daisy absolutely doesn't believe that. And who knows what Violet thinks."

Allie smiled. "Whatever Violet thinks, it's deep."

"That's for sure! If I didn't love her I might find her a little frightening."

"Come on, let's get out of here. What time is it? I could use a glass of wine. Talking about my parents always makes me want to get properly drunk. Tight, as the English say."

"Polluted, as we might say here." Poppy put her arm around her friend's shoulder. "There's plenty of wine at home."

Chapter 32

She was behind the wheel of a car. It wasn't her car. It wasn't her parents' car, either. She didn't know to whom the car belonged and she didn't care. She was tooling along what seemed like an unusually wide road. There were no other cars on the road. The windows were open and her hair was whipping around in the breeze. She was having fun. She was surprised at this. She felt relaxed. She felt in control. And then the road seemed to narrow, just a bit, but she blinked and the road was normal again and she dismissed it as an optical illusion. And then it occurred to her to wonder where she was and where she had come from and where she was going. Again, the road seemed to narrow and this time it wasn't an optical illusion, it was real. It went on narrowing so that from one second to the next there was less and less room on either side of the car and where once there was only endless road to the left and the right, now there were two blank walls of bright white light. It was like being in a tunnel that was being folded up by some giant invisible hand. She tapped the brakes. Nothing. She pushed down hard on them, but the car continued to accelerate down the ever-shrinking road.

She was now hurtling through a tight white tunnel toward a tiny, tiny dot of a vanishing point. . . . A wall? A doorway? An illusion within an illusion? Once more she frantically pumped the brakes, but to no avail and the car zoomed ahead. . . .

Evie's eyes shot open. Her heart was pounding and her nightshirt was wet with sweat. It wasn't the first time she had experienced this nightmare and she feared it wouldn't be the last. She reached for Ben and held him tightly to her chest. She would never, ever get a driver's license! She hadn't been able to be in a car since the horrific crash that had killed her mother and maimed her father without being overcome by a sense of panic and she was plagued by this terrible dream and . . .

Evie shut her eyes against the dark night. If only there was someone she could turn to, someone she could talk to or laugh with. She thought that she might go crazy with only Ben to share her life. It wasn't normal for a person to be so alone. It wasn't fair.

That girl, Daisy. The one who seemed so nice, so honest and unpretentious. Evie could imagine her listening to a friend, offering advice, maybe even laughing about silly fears. She could, just barely, imagine the two of them comforting each other about the not-so-silly fears. Maybe she could take just one little risk . . . But she would see how she felt about that in the morning.

One thing Evie knew for sure. If she did approach Daisy, and if they did become friends of a sort, she would have to lie about some things, maybe most things about herself. And she would have to hope that Daisy didn't find out about the lies. Because no one wanted a liar as a friend.

Chapter 33

Violet, Daisy, and Allie were sitting around the rectangular stone table in the garden, a pitcher of lemonade and a big bunch of green grapes before them. Grimace sat close by Violet's chair, eyeing whatever birds were brave enough to hop around on the grass within leaping distance. The rhododendrons were in full pink bloom. The roses were bravely budding. The hydrangea bushes, too, were beginning to flower; before long they would be heavy with bundles of purple-blue blossoms. Violet could smell the rosemary and the basil from the herb garden; the garden was flourishing as it had never done before. The fragrance helped calm her.

Daisy looked at her iPhone. "I thought Poppy would be back by now. Her hair appointment was at two. It's almost three thirty."

"Maybe she's enjoying some time alone, without us," Violet said. "I don't mean you, Allie. I mean Daisy and me."

Allie nodded. "Everyone needs time alone. Remember, Poppy's lived on her own for the past three years. Now she's got three roommates, even if I'm only temporary."

"But we're her family, Violet and I. We're not really the same as roommates. Though I guess I see your point."

"Familiarity breeds contempt." Violet frowned. "It's really an awful idea, but it's probably sometimes true."

"Your sister would never feel contempt for either of you," Allie said. "Of that I'm sure."

"She used to laugh a lot," Daisy said. "When we were kids. Now half the time she looks like she's in pain. It's like there's always something on her mind. Something big and dreary and important. She's getting boring. Sorry, but it's true."

"There is something big on her mind," Allie said. "Life. Her life. What to do with it. How not to waste it."

"We all think about the future and what to do with it," Violet said. *Sometimes,* she thought, *I think about the future so much I forget to notice what's happening in front of me right now.* "I wish it didn't make Poppy feel so sad."

"I think Poppy feels sad because she hasn't found her passion yet," Allie said. "She hasn't decided on her goal."

"My goal is to be a doctor," Daisy told Allie. "I've known that for sure since I was little. You know, my favorite parts of Mom's book are where she talks about all the skills a woman needed to have back before medical care was institutionalized the way it is now. Wives, daughters, mothers, everyone was a bit of a midwife and a GP and an ER nurse all rolled into one. It was pretty awesome."

"And I want to be like those women who made medicines and poultices from flowers and plants," Violet said. "I want to become a wise-woman healer. I don't have all the details worked out of course." And before someone could heal another person, they had to be healed themselves, and Violet was beginning to feel that she had not even *begun* to heal from the pain of her parents' deaths, in spite of what she told those around her. She felt her heart begin to race a bit and concentrated on calming it.

Allie was smiling. "I must say, you girls have set pretty wonderful goals for yourselves. When I was your age I never thought further ahead than the weekend and what I was going to wear to a party."

"Did you know that people have told Poppy she should be a model?" Daisy asked Allie.

"No. She never mentioned that."

"It's true. Even one of her teachers back in high school suggested she sign with an agency. But she wasn't interested."

Violet shuddered. "Mom and Dad would have hated that kind of life for her. Life is so much more than appearances."

"Well, it's an honest living for some," Allie pointed out, "but there's far more to your sister than a pretty face and an enviable figure."

"She's just not sure what, is that it?" Daisy asked.

"Exactly. Though I hope I'm not speaking out of line in telling you all this."

"Capricorns often go into community service," Violet said musingly. "Maybe that's what Poppy will do."

Daisy laughed. "Poppy? Community service? I just can't see her, I don't know, helping a bunch of strangers. And she won't even go to a town meeting. I don't think she's a joiner."

"Ssshh." Allie looked pointedly at Daisy, and Violet looked over her shoulder to see her oldest sister coming across the lawn. When Poppy reached the group she took a seat in one of the chairs gathered around the table.

"Your hair looks pretty," Violet said.

"What took you so long?"

Poppy laughed. "Thanks, Violet. And to answer your question, Daisy, I was taking a stroll on the beach."

Violet nodded. "Told you."

"What's been going on here?" Poppy asked. "Have you been plotting my overthrow?"

"Oh, no," Violet said seriously. "We've been talking about life."

Poppy laughed. "Oh, a nice light topic! And what did you decide about life with a capital *L?*"

"That life is meaningless without a goal."

Violet tried to catch Daisy's eye, but her sister wouldn't look at her. *She shouldn't have said that*, Violet thought. *It was mean.* Her sister wasn't a mean *person,* but she had these moments. . . . "That's not what we were saying," Violet corrected. "We were saying that everyone searches for her passion in life and that sometimes it's hard to find."

"Right." Allie nodded. "Sometimes we just can't see what it is we're meant to do until something strange happens or someone unexpectedly comes into our lives and reveals it. Our goal."

"Well," Poppy said, reaching for a grape, "I guess my catalyst hasn't shown up yet."

"Or else he, she, or it is already here and you just haven't recognized the opportunity," Allie suggested.

"Your vision is clouded," Violet suggested. Certainly, she felt her own vision seemed to be clouded more often than not lately. "That might be it, Poppy. Because of all that's changed so suddenly. The clouds still have to drift away."

Poppy smiled at Violet. "Maybe you're right."

"Well," Allie said, "you know my mantra, or one of them anyway. If you tell yourself you're having fun or succeeding in life, eventually you will be having fun or succeeding in life. In other words, 'act as if.' Act as if you know what you're doing and eventually, you will."

Poppy frowned. "It can't be that easy."

"Oh," Allie admitted, "it's not. It's hard work. But it pays off marvelously. I wouldn't have gotten over my disastrous marriage and only slightly less painful divorce if I hadn't adopted a downright chipper persona and lied to myself all the way through that I was on the road to full emotional recovery."

"Chipper?" Daisy repeated skeptically.

Violet nodded. "The power of positive thinking."

"Exactly," Allie said. "You do what you have to do to get past the difficult stuff."

"It sounds like mumbo jumbo to me," Daisy said. "Sorry, Allie, sorry, Violet."

"That's our future doctor talking," Poppy said. "Our rational scientist."

"Taurus people," Violet pointed out, "are very methodical thinkers. They are very focused. They don't like to take risks."

Daisy looked uncomfortable with this assessment. "Well," she said, "I guess if positive thinking works for some people it's real enough."

Violet put her empty glass on the table. "Taurus people," she added, afraid that she might have been too harsh on Daisy, "also make excellent friends."

Chapter 34

"I hope you don't mind my just showing up. I figured someone might be home."

Poppy smiled. Finding Jon Gascoyne on your doorstep, she thought, was something no one in her right mind would object to. "Not at all," she said.

"Here. These are for you and your sisters. With one extra for good luck." Jon handed her the large plastic bag he had been holding.

Poppy peered inside and laughed. "Lobsters? What a coincidence! My friend Allie is staying with us for a while and lobster is her all-time favorite. Well, I'm a fan, too. Thank you, Jon. Can I—"

"It's a gift."

Like Julie's gift of cheese in exchange for a renewal of their friendship. "A neighborly gesture?" she asked.

"Something like that."

"First you solve my lawn mower problem and now . . ."

Jon shrugged. "Glad to be of service."

Suddenly, Poppy felt almost overcome with emotion. Gratitude, simple happiness, sorrow—it was all mixed up and threatened to take the form of tears. She was glad when Jon (had he noticed her struggle not to cry?) said: "I thought I might have seen you at the town meeting the other night. Freddie mentioned something about your thinking of going."

Small towns . . . "Oh. I intended to go, but . . . something came up." Poppy felt vaguely guilty for not having gone to the meeting, let alone not having read the report about it bound to have been in the local paper.

"Things got pretty heated," Jon said with a grin.

"What happened?"

"Well, there were several topics on the agenda, but what really caused a stir was the debate about adding a traffic cop at the intersection of Main and Vine."

Poppy laughed. "Really? I wouldn't have thought the idea of a traffic cop could get people so excited!"

"The big question is about how to pay him—or her. There's money in the municipal budget, but those against the idea are arguing there are more important things to spend the money on than a guy waving cars by. And they have a point. It's not like there's been an accident at that corner for years, even at the height of summer."

"So, was anything decided?" Poppy asked.

Jon smiled. "Only to let things cool down for a week or two. You know, I remember your mother coming to the town meetings. She really had a knack for defusing tempers when people got out of control, which some invariably did."

Poppy didn't recall her mother going to town meetings and wondered what else she didn't know about Annabelle Higgins—or worse, what she hadn't noticed. But how many children—even children who were twenty-one, which was how old she had been when her mother had died—really paid attention to a parent as a person with duties and interests outside of the family?

"Well, I've got to be off," Jon said suddenly. "I'm doing a shift at the restaurant later. Two of our waiters called in sick today. Interestingly, both of them were seen partying late at Maine Street, that nightclub in Ogunquit."

"Go figure."

Jon turned to leave.

"Jon?" Poppy called.

He stopped and looked back toward her.

"Thanks again."

With a smile and a wave, Jon Gascoyne continued down the drive and Poppy Higgins, clutching a bag of wriggling lobsters, went inside.

Chapter 35

"The nurse said it's just to be sure she doesn't have pneumonia," Daisy told Mr. Wilkin for what was probably the third or fourth time that afternoon. She honestly didn't know who she was trying to reassure most—Bertie Wilkin or Daisy Higgins. "They'll take an X-ray and then she'll be right back here with you."

"Maybe."

"Mr. Wilkin," Daisy scolded. "Don't say that."

They were together in the TV room, but neither had any interest in watching the stupid game show that seemed to have mesmerized a handful of residents.

Bertie Wilkin shrugged. "At our age, Young Daisy, you can't expect to be around from one moment to the next. I know it's going to come sooner rather than later. One of us going off. And I know it's still going to be a shock."

Daisy squeezed Bertie's hand. It would be stupid to tell him not to think about losing his wife. And who was she, a sixteen-year-old, to offer any real comfort to a man in his eighties? He had known so much more of life than she had, than she ever might.

"Do you know," Mr. Wilkin said suddenly, "I fall in love with Muriella all over again, every day?"

Daisy smiled. "Was it always that way, all through your marriage?"

"No," Bertie replied emphatically. "No, it wasn't. There were times when one or both of us were unhappy. Health issues. Money troubles. The kids needing more attention than we thought we had to give. There were times—not many, mind you—when I was tempted to stray. Now, don't look shocked, Young Daisy. I wasn't always this bag of skin and bone you see before you!"

"I know that," Daisy assured him. "It's just . . . How can you—anyone, I mean, be tempted to—stray—if you're in love?"

"Ah, may you retain that innocence for many years to come," Bertie Wilkin said with a kind smile. "But then again, the sooner you understand the complexities of marriage and human feeling the better. There are strains on the human spirit, Daisy, you must know that much. Mundane strains like chores and jobs and rebelling children and leaky pipes. Larger, more existential strains, too, like loss of faith and the aftermath of a lie or a betrayal and the sudden sure feeling that you've wasted your life and it's all because of your spouse having tied you down to a life that wasn't yours to live."

Daisy thought about that. Her parents *must* have experienced tensions and troubles, but try as she might she couldn't recall ever seeing any evidence of it. "Then why do people stay together if it's so hard?" she asked.

Bertie chuckled. "Oh, many reasons, Young Daisy. Laziness. The need to punish oneself or the other. But, if you're lucky, you stay with the person you married because in spite of the occasional difficulties life is simply so much better with her. And that, I'm happy to say, is the way it is with Muriella and me."

"So, if someone gave you the chance, you would do it all over again? Marry Mrs. Wilkin?"

"Most certainly. But . . ." Bertie looked rapidly around the room and went on in a whisper. "I might have the nerve next time around to ask her not to make that awful cauliflower casserole she was so fond of."

Daisy laughed. And just then, the automatic double doors to the TV room opened and there was Muriella, being wheeled in by a nurse.

"What was that you were saying about my cauliflower casserole, dear?" she asked, smiling and reaching for her husband's hand.

Mrs. Wilkin must have supernatural hearing, Daisy thought, hiding her own smile.

"Oh," Bertie replied, studiously avoiding Daisy's eyes, "I was just telling Young Daisy how much I loved it."

Chapter 36

Traffic in downtown Yorktide was heavy and slow-moving. The sky was cloudless. Vacationers—men and women—were coming out of craft and jewelry stores loaded down with shopping bags. Kids were eating ice-cream cones. Teenage girls were strutting as if on the catwalk. Teenage boys were sauntering and not so surreptitiously eyeing the teenage girls.

Evie, who was leaning against the wall of the old clapboard building that housed two gift shops, was part of the scene but apart from it, too, not in Yorktide to have summer fun and spend money on cheap souvenirs or overpriced pottery, but to get through the day without discovery. And then, to get through the next day. If she had ever had a long-term goal, at that moment Evie couldn't remember what it might have been.

And then, Evie spotted her, looking in the window of the ice-cream shop across the street. The girl from the convenience store. The one who described herself as being clumsy. The nice one. Daisy. The girl who had wanted to hang out with her. Before she could lose her nerve Evie dashed over to her, narrowly avoiding being hit by a slow-moving car full of tourists.

"Hi," she said. "It's me. I mean, Evie. From The Clamshell."

Daisy turned from the window. It seemed to take her a moment before she recognized Evie and then she smiled. "Oh, sure. Sorry, I was spacing for a minute. Mesmerized by ice cream. Hi."

"Look, I'm on a break. Do you want to maybe grab a soda or . . ."

Daisy looked at her watch. "Okay," she said. "I've got an appointment with the eye doctor in about twenty minutes. She's down on Vine Street. And I should probably pass on the soda," she added with a frown. "I've been drinking way too much of it lately."

That was fine with Evie; she didn't really want to spend the money on a drink when she could have one for free at The Clamshell. "There's a bench over there," she said, pointing over Daisy's shoulder.

Daisy hustled off and planted herself in the middle of the bench situated under a sprawling oak tree. When Evie joined her she moved to one end. "A free bench is a hot commodity at this time of the year," she said. "All these tourists. It's funny how so many people wait all year to spend one week in your own little hometown. And half the time you don't even appreciate what you have right in front of you."

Wasn't that the truth, Evie thought. All she had taken for granted—a house, two parents, security—all gone before she had ever learned how truly to appreciate them.

"I hope I didn't sound rude the other day when you came by The Clamshell," she said to Daisy.

Daisy shrugged. "Oh, no."

"Work can get pretty stressful," Evie explained. "We get

so busy and some customers can be really rude and impatient."

"I'm sure. Actually, I've never had a job. A paying one, I mean. I volunteer at the Pine Hill Residence for the Elderly."

"That sounds depressing."

"Not really," Daisy said. "I mean, it's sad when someone you like dies and it stinks that some people never have any visitors. But it's good that the residents have a safe place to live. And there are lots of activities to keep them busy. Some are there with their husbands or wives. And there's this group of four women who all used to be neighbors. They have these fierce card games every afternoon and they argue like crazy over who's cheating and then it's time for dinner and they're best friends again. They remind me of some girls at my school. In fact, from what I can tell, the world inside the nursing home is all pretty much like the world outside of the nursing home."

"I guess. I've never actually been inside one." It was on the tip of Evie's tongue to tell Daisy that she had never known her grandparents when an alarm sounded in her head. Too much information. She had to give out information about herself—true or false—sparingly and carefully.

"So, are you new to Yorktide?" Daisy asked her. "I don't remember seeing you around until a few weeks ago."

Evie was prepared for this question or one like it. She had worked out and rehearsed her answer before the mirror in the bathroom she used at Nico's house. It was not quite but sort of the truth. Barely the truth.

"It's kind of a long story," she said, remembering to speak slowly so as not to say the wrong thing. Vigilance was all. "But I'll tell you the short version. My mom and dad died when I was ten. It was a—a fire. I spent eight years bouncing around the foster care system until I turned eighteen. Now, I'm on my own and I decided that Yorktide seemed like an okay place to live. At least for a while."

Daisy put her hand on Evie's arm for a moment. Her touch made Evie want to cry and it was with some effort that she remained dry-eyed. It had been so long since anyone had touched her like that, with sympathy.

"Wow," Daisy said. "I'm so sorry about your parents. And about the foster homes. You hear these horror stories . . ."

"It wasn't all bad," Evie said. "Not always. Anyway, don't tell anyone about this, okay? People can be weird when they hear someone's been in foster care—like you said, all those horror stories. There's, like, a stigma."

"Sure. I won't tell anyone."

"Thanks." Evie smiled. She didn't know for sure if she could trust this girl, but her need to *try* to trust her was immense.

"Not that it's any consolation," Daisy said, "but both of my parents are dead, too."

Evie's stomach dropped. Here she was pretending to be an orphan while poor Daisy really *was* an orphan. "Really?" she said, her voice a bit high with stress.

"Yeah. My mom—her name was Annabelle Higgins— died about three years ago. She had cancer. And my dad . . . My dad died just a few months ago. He had a heart attack. I was in the kitchen when it happened. He was in the sunroom. His name was Oliver."

"I'm sorry," Evie said. She wanted to touch Daisy's arm in sympathy, as Daisy had done to comfort her. But she didn't. "That's awful. Where do you live? I mean, who . . ."

"My sister Poppy is our legal guardian," Daisy explained. "By 'our' I mean my sister Violet's and mine. Violet's thirteen. I'm sixteen. Without Poppy . . . Well, we probably would have gone into foster homes, like you."

"How old is Poppy?" Evie asked.

"Twenty-five. She was living in Boston, but moved back home with us right after our dad died. He was the one who named her legal guardian."

"Did she mind coming home?" Evie asked. It was a big thing, being named someone's legal guardian. Back when she had first gone to live with her aunt and uncle there had been some talk of the Shettleworths being named her legal guardians, but nothing had come of it. Evie didn't know why.

"I think she minded at first," Daisy said. "But now I think she's kind of glad to be home, not that she's said anything to me. Anyway, it's not like she had a steady boyfriend in Boston she had to leave behind. And our house is pretty awesome. And her best friend from Boston is visiting us, so that's good. Allie's really nice and she's a way better cook than my sister!"

Evie felt a tiny flair of jealousy. If only she had someone like Daisy's older sister to rely on. Daisy and her sisters might have lost their parents, but they still had each other.

"So, where are you staying?" Daisy asked her. "Are you renting a place?"

Evie told her about the house-sitting gig at Nico's. "My boss, Mr. Woolrich—Billy—set it up for me. He's really nice."

Daisy smiled. "Yeah, he seems really sweet. And I've seen that guy Nico around town. He looks so . . . So full of himself!"

Evie shrugged. "I don't really know him. I mean, I met him once for about two minutes. He was wearing a bathrobe. And he had a towel wrapped around his head."

For some reason this bit of information and the image it conjured made them both shriek with laughter.

"Look," Daisy said when she had recovered, "we should get together again. Maybe do something."

"I don't have much money," Evie said quickly. "I mean I haven't been working long enough to really save anything."

Daisy laughed. "That's okay. I've got enough for both of us to hang out. See a movie or something."

"But I probably wouldn't be able to pay you back for a really long time."

Daisy shrugged. "There's stuff to do that doesn't cost anything, or not much, anyway. Like go to the beach. Like go to craft fairs, although to be honest, craft fairs are more my sister Violet's thing. Free open-air concerts, if we can get a ride to them. I don't have my license yet, but I'll have my permit in the fall."

A car. A car meant trembling, shortness of breath, light-headedness. All classic symptoms of anxiety she had been told, as if that made things better. Evie managed a smile. "I hadn't thought of any of those things," she said lightly. But it was no smiling matter when simple, ordinary experiences like a day at the beach or a stroll through a craft fair had become experiences that seemed impossible or out of reach.

Daisy pulled her iPhone out of her pocket. "What's your number?" she asked.

Evie swallowed. Why couldn't anything be simple? "My phone's kind of dead right now," she said. "But I guess you could call me at Nico's. I'm not really supposed to be using his phone, but . . ."

"How could he object to someone calling you? And I can find you at The Clamshell most days, right? Not that I'm a stalker or anything!"

"Right. I mean, I know." Evie gave Daisy Nico's number. "I'd better get back to work," she said, getting up from the bench. "Billy's a great boss, but I don't want to mess up."

"And I'd better be going or I'll be late to my appointment. See you soon, okay?"

"Okay." Evie watched for a moment as Daisy headed off toward the eye doctor on Vine Street and then she turned toward The Clamshell. And in spite of the anxiety parts of the conversation had produced, she didn't regret for one moment having said hello to Daisy Higgins.

Chapter 37

"I met your Jon Gascoyne in town today."

Poppy looked up from the bunch of carrots she was peeling. "He's not mine," she said. *He belongs to Yorktide.* "And how did you meet him?"

"I was chatting with the very friendly woman behind the counter at the convenience store," Allie said, "when in came this incredibly beautiful man, to whom the very friendly woman introduced me as Poppy Higgins's visiting friend from Boston. Nothing is secret in this town, is it?"

"No," Violet said quite seriously. "It's not."

"He's nice, isn't he?" Daisy said, swiping a green bean Allie had just topped and tailed.

"Very nice. Why don't you ask him out, Poppy? I mean, he was good enough to bring you lobsters and frankly, lobsters beat roses in my book any day."

Poppy shook her head. "I don't want a boyfriend, even one as generous and, yes, as handsome, as Jon Gascoyne." *That's the last thing I need right now,* she added silently. *Another complication to my already overly complicated life.*

"Well, if you don't want him, maybe I'll make a play for him."

"But he's younger than you," Daisy pointed out.

Allie raised an eyebrow. "And?"

"And an older woman with a younger man rarely works out. I mean, unless you just want a quick fling. Or unless you don't mind being called a cougar, which basically implies that you pay for sex."

"Where did you get all this helpful information about romantic relationships?" Allie asked.

"The Internet."

Allie shuddered. "Dangerous thing, the Internet. It once convinced me I had psoriasis and I've never even had a rash in my life."

"It's only dangerous if you misuse it," Daisy argued, "and I don't. Not much, anyway. Some days I spend way too much time watching videos of animals doing funny things. Like, this morning I saw this hilarious video of a kitten attacking a statue of a cat."

"I saw that, too," Violet said. "Grimace attacked the stone bird sculpture in the backyard once."

Allie frowned. "I thought you said he was so smart."

"He is. He was practicing."

Poppy shuddered. "I just hope he sticks to killing stone birds and doesn't start bringing us dead baby bunnies. Ugh."

"He won't. I've asked him not to."

"What makes you think he'll keep his promise?" Daisy asked. "That beast has a mind of his own."

"I asked him nicely," Violet explained.

"Was Mr. Gascoyne ever married?" Allie asked suddenly.

"I don't know," Poppy said. "I don't think so or Freddie would have mentioned it."

"Does it matter?" Daisy asked.

"No, just wondering."

"He would make a good husband. And a good father."

"Violet," Poppy said, "I'm not going to marry Jon Gascoyne."

Violet shrugged. "Maybe someday *I'll* marry him. The interesting thing about life is that you never know what's going to happen."

"You mean," Daisy said, "the lousy thing about life."

"Only lousy sometimes," Allie said. "Only sometimes. Right, Poppy?"

Poppy nodded; she was so grateful that Allie had journeyed north to Maine. "Right," she said. "Only lousy sometimes."

Chapter 38

Daisy had caught the summer trolley downtown. She supposed that Evie (whose last name, she had found out, was Jones), who lived much closer to the heart of Yorktide, would simply walk to their meeting place at the corner of Main Street and Vine Street. She checked her watch and the clock on her iPhone. Did Evie wear a watch? Daisy realized she hadn't noticed. If Evie didn't, then how did she know what time it was, with her phone not working?

Anyway, she had been right about Evie from the start. She *was* hiding something though for some reason she had trusted Daisy enough to tell her about her sad past. It had been right to approach Evie with an offer of friendship that day at The Clamshell. Daisy was sure it had given Evie the courage to approach her in turn.

And, they were actually having fun together. They had met at Ogunquit Beach after Evie's shift one afternoon and walked down to the Wells town line and back. One evening they had gone to a free screening of *Casablanca* at the Yorktide library. The room was packed and they had to stand through the movie, but it was worth it. Doomed, super romantic love. The story was right up Daisy's alley and she had unabashedly bawled, though Evie had been completely in control of her emotions. And one afternoon they had watched an episode of *The Daily Show* on Daisy's iPad and had laughed so hard Evie had actually started to choke. Daisy hadn't found anything so downright funny in a very long time (and she was pretty sure that it wasn't all due to Jon Stewart, as hilarious as he was), definitely not since her father had died, and even before that, as Dad seemed to grow more sad, it had been difficult to find anything really amusing, let alone downright funny. Daisy sometimes wondered how Joel, even being as sweet-natured as he was, put up with her.

Daisy caught sight of Evie coming along Main Street and waved. She noted that Evie was wearing the exact same T-shirt she had been wearing the day before. Not that Daisy was at all into fashion or style, but for some reason this struck her. *Oh, well,* she thought as Evie joined her, *she's already told me she doesn't have a lot of money.*

"Hey," Daisy said. "I had an idea. Let's see if my friend Joel is on a break. He's on the groundskeeping crew at The Starfish."

"Oh. I—" Evie fingered the hem of her T-shirt. "I guess . . ."

"You'll love him," Daisy assured her. "He's a year ahead of me in school and I'm so going to hate it when he goes away to college."

Daisy led the way down Main Street, toward the library and the town hall, and before long they turned into the lush grounds of the expansive resort. A graveled path lined with neat bunches of pink and purple flowers wound its way toward a large in-ground pool, beyond which was the ocean, sparkling in the mid-afternoon sun.

"Are we even allowed here?" Evie asked softly, glancing nervously over her shoulder. "I mean, we're not guests."

"Oh, sure. People cut through the grounds all the time on their way to the beach." Daisy grinned. "The police don't have a lot to do in this town, but they wouldn't waste their time with us!"

To the right of the graveled path was a thick green lawn on which people in bathing suits were sunning themselves on chairs and lounges. "It must cost a lot of money to stay here," Evie said.

"I guess. We're lucky we live locally and don't have to pay huge hotel bills just for a view of the ocean." *Maybe I shouldn't have said that,* Daisy thought, when Evie didn't answer. *I can't forget that Evie doesn't have all that I have . . .*

"There he is," Daisy said, "the guy with the Ray-Bans, over by the Wishing Well. There's no water in it, by the way. Purely ornamental."

"OMG, he's gorgeous," Evie whispered.

"I know. And he's smart and a fabulous musician and really nice. And gay."

"Oh. Too bad."

"For womankind. Joel!" Daisy called. "Hi!" She turned to Evie. "If he'd been wearing his earplugs he never would have heard me."

Joel looked up from the mower he was poking at, waved, and came jogging toward them.

"Hey," he said when he had joined them. "What's up?"

"Nothing much. This is my friend Evie. The one I told you about, the one who works at The Clamshell."

Joel put out his hand and after a tiny moment of hesitation (probably overwhelmed by his gorgeousness, Daisy thought) Evie took it. "Nice to meet you," Joel said.

Evie smiled. "Thanks."

"So how's work going?" Daisy asked.

"It's going." Joel laughed. "Get this. One of the guests complained to the manager that we—the grounds crew—

should be wearing nicer uniforms. Can you imagine some-one caring what the guy mowing the lawn is wearing?"

"What did he—or she—want you guys to wear? Thongs?"

Evie giggled and quickly covered her mouth with her hand.

Joel grimaced. "That could be painful, especially around the rosebushes. I don't know what she—it was a she—said specifically, but I guess chinos and a navy polo shirt just don't cut it."

"Well, we think you look fine, right, Evie? Hey, do you guys want to come over for dinner tonight?" Daisy asked. "My sister's friend Allie is making tacos."

"I'm there," Joel said. "What time?"

"Come when you get off from work and we can hang out. Evie? What about you?"

"Thanks," she said quickly, "but I . . . I promised Billy I'd come in later and help him do inventory."

"Too bad. Well, another time."

Joel glanced at his watch. "I'd better get back to work. Have fun, you two. And I'll see you later, Daisy."

Joel jogged back to his mower. Daisy watched him and felt a sharp pang of regret. Or was that a sharp pang of love? Someday someone would take Joel away from her. Someday he would fall in love. That's what happened in life. Things changed and people left.

"He's so nice," Evie said.

Daisy didn't respond for a moment. "Yes," she said fi-nally. "He's the best friend I've ever had." And then, fearing that her words might have put Evie off, she added: "But don't worry. I need a girl as a friend, too."

Evie smiled.

Chapter 39

"Coming," Poppy called, though she had no idea if anyone on the doorstep could hear someone inside calling to him. It was just something you did, call out "Coming!" when the doorbell rang.

As she hurried down the hall she thought she recognized Jon's truck through the etched glass on either side of the front door. Suddenly, she found herself smiling.

"Hi," she said, opening the door to her—to her friend?

"I'm afraid it's me again. Popping up like a bad penny."

Poppy laughed. "I never understood that expression."

"Me, neither," Jon admitted, "but I say it anyway. Look, I've got a rare free hour. I was wondering if you wanted to grab lunch at my family's restaurant. It's nothing fancy, but I can vouch for the food being good."

"Sure. I was about to vacuum the downstairs rooms, but believe me, it's a chore that can wait. Let me grab my bag."

Ten minutes later they were pulling into the parking lot of The Friendly Lobsterman ("Not my choice of name," Jon explained, cringing). Gray, weather-worn shingles. Colorful buoys hanging in clusters against the walls. Lobster traps stacked neatly nearby. A rowboat pulled up onto the pebble-covered shore of the inlet. The Friendly Lobsterman, Poppy thought, looked much like any other establishment of its kind in coastal Maine.

No sooner were they through the front door than they were met with a chorus of greetings. Jon waved to the room in general. "Look around," he whispered. "Every cliché a tourist could want."

Poppy looked. Strings of little red lobster lights were draped over the bar and across the tops of window frames. The walls were decorated with old photographs of local lobstermen and their vessels. Abandoned lobster traps and ripped nets were scattered on windowsills and tacked to walls and posts. Carved wooden seagulls and ducks were lined along shelves. By the hostess station stood a life-sized statue of a fisherman in a classic yellow slicker and hat. There was a pipe clenched between his carved wooden teeth.

"All you need now," Poppy said, turning back to Jon, "is a life-sized pirate to be friends with the life-sized fisherman."

"Don't let my father hear you say that. He'll be out buying one before the end of the day. And my mother would not be pleased. Come on. Let's take that table by the window. There's a perfect view of the marsh."

"Marshes always make me think of ancient times," Poppy said as she took her seat. "Burials. Ritual sacrifices. Bogs."

"There's definitely a sense of the primeval to a marsh," Jon agreed, "especially at low tide when you can see all the different layers of earth. Everything that time's built up."

A waitress brought menus and asked Jon how his mother was feeling. "Better, thanks," he told her. To Poppy he said, "My mom's had a summer cold. She's the worst patient ever. She hates being sick. It's like she takes it as a personal affront by—well, I don't know by whom."

Poppy laughed. "Yikes. Well, I do hope she's over it soon. For everyone's sake. Now, I'm going to have a lobster roll. When in Maine . . ."

"Fish and chips for me," Jon said. "My friend Marty caught the haddock this morning. Can't get any fresher than that. That's my brother over there, the guy in the blue baseball cap. Clark. He works with me on the boat and at the store with my mom."

Poppy's eyes widened. "He looks nothing like you!"

Jon laughed. "The milkman's son. No, really, he takes after my mom's side of the family, the Hauptmans. I'm all Gascoyne. Dad!" Jon waved to another man, who waved back and came across the restaurant to join them.

"Poppy Higgins," Jon said, "this is my father, Albert Gascoyne."

"Call me Al," he said, extending his hand to Poppy. "I knew your parents. Lovely people. I'm sorry for your loss."

"Thank you. It's nice to meet you." Al Gascoyne was indeed the physical pattern upon which Jon had been fashioned. Poppy recalled what Freddie had told her about him, that he was a true pillar of the community. She thought he had kind eyes, much like his son.

"How are those sisters of yours?" he asked.

"Doing well, thanks," Poppy said. "It's been an adjustment for us all, but we're doing okay."

"You let me or my son here know if you young ladies need anything. We're always happy to help a neighbor."

Poppy felt tears threaten and with some effort she managed to thank him. When their lunch arrived at the table, Jon's father went back to his position behind the bar.

"He doesn't need to act as bartender," Jon explained. "We have two on staff. But he likes to keep an eye on things and he feels that if the owner is visible and available for a chat his customers will feel they're being well taken care of."

"That makes sense," Poppy said, watching as Jon's father shook the hand of an elderly man in a tweed cap who had just taken a seat at the bar.

"Thanks for not mentioning the pirate."

Poppy smiled. "No problem."

"So, I know you told my dad you were all adjusting, but are things really okay on Willow Way?"

Poppy shrugged. "I guess. No one's accidentally burned down the house or run off with a boyfriend so I can't complain." *And I won't complain,* Poppy added to herself. *Not to Jon.*

"Do you miss Boston?" he asked. "Or has summer in this lovely little town in Maine erased all thoughts of the metropolis from your mind?"

The question took Poppy by surprise. "Do you know," she told him, "I haven't given Boston a thought in . . . well, in weeks. Some of the people I knew there, sure. That's why I'm glad my friend Allie is staying with us. But not the place."

Jon smiled. "I told you Yorktide could weave a charming spell."

"It's not so much that," Poppy said thoughtfully. "Not that Yorktide isn't beautiful, it is. It's just that I'm not feeling as homesick for my life in Boston as I thought I'd feel."

"I hope that's a good thing. Maybe it means you're finding enough to keep you satisfied in this new stage of your life."

Poppy smiled. "Paying bills, making sound financial investments so my sisters can go to whatever colleges they want to, cooking dinner. When I don't burn it. Trying to be—"

Their waitress appeared with their food then and took some care arranging the basket of rolls and the bottles of condiments before she left.

"Trying to be what?" Jon prompted when she had gone.

"Trying to be a substitute parent for my sisters." Poppy fiddled with her napkin. "Trying to make new friends and get to know some old ones all over again."

"Sounds like a pretty busy life. And, as I think I said when we talked at the gallery, a challenging one."

"It *is* busy and challenging, but I have help," Poppy said promptly. "Freddie for one. And Allie." *And you,* she thought. But she couldn't bring herself to say it. Jon might get the wrong idea. "I'm really pretty lucky," she went on. "My parents left my sisters and me in good shape. We're not exactly filthy rich, but we're—safe. We have a roof over our heads. We weren't abandoned."

Jon frowned. "I'd almost forgotten . . . I was in Wells the other afternoon and I drove past this young kid hitchhiking. He couldn't have been more than fourteen or fifteen. And I got the distinct impression that he was homeless. A runaway maybe. He just didn't look like a wild kid out for a day's adventure. A wild kid looking for a ride to the beach wouldn't be carrying a backpack and wearing long pants and a heavy jacket."

"Carrying his possessions. Because he has no place to leave them."

"That's what I thought. I'm ashamed to say that I didn't stop."

"Hitchhikers can be dangerous," Poppy said. "You hear stories. All those cautionary tales your parents tell you when you're young."

"And so can the people who pick them up," Jon pointed out. "No, I wasn't afraid. I . . . I'm embarrassed to admit this, but the kid was out of my mind the minute I drove by. Until you said what you did about being lucky and safe, I'd completely forgotten about him."

"What if you had stopped?" Poppy asked. "What would you have done if he told you he was a runaway? Assuming he *was* a runaway."

"Tried to convince him to let me drive him to a shelter."

"He might have refused. He might have been scared."

Jon shook his head. "I don't know what I would have done then. Taken him where he wanted to go. And then given him some money I suppose. It would be tempting to offer a kid like that a place to stay for a while, my house or my parents' house. But I couldn't foist a possibly troubled stranger on my family. A lot of runaways and homeless people are addicts. A lot have mental problems or issues with violence. None of that's their fault, of course, but . . ."

"But how do you know what's best to do for them?" Poppy said, more to herself than to Jon.

"Leave it to the experts? That seems so—so cavalier."

"I know," Poppy agreed. "At least in cities there are resources for people who need a bed for the night and a meal and a shower. And there are professionals. Social workers, health care advocates. People who know how to help without, I don't know, without accidentally doing more harm."

"But people can go homeless anywhere," Jon pointed out. "I remember when I was in middle school there was a boy in my class who started to show up in the same clothes day after day. It was clear to everyone that something was wrong. He started to smell. Sorry. He could hardly stay awake in class. In the end the school found out that his mother had thrown him out of the house weeks earlier. He'd been sleeping in a friend's garage until the friend's father told him to go home. Which he couldn't do. After that it was whatever shelter he could find. God knows how he was eating."

"Poor boy." Poppy fought a strong urge to put her hand

on Jon's where it lay on the table. "How did we get on such a sad topic?" she asked.

"My fault. I remembered the hitchhiker. I hope I didn't ruin our good time."

"Not at all!" she assured him. "I'm glad you told me about your experience."

"Next time I promise I'll only talk about happy or neutral topics."

Poppy smiled. "That might be boring!"

"Maybe. So." Jon gestured to Poppy's empty plate. "How was the lobster roll?"

"Excellent. But I do want to try the fish and chips."

"Like I said. Next time."

Jon waved to the waitress for their check. And Poppy thought, *Next time*.

Chapter 40

Violet sat at the kitchen table with Grimace. She was eating a bowl of cold cereal. He was lapping up a bowl of cold milk. Daisy was still asleep and Poppy had gone out early to her favorite farm stand to get a jump on the tomatoes and curly kale. For some reason Violet had picked up the day's copy of the *New York Times* (still delivered though rarely read) to flip through while she ate her breakfast. On the front page of the paper there was a story about homelessness. Violet started to read, and this is what she learned. That homelessness was rampant in certain areas of the United States. That sometimes people weren't even aware that the person they regularly saw at church or walking through the park or getting onto the city bus was homeless or nearly so. That children without homes suffered terribly from the experience, and sometimes never really recovered from the trauma. Every right-minded person, the writer said in conclusion, should consider the situation a disgrace.

With a shaking hand Violet put down her spoon and fled the kitchen, Grimace at her heels. Once inside the haven of her room she lay on the bed, her arms at her side, her palms flat against the mattress, her eyes staring unseeingly at the ceiling. It had never, ever occurred to her that she might one day be homeless. But the article said it could happen to anyone and while in the past Violet had never been one to leap to negative possibilities or to anticipate catastrophe, now . . . Now the image of an uncertain future loomed large in her mind. What had prompted her to open the newspaper? Had the universe been sending her a message—or a warning?

Violet closed her eyes and tried to breathe deeply, but the worry continued to grow. Maybe if she knew the specifics of her family's financial situation she would feel more assured. But even if she asked someone to explain—like Freddie— she doubted she would understand. Math was not her best subject. She opened her eyes again and the ceiling and the scarves draped across it refused to come into perfect focus.

What if something happened to her family's money and they had to leave this house Violet loved so much? Where would they go? Freddie and Sheila might take them in for a while, but they were old and might not want the responsibility. What if something happened to Poppy, and she could no longer take care of her sisters? Would the girls be separated? Would Grimace be taken away from her?

Suddenly, Violet realized that she couldn't move her arms or her legs. She couldn't even *feel* them. The ceiling, no, what she could see of the entire room, was out of focus. She felt dizzy. Her heart was pounding and her breath was coming in short and painful gasps.

Grimace leaped onto the bed and pawed at her arm, all the while making frantic little sounds in his throat. He was afraid for her. Violet was afraid for her, too. *Am I dying?* she wondered. *But I don't want to die.*

For what seemed like an eternity Violet lay immobile on her bed, waiting for whatever it was that was going to happen to happen. Finally, she realized that she could feel her arms again. Tentatively she tried to move her right hand. It moved. Then she tried her left. That, too, moved. With a whimper of relief Violet realized that her vision was clear and that her heart had slowed. Grimace, sensing that the worst was over, settled in a lump beside her and was quiet.

Violet knew only one thing for sure. She would tell no one about what had happened. Poppy would insist she go to the family's doctor who would probably put her on some scary medication that might dull her imagination and maybe even damage her ability to think clearly. There *was* that nice woman from the local family owned drugstore downtown. Back when Violet's mother had been undergoing chemotherapy she had recommended a very effective natural remedy for nausea. But if Violet went to Ms. Hollister for help then Poppy might find out and others, too. Gossip was notorious and inevitable in a small town like Yorktide.

No, Violet thought, she would handle this all on her own. Slowly, she got off the bed and went to the bookcase for the volume of ancient and contemporary herbal remedies. The book would tell her what she could take to calm her nerves, to stop these negative thoughts from harming her.

Ashwagandha root, the book said, was used in the Indian tradition of Ayurveda. It was added to calming serums to treat anxiety, panic attacks, and depression. Sometimes it was used with brahmi or bacopa. Violet had never heard of brahmi before. Valerian root, she read, was used as a sleep aid and to reduce anxiety, but you had to check with a doctor before using it. Ginseng root was a possibility, as was L-theanine, an amino acid found in green tea. Perfect, Violet thought. How could Poppy object to her drinking green tea? It was definitely worth a try. And there was meditation. She could spend more time trying to meditate, to sit quietly and clear her mind, to focus only on her breathing. It hadn't worked a few minutes ago, but . . .

Violet pricked her ears. It was Daisy coming out of her room and heading down the hall toward the bathroom. She remembered that she had left a half-eaten bowl of cereal on the kitchen table. If Daisy or Poppy found it they would be concerned; Violet never left anything half eaten and she always put her dishes in the sink. Dropping the book of herbal remedies, Violet hurried back downstairs to remove the evidence of her distress.

Chapter 41

"But you don't need a new phone," Poppy argued, putting a carton of orange juice back into the fridge. "You've only had that one for a few months."

Daisy crossed her arms over her chest. "We can afford it, can't we? You haven't lost all of Dad's money, have you?"

Violet was in her room, wisely, Poppy thought, avoiding the fray. Allie, reading the current edition of the local paper, was a silent witness to this . . . discussion.

"Daisy, don't be ridiculous. Of course we can afford it and no, I haven't lost a dime of the family's money. But that's not the point. The point is you don't need a new phone when the one you have works perfectly."

"But I . . . Look, Poppy, I really want this."

"You can't always get what you want in this life, Daisy."

"Like I don't know that?" Daisy retorted, unfolding her arms and throwing them into the air. "I want Dad and Mom to be alive again, but I'm not going to get that wish, am I? The least I can have is a stupid new phone!"

Poppy sighed and turned to her friend. "Allie, back me up here. Daisy's being dramatic again."

"No thanks," Allie said, not looking up from the paper. "I make it a policy to stay out of family squabbles."

"But—"

"Nope. You'll thank me for keeping my opinion to myself, trust me."

Poppy wasn't at all sure about that. "Daisy," she said, "the answer is no and that's final."

Poppy left the kitchen without another word. Behind her, she heard Daisy continuing to grumble, but continued silence from Allie. She went upstairs and put her hand on the doorknob of the master suite and then she turned and walked down the hall to her old bedroom. She closed the door behind her and slumped onto the twin-sized bed. It had been rude to walk off as she had. But didn't she have a reason to be rude on occasion? Didn't everyone?

Well, Poppy thought, letting her shoulders sag, maybe there was no good excuse for rudeness, no matter the provocation. It was just that these past few months had given her a taste of what it meant to be a parent and at times—like now—she felt utterly exhausted by the experience.

Poppy's eye fell on the faded poster of a boy band she had been obsessed with back in high school. The image of the baby-faced kids made her feel uncomfortable. She really should take the poster down and throw it out. It was a relic now and of no use to anyone. Unlike her old rag doll, Annie. Poppy reached for Annie where she rested against the bed pillows. She would never throw Annie away, no matter how limp and bedraggled she became.

Photographs. They were memories made tangible, also to be cherished, like the photograph of Julie and Poppy that sat on the dresser. It had been taken on a class trip to a petting zoo in Wells when they were about eleven. There had been this one aggressive goat who kept trying to get a mouthful of Julie's sweater. . . . Poppy smiled at the memory though she had been slightly terrified at the time. Julie had thought the whole thing hilarious.

The boy band. The rag doll. The photograph. She was surrounded by bits of the child that she had been. The child she still was, at least in part. A child who was playing at the adult game of parenthood.

Poppy sighed and gently straightened a strand of Annie's yarn hair. What would happen if one of her sisters got really sick? What if one of them required drugs given through a PICC line? What if one of them had an open wound that needed to be cleaned and dressed? Poppy felt weak at the knees just thinking of being called upon to fake nursing skills. How did anyone ever decide to have children, knowing they might one day be called upon to save their lives? All Poppy could do was to pray to who or whatever might be out there guiding or determining human life that neither Daisy nor Violet would be forced to rely on her as nursemaid because she would undoubtedly fail her sister miserably.

Suddenly, Poppy remembered something her mother used to say. Worry was interest paid on a debt that might never come due. Annabelle was right. Poppy got up from her old bed, put Annie back against the pillows, and left the room. Both Daisy's and Violet's bedroom doors were closed; she could hear Daisy's clarinet and Violet talking, no doubt to Grimace. She continued on downstairs and found Allie in the sunroom, reading the first of Oliver Higgins's books.

"You were right," she said without preamble. "I'm here to thank you for keeping your opinion to yourself. And to apologize for being so unreasonable."

Allie put aside the book and smiled. "No worries. Sit. Have some wine. And FYI, don't try to read your father's work under the influence of alcohol. It's a mistake. I don't think I understood one word of the three pages I managed to get through."

"I can't make out his work sober." Poppy sank into the comfortable chair next to Allie's. "You know," she said, "sometimes I think I've gotten it all under control, that I've made my peace with the changes in my life, and then suddenly, I find myself acting like a ten-year-old."

"Hardly a ten-year-old. Anyway, family tensions always bring out the worst in people. We'd never treat our friends the way we sometimes treat our family. If we did, we'd have no friends."

Poppy smiled. "You're right about that."

Chapter 42

"I'd love to get a peek at what's inside that house," Joel said, craning his neck to get a view through the windshield. "His art is so—unique—I imagine his home is pretty interesting, too."

Joel, with Daisy in the passenger seat, had pulled up outside The Clamshell just as Evie was leaving for the day, and offered her a ride home. Evie, in spite of her dread of riding in cars, had accepted his offer. Standing for five or six hours at a time was tiring, especially when you were wearing thin-soled sneakers. Her feet—and her back—could use the rest. Besides, it was a short ride home and they wouldn't be anywhere near a highway, which was what really terrified her.

Evie laughed and unbuckled her seat belt. "Not really," she said. "It's all pretty normal."

"Do you think we could come in, just for a few minutes?" Joel asked.

Evie hesitated. Nico had made her promise not to have anyone over to the house, but she was sure that Joel and Daisy were not the sort of people to steal a valuable knickknack or to write on the walls with indelible markers. If she let them come in for only a minute or two, Nico would never know. . . .

"Sure," she said. "But could you park in the back?" Evie buckled her seat belt again and Joel drove around to the back of the house. "We have to use the front door," Evie explained, as they got out of the car. "There's a deadbolt on the back door. Sorry." *Why didn't I think of that?* she chided herself. *What does it matter if Joel parks in back when we have to go in through the front?*

With a rapidly beating heart Evie unlocked the front door, and with a final glance over her shoulder, ushered Joel and Daisy in ahead of her. Quickly she closed and locked the door behind them.

Joel stood in the center of the living room. "It's . . . It's big," he said. "And the site is nice enough, though with all the pine trees he must get very little sun in his garden, assuming he keeps one; I didn't notice a garden when we parked. But it's so . . ."

"Bland," Daisy said. "It's nothing like his art."

Evie smiled. "I told you."

"Still," Joel said, examining Nico's sparse collection of books, "it's cool you can stay here for free."

"I don't have to do much, either. I just have to bring in the mail and sort through it. The junk goes in the recycling bin and I take it out to the curb once a week. And the garbage. And I have to answer the phone when I'm here and check the voice mail in case there's an important message. And of course I can't mess up the place." Evie laughed. "And there's a view of the ocean—if you can survive the stairs to the tower room and have a pair of binoculars."

"That probably raises the value of the house by tens of

thousands!" Joel exclaimed. "Nico must be doing all right if he can afford this place."

Daisy harrumphed. "I wonder who buys his stuff? I think it's hideous."

Evie was about to agree with Daisy when she heard a car in the not-so-distant distance.

"Oh my God," she cried. "Someone's coming! I'm not really supposed to have anyone here. . . ."

"Don't worry," Joel said, grabbing Daisy's hand and hurrying toward the back door of the house. "We're already gone. I'll take the back road."

Evie slammed the deadbolt into place when they had gone and then hurried back to the living room. She peered through the window that faced the main road. Nothing but dirt and rocks and trees and ferns and chipmunks. No car. No witness to her crime.

"False alarm," Evie whispered, but it had scared her. If she had been caught having friends in Nico's house she might lose her temporary home. . . . Suddenly she remembered what Daisy had said about the police when they had gone to The Starfish to see Joel. Something about them not wasting their time bothering teenage girls . . . But what about teenage girls who defied the rules of their employer? Could the police forcibly evict her from Nico's home?

Evie dropped into a chair and put her head in her hands. Everything was so fragile. The security she had found was so temporary and depended on her following the rules, unlike life in a family where you could make a mistake and still be loved and have a warm bed in which to sleep and healthy meals to eat.

Then again, Evie thought, she had made no mistake and broken no rules, and yet her home and her family had been wrenched from her. . . . Was there no real certainty in life, no real safety no matter how hard you worked to create a sense of security? It was an awful thought, the possibility of never being allowed to rest, never being allowed to let her guard down. Like the night she and Daisy had gone to see *Casablanca*. She had been so moved by the sad love story, so reminded of her mother though she couldn't say exactly why, that she had been on the point of pouring out her own true sad story to Daisy. It had taken a supreme effort not to break down, not even to allow one tear to stain her cheek. . . .

And the only reason she had said no to Daisy's invitation to dinner the day they had gone to The Starfish (and she *loved* tacos) was that she was still unsure of how smart it was to get close to too many new people. What about the adults at Daisy's house, that friend of Poppy's Daisy had mentioned, and maybe others? What if they started asking questions she couldn't answer? What if she couldn't come up with lies quickly enough, what if she couldn't keep the lies straight? It was hard enough to watch everything she said to Daisy and Joel, people her own age. Adults, even the nice ones, could be tricky. Parents, even her laid-back mother, were always asking questions, always on the lookout for potential problems so they could stop them in their tracks. Teachers were always suspicious of bad behavior. Even if an adult knew you were officially an adult, too, it wouldn't stop them from—from meddling. Why did adults always think they knew better than kids? A lot of time they didn't. Look at her father, for example. What did he know that she didn't? Nothing.

Evie rubbed her eyes. She wondered if she was getting paranoid. That couldn't be good. It was smart to keep an eye out for trouble, but it was stupid to see trouble everywhere you looked. You could make bad mistakes that way.

Wearily, Evie rose from the chair and wandered into the

kitchen. She supposed she should eat something. There was a container of leftover Chinese food in the fridge. Billy had treated the staff to takeout the other day. "A change from our little menu," he said. Evie opened the fridge and stared blindly at its meager contents. And then she closed it. And then she went upstairs to her bedroom. The bedroom that was *not* really hers.

Chapter 43

"And then I have to pick you up?"

Daisy rolled her eyes at her older sister. "Yeah. You know I can't walk home. It's almost six miles along Shore Road. There's no pedestrian walkway. Anyway, why is this suddenly such an issue? You've been driving me every Tuesday afternoon since you moved back from Boston."

"It's just that I had plans," Poppy said, leaning back against the kitchen counter.

"What plans?"

"I was going to see a movie at the Leavitt."

Seriously, Daisy thought. *A movie trumps my job with old people?* "Why can't you go to a later show?"

"There's only one show a day," Poppy told her, "and today is the last day it's playing. It's an Iraqi film, a love story. Allie saw it and she said it's wonderful. Why can't you ride your bike to Pine Hill?"

"Because I don't have a bike," Daisy said. "I haven't had a bike since middle school."

"Why not?"

Daisy gathered what remained of her patience. "Don't

you remember how I was never good on a bike? Don't you remember when I fell off my tricycle and broke my ankle?"

"I guess I forgot."

"And then I need to be picked up at four."

Poppy sighed. "Can't you get a ride home from someone, one of the other volunteers? I really don't want to miss this movie. Who knows when it will show up on Netflix."

"Maybe," Daisy admitted. "But I can't be sure anyone else is going to be leaving when my shift is over."

"There's no bus?"

Daisy stamped her foot in frustration. "Poppy, where do we live? This is not Boston. You *know* there's no public transportation. And the trolleys don't count. They only go to the tourist places and the hotels. You *know* that."

"Pine Hill doesn't have a shuttle you could use? Not all of the employees can have a car."

"Are you trying to drive me crazy? No, Pine Hill doesn't have a shuttle."

Poppy stood away from the counter. "Fine, all right, I'll get my keys."

The sisters were silent on the drive to the Pine Hill Residence for the Elderly. *Thanks for the major sacrifice,* Daisy thought angrily as she got out of the car. What had come over her sister, anyway? Some weird hormonal episode? Poppy wasn't usually the perverse and difficult one in the Higgins family. *She* was!

"I'll have my driver's permit soon," Daisy said, leaning in through the window on the passenger's side. "So you won't have to waste your precious time."

"Daisy," Poppy began, "I didn't say—"

"And you'll have to buy me a car. We won't be able to manage with just one."

Her sister opened her mouth again, but Daisy abruptly turned and ran up the path to the main building. *Bitch,* she thought. Refusing to let her get a new phone. Making a stink about driving her to work. If she, Daisy, were in charge of the family . . . But that was a ridiculous notion. And a frightening one. And suddenly, Daisy felt bad that she had called her sister a bitch, even if only in her head. Her parents had never, ever used foul language, and Daisy wanted to do her parents proud.

Chapter 44

"What have you been up to since I saw you last?" Julie asked when they were settled at Julie's kitchen table with home-brewed iced tea and home-baked granola bars.

"Contemplating my future," Poppy told her. *And being an idiot with Daisy.*

Julie laughed. "Most people would answer that question by saying something like, working on my garden or playing tennis every afternoon, or even binge-watching *Orange Is the New Black*."

"Sorry."

"Don't be. And? What's it like, contemplating your future?"

"It's like struggling through one big jigsaw puzzle with too many missing pieces. Or something like that. I'm not good with metaphors. Or was that a simile?"

"Whatever it was," Julie said, "contemplating the future sounds tiring. That's probably why I try not to do it."

"But you must think about the future to some extent," Poppy argued. "I mean, like where are the kids going to go to school. And, I don't know, are you going to grow the cheese business."

"Sure, but that's called planning. That's practical stuff. The existential stuff I leave to people like you. Sorry. That didn't sound right."

"No, I know what you mean. People like me who haven't found their calling. People who still haven't settled down with a person or a career or better yet, both. People without a vision of what they want their life to look like."

Julie smiled. "I'm not sure I'd say I had a vision—or a calling, for that matter—but I did always know that I wanted to get married and have kids. There was never a doubt in my mind. And then when I met Mack, well, it was so easy. That sounds smug, but I don't mean it to. What I mean is, we fell in love and we stayed in love and then we got married. Like I said, easy. I guess I'm pretty lucky."

"I've never been certain about anything," Poppy said. *A character flaw?*

"That's not true. Back in middle school you told every-one who asked that you were going to be a kindergarten teacher. And then in high school you were totally certain you were going to be a graphic designer."

Poppy was stunned. "Really? I can barely remember those days and they weren't so long ago." *A kindergarten teacher? A graphic designer? Who was that girl?*

"A lot of tough stuff has happened to you since then."

Suddenly, Poppy felt embarrassed. She feared that Julie would find her annoyingly self-obsessed if she kept going on in this way. "How are your parents, Julie?" she asked. "I'm sorry I haven't asked before now."

"They're good. Mom's still working at the Beachplum, you know, that motel along Route 1 in Wells. I wish she would quit—she's too old to be cleaning up other people's messes—but she says she likes to keep busy so . . . And Dad spends most of his time making these fancy birdhouses."

"Like the one out there?" Poppy asked, pointing to a yellow and green construction hanging from the branch of an apple tree in Julie's side yard.

"That's one of Dad's, yes. He's pretty talented, I think. He's been selling his birdhouses at a few of the shops in town and in Ogunquit."

"I guess building birdhouses makes sense after all those years in construction! Please give them both my love. They must be thrilled about the new grandchild."

"Dad's convinced it's a boy," Julie said. "Mom's convinced it's a girl. Well, one of them has to be right!"

"You mean you don't know the sex of the baby?" Poppy asked. She had always imagined she would want to know the sex of her unborn child as soon as possible.

"Mack and I like to be surprised," Julie explained. "Though after Virginia was born, I really had my fingers crossed for a boy. To have at least one of each seemed perfect. And then came Michael."

"So the third one is the icing on the cake," Poppy said. "He—or she—is under no pressure."

Julia laughed. "You could put it that way."

At that moment Virginia and Michael came dashing through the kitchen, the phone on the counter rang, and the oven timer went off. "Don't run in the house," Julie said, as she picked up the receiver with one hand and turned off the timer with her other. "Hello?" she said into the phone as she removed a pound cake from the oven. "Yes, we'll be there. Thanks."

Julie came back to the table and lowered herself into her chair. "Sorry. That was my ob-gyn's office confirming my next appointment. Just a checkup."

"How do you do it?" Poppy asked.

Julie laughed. "Do what?"

"All this. Everything. The kids, the farm, the house, a husband, a new baby on the way . . ."

"Don't forget the cheese-making! Really, Poppy, it's just life. My life. I just live it."

"You chose it," Poppy argued. "That's why it's easy for you to live it, even when it's chaotic. But what happens when your life isn't of your own choosing, the big parts of it anyway, like where you live or the job you have to take. How do you live a life you didn't ask for?"

"There are always some parts of life you didn't ask for. Do you think I wanted my son to be born deaf? Life isn't always a bed of roses."

"Oh, I know," Poppy said. "I guess I'm being self-pitying again. A self-pitying wretch. And no one likes one of those."

"I like you, Poppy. And you're not a wretch of any sort. Your problem is that you think too much."

Poppy laughed. "How do you *not* think too much?"

"Once you have kids you'll find out! Most of the time, you just have to do something right then and there because it's what's called for. No time for debate."

"*If* I ever have kids of my own. Looking out for Daisy and Violet is exhausting enough to put me off the idea for good. It seems I'll be buying Daisy a car before long. And then there's her college applications to get through and figuring out financing . . . And then there's Violet, who's told me she's not sure she wants to go to college!"

"Don't worry. It will be totally different once you're married and have someone to help you make the big decisions."

"If I ever get married!"

"You will."

Poppy shrugged.

"There *is* Jon Gascoyne . . ."

"Jon? I doubt he has any interest in me. He's never asked

me out." He had only taken her to his family's restaurant, where he had introduced her to his father, and he had brought her lobsters and he had sorted out the problem with the lawn mower and he had said nice things about her parents.

Oh, Poppy thought now. *Why haven't I seen . . .*

"Dating—candlelight dinners and all the artificial fuss—isn't Jon's way," Julie was saying. "He's the kind of guy who wants to get to know a woman in natural, day-to-day situations."

Poppy smiled. "But all the 'artificial fuss' can be fun." *Not necessary,* she added. *But fun.*

"I know. I vaguely remember the dates Mack and I used to go on. Not that he had much money to take me anyplace fancy. But getting dressed up was enjoyable. Look, all I'm saying about Jon Gascoyne is that he's—he's an intentional guy. He doesn't waste his time. His taking you to lunch at The Friendly Lobsterman—don't look so surprised, everyone knows about that—had a purpose behind it, mark my words."

Poppy didn't know quite how she felt about this. If Julie was right and Jon really was courting her in this slow and old-fashioned way . . . But he hadn't even touched her, not once. She tried now to remember if their hands had ever accidentally made contact, when she was handing him a glass of lemonade, when he was giving her a bag of squirming lobsters, the time they had eaten lunch at his family's restaurant and she had so wanted to place her hand over his. No, she thought. She would have remembered something so . . .

But if he *was* interested in her, why didn't he come right out and tell her? Like her ex-boyfriend in Boston, Ian, had. Like all of her ex-boyfriends had. "I'm into you," they had announced. No slow, old-fashioned approach. Just a statement of fact. A statement of desire. But what would she say to Jon if he did declare himself? (She felt slightly ridiculous using that term, but . . .) She liked Jon, she found him attractive and kind and smart and fun, but . . . In spite of all the good things in her life—the house and her sisters and good friends like Freddie, Sheila, Allie, even Julie—life still felt so precarious.

"Poppy? You look like you're a million miles away."

"Sorry. I was just thinking. Anyway, Jon knows I have no intention of sticking around once Violet turns eighteen. I doubt he'd want to pursue a relationship with someone who's already told him she's leaving town in a few years. He made it pretty clear to me when we first met that his future is in Yorktide."

"Hmm."

"What do you mean by 'hmm'?"

"I mean nothing by it. Anyway, the pound cake should be cooled by now. How about a slice?"

Chapter 45

Evie looked at her image in the mirror by the front door and adjusted the tortoiseshell sunglasses Daisy had given her the day before. Evie had lost her one pair and Daisy had insisted she take hers. She had been so nonchalant about it, too. "I have, like, a bazillion pairs, no worries." Would she have said something else if she knew the truth? Would she have seen giving Evie a pair of her sunglasses as an act of charity, not as an act of friendship? Would knowing that Evie was a homeless runaway change the way Daisy felt about her? Of course it would.

Evie took off the sunglasses and put them on the little table under the mirror. It was so much worse once having had stuff and then losing it all, than never having had stuff to begin with. Now, when things in the Lost and Found box at The Clamshell went unclaimed after a week, Evie took them before any of the other employees could, even if it was something for which she didn't have an immediate need. You never knew when a hair band or a sun visor or a half-used bottle of sunblock might come in handy. In such a short space of time she had gone from being a kid whose every need and most desires were met by adults to a person who had to think hard to anticipate every possible necessity—forget about desires—and, in spite of her inexperience, find some way to meet those necessities. She wasn't even sure a sixteen-year-old brain was physically *able* to function like an adult's!

Still, she couldn't afford to feel sorry for herself. Other people had it worse than she did. Look at all those people in parts of the world that were torn apart by war every few years. Her situation was heaven compared to theirs and she had to remember that. Because if she did succumb to self-pity she was afraid she would start to make big mistakes and poor judgments, and worst of all, be found out. And what then? Be sent back to her aunt and uncle? Be put into foster care? Be returned to her father, wherever he was?

Evie sank onto the couch. At least Nico had a television and complete with Roku, too, so she was able to pass the time after work and before she went to bed watching old French language movies and reruns of *Psych*. It was great good luck, given Nico's limited book collection and the fact that Evie had no access to the Internet unless she used the computer in the public library, but there was a strict limit to the time you were allowed and it wasn't like the library was just next door to The Clamshell. And even if it were right next door she wouldn't be able to check out books or DVDs because she didn't have a library card! Without Nico's television she thought she might go mad, alone with her own thoughts.

Though it wasn't her habit she clicked through to the local news station, which was in the middle of a weather report. More clear and sunny skies. At least that was good news as Evie didn't have an umbrella and she hadn't seen one in Nico's hall closet, where things like umbrellas were usually kept. And then, the anchor introduced a report on the homeless population in Maine and suddenly Evie was watching a social worker from a shelter in Portland explain to the reporter that homelessness could happen to anyone. "Bad luck," she said, "some terrible misfortune, a sudden economic collapse, and the next thing you know you're on a downward slope."

Evie swallowed hard. A car accident that killed your mother. Your father's subsequent addiction to prescription painkillers. Distant family that didn't really want you around. She reached for the remote on the couch beside her—she couldn't bear to watch this report!—and then withdrew her hand.

The reporter now sat down at a cafeteria-style table next to a woman Evie thought might be about Mr. Woolrich's age.

"I have nothing to hide, not anymore," the woman said abruptly, before the reporter could ask her a question. "But I'm not going to give my real name. Let's say that I'm called—Marion."

Another person who had been forced to leave behind her real name, Evie thought. *Another person like me.*

The reporter asked Marion to share her story and briefly, Marion did. She had once been married to an affluent man, but he had turned out to be a crook, and not a very successful one at that. He lost most of their money and had been sent to jail on charges of corruption. Marion had been forced to sell what was left of their estate and then to repeatedly downscale until there was nothing at all remaining of her once easy and comfortable lifestyle.

"The shame was awful," she said. "I thought I would die of it. At times, I wanted to die."

"But you survived," the reporter said.

Marion laughed. "And this is what I'm reduced to. Once,

if you can believe it, I would give dinner parties for twenty with caviar and champagne to start and handmade chocolates and expensive brandy to finish the night. I loved the fact that I could be so openhanded and generous. And now, I'm lucky to keep aside an extra package of crackers to offer to a fellow . . . A fellow woman without a home."

The reporter then asked if Marion had turned to her family for help when things began to go sour.

"There wasn't anyone by then," Marion replied. "My parents were long gone and I'd had no children. I'd lost touch with my sister when I married. We'd had a falling-out. She thought I was making a mistake marrying the man I did. Well, in the end she was right."

The reporter asked about friends, and still Evie watched and listened.

Marion laughed bitterly. "Friends might be happy to put you up for a night or two, but who is going to adopt to what amounts to a sixty-three-year-old dependent? Or give money to you when it's clear you're always going to need more, and more? Even if you were always generous with them in the past . . . No. When you're destitute, you have no friends. Not anymore."

The reporter then asked Marion how she felt about the shelters she frequented.

"The shelters I'm forced to frequent, you mean. I know I should be grateful and I am of course, but . . . There can be trouble. I woke in the middle of the night one day last week to find a man groping at me . . ." The woman turned away from the probing eye of the camera for a moment. "The staff does their best," she went on when she had recovered her composure. "They're angels. But they can't do everything that's needed."

Evie still desperately wanted to turn off the TV, but she

couldn't make her finger hit the power button on the remote. She had to know more. Like probing a wound. Like seeing into her own dismal future.

The reporter thanked Marion and moved on to a man sitting at an adjacent table. His name was Tommy. He told her that he had grown up in a family that had been homeless on and off for years. When he was seventeen, he had left his parents and struck out on his own. Evie couldn't at all guess how old he was. He had no top teeth. He was very skinny and there were dark bags under his eyes. He was wearing a Boston Red Sox T-shirt.

"It's a cycle," Tommy was telling the reporter. "What they call a vicious cycle. My mother and father had nothing, no money, no education, no one to help them out when they lost jobs, which they did when they was drinking. Now I got nothing. No way out. That's what I tell anyone who asks me. No way out."

"How old are you, Tommy?" the reporter asked.

"I was twenty-eight last month."

Evie was shocked. So young, so deteriorated, so without hope. Finally, finally, she felt able to press the power button on the remote and the screen went blank. She sank farther into the couch and thought of her father, wherever he was. A man who had lost everything. A man who might, like Marion, be ashamed. A man who might, like Tommy, be caught in a vicious cycle. And there it was in Evie's heart, a glimmer of sympathy for what her father had suffered, for what he might be suffering now.

The police had investigated the accident that had killed her mother and had concluded beyond a shadow of a doubt that her father was innocent. The medical staff attending to her father had assured her time and again that he wasn't to blame, that it had all been just a terrible accident, a mischance. "These things happen," one nurse had murmured over and over as Evie stood staring down at her father in his bed. "No one is to blame."

But Evie hadn't believed any of them. She had felt she couldn't afford to believe them though now, at this great distance, alone in a stranger's house, Evie wondered if it had been wrong not to believe in her father's innocence. But if he was indeed innocent, why had he allowed himself to get addicted to those painkillers, to lose his job, his house, his daughter! Guilt. His guilt had driven him to it. His guilt for having killed his wife. Or his *belief* that he had killed his wife, no matter what the authorities said?

Guilt. Innocence. Evie clutched her head in both hands. What if some day she saw her father on a TV show like the one she had just watched? What if some day she had no other choice but to take refuge in a shelter and what if her father was staying at the same one? "Hi, Dad, what a coincidence!" The thought made her feel sick.

Evie ran up to her temporary bedroom, jammed the chair under the doorknob, and, clutching Ben, she burrowed down under the covers on the bed. She wasn't sure how long she could go on like this. Maybe she should just give up and go back to her aunt and uncle's house. Of course, they might not take her in; they were probably really mad at her for running off. But if they did take her in it would only be for two years, until she turned eighteen, and then . . . And then she would be right back to where she was now. Alone.

Chapter 46

The letters charged at her, huge and densely black, capital letters zooming toward her face and only at the very last moment darting off to the left or to the right. And all the while she was dodging the *M* and the *B* and the *Z* she was desperately trying to free her father, prisoner in a jail cell of black and white squares. All the while she was desperately trying to solve the crossword puzzle that stretched across the sky before her. "I can't think, I can't think!" she cried. "Five down, ten across, a thirteen letter word." From inside the bars of the puzzle her father tried to speak. He was trying to help her. He opened his mouth to give her a clue, but not a word would come out. His lips refused to form the words that would save him. And then he shook his head. *It's hopeless,* he was thinking. *I can't help you!* "But it can't be hopeless" she cried. "If only I can think harder I can get you out!" But the theme of the puzzle, she couldn't discern the theme! First it was one thing and then it was another and still one by one the white squares darkened, blotting out the sight of her father, inexorably imprisoning him, burying him behind the blackness and still Daisy, pulling her hair in frustration, couldn't find the right words to set him free. . . . Only three white squares left. Two. Only when the final white square was beginning to darken did Daisy wake, haunted by the image of only her father's anguished eyes peering out at her from his doom.

"It's that time of year again," Joel said.

Daisy was slumped in one of the Adirondack chairs her father had loved so much, sweating. Joel, looking cool as the proverbial cucumber and entirely unwrinkled, was sitting next to her in his own chair. Just out of earshot Violet was crouched among her herbs. So hot. So humid. *Why am I out in this goop?* Daisy wondered. *Why am I not inside with the air conditioning blasting?*

"What time of year again?" she asked, not really interested in the answer.

"Time for the annual summer party for the groundskeeping crew at The Starfish Hotel and Resort. Swimming in the outdoor pool, free food, decent music if you can stand technopop. So, how about it? You'll be my plus one again?"

At the moment, the idea of going to a party with a bunch of happy, nicely dressed and probably un-sweaty people didn't appeal to Daisy at all. She was still haunted and depressed by that maddening dream. The awful, Daliesque dream in which she hadn't been able to release her father from his doom.

"Why don't you ask Evie, instead?" she suggested. "She has so little and she works so hard. She deserves a fun night out."

Joel frowned. "You don't mind? You had such a good time at the party last year."

Last year my father was alive . . . "No," Daisy said honestly. "I don't mind at all."

"Okay. That's nice of you, Daisy. I'll pop over to The Clamshell right now."

When Joel had gone Daisy finally went inside the house, leaving Violet, who didn't seem fazed by the dense wet weather, to her plants. She wandered into the sunroom. Her father's favorite room. She sat in his favorite chair. She felt depressed. She also felt a sort of free-floating anger, but she couldn't locate its source. Without a second thought she took her cell phone from her pocket and placed a call to Pine Hill. The receptionist put her through to the office of the volunteer coordinator. "This is Daisy Higgins," she told the administrative assistant who answered the line. "I'm calling to say that I'm resigning from the volunteer staff." The admin was sorry to hear the news and asked for Daisy's reason. Daisy told her that it was personal. The admin didn't press her.

The minute—no, the second—Daisy ended the call she regretted her action. What had she been thinking? She had never done anything so ridiculous. She had consciously thrown away a part of her life that gave her genuine pleasure and more importantly, especially since her father was gone, a part of her life that had given her a real sense of purpose.

Why, she wondered, feeling tears come to her eyes. Why had she done it?

Chapter 47

"So, it's a week from Saturday, from seven until ten. It should be a lot of fun. Well, some fun," Joel amended. "The music's usually pretty awful. But we'll have a perfect view of the water—what you can see of it at night."

Evie's initial flush of excitement was rapidly followed by a sort of horror. It was impossible. How could *she,* Evie Jones, go to a party? Evie Jones couldn't be part of a crowd. She didn't even exist. "I don't have a bathing suit," she said lamely.

Joel shrugged. "I'm sure you can borrow one from Daisy. Besides, not everyone goes swimming. You could wear whatever you have. Shorts and a T-shirt would be fine. There's no dress code."

Still Evie hesitated. Hanging out with so many people could be dangerous; what if she got nervous and let something slip, something important, like her real birthday or her real name? She had already made a mistake by having Daisy and Joel to Nico's house. For days afterward she had expected to find one of Nico's friends at the front door, saying he had seen Daisy and Joel at the house, telling her that he had called Nico in Tangiers and that Nico had told his friend to throw her out. The friend, of course, would be accompanied by a burly policeman.

"Say yes," Joel coaxed. "There's always a big spread—including lobster rolls, but maybe you've had your fill of them working here—and generally my coworkers are decent people. It'll be like being on a mini-vacation."

Evie knew further resistance was hopeless. Joel was trying so hard to convince her to come along she felt it would be insulting to turn him down. He might not want to be her friend any longer. "Okay," she said. "I'll go. Thanks, Joel."

"Great. I'll pick you up at seven." With a wave Joel was off and Evie went back to her station behind the order counter at The Clamshell, where it suddenly occurred to her that Daisy must have put Joel up to asking her to the party. Daisy was much closer to Joel than she was and would have been his obvious first choice. Evie wondered how she felt about Daisy's gesture. She could try to convince herself that she didn't need special attention, that she didn't want it. But that would be a lie. She had been so blue after seeing that awful show the other night about homelessness. Maybe a change in routine—thanks to her friends—would nudge her out of her depression. At the very least she could finally get her fill of something other than fish and chips, coleslaw, and the occasional Chinese takeout.

Chapter 48

"Carpe diem."

"What?" Daisy asked. She and Poppy were in the kitchen. Poppy was prepping for dinner. Daisy was slumped on a stool at the counter, doing not much of anything.

Poppy looked up at her sister. "I didn't know I'd said that out loud. I was just thinking. My parents—our parents— both died young. Too young. Who's to say I won't die young, too?" *Or that Daisy or Violet won't* . . . "I've only got this one life and here I am, wasting it."

"Peeling potatoes *is* a waste of time, isn't it? The skin is perfectly edible and it has a lot of fiber."

"I'm not talking about peeling potatoes, but you're right. Why am I doing it?" Poppy put down the vegetable peeler. "No, I meant that I'm wasting my life by not doing anything important, anything meaningful."

Daisy frowned. "Gee, sorry being our legal guardian is such a *waste* of your time. I'm sure Violet and I don't mean to be ruining your life."

"I don't mean that you're the waste. Really, Daisy, don't be so touchy. I mean that I want my life to be meaningful like Mom's and Dad's were meaningful, out there in the world, affecting the lives of thousands of people for the better. I feel I've done absolutely nothing of *public* value since graduating from college."

"I thought you liked your job in Boston," Daisy said. "You were writing articles that lots of people were reading."

"I wrote about fluff topics, Daisy. What café made the best decaf latte. What nightclub served the weirdest cocktails. Nothing that made a significant difference in anyone's life. I guess what I'm saying is that I want to have a calling. But a calling just comes to you, I think. I don't think you can force one."

"Not everyone can be a superstar, you know," Daisy said.

"Thanks," Poppy said dryly. "I do know. And I'm not saying I want or need to be famous. Look, you've always known you want to work in the medical profession. Even Violet already knows what she wants to do with her life. Me? I keep drawing a blank."

"Maybe you should see a career counselor. Or take one of those standardized tests that tell you what you'd be good at." Daisy grinned. "Maybe your calling is to be an accountant."

"Ha."

Poppy went back to peeling the potatoes (vowing it would be the last time she bothered) and Daisy occupied herself by kicking the counter with her sneaker, one of her more annoying habits in her sister's opinion. And then the kicking stopped.

"You know," Daisy said suddenly. "When you left for Boston, I was really upset. I think I actually hated you for a while."

Poppy felt her eyes widen in surprise. "I had no idea you were upset. Mom didn't say anything to me about it."

"That's because I didn't tell her. I didn't tell anyone, not even Dad, that I felt you were . . . abandoning me."

"But why?" Poppy asked. "Why hide how you were feeling?"

"I'm not really sure," Daisy admitted. "Maybe because I'm stubborn. That's not really the right word. Perverse? Maybe because I don't like anyone to know when I feel weak or vulnerable or sad. Anyway, what would you have done if you had known I didn't want you to move away? Stay home?"

"No," Poppy said, "but I might have been able to offer you some comfort."

Daisy shrugged. "I was only being silly, anyway. Everyone leaves. Nothing stays the same for long."

Poppy sighed. "I can't argue with that."

"And that," Daisy pointed out, "means that this stasis and indecision or whatever it is you feel won't last forever."

"You're right I suppose."

Daisy grinned. "I'm smart."

"That, too. You're way smarter than I am."

"That's your problem, Poppy. You're always putting yourself down! It's like a reflex. Where did that come from? Not from Mom and Dad. They were, like, ridiculously supportive of us."

"I know."

"Even when we were just being ordinary kids they acted as if we were . . . How can I say it? It's not that they spoiled us . . ."

"No, you're right. They didn't spoil us, but at the same time they didn't push us to be people we weren't. They just—accepted each of us. Is that it?"

Daisy nodded. "Yeah. That's it. And you know what? I think that's pretty rare."

"Me, too."

Daisy grabbed a banana from the fruit bowl and loped out of the kitchen.

Poppy now began to cut the potatoes into chunks. She was pleased by the conversation she had just had with her sister. She felt it had been a bit of a breakthrough; she felt now that maybe she and Daisy might become real allies in the new life the family was forging. And maybe the conversation had been possible because a day earlier she had apologized to Daisy for being such a grump about driving her to and from her volunteer job. Really, Poppy was a bit ashamed of her behavior. She wasn't supposed to let a bad mood affect her conduct toward the girls—the children—who were in her care.

Poppy dumped the potatoes into the pot of water boiling away on the stove. Bad moods aside, Poppy thought, she was still not going to buy Daisy a new phone until the old phone died. Supportive she would be, but she would not ruin her parents' good work by giving in to her sister's unreasonable demands!

Chapter 49

Monterey Jack cheese. Pickle relish. Whole wheat bread. It was just after noon and Violet was in the kitchen making herself lunch. She might be feeling anxious and her spirits might be depressed, but her appetite was still strong. Violet was grateful. She really enjoyed food.

After what had happened to her the morning she had read the article in the *New York Times,* Violet had made it a point to research the topic of anxiety, both on the Internet and in a book she had found in the study. She knew now that she had had a full-blown panic attack.

Anxiety, the experts said, was a natural response to danger, like an alarm that went off when you felt you were being threatened or when you found yourself in a stressful situation. The problem with anxiety was that while it could be productive by keeping you alert and focused, it could also get out of control and take over your life. And Violet was determined not to let that happen. So she had bought a box of green decaf tea and was drinking three to four cups a day. Trouble was, she wasn't sure if she was feeling any calmer or if she was only convincing herself she was feeling calmer because she wanted to be. And maybe that was okay. It was called the placebo effect. If you got the result you wanted, did it really matter *how* you got it?

Daisy came tramping into the kitchen and grabbed a bottle of water from the fridge.

"Hi," Violet said. "Do you want a sandwich?"

"Hi. And no thanks. I had two corn muffins this morning. I feel like I've swallowed a brick. I don't know what I was thinking."

"That they were delicious," Violet said. "Allie's a really good baker."

"And I have no self-control!"

Violet didn't think that was true, but Daisy liked to exaggerate. "Isn't it about time for that party Joel's boss throws every summer?" she asked. "Or did you already go and I spaced on it?" That was possible, Violet thought. Keeping focused on day-to-day stuff wasn't all that easy these days.

"No," Daisy said. "It's coming up soon."

"Are you going?"

"No. Not this year."

"Why not? Didn't Joel ask you?"

"Of course he did. I just don't feel like going, that's all."

"Oh." Violet thought that she understood. If someone invited her to a party right now she wouldn't be in the mood for it, either. Not that she had ever been at a party before, not one without her parents or with Freddie and Sheila, like the gallery opening they had gone to earlier in the summer. Once, back when she was little, a girl in her class had invited her to her birthday party, but when Violet and her mother had gotten to the door of the girl's house, Violet had refused to go in.

"I told him he should take Evie," Daisy said, breaking into Violet's thoughts. "I've told you about her. Our new friend, the one who works at The Clamshell."

Violet took a bite of her sandwich, chewed, and swallowed. "Why did you tell him to take Evie?" she asked then.

Daisy shrugged. "So he wouldn't have to go alone, I guess."

"Did Evie say yes?"

Daisy laughed. "Joel said he really had to coax her, but in the end she agreed."

"Why didn't *she* want to go?" Violet asked.

For some reason Violet couldn't figure Daisy wouldn't meet her eye. "She's a bit shy."

Violet finished her sandwich and contemplated making another one. She hadn't been sleeping well in the past weeks and often by mid-afternoon she could barely keep her eyes open. She decided that yes, she would make another sandwich. Food was fuel. She reached for the package of bread.

"Are you feeling okay?" Daisy asked, now watching her closely.

"Of course," Violet replied quickly. Too quickly?

"It's just that you look, I don't know, kind of tired I guess."

And suddenly Violet felt her temper rise in her and she was scared. She almost never got angry and when she did it was about really terrible things like an injustice, like the time a boy in her second grade class had pushed a smaller boy to the ground just because he could. She never got angry about a totally innocent question posed by someone she knew loved her. She took a breath and answered carefully.

"I guess I am tired. I stayed up late last night reading."

"Don't tell Poppy that," Daisy advised. "She'll try to send you to bed right after dinner."

"No," Violet said, assuring both her sister and herself. "I won't say anything."

Chapter 50

The pool, Evie noticed, didn't seem to be a big attraction; only a few people were standing around in the shallow end. Much more popular was the table laden with the kind of food easy to eat without utensils—cold shrimp, mini-quiches, chunks and slices of fruit, pigs in a blanket, and, as Joel had promised, lobster rolls. There was beer and wine for those over twenty-one, bottled water and juices for the others. The DJ had set up his equipment at the far end of the pool; he had attracted a group of female guests who were staring at him like he was a real celebrity, not the local college sopho-more with failing grades and bad skin Joel had told Evie he was. Evie guessed there were about forty people in all, not really that many, but she felt as if she were in a much larger, louder, and possibly dangerous crowd. And she was defi-nitely one of the youngest there. At least, she felt that way and it was strange that she felt so immature in comparison to the other guests because Evie strongly suspected that not one of them had gone through the terrible experiences she had—losing her family, living on the road . . .

"See that guy over by the food table, the one stuffing a

lobster roll into his mouth?" Joel whispered. "Can you believe what he's wearing? It's like . . . It's like something from the eighties. Like something the guys in Duran Duran would have worn. I wonder who he came with."

Evie laughed. The guy's outfit—a cobalt blue suit in some shiny material; two massive sparkly brooches pinned to the jacket's narrow lapels, the sleeves of which were pushed up to the elbows—really was a pretty outrageous throwback. She only hoped that no one was looking at *her* as critically. Daisy had lent her a brand new T-shirt (it was the softest cotton Evie had ever felt) and a lightweight cotton jacket, and she was wearing her best pair of jeans. Well, the better of the two pair she had with her in Yorktide, and even so, the exterior seam of the left leg was beginning to tear. The only shoes she had to wear were sneakers or flip-flops and she had gone with the latter because they were cleaner. The other girls were far better dressed than Evie was and at first, she felt embarrassed. But Joel was such a great date—yes, even though he was gay Evie thought of this night as her first date—chatting with her, introducing her to people, bringing her drinks, and making her laugh that before long she almost forgot her misfit status and began to enjoy herself.

"I wonder if he crashed. It's kind of a small party for someone who wanted to crash. No place to hide." Joel shrugged. "As long as he leaves some food for the rest of us. Speaking of which, did you get enough to eat?"

Evie nodded. "I had plenty, thanks, Joel."

"Good. Look, I'm going to run inside to the gent's. Be back in a minute."

It was only as Evie watched him go off that she began to feel exposed again, like the misfit and outsider that she was. A misfit and outsider who couldn't help but overhear snatches of the conversations going on around her.

The guy in a T-shirt and cargo shorts and flip-flops to a guy in a similarly casual getup: "Can you believe my parents are so lame? I mean, telling me they're not going to pay for me to go to Mexico on winter break. What am I supposed to do between semesters, work?"

The girl in a bright pink sundress to a girl in a bright purple sundress: "Oh, my God, I got the cutest skirt the other day at Express. It was on sale for, like, sixty dollars. I wish they had it in black 'cause I would have gotten that, too."

Evie willed her ears to shut. She was so far removed from the society these kids inhabited, with their nice homes and functioning parents to complain about and good schools to go to and money to spend on stuff that was completely unnecessary.

"Hi. You came with Joel, right?" Evie jumped. She hadn't seen the girl approaching though now she couldn't imagine how she had missed her. She had a figure like Kim Kardashian's and hair to match. She was wearing a pristine white crop top, white jeans, and fuchsia-colored high-heeled sandals.

Evie nodded.

"I'm Natalie. My boyfriend's on the groundskeeping crew. How do you know Joel?"

"I met him . . . through a friend," Evie said, amazed that her voice was steady.

"Joel's a real sweetheart. Look, a bunch of us have been talking about going out after the party, maybe hitting a club. Why don't you and Joel join us?"

"No," Evie blurted, then, horrified, she said, "I mean, sorry, we can't. We have plans. Sorry."

Natalie shrugged and walked off. She probably thought Evie rude and Evie was sorry for that, but what else could she have done? She was already risking so much trusting Daisy and Joel. She only hoped that if Joel learned of the invitation he wouldn't be mad at her for turning it down without checking with him.

And then Joel was back at her side.

"Sorry it took so long," he said. "I was waylaid by my boss. Seems one of the riding mowers is broken though no one reported it. He wanted to know if I knew who was using it last. I mean, I'm not a snitch. Even if I did know I wouldn't tell him!"

"Oh."

"Are you okay?" Joel asked, peering down at her.

"Yes," Evie protested. "I'm fine."

"You don't look fine. Did anyone bother you? That chucklehead Frank, the guy in the madras shorts, thinks he's God's gift to girls."

"No, he didn't bother me. No one did."

"Then what's wrong?" Joel asked.

"Nothing," Evie insisted. "It's just that it's been such a long time since . . . since I've been to a party like this." *Another lie. I've never been to a party like this.*

Joel smiled sympathetically. "Music too loud?"

"Maybe."

"Told you it was awful. Look, why don't we call it a night?"

"I'm sorry, Joel," Evie said hurriedly. "We don't have to go, really. I'm fine."

"It's no big deal," he assured her. "Look, I work with these guys every day and most of them are getting drunk. I've seen enough of them for a lifetime."

He held out his hand and she gave him hers. It had been so long since anyone had held her hand that the sensation of warmth and support almost made her drop to her knees with gratitude.

Chapter 51

"I can't believe Freddie's going to be eighty." Poppy shook her head. "I never think of her as old, you know. I mean, she's still working full-time! Where does she get the energy?"

Poppy and Violet were at the table in the sunroom making plans for the party they were giving for their friend's birthday, which happened to coincide with Independence Day.

"You're only as old as you feel," Violet recited. "People say that, but I don't think it's always true, do you?"

"I don't know. Some days, I feel twenty-five in the morning, eleven at noon, and ninety-five at bedtime. And sometimes, it's the reverse. All ages of man. Or, in my case, woman."

"I don't think I feel any age at all. I just feel like—me." A person who was hiding a secret for the first time in her life.

"That's probably a good thing," Poppy noted. "Just feeling like you. Our culture is obsessed with youth. Antiaging. What's that about? Like getting old is always a bad thing?"

Violet didn't think she needed to respond. Getting old

was an experience—a gift—neither of their parents had been allowed. Poppy knew that as well as she did.

"I thought I'd do a centerpiece of green and white flowers," Violet said. "Freddie's favorite color is green so she'll like that. Maybe some snowball viburnum and Queen Anne's lace—there's the tiny ruby inside the blossom and ruby is Freddie's birthstone—and maybe some ivy and sage leaves and white roses. I'll have to buy some stuff, of course."

"Sure. I'll take you to the florist later if you want. Should we get balloons do you think? It might be fun, given Freddie's not exactly a kid."

"You mean like the Mylar kind that have Hello Kitty or SpongeBob on them?"

"Yeah. What do you think?"

Violet shook her head. "It's not Freddie's kind of humor."

"Yeah, you're right. Maybe just some regular balloons?"

"Okay. And I'm also going to make a corsage for Freddie. I'm thinking of using green hydrangea for that, if I can find some small enough. I know corsages are kind of old-fashioned and formal, but . . ."

"I think it's a great idea, Violet." Poppy tapped the pencil she was using to make notes against the table. "I can't believe it's already July. I've been back home for almost five months."

Violet nodded. "And Dad's been gone for almost six."

"Yes. Look, Violet, do you want to go to the parade this year?" Poppy asked suddenly.

"Sure. Why wouldn't I?" Because, she thought, she was terrified of having a panic attack in public. She had been thinking about the parade for days and the anxiety it might trigger, but she refused to allow herself to be made a victim of bad thoughts and feelings. She refused.

"I don't know," Poppy said. "Because . . ."

"Because both Mom and Dad are dead and it might bring

back memories of us all going to the parade together and that will make me sad?"

"Yes," Poppy said. "I guess that's what I meant. I know it will probably make *me* sad."

"And because there'll be a lot of people and some of them might still want to stare at us and whisper about how awful we must feel?"

"That, too."

"I don't care about people like that," Violet said, with more conviction than she felt. "I love the parade. A parade is a celebration. Communal rites and rituals are important for everyone. I really want to go."

"Then we'll go," Poppy said. "Well, I'm not sure about Daisy, but you and I will definitely be there."

"Daisy will come, too," Violet said.

"How do you know for sure?" Poppy asked with a smile. "She can be moody and contrary when she wants to be."

"I just know she'll come." *Because,* Violet thought, *Daisy always tries to do the right thing.*

"Well, I hope you're right. Now, what about Freddie's cake?"

"I think," Violet said, "that we should talk to Allie about that."

Chapter 52

"My favorite float was the liberty bell made all of roses. It was beyond awesome!"

Her younger sister's enthusiasm made Daisy smile. The Higgins family had gone to the Independence Day parade that morning, Poppy, Daisy, and Violet. Daisy had been wary of being on display—come see the three orphaned Higgins girls!—but for the sake of Violet, who had always loved parades and festivals of all kinds, she had squashed her fears and gone along, small American flag in hand. In the end, very few people had paid Daisy and her sisters any real notice. Either time really was making them less interesting to the sort of people who loved other people's misery or the high spirits associated with Independence Day had managed to take precedence over any remaining bits of morbid curiosity.

Daisy had asked Evie to join them at the parade, and then after, at the house, for Freddie's party—Poppy had said it would be fine—but Evie had taken on two extra shifts at work, giving coworkers the holiday off and allowing her to make extra money. Joel was spending the day with his large

Gascoyne family but said he would stop by later if he could sneak away.

Now they were gathered in the garden behind the Higgins house, the three sisters, Allie, Freddie, and Sheila. Poppy and Violet (with Allie's help, Daisy suspected) had succeeded in making Freddie's favorite pastry, the petit four, into a tall, rectangular cake. Allie had made fish tacos, another one of Freddie's favorites, and there was guacamole and chips and some amazingly delicious warm cheesy dish Sheila had brought. The adults were drinking martinis, except for Poppy, who never drank anything harder than wine. Daisy and Violet were drinking super-spicy virgin Bloody Marys; Daisy had already sneezed four times from the black pepper. And Violet had outdone herself with the beautiful centerpiece and Freddie's corsage. If the corsage, made largely with hydrangea blooms, was a bit large to be sitting on someone's shoulder, no one was saying.

Allie raised her glass. "Thank you for letting me celebrate your birthday with you, Freddie."

"Any friend of Poppy's and all that. And you make a superb martini."

"I took a course in bartending once, just for the fun of it. Every once in a while it comes in handy. I also took a woodworking class at around the same time. But so far, I haven't been called upon to build anyone a shelf."

"I could use another bookcase in my room," Daisy said. "Half of my books are stacked on the floor."

"Maybe you need to stop collecting so many books," Poppy suggested.

"Why ever should she do that?" Sheila asked. "It's a fine passion, book collecting. How many people even read books these days, I mean real books, ones with covers and paper pages you turn between your fingers. Everyone's on those machines. . . ."

Freddie laughed. "You're a dinosaur, my dear."

"Speaking of dinosaurs, Freddie, how does it feel to be eighty?" Poppy asked with a grin.

"It feels just fine," Freddie replied with alacrity. "My feet are an abomination, my back aches, my skin is mottled like a—like a something—my eyesight is terrible, and on some days I'm hard-pressed to remember my own name. Slight exaggeration there. But I'm alive and that's what really counts."

"Hear, hear!" Sheila raised her glass. "To my beloved ruin. To love among the ruins!"

"To getting old," Daisy said. She thought of Muriella and Bertie, how happy they were in spite of illness and weakness. And she realized that so far, no one had mentioned those missing from the celebration, those who hadn't been granted the gift of a long life. Annabelle and Oliver Higgins.

"Do you mind sharing your birthday with a country?" Allie asked.

Freddie raised an eyebrow. "I prefer to think the country is sharing its birthday with me!"

"Now that displays a healthy dose of self-esteem," Sheila said. "Or a pathologically over-inflated ego."

"Ha. I think I will have another of those delicious martinis."

Allie got up to prepare the drink at the small side table that served as the bar. When she rejoined the group at the table, Violet said, out of the blue: "I wish Mom and Dad were here."

There was a heavy beat of silence. Daisy felt tears smarting at her eyes and wished her younger sister hadn't voiced what probably everyone gathered was feeling. Sometimes it was just better to keep your mouth shut and the feelings safely inside.

"I think," Freddie said quietly, "that we all wish Annabelle and Oliver were with us today."

"If wishes were horses . . ."

"What was that, Daisy?" Allie asked.

Daisy shook her head. "Nothing. Sorry. Look, can we cut the cake now?"

Chapter 53

There were still a few minutes before Poppy had to leave so she busied herself straightening the pile of correspondence on the kitchen counter (another sympathy card had trickled in only that morning) and reminding herself that she had vowed to remove all of her paperwork to the study. On the top of the stack of brochures from the bank, advertising new services, and the odd takeout menu Poppy found the letter from Adams College, requesting her membership on the scholarship committee. Poppy frowned. She was still hesitating about making that commitment. A representative from the committee, a Dr. Dolman, had called her that morning and though he was perfectly polite he made it clear that the committee was eager for her answer. He reminded her that if she turned down the offer of a position they would have to start looking elsewhere for another suitable candidate, and that might take some time. She had promised Dr. Dolman that she would make a final decision very soon. "How soon?" he had asked, to which Poppy had replied, "Very."

It had been a lot easier to make the decision to attend

tonight's town meeting. Freddie was right. It wouldn't hurt
for her to make an effort to be more of a part of the Yorktide
community, at least for the few years she was committed to
spend as a resident. Earlier in the day Poppy had spent over
an hour on the town's official Web site, hoping to get edu-
cated about the issues most recently debated at the meetings.
In addition to the traffic-control question Jon had told her
about, tonight's agenda included a proposed increase in the
area required for the development of a privately owned lot
of land. That didn't sound terribly exciting, but as Freddie
had pointed out, Poppy's personal interests weren't really
the point.

Seven o'clock. Time to get going. Poppy checked her bag
for the essentials—tissues, lip balm, wallet, and keys—and
grabbed a bottle of water from the fridge. She called out a
farewell to Allie and her sisters, who, after an early dinner,
were watching a movie in the living room, but given the roar
of the action on the screen she doubted they heard her.

The lot outside the town hall was already crowded when
Poppy arrived twenty minutes later; she got one of the last
spots available and hurried inside. Almost all of the seats
were filled and Poppy found the din of voices momentarily
deafening. A quick glance around the room told her that
Julie and her husband, Mack, were there, as was Jon, his father and his brother Clark, and a woman Poppy took to be
Clark's wife. A sudden crisis with one of her longtime
clients had prevented Freddie from attending; she had told
Poppy she was counting on her to make a full report afterward. (Poppy had come to the meeting equipped with a good
old-fashioned pad of lined paper and a pen.) Poppy also recognized Billy Woolrich, the owner of The Clamshell, and
the woman who owned the town's only high-end art gallery.
Annabelle and Oliver Higgins had bought several paintings
from Anna Ross over the years and Poppy remembered

going with them to openings at the gallery. She had found the gallery atmosphere so exciting. She had enjoyed watching people interact, how they studied the paintings and the sculptures. And it occurred to her that in the three years she had lived in Boston she hadn't gone to one gallery show. And though the city and its surrounding towns offered a large number of museums—the MFA, the DeCordova, the Isabella Stewart Gardner, the museums at Harvard, the ICA—she had probably only visited each one once, if that. How odd.

What the heck was I doing with my spare time for all those years? she thought, threading her way through the crowd of locals toward a free seat. Shopping. Going out for drinks. Dancing at clubs. Poppy felt a shiver of embarrassment pass over her. *Certainly not being very productive.*

Someone tapped her shoulder and Poppy twisted around in her seat. "Poppy Higgins," the man said with a smile. "Why I haven't seen you since you came back to Yorktide! How are things at home?"

"Mr. Hillman, hello!" Poppy offered her hand to the man who had cut her father's hair for over thirty years. Oliver Higgins's hair might have been wild, but there was a method to its madness. "Fine, thank you. We're all doing well."

When Poppy turned back, the woman seated to her left leaned over. "It's good to see a representative of the Higgins family here with us," she whispered. "Stand together is what I always say."

Poppy smiled in reply. She couldn't for the life of her recall the woman's name, but she recognized her from the old-fashioned, independently owned drugstore in town. When Annabelle Higgins had been suffering the side effects of chemotherapy, this woman had kindly recommended a variety of natural remedies to ease the nausea. Violet, Poppy thought, probably knew the woman by name.

The meeting was called to order and Poppy was swept up in the opinions expressed and the heated arguments that Jon had warned her would break out. After an hour and a half—which seemed to fly by—one of the Selectmen called the meeting to a close without, it seemed to Poppy, having resolved much of anything. She wondered if all politics, whether in cities or small towns, progressed at a snail's pace and suspected that it did.

As the crowd slowly made its way toward the door—those who weren't interested in hanging around to rehash the evening's high and low points—Poppy saw that Jon Gascoyne was walking toward her.

"Any interest in joining me at The Blue Mermaid for a drink and a bite to eat?" he asked.

Poppy smiled. "Sure. I think I worked up an appetite trying to follow all the arguments pro and con. Plus, I've never been to The Blue Mermaid."

"What? Then come on. It's the go-to place for us townies, especially after events like tonight's."

The bar, located just a few doors away from the town hall, was filling up rapidly. Jon and Poppy grabbed the last table for two in a room decorated with gleaming brass lighting fixtures, a collection of ships' wheels, and oil paintings of storm-tossed seas set in elaborate wooden frames.

"So, are you glad you came this evening?" Jon asked when they were seated.

"Yes," Poppy admitted. "I really am. And I have to say, I was touched by the good feeling people showed me, even if it was only because of the esteem in which my parents were held. And it was a bit like theater in some way I can't describe. Entertaining." Poppy laughed. "Anyway, if I hadn't come Freddie would have never let me forget it!"

Jon grinned. "She can be . . . tenacious. So, do you feel like a real member of the community now?"

"I don't know if I've earned that title quite yet! But it felt nice being with all the others. I mean, I haven't forgotten about the downside of small-town living—I think the small town invented the busybody!—but I think I'm beginning to understand the upside that my parents realized long ago."

"I'm glad. Life's too short to be unhappy about things like the town you live in." Jon nodded toward the bar. "I'll go up and get us some drinks. For you?"

"White wine, thanks."

"You know," Jon said, leaning toward her across the table, "they have the most amazing cheese fries here and you did say you were hungry. Now, before you lecture me on fat and cholesterol, let me just say that life is short and there are occasions on which cheese fries really shouldn't be rejected."

Poppy laughed. "Don't worry, I wasn't about to lecture you—or to say no to an order of these famous cheese fries."

"I knew there was a reason I liked you. I'll be right back."

Jon dashed off. *Hmm,* Poppy thought, aware that she was smiling. *He likes me.*

Chapter 54

Evie was standing at the fryer, her back to the door, when she heard familiar laughter. She whirled around, spatula in hand, to find her parents standing at the counter, placing an order for food. Her father's arm was around her mother's waist. Her mother was beaming up at him. The spatula dropped from Evie's hand and she dashed toward the counter. "Mom! Dad!" she cried. "What are you doing here?" Her parents looked at her blankly. "Excuse me," her mother said. "But do we know you?" Evie laughed. "Of course you do! I'm your daughter!" It was only then that Evie noted her parents were much younger than they should be, maybe only twenty-one or -two. "We have no daughter," her father explained, very seriously. "We had one, but she died." Her mother began to weep and her father hustled her out of the restaurant. "Wait!" Evie cried, wanting badly to hurry after them. But Billy stopped her with a heavy hand on her shoulder. "Let them go," he said. "Can't you see they're grieving?" Evie whirled on him. "But what about me?" she demanded. "What about me?" Billy shrugged and turned away.

And then Evie woke. She was shaking. The dream had seemed so real. But it wasn't real, she told herself. It wasn't real. Because she wasn't the one who had died.

Evie sat up against the pillows and turned on the bedside lamp. No, she wasn't the one who had died. She was the one who was left to live with the memories. . . . It was why she hadn't been able to bear the thought of spending the Fourth of July with Daisy and her family and their friends. All those memories of the annual party on Crescent Way, her father and the neighbor to their left, Mr. Acton, acting as chief grillers, her mother providing quirky decorations from her shop, the Spinelli family bringing side dishes, old Mr. and Mrs. Fitzpatrick, with their ancient dog Buster tagging along, providing the soft drinks. At the end of the evening the families would drive to the little park in the center of town to watch the fireworks display. It had all been so much fun, playing with the Acton and Spinelli kids, sneaking hot dogs to Buster, oohing and ahhing over the colorful fireworks.

But it was all over now. That was the past. It had been much better spending the day at The Clamshell than pretending to have a good time, like she had been pretending for the past three summers. Certainly, going to the pool party with Joel had been mostly a mistake, in spite of his being a wonderful date. How many of the other teens at the party had lost their parents as she had. . . .

The accident had happened in early May. Evie was in history class when the school counselor came to the door of the room, asking for Evie to accompany her. She remembered feeling puzzled but not really concerned. She had done nothing wrong so she couldn't be in trouble. It was only when the counselor ushered her into his office and Evie saw the policeman and one of her father's colleagues, a young woman named Emma Travis, that her heart sank into her stomach. Emma suggested that Evie sit. There had been an accident. A car accident. Her parents were in the hospital.

"Dad was driving," she said to Emma, as if it mattered. "Mom doesn't really like to drive."

The policeman nodded.

Emma took Evie home after that. Evie had only a very vague memory of that afternoon and of the days immediately following. She knew she had been numb most of the time; she didn't remember crying, but she might have. They—all these strangers!—hadn't let her see her mother at all, and she had only been allowed to see her father two days after the first emergency surgery to save his left leg. He was too sedated to say anything and Evie couldn't even be sure he recognized her.

Emma moved in to the house on Crescent Way just until Evie's parents' condition became clear; Emma had her own family obligations to return to. It felt weird being alone in the house with Emma, even though she knew Emma from her father's company picnics and Emma and her fiancé had been to dinner at the house a few times. But Emma was respectful and slept on the couch in the living room—not in Evie's parents' room—and she was very quiet and didn't ask Evie questions she couldn't answer, stupid questions like "How do you feel?" and "Are you hungry?"

And then had come the news of her mother's death. Emma told her with tears streaming down her face. She had been Evelyn's friend, too. Only then had Evie demanded to know the details of the accident. And that was when she decided that her father had killed her mother. "Dad's a murderer," she had said coldly. She remembered that moment now with some shame and a bit of regret. Her words had shocked poor Emma. "Don't say that!" the woman had cried. "It's not true!" A better instinct had kept Evie quiet then, but the words and the conviction that fueled them continued to echo in her head, even now, even three years on. Brutal, damning words. A brutal, damning conviction. But was the conviction a truth?

Unsettled by that question, Evie threw back the covers and got out of Nico's guest bed. There was no point in trying to go back to sleep so she might as well get up and do something productive. Like clean the bathroom. It was the chore she hated the most and she had been avoiding it for the past week. But what if Nico suddenly showed up? What sort of new trouble might she be in then?

Chapter 55

"Wait a minute," Poppy said, turning from the white-board in the kitchen. "It's Thursday. Why didn't you ask me for a ride to Pine Hill on Tuesday? Aren't you working this week?"

Daisy felt a wave of embarrassment come over her. She didn't look directly at her sister when she said no.

"Since when do volunteers get vacation?"

"They don't," Daisy said. "I quit."

"You quit? But why?" Poppy asked. "I thought you really liked working with the elderly."

"I did. A lot. But you were making such a stink about having to drive me there and back. . . ." Daisy couldn't go on. She thought about the good conversation she and Poppy had the other day, when she had been honest about the re-sentment she had felt when Poppy moved to Boston, and wondered why she was acting so childishly now.

"You didn't have to *quit*!"

"Well, what was I supposed to do?" Daisy asked, simply unable to check her irrational irritability. "Just go on arguing with you all the time?"

Poppy took a deep breath. "Call Pine Hill and tell them you want to come back to work. I'll drive you and I won't complain. If for some reason I really can't be available I'll find someone else to take you or pick you up."

"Thanks," Daisy said. "Really. Sorry I raised my voice just now."

Poppy looked at her watch. Oliver's watch. "Gosh," she said. "If I'm going to make the bank before it closes I'd better get going. I'll be back by five, okay?"

Daisy nodded and sank into a chair at the table. What a mess she had made. She had felt bad about quitting her job at Pine Hill from the moment she had gotten off the phone with Ms. Beverly, the volunteer coordinator's administrative assistant. But she had been too embarrassed to call back and say that she had changed her mind. She had suffered because of the impulsive decision—she missed talking with Muriella and Bertie—and so had the nursing home, which was always short of volunteers. It had been a totally infantile thing to do. In some stupid way she had wanted to punish her sister, but she had only succeeded in punishing herself and other, innocent people.

But I am a child, Daisy thought. *Not an infant, but a child. Except I'm not allowed to act like one anymore.* Because how could you be a child when there was no parent? One defined the other, didn't it, like there couldn't be right if there wasn't wrong? Poppy might be her legal guardian, but she could never be a true parental figure for Daisy—someone she could totally rely on for things both big and small, someone she could be comforted by, someone she could learn from and admire. Daisy frowned. Wait a minute, she thought. Why *couldn't* Poppy be a true parental figure? Maybe she hadn't been giving Poppy enough of a chance; maybe she had to put some faith in her. It had been scientif-ically proved that praise and appreciation went further in motivating a person than complaints and criticism. It certainly always had for Daisy. She decided. She would make a real effort to thank her sister for the good things she did for the family, rather than point out the things she had failed to do. And just for good measure she would finally dust the baseboards in the upstairs hall. It was only something she had been promising Poppy she would do for the past week.

Daisy leaped to her feet before she could change her mind.

Chapter 56

"I'm glad you were interested in coming with me," Sheila said. "Freddie hates this sort of thing."

Violet managed a smile. She had woken at two o'clock that morning from the dream about the weird garden, and this time, it had been more frightening than ever. This time, she had killed both of her parents by giving them each a goblet of poisonous tea. What was unclear in the dream world and now in the waking world was if she had known the tea was poisonous when she offered it. And the demon in the well had been covered in what Violet could only call gore. In spite of the comforting warmth and bulk of Grimace, curled up under her left arm, she hadn't been able to get back to sleep, but had lain awake until six when Grimace had announced with his usual earsplitting howl that it was time for breakfast.

It was almost noon now and Violet still felt groggy. She had avoided drinking any of the decaf green tea (the poisonous tea from the dream?) that morning because she thought it might knock her out entirely and she really wanted to go to the craft show with Sheila. Sheila had shown her a brochure advertising some of the artists who would be selling their work and a stained glass artist named Kashmir had drawn her attention. Violet had been envisioning a beautiful piece of stained glass for her room, which had a south-facing window where the piece would glow with the light.

"Freddie's probably going to hate this," Sheila said. They had stopped at a booth where a man was selling hand-printed silk scarves and Sheila had picked up a scarf in shades of taupe and gray. "She has a thing about long floaty scarves. Maybe they remind her of snakes. She's terribly afraid of snakes, you know. Or maybe they make her think of Isadora Duncan. Wasn't she the dancer who was accidentally strangled to death by her scarf? But I'm buying it anyway. She'll just have to look away when I'm wearing it."

Violet smiled, as she was meant to do. Sheila often complained about Freddie, and Freddie often complained about Sheila, but everyone knew they totally loved each other. It was just a little game. Annabelle and Oliver Higgins had played little games with each other, too. Like how her mother had teased her father about his incompetence with a hammer and nails and how her father had teased her mother about her inability to master the art of eating with chopsticks.

The memory of her parents' good-natured banter made Violet feel sad. At least she hadn't had a full-blown panic attack again, and the Independence Day parade had brought no memories other than happy ones. She was grateful for that.

Sheila paid for the scarf and they moved on along the double row of booths. It was interesting, Violet thought, how so many people felt the urge—the need—to create. Not much of what Violet saw struck her as particularly new or special, but she liked being around creative energy. She really believed that there was value in the effort of creativity alone. It was good for the soul.

"Stop, Violet. I have to look at these earrings!" Sheila made a dash across the path to a booth where a woman was selling handcrafted jewelry. Violet followed her, and while Sheila examined several pairs of dangling silver earrings, Violet watched the stream of people passing by. There was always something interesting to see if you knew how to look for it. Like the man walking by with that magnificently carved walking stick. It was taller than he was and Violet thought it might be made of oak. Or like the woman carrying a teeny dog wearing a teeny costume of a teeny frog. Or the girl standing before the booth across the way . . .

For one powerful moment Violet was absolutely sure that she knew the girl and that she had always known her. And then, the certainty was gone, replaced by an inexplicable feeling of loss. The girl was about her own age and wearing a long loose dress like the sort Violet often wore, and a large cross-body bag made from scraps of different materials and varying patterns. Violet wondered if the girl had made it herself. It would be awesome to know how to sew.

"Do you know her?" Sheila asked.

Violet turned back to face her friend. "Who?" she asked.

"That girl across the way. The one you've been staring at, by the awful pottery."

Had she really been staring? "No. For a second I thought she looked familiar, but I don't know her."

"That's a beautiful pendant she's wearing," Sheila said, "though it looks awfully heavy. I could never stand anything heavy around my neck. It makes me feel like I'm choking. I'll stick to floaty scarves."

"It's an image of Isis, the Egyptian goddess," Violet explained. "She's the patron of nature and magic. She's also the protector of the dead and of children."

"I suppose I should have known that. I've certainly watched enough shows about Egyptian tomb treasures and the like."

Violet looked back one more time to see the girl joined by a woman who put her hand on her shoulder and smiled. Her mother, Violet thought. She could always tell a mother and daughter, even when they didn't look all that much alike. This mother and daughter, though, did look alike. They each had curly red hair, for one. Violet looked away.

"Come on," Sheila said. "I've decided I don't need another pair of earrings."

Violet followed her friend along the row of booths. "I don't know how some people have the nerve to call their work art," Sheila was saying. "Look at that abomination. That metal . . . thing. Who in God's name would buy that?"

Violet was only half listening. Seeing that girl with the Isis pendant had caused her to experience a totally new and unexpected sense of longing for a friend her own age, not someone to replace Sheila, but someone who could bring another element to her life, an element she hadn't known had been missing. What that element was, exactly, Violet couldn't say. She was very, very grateful for all that she did have, but now it occurred to her that she might need something more, *someone* more. . . .

"Look!" Sheila said excitedly. "There's the stained glass artist you were telling me about."

"Good," Violet said, glad for the distraction from her confusing thoughts. "And then let's get something to eat. I'm starved."

Chapter 57

"It looked like a family," Daisy said, digging her hand into the sand. "Like a *happy* family."

Joel, sitting beside her, shook his head. "I know. But whose happy family?"

Twenty minutes earlier Daisy and Joel had left Nico's house in a state of minor confusion that had now morphed into a state of major confusion. What had happened was this. It was Evie's day off and after lunch at The Friendly Lobsterman (Joel's treat since he got the family discount) they had driven Evie back to Nico's house, where Daisy had begged to come in to use the bathroom.

"Why didn't you go at the restaurant?" Joel had asked.

"Because I didn't need to go then. But I do now. Too much soda. I'm going to bust any moment."

"Okay," Evie said, climbing out of the back seat. "But be fast. You know I'm not supposed to have people in."

Once inside, Daisy dashed to the powder room, while Evie went up to Nico's bedroom to check his voice mail. When Daisy finally joined Joel in the living room he greeted her by putting his finger to his lips and shaking his head. Then he beckoned her to where he stood by the fireplace.

"Look," he whispered, pointing to a messy stack of papers piled on the mantel. "This stuff must have fallen off the mantel. I came over to pick it up." He held out two laminated cards. "From a high school in Vermont," Joel went on, glancing nervously toward the stairs. "The name says Sophie Steuben. This one is dated this year and this one from the year before."

"But the photos are gone!" Daisy hissed. "They've been cut out."

"And there's this." Joel put the identification cards back on the mantel and took a photograph from the stack. "Look at the girl. Doesn't it look like—"

Thundering footsteps alerted them to Evie's return. Joel stuck the photo back in the stack of papers and pulled Daisy into the middle of the room.

"He had ten messages! And that's just since this morning."

"Any creditors?" Daisy asked, hoping that her voice didn't betray her anxiety.

Evie frowned. "That's an odd question."

"We should be going," Joel said, already moving toward the door. "Thanks for letting Daisy use the bathroom. I'm trying to break her of her soda habit, but . . ."

Joel had then driven to the beach with no protest from Daisy. She couldn't go home just yet, not with this mystery unsolved.

"Why cut out the picture and save the rest of the card?" she wondered.

"I have no idea. Have you ever seen Evie's handwriting?"

After a moment Daisy shook her head. "No, I don't think so. Why?"

"Because if one of us had we might be able to compare it to the handwriting on the cards."

"Meaning, you think that maybe Evie Jones is really Sophie Steuben?" Daisy asked. "Or that she *was*?" The thought that her new friend might be deceiving them was disturbing.

Joel shrugged.

"Anyway, a signature isn't really a good indication of a person's handwriting. I mean, my signature is a scrawl, but in general my handwriting is fine. So even if . . ."

Daisy found she couldn't go on.

"You know," Joel said suddenly. "I really didn't mean to snoop. All I did was pick up the stuff that had fallen off the mantel."

"I know. And how could you not have noticed the damaged cards?"

"The girl in the picture. She could be Evie. Did you see the eyes?"

"I only got a quick look," Daisy admitted. "Just enough to see that all three people were smiling."

"How old would you say the girl was?"

Daisy shrugged. "Eleven? Twelve? Why?"

"Didn't you tell me that Evie said her parents died in a fire when she was ten? And don't look so guilty, I haven't told anyone. We're the only two who know the truth."

"Yes. She said she was ten. But . . . Maybe the adults in the photo aren't her parents. Maybe they're foster parents. Or relatives." But some instinct told Daisy that the people in the photo, whoever they were, were father, mother, and daughter.

"Maybe," Joel said after a moment, "the ID cards and the photograph have nothing to do with Evie. Maybe they were left behind at The Clamshell. People are always losing things in restaurants and not claiming them. Maybe some woman dropped her bag and the cards and the photograph fell out and she didn't notice they were gone."

"But what would Evie want with them?"

"I have no idea," Joel admitted. "I'm just trying to consider all the possibilities. Maybe Nico knows someone named Sophie Steuben. Maybe she's a niece or something. Though why he would have her outdated, vandalized high school ID is beyond me."

"Does Nico have a housekeeper?" Daisy wondered. "Maybe the stuff belongs to her. Maybe she has a daughter named Sophie Steuben."

"Possible. Evie never mentioned a housekeeper, but that doesn't mean Nico doesn't have one. Anyway, back to the photograph. We think the girl in the picture is eleven or twelve, right? Evie's eighteen. People change so much over time. How could we ever tell if they're the same person? And what does it matter?" Joel rubbed his forehead. "Why is this any of our business?"

"Because we made an emotional investment in Evie's friendship," Daisy said. "You know, it's the fact of the missing photos on the ID cards that really puzzles me. Was whoever cut them out angry? Or did she—or he—only want to reuse the pictures?"

"This is too weird," Joel said forcefully. "I think we should just pretend we never saw anything out of the ordinary. Because maybe it *is* all ordinary."

"But what if Evie is in trouble?" Daisy countered. "What if she needs our help?"

Joel sighed. Daisy thought he sounded annoyed. "What makes you think she could be in trouble?" he asked. "You're always assuming that everyone needs help!"

"Just, what if?" Daisy pressed. "Look, I was right in the beginning, when I didn't know Evie but I sensed that she was hiding something."

"Fine. But if she does need help, shouldn't she come to *us,* not the other way around?"

"What if she's too scared to come to us?"

"Why would she be scared?" Joel said. "We're her friends."

"Look," Daisy argued. "The fact is that she hardly knows us. And we hardly know her. Here *we* are wondering if she's been hiding something from us. Why should she think she can trust us when we're not sure we can trust her?"

Joel nodded. "Good point. I guess we can't just forget what we saw. But I'm worried she'll be angry if we confront her."

"I think," Daisy said, "that we have to take that chance."

Chapter 58

"Evie," Daisy asked, looking down at her hands folded in her lap. "Who is Sophie Steuben?"

Daisy, Joel, and Evie were sitting at a picnic table outside The Clamshell. Evie was on break. And her blood had just turned cold. "I don't know anyone with that name," she said quickly. *Too quickly,* she thought. *Stupid.*

Daisy looked up now. Her expression was worried. "Because the other day, when we came in so I could use the bathroom we saw—"

"You were snooping!" Evie cried.

Daisy reached across the table, but Evie snatched her hand away. "No," she said. "Honestly, we weren't!"

Joel, sitting next to Evie, took a deep breath and turned to her. "This is what happened. You had gone upstairs to check Nico's voice mail and I saw a bunch of papers on the floor by the fireplace. I figured they must have fallen off the mantel, so I just picked everything up to put it back."

Evie felt nauseous. This was a nightmare. "And you couldn't help but look," she said flatly.

"Yes," Joel said. "I'm sorry. I didn't mean to. You know how your eye just catches something."

"What did you see, exactly?" Evie asked.

Daisy told her. "Was it you and your parents in the photo?"

"Yes," Evie said shortly. The photo had been taken less than a year before the accident, back when they were all so happy. Why hadn't she left it behind at her aunt and uncle's? And those stupid ID cards! Why hadn't she thrown them out after cutting away the pictures to use if she needed more false identification someday?

Evie did some rapid thinking. She could continue to swear that she didn't know anyone named Sophie Steuben. They couldn't prove that she did. She could say the damaged cards must belong to Nico; maybe he was using them in one of his crazy assemblages. They might believe her. And they might not believe her. Either way, something in her gut told her that if she didn't tell Daisy and Joel at least a part of the truth then the friendship they had been constructing over the past weeks would fall apart. And that was something she really didn't want to happen.

Still, for another moment Evie could say nothing. It occurred to her that Daisy might have told Joel the phony story about the fire and the foster homes. And if Daisy *had* betrayed her, Evie had absolutely no right to be angry. After all, she had told Daisy a lie. Daisy didn't yet know it, but Daisy had every right to be angry with *her*.

"Evie?" Joel prompted.

"I didn't tell you the real truth, Daisy," Evie said carefully, crafting the story as she went along. "My parents didn't die in a fire when I was ten. My mother died of cancer a few years ago. And I wasn't in foster care. My father always used to drink, but after my mother died he got worse. He couldn't take care of me, so he sent me to live with some old friends of his, but . . . but the man tried to . . ." Evie looked down at the table. This lie was hard to say aloud. "He tried to rape me and I had no choice but to run away."

Daisy put her hand to her heart. "Oh my God, that's so awful, Evie. Or should I—"

"No," Evie said fiercely. "Don't call me Sophie. She's in the past. Those things you found. I should have thrown them away. I will."

"Why didn't you tell me the truth?" Daisy asked gently.

"Because I was scared of . . . Scared of him finding me. The more people who know who I really am . . ."

"How long have you been on your own?" Joel asked.

Stay calm, Evie told herself. "I was only sixteen, I mean seventeen, when I left those people, but I'm eighteen now, like I told you. Everything's okay. Anyway, you have to keep this a secret." Evie looked pleadingly to Daisy. "Don't even tell your sisters."

"I'd rather die than reveal your secret," Joel said earnestly.

Evie smiled. "Thanks."

"I promise, too," Daisy said. "But why would my sisters care? I mean, you're not doing anything wrong. You're an adult. And you have nothing to be ashamed about."

Oh, yes, Evie thought. *I do!* "I know, but . . . It's just that I don't want people knowing about what happened to my family . . . It's . . . It's embarrassing."

"Don't worry, Evie," Joel assured her. "Your secret is safe with us."

"Look, I've got to get back to work so . . ." Evie got up from the picnic table. The others rose with her.

"We'll see you later, Evie," Daisy said. "And don't worry. Everything's all right."

Evie watched for a moment as her two friends—could she still call them that?—walked to Joel's Volvo. And she found herself wondering if she had wanted to be found out.

If she hadn't, why had she been so careless with those ID cards and the photo? Maybe, she thought, walking toward the restaurant, she should just run off again, before she got herself further embroiled in lies. Take what money she had managed to save and cut her losses, as she had heard her father say. Start over somewhere new.

But even as Evie contemplated this action, she knew that she just didn't have the energy.

Chapter 59

*So, Poppy, Boston is hot and dirty and
miserable. Work has dried up, as it usually
does in summer, and here I am, alone and
forlorn—everyone but me has escaped the
city!—and dreaming of a few days in the
fresh air to restore my energy before the
grind gets geared up again and the college
kids invade (with their obnoxious parents!)
and another year can be checked off as
done. Finished. So, show pity on your old
companion and check in when you can from
your vast (?) family manse. Ian.*

Why not, Poppy thought, regarding the e-mail. Things
on Willow Way were going pretty well. Daisy had signed
on again at the nursing home so that little drama was
over, and in the past few days she had gone out of her
way to thank Poppy for doing everyday things, like
putting dinner on the table and taking the trash to the
curb on pickup day, and whatever that was about, Poppy
was grateful. As for Violet, she seemed her usual self,

busy with the garden and taking care of Grimace. And Ian could be a lot of fun. He knew a lot of interesting people.

Without further consideration, Poppy typed a reply.

> *Ian, you poor abandoned thing! Why not*
> *get in the jalopy of yours and come spend a*
> *week or two with me and mine? Let me*
> *know. P.xx*

Poppy hit send and closed her laptop. Come to think of it, the people Ian knew weren't really *all* that interesting, and they weren't here in Yorktide. And she hadn't known any of them that well. There was that girl, the one who worked at a Starbucks; what was her name? And there had been that guy Nate, the one who had worked at the boutique, the one who got creepier and creepier on reflection. And did she really want Ian around when there was Jon . . .

Jon. Poppy put her hand to her forehead. She felt swamped with regret. She had acted on impulse; she hadn't used her head at all! If only there was some way you could retrieve a wrong-headed e-mail! Now she would have to hope it got lost in the ether. But maybe all wasn't lost. If the e-mail did find its way to Ian, and he did accept her invitation, she doubted he would stay for more than a few days. He would probably get so bored with the quiet life the Higgins girls lived he'd hightail it back to Boston, like an addict needing a fix. She could only hope.

Anyway, Poppy thought, what *about* Jon? They weren't a couple. And Ian was only a friend, not a romantic rival; they hadn't slept together in over a year and she had no intention of sleeping with him again. And she had no proof that Jon thought of her in romantic terms. Sure, he had said that he liked her, the night of the town meeting. But that had probably been something you would say to anyone who agreed to share cheese fries with you. And lobsters.

Poppy got up from the kitchen table. She was making a proverbial mountain out of a molehill. Still, she didn't look forward to telling Allie that she had invited Ian to visit. Allie had met him a few times in passing and she had made no bones about her dislike. And if Allie found Ian to be objectionable, there seemed to Poppy a good chance that her sisters would, too.

Chapter 60

"Do you want any sunblock?" Daisy asked.

Evie shook her head. "No, thanks. I'm good."

The girls were at Ogunquit beach, sitting on a blanket Daisy had brought from home. (Evie didn't dare take anything of Nico's from the house.) Daisy had her knees up and her arms around her legs; she was wearing cut-off jean shorts and a big loose T-shirt. Evie wondered if it had belonged to Daisy's father. She had once liked wearing her father's flannel shirts around the house though they swamped her. But that was in the old days and the old days were dead and gone.

The sun was seriously bright and Evie was very glad for her new sunglasses. Daisy's old sunglasses. The beach was crowded. There were families, moms and dads with impossibly cute little kids. (Evie wondered, Did being at the beach automatically make little kids and dogs cuter than when they were elsewhere?) There were couples of all ages. There were groups of friends, all girls, all boys, and mixed groups. If she were a normal teenager, Evie thought, she might be one of a group of girls like the one to her left, with little to worry about other than getting a tan and convincing a guy she liked to notice her. To be fair, maybe the girls in that group did have a lot to worry about, like parents getting divorced, or a sibling with cancer. The thing was you could tell so little about a person just by looking at them. Not always, but often. How many people who saw Evie Jones during an average day had any idea of the sort of life—the sort of lies—she was living?

"Oh my God," Daisy said under her breath. "Look at that guy in the white bathing suit. Could he be any hairier?"

Evie laughed. "Ugh, the missing link."

"Not that making fun of someone is right. It isn't. But he's just so—so hairy! Can I say something?" Daisy asked suddenly.

Evie felt her stomach drop. Ever since Daisy and Joel's confrontation outside The Clamshell she had been expecting some sort of repercussion from her friends. "Sure," she said. "Okay."

"I have to admit that I was a little bit hurt when I found out you had lied to me about your past. I mean, we're friends. But then I realized you probably felt that you had no choice, back when we first met. I thought about it and I realized that I probably would have done the same thing. So I'm not hurt anymore."

"Thank you," Evie said genuinely. "Thank you for understanding. And I am sorry. I don't like to lie."

"Do you think anyone really enjoys lying?" Daisy asked. "That's a silly question. Some people probably get a kick out of it. Some people probably enjoy tricking people."

"And some people can't help lying because they're sick."

"And little kids lie because they're testing the limits of their power. Seeing what they can get away with. I remember taking money from my mother's dressing table once. It was sitting right there, a five-dollar bill. It was like I couldn't resist. Then, when she asked me if I had taken the money, I lied and said that I hadn't. I remember being absolutely petrified, but for some reason I just wouldn't tell her the truth. The more she asked the more I lied and the more I began to believe the lie!"

"What happened?"

Daisy laughed. "Finally she said that if it wasn't me who had taken the money then it must have been Poppy—Violet was just a toddler—and I caved. I couldn't let Poppy get in trouble for something I did."

"Were you punished?" Evie asked.

"My parents didn't believe in punishing us. They didn't have to. I remember my mother looking so disappointed in me and believe me, that was punishment enough. Anyway," Daisy went on, "I think you're really brave, to have gotten away from a bad situation. It must have taken a lot of guts."

Evie wasn't sure it was guts that had convinced her to leave her aunt and uncle's house. And it *hadn't* been a bad situation, not really. . . . But she had told a lie—another one, about the abusive man—and now she was committed to it. "Thanks," she said, folding and refolding the edge of the blanket. Lately she had noticed that she had developed a habit of fiddling with things. It was probably a sign of anxiety.

"You know," Daisy went on, "the administration at school tried to get me to see a grief counselor when Mom died. But I said no. Violet refused, too. I guess people left Poppy alone because she was older. But sometimes I wonder if I made the right choice. Dad never would have compelled us to talk to a professional so the decision really was Violet's and mine to make. But maybe we were both too young to know what was best."

"I had no choice," Evie said. "The people at my school forced me to see a counselor after my mother died. Because my father wasn't . . . He wasn't any help. And neither was the counselor. I don't think I said one word to him all the times we met. What was I supposed to say?" *All the things I was feeling. Like anger. Like hate. Like the fact that I wanted the impossible—for the accident never to have happened.*

"The thing about when someone close to you dies," Daisy said musingly, "is that everyone is suddenly so *nice* to you. It drove me crazy. It was bad enough when my mother died. I mean, everyone always assumes a kid's going to go completely insane if her mother dies. But then when my father . . . Then it was worse. People were either ridiculously nice or they just ran the other way. I mean, what could anyone possibly say to me or my sisters that would make any sense? That we're better off without our parents? Of course we aren't!"

Evie nodded. "I know, right? Everyone always *looks* at you, like they're waiting for you to explode or break down or something. I wanted to say, leave me alone. Let me get on with my life without being watched every minute, like I'm some sort of freak."

"Imagine how it is when you lose *both* of your parents."

"In a way, I have."

"Oh," Daisy said. "Right."

"But I'm not living at home, I mean, back where I grew up, so no one knows that I'm sort of an orphan unless I tell them. Well, that I *was* a sort of orphan, before I turned eighteen." *No one knows that I'm an unaccompanied teen.*

"Right. Sometimes I feel like I've got this big neon sign over my head: ORPHAN GIRL. I hate knowing that people feel sorry for me. Is that terrible?" Daisy asked. "I mean, I suppose I should feel thankful that people care. Except that not everyone *does* care. Some people just want to approach you because you're like a dark celebrity or a really bad car accident they have to stop to see so they can be part of the excitement."

A really bad car accident . . . It took Evie a moment before she felt calm enough to speak. *Remember,* she told herself. *It was cancer.*

"It's like, you'll always be The Girl Whose Mother Died of Cancer. Anything wrong or stupid you do in your life, people will say: Oh, it's probably because she lost her mother so young. And maybe your motives for doing something wrong or stupid had nothing at all to do with your dead mother! Or your father," Evie added hastily. "Maybe you just made a mistake. Maybe you just listened to some bad advice."

Daisy laughed. "And if you do something great someday, it'll be: Can you imagine she's so successful when she lost her parents when she was just a kid? It's unbelievable!"

"It stinks," Evie said, "that you're defined by the stuff that happens to you. There was this girl from middle school, she's a year older than me, and when she was about twelve she was anorexic. She got better, but I remember being in the lunchroom and kids commenting on what she was eating and wondering when she was going to get sick again. I remember thinking: I wonder if she knows everyone's watching her, waiting for something to go wrong. I remember thinking it was horrible. It was like, no one had faith in her. How can you have faith in yourself—how can you know you're going to survive—if everyone around you expects you to fail?"

Daisy shook her head. "You can't. But you know, Evie, if you never go home again and if you don't tell people about what happened in the past, the cancer and that disgusting man, you can be free of all that negative expectation. You can be whoever you want people to think you are. No stigmas attached. You can be defined only by what you choose to do in the present."

"You mean," Evie said, "I can lie. I can be totally alone with my lies."

Daisy frowned. "That doesn't sound very good, does it? You could never get married because how could you really love someone and spend the rest of your life with him and be lying all the time? Besides, with the way life is something bad or weird is probably going to happen again and then you'll be The Woman Who Was in a Car Wreck or The Woman Who Was Robbed at Gunpoint." Daisy smiled. "Or, The Woman Who Won the Bazillion-Dollar Lottery."

The Woman Who Was in a Car Wreck. Evie forced a smile. "I wish I'd win even a thousand-dollar lottery! Anyway, I'm sure a lot of people live under an alias. People in the witness-protection program, for one. But . . . But I don't think that I could."

And yet here I am still lying to Daisy . . . and it feels bad. I'm doing it to protect myself, but still . . . If someday I tell her the whole, real truth—about the car accident and Dad's getting addicted to painkillers and our losing the house and my running away from my aunt and uncle's house and Dad's being homeless—will she hate me for lying to her? Will she hate me for not trusting her? And will she want nothing to do with me, someone essentially homeless?

Someone, Evie thought, like that poor sixty-three-year-old woman on the television show, the woman who called herself Marion. Or that poor guy Tommy. This was an unforeseen consequence of her plan (if it could be called that), coming to care for someone and having to worry about keeping her friendship and respect.

Suddenly, Daisy jumped to her feet. "Well," she announced, "I for one have had enough of depressing for today. I need some retail therapy."

Evie smiled up at her. "I thought you didn't really like to shop."

"I don't. Except for books. Have you been in the little shop on Clove Street? The Bookworm. It's awesome."

Evie got to her feet and brushed sand from her legs. How was it that even when you sat on a blanket sand got all over your legs? "Do they have a sale section?" she asked. Maybe she would find a discounted book written in French. . . .

Chapter 61

Poppy looked at the man standing at the front door and tried very hard to convince herself that her invitation to Ian had been a good deed and not a stupid one. An old friend was in need of a change of scenery. She had offered to provide that change of scenery.

"Come in," she said. "How was the drive?"

Ian stepped over the threshold and dropped his beat-up leather travel bag on the hall floor. "Once I was out of Boston, no worries," he said. "In Boston, the usual nightmare."

Now he came forward, arms open, and reluctantly, Poppy hugged him back.

"So, where's my present?" she asked when she had pulled away, quickly but not quickly enough to allow him to sense that in spite of her generous invitation she didn't really want him at the house on Willow Way.

"What do you mean?" Ian grinned. "I'm not enough?"

"The handmade soap I like, the organic stuff that smells like lilacs. You know, from Scents and Sensations. You said you'd bring me a bar."

Chapter 62

only have fifteen minutes," Evie told them, glancing
at The Clamshell.

Long enough for me to convince you to take a road trip
Daisy and me to Portland next Wednesday."

Portland. Evie was pretty sure you had to take a highway
et there. "I'm working all day Wednesday," she said.
uble shifts. Sorry."

el shrugged. "Then we'll go another day. I've covered
few guys this summer—mostly recovering from hang-
—so my schedule's relatively flexible. What day are
ff?"

m not sure. I'd have to check. Sometimes Billy doesn't
e schedule until the last minute."

ll then," Daisy said, "when you find out we'll make a

felt her heart begin to race. Portland was a pretty big
police there might have her on file as a missing
d if they did, they would have her photograph. The
olice were far more likely to be on the watch for a
een than the police in Yorktide.

Ian smacked his forehead. "Sorry, Pop. I totally spaced.
Maybe next time."

She hated when he called her Pop, but she let it go. His
beard was longer than she remembered it. He was vain about
the beard, and about his hair, which he wore long enough to
pull into a ponytail or a bun on the top of his head. A lot of
women found him attractive. Certainly, Poppy once had, attractive enough to sleep with. He had a good body and a sort
of cool, hipster thing going and you could make all sorts of
fun of hipsters, but they did have a certain style that made
certain types of women (which ones, Poppy wondered now;
silly ones? shallow ones?) assume there was serious substance underneath. But a beard and skinny jeans did not a
man make. . . .

"Come into the kitchen," she said, leading the way through
the house. No sooner had they entered the room than Daisy
and Violet came thundering in after them.

"I heard the doorbell," Daisy said.

"Was it Grimace's special catnip toy? UPS is supposed to
deliver it today."

Ian laughed. "I hope I'm not a toy for whoever this Grimace is. Doesn't sound like fun."

"Who's this?" Violet asked, with a note of suspicion in
her voice.

"This is my friend Ian," Poppy explained. "From Boston.
He's come for a visit."

Daisy looked on the edge of truculence. "I didn't know
you had another friend visiting."

"I told you about Ian," Poppy said. "I'm sure I did."

Violet shook her head. "No. I would have remembered."

"Me, too."

Poppy felt ridiculously embarrassed. "I'm sorry." She knew
she had told Allie . . . *And maybe it was her reaction that*

stopped me from telling my sisters, Poppy thought, remembering Allie's frown of disappointment.

"Are you going to introduce me?" Ian asked.

"Of course. Ian, this is Daisy and this is Violet."

"And who's this Grimace character?" he asked.

"He's my cat."

"Strange name for a cat."

"No," Violet said. "It's a perfect name."

This was followed by a deafening silence, which Daisy finally broke.

"What's for dinner?" she asked.

Poppy laughed a bit wildly. "You know, I haven't even thought about it. Maybe Allie can handle dinner tonight."

"Wait, Allie is here, too?" Ian asked.

"Didn't I mention that in my e-mail?"

"No."

Why didn't I? Poppy thought. *Then Ian might not have come!* "Well, she's here."

Ian snorted. "*This* should be a blast."

"We'll go and find Allie now," Daisy announced and she and Violet left the kitchen as quickly as they had come.

Poppy didn't know what to say or to do next. She wondered how long she had to wait before asking Ian to leave. She didn't want to be impolite. Maybe she could concoct a phony family emergency. Daisy and Allie would go along though Violet, who was congenitally unable to lie, would somehow spill the beans. Maybe she could . . .

"Hey. You in there?"

Poppy startled. "Yes," she said. "Sorry. Follow me and bring your bag." Poppy led Ian out of the kitchen and down the hall to the study. "You can stay in here. The couch doesn't pull out, but it's comfortable."

Ian's eyebrows rose. "No beds free?"

"No. Sorry." That was a lie; her old bedroom was unoc-

cupied and she had planned on letti
now the thought made her cringe. "I'll
The bathroom is down the hall. There's
but you'll have it to yourself."

"Girl world is off limits then?"

"Yes," Poppy said, not able to meet
ner's at six thirty."

Ian laughed. "That's, like, the middle o

"That's when we eat."

"All together, around the table, one big

"Yes." *At least,* Poppy thought, *one big f*

Ian shrugged and pulled a cigarette case
pocket. He rolled his own. "All right," he
Rome."

"There's no smoking in the house."

"Really?" Ian said in a tone that implied: Are you
kidding me?

"You can smoke in the backyard, I guess,
glass or something for the ashes and butts.
me if she finds cigarettes in her garden."

Ian put the cigarette case back in his pock
to head to the kitchen. Behind her, she hear

"We'll go to that famous cupcake place," Joel was saying, "the one that was on the Food Network or something. Come on, no one can resist a cupcake."

"It'll be fun." That was Daisy. "Everyone needs a change of scenery once in a while, right?"

Joel rolled his eyes. "You can say that again! I need my cage rattled in a big way. I am so sick of pretty flowers and velvety lawns."

"All right," Evie said finally, more because she felt Daisy and Joel would continue to press her until she said yes than because she thought the trip a good idea. Besides, she could always back out at the last minute. "You convinced me."

"Good," Joel said, "then it's settled. Just tell us the day you're free and we're on our way."

"You know," Daisy said, "I haven't taken a road trip since . . . Since my dad took Violet and me to Salem last summer. We did the witch tour. Violet was pretty upset about it all, actually. She said she could feel the unhappiness and fear of the women who were unfairly condemned and killed."

"Poor Violet. Anyway, I'm not sure it's considered a road trip when you're with your parents. I think road trip implies you're with your friends."

Daisy laughed. "Then the last time was when you and I went to that awful county fair."

"Hey, it wasn't my idea. You made me take you." Joel turned to Evie. "It was really pathetic. Two skinny cows, a mangy workhorse, carnival rides from like the last century, and the only stuff to eat was greasy fried dough."

"And cotton candy," Daisy added.

"Blue cotton candy. What's that about?"

Evie smiled and tried to seem interested in her friends' banter. As long as they didn't ask about her own road trip history. She didn't feel up to constructing another lie. Because she was sure that a few weeks alone on the road, on foot, didn't count.

"Hey," Joel said. "Big news. I'm applying for this scholarship my sax teacher told me about at my last lesson. It's huge, ten thousand dollars toward private lessons with staff from the Berklee College of Music. There's a lot of competition, but with a little luck I just might get it."

"Joel, that's amazing!" Daisy cried.

"It'll be amazing only if I *get* the scholarship! I know a life in music is going to be hard, but it's not like I need to be famous. I just want to play music and make enough money to go on playing it."

"Well, I'd offer to lend you money, but when I'm a doctor I'm pretty sure I'll be paying off student loans until I'm ninety!"

"We'll both be living lives of sacrifice for our art! So, Evie," Joel asked, "what do you want to do with your life?"

Evie felt as if she had been slapped. How could she possibly answer that innocent but devastating question? She had no education, no family, and no money. She had no *right* to dream about her future. Once, before the accident, she had thought about teaching language or going into the field of diplomatic relations, but now . . . Now survival seemed her only goal.

"Oh, Evie," Daisy said quietly. "I'm—we're—so sorry."

Evie shrugged. "It's all right."

"I'm an idiot," Joel said. "I didn't mean . . ."

"Really," Evie lied, "it's fine. I'll be fine. I'll . . . Don't worry about it."

Daisy looked to Joel. "We should probably go. I told Poppy that I'd . . . that I'd do the laundry."

Evie turned toward The Clamshell. "Yeah. My fifteen minutes is up anyway. . . ." With a halfhearted wave, she left Joel and Daisy and went back to work. She loved her new

Ian smacked his forehead. "Sorry, Pop. I totally spaced. Maybe next time."

She hated when he called her Pop, but she let it go. His beard was longer than she remembered it. He was vain about the beard, and about his hair, which he wore long enough to pull into a ponytail or a bun on the top of his head. A lot of women found him attractive. Certainly, Poppy once had, attractive enough to sleep with. He had a good body and a sort of cool, hipster thing going and you could make all sorts of fun of hipsters, but they did have a certain style that made certain types of women (which ones, Poppy wondered now; silly ones? shallow ones?) assume there was serious substance underneath. But a beard and skinny jeans did not a man make. . . .

"Come into the kitchen," she said, leading the way through the house. No sooner had they entered the room than Daisy and Violet came thundering in after them.

"I heard the doorbell," Daisy said.

"Was it Grimace's special catnip toy? UPS is supposed to deliver it today."

Ian laughed. "I hope I'm not a toy for whoever this Grimace is. Doesn't sound like fun."

"Who's this?" Violet asked, with a note of suspicion in her voice.

"This is my friend Ian," Poppy explained. "From Boston. He's come for a visit."

Daisy looked on the edge of truculence. "I didn't know you had another friend visiting."

"I told you about Ian," Poppy said. "I'm sure I did."

Violet shook her head. "No. I would have remembered."

"Me, too."

Poppy felt ridiculously embarrassed. "I'm sorry." She knew she had told Allie . . . *And maybe it was her reaction that stopped me from telling my sisters,* Poppy thought, remembering Allie's frown of disappointment.

"Are you going to introduce me?" Ian asked.

"Of course. Ian, this is Daisy and this is Violet."

"And who's this Grimace character?" he asked.

"He's my cat."

"Strange name for a cat."

"No," Violet said. "It's a perfect name."

This was followed by a deafening silence, which Daisy finally broke.

"What's for dinner?" she asked.

Poppy laughed a bit wildly. "You know, I haven't even thought about it. Maybe Allie can handle dinner tonight."

"Wait, Allie is here, too?" Ian asked.

"Didn't I mention that in my e-mail?"

"No."

Why didn't I? Poppy thought. *Then Ian might not have come!* "Well, she's here."

Ian snorted. "*This* should be a blast."

"We'll go and find Allie now," Daisy announced and she and Violet left the kitchen as quickly as they had come.

Poppy didn't know what to say or to do next. She wondered how long she had to wait before asking Ian to leave. She didn't want to be impolite. Maybe she could concoct a phony family emergency. Daisy and Allie would go along though Violet, who was congenitally unable to lie, would somehow spill the beans. Maybe she could . . .

"Hey. You in there?"

Poppy startled. "Yes," she said. "Sorry. Follow me and bring your bag." Poppy led Ian out of the kitchen and down the hall to the study. "You can stay in here. The couch doesn't pull out, but it's comfortable."

Ian's eyebrows rose. "No beds free?"

"No. Sorry." That was a lie; her old bedroom was unoccupied and she had planned on letting Ian stay there, but now the thought made her cringe. "I'll get sheets and towels. The bathroom is down the hall. There's a shower but no tub, but you'll have it to yourself."

"Girl world is off limits then?"

"Yes," Poppy said, not able to meet his eye. "It is. Dinner's at six thirty."

Ian laughed. "That's, like, the middle of the afternoon."

"That's when we eat."

"All together, around the table, one big happy family?"

"Yes." *At least,* Poppy thought, *one big family.*

Ian shrugged and pulled a cigarette case from his shirt pocket. He rolled his own. "All right," he said. "When in Rome."

"There's no smoking in the house."

"Really?" Ian said in a tone that implied: Are you freakin' kidding me?

"You can smoke in the backyard, I guess, but bring a glass or something for the ashes and butts. Violet will kill me if she finds cigarettes in her garden."

Ian put the cigarette case back in his pocket. Poppy turned to head to the kitchen. Behind her, she heard Ian chuckling.

Chapter 62

"I only have fifteen minutes," Evie told them, glancing back at The Clamshell.

"Long enough for me to convince you to take a road trip with Daisy and me to Portland next Wednesday."

Portland. Evie was pretty sure you had to take a highway to get there. "I'm working all day Wednesday," she said. "Double shifts. Sorry."

Joel shrugged. "Then we'll go another day. I've covered for a few guys this summer—mostly recovering from hangovers—so my schedule's relatively flexible. What day are you off?"

"I'm not sure. I'd have to check. Sometimes Billy doesn't post the schedule until the last minute."

"Well then," Daisy said, "when you find out we'll make a plan."

Evie felt her heart begin to race. Portland was a pretty big city. The police there might have her on file as a missing person and if they did, they would have her photograph. The Portland police were far more likely to be on the watch for a runaway teen than the police in Yorktide.

"We'll go to that famous cupcake place," Joel was saying, "the one that was on the Food Network or something. Come on, no one can resist a cupcake."

"It'll be fun." That was Daisy. "Everyone needs a change of scenery once in a while, right?"

Joel rolled his eyes. "You can say that again! I need my cage rattled in a big way. I am so sick of pretty flowers and velvety lawns."

"All right," Evie said finally, more because she felt Daisy and Joel would continue to press her until she said yes than because she thought the trip a good idea. Besides, she could always back out at the last minute. "You convinced me."

"Good," Joel said, "then it's settled. Just tell us the day you're free and we're on our way."

"You know," Daisy said, "I haven't taken a road trip since . . . Since my dad took Violet and me to Salem last summer. We did the witch tour. Violet was pretty upset about it all, actually. She said she could feel the unhappiness and fear of the women who were unfairly condemned and killed."

"Poor Violet. Anyway, I'm not sure it's considered a road trip when you're with your parents. I think road trip implies you're with your friends."

Daisy laughed. "Then the last time was when you and I went to that awful county fair."

"Hey, it wasn't my idea. You made me take you." Joel turned to Evie. "It was really pathetic. Two skinny cows, a mangy workhorse, carnival rides from like the last century, and the only stuff to eat was greasy fried dough."

"And cotton candy," Daisy added.

"Blue cotton candy. What's that about?"

Evie smiled and tried to seem interested in her friends' banter. As long as they didn't ask about her own road trip history. She didn't feel up to constructing another lie. Because she was sure that a few weeks alone on the road, on foot, didn't count.

"Hey," Joel said. "Big news. I'm applying for this scholarship my sax teacher told me about at my last lesson. It's huge, ten thousand dollars toward private lessons with staff from the Berklee College of Music. There's a lot of competition, but with a little luck I just might get it."

"Joel, that's amazing!" Daisy cried.

"It'll be amazing only if I *get* the scholarship! I know a life in music is going to be hard, but it's not like I need to be famous. I just want to play music and make enough money to go on playing it."

"Well, I'd offer to lend you money, but when I'm a doctor I'm pretty sure I'll be paying off student loans until I'm ninety!"

"We'll both be living lives of sacrifice for our art! So, Evie," Joel asked, "what do you want to do with your life?"

Evie felt as if she had been slapped. How could she possibly answer that innocent but devastating question? She had no education, no family, and no money. She had no *right* to dream about her future. Once, before the accident, she had thought about teaching language or going into the field of diplomatic relations, but now . . . Now survival seemed her only goal.

"Oh, Evie," Daisy said quietly. "I'm—we're—so sorry."

Evie shrugged. "It's all right."

"I'm an idiot," Joel said. "I didn't mean . . ."

"Really," Evie lied, "it's fine. I'll be fine. I'll . . . Don't worry about it."

Daisy looked to Joel. "We should probably go. I told Poppy that I'd . . . that I'd do the laundry."

Evie turned toward The Clamshell. "Yeah. My fifteen minutes is up anyway. . . ." With a halfhearted wave, she left Joel and Daisy and went back to work. She loved her new friends—she thought that *love* was the right word—and she didn't know what she would do without them. But sometimes, it was very hard to spend time with them. Pretending to be just like them—pretending to be just an average kid—was so terribly tiring.

Yes, Evie thought, opening the door to the restaurant. She would back out of the trip to Portland at the last minute.

Chapter 63

Violet was examining a basil plant in the garden when she heard Grimace hiss loudly. She stood up and saw that her sister's friend Ian was standing a few feet away, his hands in the air as if in surrender. Grimace was staring up at him, fur on edge.

"He doesn't like you," Violet stated unnecessarily, as she scooped up Grimace. He sat heavily in her arms, glaring fixedly at Ian.

"Well," Ian said, lowering his hands, "I don't like him, either."

"He knows. He doesn't care."

Ian grinned. "Do *you* like me?"

"Not really," Violet said promptly. "No."

"Really? But I'm such a likeable guy."

"Not to me, you're not. But it doesn't matter because you don't like me, either. Not everybody likes everybody. It's perfectly normal."

Violet went back inside the house, leaving Ian to process her last words. She deposited Grimace on the kitchen floor next to his bowls of food and water and went to the fridge in search of grapefruit juice.

She wondered what her sister had ever seen in Ian. He was so . . . so insubstantial. She had heard Poppy telling Allie that there was absolutely no romantic attachment between them any longer. Which Violet thought was a good thing, but she couldn't at all figure out why Poppy still considered Ian friend enough to invite him to stay in their home. It was a puzzle all right, one Violet, for all of her uncanny insight into the workings of the human heart, simply couldn't solve.

Daisy came bounding into the kitchen, knocking into a chair as she did. "Ow. Guess what?"

"About what?" Violet asked reasonably. "Animal, vegetable, or mineral? Past, present, or future?"

"Never mind. Joel and I and our friend Evie are going to Portland one day next week. Do you want me to bring you anything from that stone shop you like? Stones 'n' Stuff. It was really nice of you to get me that piece of stained glass at the craft fair. I've never seen such a bright green."

"I'm glad you like it," Violet said. She had bought an abstract piece for Poppy, too, and for herself she had chosen the image of a black and white cat bearing an uncanny resemblance to Grimace. Since she had hung it in her window, Grimace had spent many hours staring at it. "But no thanks. I like to choose my own stones. A stone speaks to me and I bring it home."

Daisy shrugged and took an apple from the bowl on the counter. "Okay. But if you change your mind . . ."

"Daisy," Violet asked, "why hasn't Evie ever been to the house? None of us have met her."

"I've asked her a few times, but she's pretty much always working. She makes me feel lazy!"

"She can't work at night. The Clamshell closes at seven. Does she have a second job?"

"No. But sometimes she stays at The Clamshell to help close up." Daisy shrugged. "Maybe Mr. Woolrich gives her some extra money."

"She lives all alone at that artist's house? The big house with the tower?"

Daisy chewed the last bite of her apple and tossed the core in the small compost bin by the sink. "Yeah. Violet, why are you asking all these questions?"

"I'm just curious," Violet said. "Where's she from?"

"Um," Daisy said, going over to the fridge and staring in it. "I forgot. Somewhere in New England. Vermont, I think. Maybe Connecticut." Daisy shut the door to the fridge and wandered over to the cupboard where they kept things like chips and cookies.

"Is she going back to school in the fall?"

"She's out of school. I mean, she graduated high school."

"Oh."

Daisy shut the door to the cupboard and turned back to Violet. "Violet, why is any of this your business?"

"Were the questions too personal?" Violet asked. She thought they had been fairly neutral, but her social perception was pretty off lately. . . .

"No. It's just . . ." Daisy sighed. "Evie's a private person, okay?"

"Okay." Violet might have asked one more question, but the sudden arrival in the kitchen of Ian prohibited her.

"What's up, ladies?" he said, casting a wary eye toward Grimace, who was chewing noisily.

"Ladies?" Daisy said with a laugh. "Could you be any more condescending?"

Ian opened the door to the snack cabinet, as Daisy had done

a moment earlier. "So you're not ladies," he said. "What are you then? Chicks?"

"Women," Daisy retorted, going over to the cabinet and shutting the door against Ian's gaze. "People. Human beings. And how about paying for some of the food you've been consuming."

The sudden look on Ian's face—a flare of fury, Violet thought; she suspected he was going to say something really nasty—made her step between him and her sister.

"Are there any peanuts in there?" she asked, reaching up to open the cabinet again. "I really love peanuts. I think peanuts are pretty much everyone's favorite nut."

It was lame, but it worked. Ian turned and left the kitchen without another word, followed a moment later by Daisy, who once again knocked into a chair on her way out.

Suddenly, Violet felt enormously tired. People could be such a drain on her energy. She wanted to like them all and to help them, but more and more she was feeling the need of someone to help *her*. Grimace, finally finished with his snack, smashed against her leg in agreement.

She was, after all, only thirteen.

Chapter 64

"Darn," Poppy said under her breath.

"What?" Ian asked.

"Nothing."

But it wasn't nothing. It was Jon Gascoyne, making his way through the throng of vacationers crowding Main Street. Of course she had known there was a chance she and Ian would run into him. But she had hoped very hard that they wouldn't.

"Fancy running into you," Jon said, joining them where they stood in front of the homemade candle shop. He was wearing a pair of knee-high rubber boots over a pair of work pants and a sweatshirt that had seen better days.

"Hi, Jon," Poppy said. "This is an old friend, from Boston. Ian. Ian, this is Jon."

Jon put out his hand and Ian shook it. "Hey," Ian said.

Poppy thought she saw a look of disappointment flit across Jon's face. She wondered if he thought she was dating Ian. *Please don't let him think that!*

"Have you been to Yorktide before?" Jon asked into the silence that had followed the handshake.

"When I was a kid, I think. I don't really remember. Guess it didn't make an impression."

"Ian's just up for a few days," Poppy said.

"Are you showing him the sights?"

Poppy laughed. *Why am I laughing? Because this is a little nightmarish farce.* "I'm afraid I haven't been a very good tour guide."

"You should at least see the Nubble Lighthouse," Jon suggested. "It's very popular and for good reason."

"Not really a fan of lighthouses," Ian said, looking off over Jon's shoulder.

"Well," Poppy said, "we should . . ."

Jon nodded. "Enjoy your stay, Ian."

Ian didn't reply. Poppy watched as Jon walked toward his truck, parked outside the drugstore.

"When do we eat?" Ian asked.

"So, what's he do?" Ian asked, taking a long swallow of his beer.

"Who?" Poppy asked.

"The guy we ran into earlier. The Gorton's Fisherman."

Poppy stiffened at the implied insult. "Jon. A lot," she said. "He's a lobsterman primarily. His parents own a restaurant and a fish market and he works at both of them. And he's involved with town stuff."

"He's a politician?" Ian said with ill-concealed disdain.

"No. I mean, he and his family are—concerned. They do good things for the town. They volunteer and contribute. They give back."

"Sounds pretty dull to me, but whatever floats the lobsterman's boat. What does his wife do, weave his nets and scale his fish?"

Poppy wondered. What *would* Jon's wife do, besides be thankful she was married to such a good man?

"He's not married," she said shortly.

"Let's go out tonight," Ian said, clearly bored with the topic of Jon Gascoyne. "I feel like I'm growing barnacles hanging around the house every night after dinner."

"There's not really much to do at night in Yorktide," Poppy told him. "But there are a few clubs in Ogunquit."

"That's cool. I hope they stay open past eleven."

"They do, but I think I'll pass, Ian. I'm not really into going to dance clubs these days."

"Sleepy small-town life affecting you? Tucked up in bed by nine?"

Was it even worth reminding him that she was still in mourning for the sudden loss of her father? Was it even worth pointing out that she was responsible for two minors now? Was it even worth trying to explain to him that she was changing and hopefully for the better?

No, Poppy thought. It probably wasn't.

"Early to bed and early to rise," she said with a false smile.

"I'll do a shot for you," Ian promised.

"I don't drink hard liquor. You know that." But of course he wouldn't have remembered.

And then she realized that Ian would need the alarm code if he were going to be out late. Well, there was no way she was going to give it to him. She doubted he was clever enough to have any criminal intentions, but she wasn't going to give him the gift of her trust. She would have to wait up until he got home from wherever he had gone, let him in, and then set the alarm. . . .

She wished she hadn't invited him! But she couldn't just throw him out. Her parents had been very firm about the courtesy one showed to guests, especially those one had invited. Again she wondered how long it was before she could politely ask him to leave. Where was Emily Post when you needed her?

Ian was regarding her over the rim of his almost-empty glass.

"What?" she asked.

"You've changed since you left Boston. Where's the Poppy I used to know?"

"Gone."

"But not forgotten, I hope."

Poppy shrugged. What was there to remember?

"You're less . . ."

Poppy didn't prompt him. What he thought of her didn't matter in the least. Besides, she was not less anything. She was *more* of a complete person. "Let's get the check," she said, gesturing to their waiter. "I've got things to do at home."

Chapter 65

In the end, Evie hadn't the nerve to back out of the road trip to Portland. Joel and Daisy were so excited about the excursion that Evie thought her pulling out at the last minute might ruin their fun. Besides, they would probably know she was lying about having a stomachache or whatever ailment it was she claimed to be suffering. Joel and Daisy knew she was a liar.

The ride north on 295 had been difficult for Evie, as she had known it would be. She sat in the back, behind Daisy in the passenger seat, her seat belt securely fastened, clutching the armrest, and hoping that neither Joel nor Daisy would notice her distress. Neither had. At least, neither had said anything.

When they reached the city, Joel put the car in a municipal lot and steered them in the direction of Deering Oaks Park, where there was a music festival happening. Evie had never been to Portland, but Daisy and Joel seemed to know the city well enough not to have to ask anyone for directions. That was good. The last thing Evie wanted was for someone to get a good enough look at her face to recognize

her from a missing person poster. Assuming there had ever
been any such posters in the city. After all, she had gone
"missing" in Vermont.

They didn't stay long at the festival. The band that was
playing at the time of their arrival was, according to Joel, insanely bad and according to Daisy, insanely loud. Evie hadn't
found them all that bad or all that loud and she would have
been happy to sit on the grass and listen for a while, but she
tramped out of the park with her friends and on toward
Longfellow Square. Beggars, she thought, can't be choosers.
It was something she had heard her uncle say a few times and
she had always wondered if it wasn't in reference to her.

"Let's walk down Congress Street," Joel suggested. "We
can grab a slice of pizza at Otto's on the way."

They did grab a slice—Daisy had two—and sat at a small
table outside the restaurant, watching people pass by. A fair
amount of them had what looked like ID tags hanging
around their necks. "Cruise-ship passengers," Daisy told
her. "I guess if they get lost or hurt the police know where
they came from." Evie did not find this idea entirely comforting. There were also a lot of people dressed like the men
and women in her father's office—his former office—dressed.
Business casual, it was called. And then there were some people who looked pretty down-and-out. A skinny guy about
Joel's age was sitting against the building next to the pizza
place with a cardboard sign on which was printed in spindly
black letters these words: HOMELESS. NEED HELP.

"It's too sad," Joel said softly. "That guy can't be older
than me and he's living on the street. We are so lucky."

Am I lucky? Evie wondered. How different was her situation from that guy's? In a way, wasn't *he* the lucky one? He
had fallen as far as there was to go. There was no more
doubt and uncertainty to contend with. While she . . . While
she lived every day not knowing how and when she would

lose what little security she had. Evie felt sick to her stomach and pushed the rest of her pizza away uneaten.

"Not hungry?" Joel asked.

Evie shrugged. "I had a big breakfast." She would not let her friends see her distress. She would not.

A girl wearing a pair of short shorts and a torn tank top stopped to talk to the guy, whom she seemed to know. She held a matted-looking dog on a frayed piece of cord. After a moment, the girl sat down on the sidewalk next to the guy. The dog dropped and put his graying muzzle on her lap.

"That poor dog," Daisy murmured. "I wonder when he last had a decent meal."

Evie felt anger rise in her breast. Why did some people respond with more ready sympathy to animals than to humans in distress? Because there was this underlying assumption even in the best, most kindhearted people like Daisy that a human being in distress could have—should have—prevented it from happening, should have been smarter than to let bad things happen to them. It was entirely unfair!

Before her irritation could erupt into words, Evie took a deep breath. She shouldn't assume that Daisy cared more about the dog than about the guy and the girl. Look how generous Daisy had been to her this summer. . . . Still, Evie so wished she hadn't come along on this trip, but she was stuck now, with no way home—rather, back to Yorktide—unless with Joel and Daisy.

When they were finished with lunch—and after Joel and Daisy had given the homeless guy and his friend some money—they continued down Congress toward Monument Square. Evie tried to focus on the interesting storefronts, but nothing really held her attention. She just wanted to be—not there. When a police car went speeding by, siren blaring, she threw her hands over her ears and hunched her shoulders, as if these gestures would somehow render her invisible to watchful eyes.

"You really are sensitive to noise," Joel commented when the police car had disappeared.

Evie managed a smile.

"Do you realize we've passed, like, three or four tattoo parlors in one block?" Joel said.

"We have?" Daisy asked. "I didn't notice."

"Some of them are on the second floor. See that one up there? Hey, why don't we get a tattoo?"

Daisy laughed. "One giant one covering all three of us?"

"The Three Stooges? No, silly. One for each of us. But wait. I think you might have to be eighteen to get a tattoo on your own."

Daisy turned to Evie. "Evie, you're eighteen. You could get a tattoo!"

Evie tried to laugh off the suggestion. "No thanks," she said. It wasn't that she was opposed to the idea of getting a tattoo (she thought that one day she probably would). But to try to get one now she would probably have to show her fake ID and risk being found out. Could she be arrested? Would Daisy and Joel also be in trouble? Sure, they knew she was using a false name, but they still thought she was really eighteen. They just didn't understand the seriousness of her situation. Evie felt irritation rise in her again, in spite of the fact that she was the author of her friends' ignorance.

"Come on," Daisy urged. "Let's see, what would you get? A heart? A rose? A skull?"

Joel laughed. "I don't see Evie as the skull type!"

"No," Evie said, with more force than she intended. "Stop it. I mean it. I hate tattoos."

Joel shot a look at Daisy; Daisy looked down at her sneakers.

"Sorry," Evie said, and she was. "It's just that I've got

this terrible fear of needles. Even the *thought* of a needle makes me freak out."

Daisy looked up and smiled. "It's a pretty common fear," she said. "Hey, I think it's time for the cupcakes Joel promised us. I'm starved."

"And you just had two slices of pizza!" Joel turned to Evie. "The place is down on Fore Street, in the Old Port. There are some awesome shops on Exchange and Commercial. Se Vende is my favorite. We can browse if you want."

Evie didn't really see the point in browsing when there was absolutely no way she could afford anything other than the very basics (was a cupcake a basic?), but she agreed to the plan. These people were her friends. They were her only friends. And she would cherish them for as long as she had them. Nico would be back at the end of the month and after that . . . After that, unless some major miracle occurred, she would have to be moving on.

They passed a nicely landscaped square called Tommy's Park where they saw two young mothers breastfeeding their babies, a man in a business suit sitting on one of the benches and talking into his iPhone, and a small group of cruise-ship passengers eating ice-cream cones. Passing through the square, muttering to himself, there was one very old man in a bulky army-style jacket, pushing a rusty shopping cart filled with plastic bags, some torn. Evie assumed they were stuffed with his possessions.

"Someone should be taking care of him," Daisy said fiercely. "He should be in a place like Pine Hill, getting three meals a day and sleeping in a clean bed."

Joel frowned. "Nursing homes and assisted living places cost a lot of money. The good ones, anyway. That's the problem. If your family can't take you in, then what?"

Evie said nothing because she couldn't speak. The sight of the old man had made her think of her father, possibly alone, probably in need of help. Maybe homeless. How was her father eating? Was he able to get his meals at a shelter? Where did he keep his clothes if he didn't have a place to live? Did he even have any more clothes than those on his body? Were his shoes worn through? Where did he sleep? Huddled under a dirty collection of newspapers in some doorway? Was he frightened?

By the time they reached the bakery on Fore Street Evie's spirits had tumbled dangerously low and it was all she could do to keep from bursting out in tears. Joel asked her what kind of cupcake she wanted. She chose the chocolate mint chip though she wasn't even a fan of mint. Joel insisted on paying for the girls. "My parents taught me how to be a gentleman," he told them. "Daisy, you've got icing on your nose."

Daisy laughed and wiped at her nose with a paper napkin. "I am such a goof!"

Evie managed a smile, as if she were really one of the group. But she wasn't. She was essentially alone. Like the homeless boy. Like that old man with the shopping cart. Like Marion and Tommy from the television show. There was never any escape from the harsh reality that was her life, not here, not even back in Yorktide. No cupcake in the world, no matter how delicious, could change that.

She hoped they would be going home soon.

No, not home. She had no home.

Chapter 66

It was going on eleven when Ian ambled into the kitchen, scratching his stomach through a flimsy T-shirt. "Any coffee?" he asked.

Daisy looked up from her crossword. "Good morning to you, too."

"Is there?"

"There was," she said. "Like, at breakfast time." If he asked her to make him a pot she was going to have to smack him. The thought had its appeal.

Ian opened the door of the fridge and proceeded to stare at the contents.

"Don't keep the door open so long," Daisy snapped. "You know what's in there." *You're in there often enough. . . .*

Ian shut the door and came over to the counter.

"What's that you're doing?"

Daisy sighed. "A crossword puzzle."

Ian laughed and ran his hand through his long, bed-mussed hair. "I never could do those. My brain doesn't work that way."

Daisy wiped a nonexistent strand of hair from the page

before her. "Hmm," she said. And then, she couldn't help herself. "In what way *does* your brain work?" she asked.

Ian shrugged. "Not that way."

A brilliant riposte, Daisy thought, barely able to hide a grin of satisfaction.

"I think I'll go into town and get some breakfast," Ian said, ambling out of the kitchen.

When he was gone, Daisy put the cap on her pen (she was good enough by now to have abandoned a pencil) and brooded. What had her sister ever seen in Ian? He was such a loser. At least she wasn't dating him any longer. Now, in Daisy's opinion, Poppy should be dating someone like Jon, who was most certainly not a loser and who wouldn't abuse the hospitality of a so-called friend by leaving dirty towels on the floor of his bathroom (Daisy had checked) and not re-placing the milk when he had drunk the last of it.

Suddenly, Daisy realized that she felt kind of bad for her sister. Poppy was a good person who didn't deserve being saddled with a so-called friend like Ian. And it occurred to Daisy that maybe Poppy hadn't had her act together in Boston as smartly as she had assumed her sister had. Maybe Poppy had been lonely away from home. Maybe in spite of her physical beauty she had suffered from low self-esteem. Maybe she still did. All sorts of scenarios might be possible. Sure, since Poppy had been home the sisters had grown a bit closer; proximity alone helped the process of getting to know a person either for the first time or all over again. But Daisy was aware that there was still a significant gap that needed to be filled.

She heard the front door slam. Ian. Why did he always have to let the door slam? It wasn't a guy thing. Her father had never let a door slam. It was a rude thing, that's what it was.

Chapter 67

Day five and counting. Surely, Poppy thought, after the seventh day she could ask Ian to leave without appearing totally rude. Though why she was so concerned with his feelings she would never know.

They were in the garden. Poppy was trying to read a novel Julie had recommended, but the very presence of her unwanted houseguest stretched out on a lounge chair a few feet away prevented her from concentrating.

"Why don't you come down to Boston for a few weeks?" Ian suggested suddenly. "You could probably stay at Allie's. My place is a mess. Have some fun. Shake the cobwebs off you. You're atrophying here, Poppy."

Atrophying? "I thought you said Boston was miserable."

Ian shrugged. "Not necessarily at night."

"No thanks. You might have noticed that I have two minors to care for."

"Well, wait until school starts. They'll be busy all day. They won't need you."

Poppy laughed incredulously. "They won't need me?" Her gut told her it would be a total waste of time to enumerate for Ian all the simple and the not-so-simple daily duties it was her responsibility to enact. Making sure Daisy and Violet ate a good breakfast. Packing their lunches. Planning and cooking dinner. Maintaining her sisters' after-school schedules, everything from Violet's music lessons to Daisy's jazz band rehearsals to Violet's soccer practice (something Violet tolerated as it was mandatory she participate in some sport), to Daisy's volunteer job. And then there were doctors' appointments to be met and the household to be run and the checkbook to be balanced. And, just maybe, there was being a shoulder for her sisters to lean on after a tough day.

"Yeah," Ian said. "You can, like, have those old women you told me about, what's their names, check in on them once in a while."

"That won't be possible," Poppy said evenly. She had deliberately kept Ian from meeting Freddie and Sheila. She didn't think she could survive their inevitable censure. And she wondered, Would Jon Gascoyne ever in a million years suggest she choose to be derelict in her duties to her sisters? Would any right-thinking person suggest such a thing? And suppose she was stupid and careless enough to run off to Boston for a lark, what would Freddie and Sheila and Jon and Joel and Allie and Julie think of her? The idea made her shudder. Besides, she realized, she had not one tiny bit of interest in leaving her home on Willow Way, not for all the enticements Boston or any place else might offer.

Ian stretched his arms over his head and yawned. "Suit yourself."

I will, Poppy thought. *Thanks.*

"Your sister is pretty weird, you know."

"Which one?" Poppy asked warily.

"Violet. Daisy's just your typical moody teenager."

Poppy bristled. "They've been through a lot. And Daisy is certainly not typical."

"Whatever. Anyway, your dad's death might explain Daisy but not Violet."

"I'd appreciate it if you didn't speak ill of my sisters."

Ian laughed. "I'm not 'speaking ill'—really, what an archaic expression. I'm just stating observable facts."

Poppy closed her book with a snap. "Then shut up."

"Dude, there's no need to—"

"Yes, Ian, there is a need. And don't call me 'dude.' I'm not a guy."

"Whatever." Ian got up from the lounge. "I think I'll go into town for a few beers."

"Will you be back for dinner?" Poppy asked. *Of course he will,* she thought. *Because I'm paying for the food.*

Ian laughed. "Of course. Why wouldn't I be?"

Poppy watched him walk around to the front of the house with a feeling close to revulsion. Though the memory was unwelcome she recalled the first time she had met him. It was shortly after her mother had died and she had decided to take a walk through the Commons. Ian had been leaning against a tree, listening to three guys playing acoustic guitar. They were pretty good and Poppy had stopped to listen, too. Ian introduced himself and after some conversation they had gone for a drink. And that was that. Now, three years later, Poppy wondered if her grief, her anger at herself for failing her mother by not being with her at the end, and her guilt about moving back to Boston and leaving her sisters had all worked together to badly cloud her judgment. Could it be that she had been punishing herself in some way by choosing Ian as a lover and a friend?

Her cell phone rang, mercifully interrupting her train of thought. It was Julie. Good, she thought. Someone entirely nice and normal. Someone of substance. The perfect antidote to Ian.

"Julie?" she said. "Hi."

Chapter 68

"But you said you weren't coming back until the end of August." Evie knew her voice was shaking. "That's almost three weeks from now."

Nico sighed. "I know what I said, but things changed. Tangiers was a bore. I just had to leave and return to the beauty of home."

Evie didn't know much about Tangiers, but she knew enough to decide that anyone who said he found it a bore was probably lying. And she thought that Nico's home was anything but beautiful (except in tiny bits and pieces). But there was no point in pursuing that part of the conversation.

Evie stared at the man before her. The one and only other time she had seen him had been the day she knocked on his door to ask for the job of house sitter. He had opened the door little more than an inch or two, enough for Evie to see a bit of a figure swamped by a huge white terrycloth robe, with a white terrycloth towel wrapped around his head.

"You're the one Billy sent," he had said.

"Yes. I—"

"What Billy wants, Billy gets. You have the job. I'm

leaving tonight. Come back in the morning and the lady in the house to the left will let you in."

Evie had been about to ask if there was any way she might stay at the house that night—he would be gone, after all—when he closed the door.

Now she had the opportunity to study her absentee employer. He was a small man, barely as tall as Evie, and skinny. His hair was very dark and very thick and he wore it pulled severely back from his face. Evie suspected he was wearing eyeliner, but she couldn't be sure; his eyes, actually, were very nice. In fact, if it weren't for the expression of intense weariness or martyrdom on his face, he would be a handsome man. But Evie couldn't get past the expression. Or her sense that he was probably about to throw her out.

"So . . ." she began, but didn't quite know how to ask the all-important question. *What about me?*

"So, I'm afraid you'll have to be on your way, the sooner the better."

"But can't . . . Do you think I could stay on for just a bit? I won't be a problem. I'm quiet. I could do some cleaning and . . ."

Nico sighed again. "Impossible, my dear. I must be alone to work. I must be alone to *live*."

"But—"

"No buts. Anyway, I've already invited a few dear friends to join me here tomorrow. There'll simply be no room for one more. Here." Nico dug into the back pocket of his jeans and pulled out his wallet. He extracted three twenty-dollar bills from it and thrust them at Evie. "This should . . . Well, it should do something."

Pride warred with reason. Evie wanted nothing more than to throw the money back at Nico and tell him he was a skinny idiot jerk. And how did he reconcile the need to be alone with a house full of guests? A skinny idiot lying jerk!

But reason prevailed. Sixty dollars wasn't much, but it would buy her a new T-shirt at the thrift store in town and a new pair of socks, which she badly needed as the heels on one of the two pairs she owned were pretty much threadbare and she had gotten a bad blister the other day, and also, she hoped, a new hoodie to replace the stained one she was always embarrassed to be seen in.

"Thanks," she said, hating the word and the false intent behind it. "I'll go pack my stuff."

"And I'll go lie down for a while. This encounter has exhausted me."

And off Nico went to his bedroom.

Chapter 69

Violet was watering the plants in the sunroom when Ian wandered in. Grimace, from his perch atop the breakfast table, growled.

"That beast has pretty strong opinions about people, doesn't he?" Ian moved back toward the door a bit.

"Yes," Violet said. *As do all discriminating creatures.* And then she pointed at his right arm; the sleeves of his plaid shirt were partly rolled up. "I've been meaning to ask you what that's supposed to be."

Ian laughed. Violet thought it sounded like a condescending laugh. "It's a skull, of course."

"It doesn't look like a skull. What's it a skull of?"

"A human. It's the skull of a human." He said this as if he were talking to someone very stupid, which Violet was not.

"Nope," she said. "Can't be."

"Yes," Ian said—now he sounded annoyed—"it can be and it is. I designed it myself."

"You should probably take some drawing classes. I mean that as constructive criticism. What's that other one?"

Ian pushed up his left sleeve to reveal a series of Chinese

characters winding their way down his forearm. "Just a bit of ancient wisdom," he said.

"What bit?" Violet asked.

Ian quoted sententiously. "A wise man makes his own decisions. An ignorant man follows public opinion."

"That's not what it says." Violet had never considered herself a mean or nasty person, but at that moment she was having a very hard time maintaining her composure when what she wanted very badly to do was burst out in derisive laughter.

"Yes, it is. The guy who did the inking told me. He had a book of quotes from the ancient Chinese. The real stuff."

"The book," Violet explained, "was wrong. I don't know what your tattoo really says, but it's not what you think it is."

Ian sneered. "You're lying."

"I never lie. I've been told that I should learn. I hurt people's feelings sometimes."

"How would you know what this says?" Ian demanded. "You don't know Chinese."

"I can recognize a little from a book my dad had. I have a very good visual memory, you see. It's partly why I do really well on tests. The book is just over there, on that bottom shelf. I can show it to you if you want. The phrase you think is on your arm is on page twenty-three. No, twenty-four. But you shouldn't be too upset. The man who did the inking probably didn't know his source was wrong."

Ian pushed down his sleeve. "I don't need to see the book," he said, and stalked out of the sunroom.

Violet put her hand over her mouth and giggled. Maybe, she thought, Ian's tattoo meant, "The naive man is often made a fool." Whatever it said, Ian and his awful tattoos had given Violet the first really silly, lighthearted moment she had had in weeks. She looked to Grimace. "It's funny," she said to him, "the way that life works."

Chapter 70

"Evie! Hey. Come in." Daisy stepped back from the door and gestured for Evie to follow her inside.

"I'm sorry for just showing up," Evie said. "I remembered you told me where you lived, so . . ."

"You don't have to apologize." Daisy laughed. "This place is like a train station, people always coming and going. So, what's up? You looked stressed."

"The thing is . . . Nico showed up this morning. He wasn't due back until the end of the summer, but he cut his trip short. And he said I can't stay at his house any longer."

Daisy frowned. "What are you going to do?"

Evie fiddled with the hem of her T-shirt. "Well, that's a bit of a problem. See, I don't really have money for rent. . . . The rents are so high in summer. . . . I told you I haven't been working long enough to save much. I had figured that in the fall, when the tourists are gone, it might be easier to find an apartment I could afford. . . . But now . . ."

"Why don't you stay here?" Daisy suggested promptly. "We've got plenty of room."

"Really? It would only be for a little while. I'm . . . I'm

expecting a check from my mother's estate and once that finds me, I'll have plenty of money for rent somewhere downtown."

Daisy immediately wondered how a check would find Evie if she was on the run and using a false name, but she didn't push the point. She *wanted* Evie to stay with them. Being friends with Evie, keeping her secret and helping her in small practical ways, had given her a sense of purpose, a sense she had lost when she lost her beloved father. After her mother's death she had taken on her father's happiness as a sort of cause, a reason to get up in the morning. When he had died and Poppy had come home to be guardian, well, things had changed.

"Of course you can stay," Daisy said, putting a hand on Evie's shoulder. "For as long as you like. I mean, well, I'll have to ask Poppy, but I'm sure she'll say yes. Wait here. She's in the kitchen. I'll go ask her now."

Daisy dashed off to find Poppy. If idiot Ian were welcome, why wouldn't Evie, who was perfectly nice, be welcome, too?

Poppy was chopping onions; a pile of cut green peppers sat in a bowl nearby. "I'm getting pretty good at the sous-chef stuff," she announced. "I haven't sliced off the tip of a nail in days."

"Good. Poppy? I have a big favor to ask. An important one."

Poppy put down her knife. "That sounds ominous."

"No, I don't mean it's anything bad. It's about my friend Evie, the one staying at Nico's house for the summer. The thing is he came home unexpectedly and basically threw her out."

"That wasn't very nice of him."

"No, it wasn't," Daisy agreed. "Anyway, I told—I mean, I was thinking that she could stay here with us for a while, until the tourists leave and rents drop. I know you've never met her," Daisy went on hurriedly, "but that's only because she works so many hours at The Clamshell, but she's really nice. Joel can tell you, she won't be any trouble."

Poppy shrugged. "Sure. I don't see why not. Why don't you get my old bedroom ready for her?"

Daisy laughed with relief. "Thanks, Poppy, really. She'll help out around the house. She won't be a burden at all."

"I'm not really worried about that. No one could be a worse houseguest than Ian."

"That's the truth!"

Poppy picked up her knife again. "Evie can be an honorary Higgins. The more the merrier. Plus, it's what Mom and Dad would have done."

"Really?"

"Don't you remember the time one of Mom's old friends from high school stayed with us for an entire summer?" Poppy asked. "Well, you were pretty young then."

"No, I vaguely remember . . . Yeah, what was her name? Her marriage had just broken up or something. . . . She had the most amazing red hair."

"Stacy. Stacy Street. She sent a card when Mom died."

"She wasn't at the funeral?" Daisy asked.

"She lives in Hong Kong now," Poppy explained. "With her second husband. Anyway, she was in a bad way that summer, totally at a loss. Mom and Dad took her in without question. It must have been difficult for them in some ways. I remember Stacy always seemed to be crying or about to cry. But they were so good to her. They really helped her get on her feet again."

"Hospitality is a Higgins family tradition. Oh, Evie's waiting! Thanks, again, Poppy."

Daisy dashed back to Evie, still waiting in the front hall. "She said it's fine!"

Evie smiled, but Daisy saw tears in her eyes, too. "My stuff is still at Nico's. It's not much. . . ."

"Wait a minute. How did you get here from Nico's?"

"I walked."

"That's an insanely long walk!" Daisy reached into her pocket for her cell phone. "Look, let me see if Joel can pick us up and take us to Nico's right now. If he can't I'll see if Allie can. We're having chili for dinner and you definitely don't want to miss the famous Higgins chili."

Chapter 71

Evie was safely installed in Poppy's old bedroom, though how she was going to stand looking at the poster of that stupid boy band still on the wall, Daisy just did not know. Still, it had to be better than sticking around at Nico's house unwanted until she found a room somewhere she could afford.

Daisy and Joel had waited in his car outside the house while Evie had gone in to grab her things.

"I'm dying to get another glimpse of this guy Nico," Joel had said when Evie had been gone for a few minutes. "Can you believe I've only seen him once?"

"I don't think he likes to mingle with we townies," Daisy said. "Just my observation."

Twenty minutes later Evie came out of the house and climbed into the back seat of Joel's car.

"Was he there?" Joel asked.

"Taking a beauty nap," Evie replied, with the ghost of a smile. "I could hear the snoring."

The ride back to Willow Way was oddly silent. Daisy was pleased that Evie would be staying with her and her family, but the fact remained that the situation couldn't last forever and what might happen once Evie moved on was kind of scary to think about. Evie, too, must have been thinking much the same thing. The future, what any of them could see of it, was murky.

After Joel had dropped them off, Daisy had introduced Evie to her sisters and to Allie, and had then shown her to what would be her room. She had just left Evie to put away her things, which certainly wouldn't take long as she had so little with her, just one large backpack. No iPad. Only two pairs of socks and two pairs of jeans. No books. Watching Evie pull her few belongings from the backpack it had occurred to Daisy for the first time that Evie, who wasn't a permanent resident of Yorktide, might not be eligible for something as ubiquitous as a library card. She had never thought about the fact that someone might be denied a library card. Why should she have? Well, Daisy thought, assuming Evie did want to read, she had come to the right house! They were tripping over books in the Higgins homestead.

Daisy stopped in the upstairs hall outside of what had once been her parents' bedroom. The door was closed. She hesitated for a moment and then she opened the door and went inside. It was the first time she had been in the room since she had taken her grandfather's tiepin from the safe. A quick glance around the bedroom and the adjoining bathroom told her that Poppy hadn't made any major changes. There was a lamp she had brought with her from her Boston apartment, and she seemed to have replaced the bedding— neither Annabelle nor Oliver would have chosen the pattern that Poppy had chosen. Daisy's parents might walk into the room at any moment and find themselves at home.

It was a disconcerting thought, but Daisy realized that only weeks ago such a notion—her father alive and well and walking into his bedroom—would have sent her spiraling into grief. But now . . . The loss of her father didn't hurt quite as much as it had. Yes, a melancholic sadness still haunted her, but it wasn't as sharp and biting as it had been. Her grief had mellowed, probably for several reasons. One of which, Daisy thought, might be her new friendship with Evie, and the sense it brought with it that she was doing good for someone.

Daisy quietly opened her father's closet. It was a waste, really, all those expensive, beautifully tailored shirts and suits, the cashmere sweaters and silk ties, the leather shoes handmade for him in Italy. All just sitting there, tucked away and unseen. She closed the closet and moved over to his dresser. She opened the top drawer and looked down at the neatly folded linen handkerchiefs, all of which bore his initials in elaborate embroidery. His wallet was there, too. His house keys. And a stack of thin leather bookmarks Daisy had made at summer camp one year. She picked up one of the bookmarks—appropriately enough she had tooled a daisy onto its surface—and thought it might be okay if she took it to her own room to use. Carefully, she closed the drawer again and slipped the bookmark into her back pocket.

Poppy had been given so much responsibility, and with so little warning. Maybe, Daisy thought now, she could offer to be the one to go through their father's clothes and select what would go to charity. As long as Poppy didn't take her offer of help as criticism of her own failure to handle the chore . . . Wait, Daisy thought. She would wait a bit before suggesting that she would deal with their father's clothing. The truth was she wasn't entirely sure that she was ready, either.

One step at a time. And the next thing on Daisy's agenda was chili, which with Allie's coaching, Poppy had really mastered. Daisy left her parents' old room—Poppy's room now—careful to close the door behind her.

Chapter 72

"That chili really was amazing. And the salad wasn't bad, either. Funny, I've never been into salads before. All that cold green lettuce."

Daisy laughed. "With all the good stuff Allie adds to a salad it's not even like eating a salad!"

Evie and Daisy were in Poppy's old room. Evie's room now. For a while. Poppy had given permission for Evie to take down the old poster of the boy band and she had. Otherwise, Evie hadn't changed anything and she wouldn't. It wasn't really her room to—to inhabit.

"Your house is really great," she said now to Daisy. "It's like a manor house in some wonderful movie."

"To the manor born. Why do I know that expression? I must have read it somewhere."

"I used to like to read," Evie said. "Well, I guess I still do. Or would. If—"

"If what?"

Evie shrugged. "If things were different. If my mind wasn't so busy all the time with practical stuff."

"Well, here's a good thing. While you're staying with us

you don't really have to worry about practical stuff—not much, anyway—so you can do all the reading you want."

Evie smiled. Maybe, she thought, there were some foreign-language books in the sunroom or the study. That would be awesome.

"Um, is this really all you have?" Daisy asked. "What we picked up at Nico's yesterday? I don't mean anything insulting by that. . . ."

"I know. And yeah, it's just the stuff I brought with me when I . . . But I don't really care. Things don't mean a lot to me. Possessions."

"Really? They mean a lot to me. Some things, anyway. Look, come to my room. I want to show you something."

Evie followed Daisy two doors down the hall, where Daisy took a square black box off a shelf of her bookcase. "It's a conservation box. It helps keep old papers from rotting away. Here," she added, handing Evie a pair of plastic gloves. "You don't want any oil or dirt on your skin to get on the paper."

Wearing her own pair of gloves, Daisy opened the box and lifted out a piece of yellowed paper. "This belonged to my mom," she said. "We each chose something special of hers to keep when she died. Violet chose her gardening hat and Poppy took a bracelet. This is what I wanted."

"What is it?" Evie asked, thinking of the locket she wore around her neck and gently touching the old paper. "I mean, it looks like a letter, but . . ."

"It is. It dates from the Civil War," Daisy explained. "It was written by this woman, look, here's her signature, Clementine Wallace, to her son, Abraham. He was a soldier in the Northern army."

Evie squinted. "It's kind of hard to read the handwriting."

"I know. It's pretty faded and people's handwriting was

different back then. But Mom could read it. Basically this woman, Clementine, is worried sick about her son. Listen to this line. 'My beloved Abraham, I am sending you the shirt you asked me to mend, as well as a new pair of socks as I am sure such amenities are not to be had—' The next word is too badly faded for me to make out. Even my mom couldn't read it. Anyway, the next line reads: 'Your brother recovers from an ague that kept him to his bed for nigh three weeks.'"

"What's an ague?" Evie asked.

"It's an illness, like a fever with chills and sweats. And then she goes on: 'Every evening I stand by the front gate and look down the road in the fond hope that I will find you coming home to us.' Can you imagine?" Daisy said, carefully replacing the letter in the box. "Knowing that your child is out there in awful conditions, getting shot at or stabbed with a bayonet. Getting dysentery. Having a limb cut off without anesthesia. And there's absolutely nothing you can do about it but pray. If you believe in God and I think pretty much everybody did back then."

"And nothing has really changed, has it?" Evie said after a moment. "I mean, parents love their children and children love their parents." *Or they want to . . .*

"Yeah. Look, I'm really sorry about your dad. I wish . . ."

"I know," Evie said quickly, wondering how Daisy had possibly known what she was thinking. "Me, too. I think I'll go see if Poppy needs any help with anything."

Daisy laughed. "She'll find some chore that needs doing! And if you run into Ian, don't let him talk you into doing his laundry!"

Evie left Daisy's room and went downstairs, noting as she went the pictures on the walls, the colors of the curtains, the pattern on the stair runner—all the details of the home that would be hers only for a time. She was reminded yet again of all that she had lost. And she had lied to Daisy yet again. Possessions *did* mean a lot to her, now more than ever, possessions and a place to come home to at the end of the day. Evie felt a rush of envy, followed by a wave of sorrow, followed finally by a fierce determination to regain a life of certainty. *I will have a home of my own again,* she vowed, as she went to find Poppy. *I will.*

Chapter 73

The occupants of the Higgins house, both permanent and temporary, were seated at the table in the rarely used dining room. Allie had suggested to Poppy that they gather there for dinner just for the change.

"Besides," she had said. "Our brood seems to be ever growing. We're getting a bit crowded at the kitchen table."

And that was a point. Poppy looked around at the others at the table. Except for one person she was happy they were all there together.

"If I were you," Daisy was saying to Ian, "I'd be scared. You're outnumbered in this house."

"Because I'm a man?"

"Because you're a guy," Daisy corrected.

Ian didn't seem to take offense. He poured another glass of wine and grinned. "I think I can take care of myself. Unless you're like, The Witches of Willow Way."

"Nothing is impossible," Daisy shot back.

Poppy raised her eyebrows at her sister. Ian was, after all, a guest and that made him in some way vulnerable. It was the host's job to protect her guest, not to attack him. No matter how obnoxious he was.

"What's your sun sign?" Violet asked Ian. "I'm usually very good at telling that about someone, but with you, all I'm getting is static."

Ian shrugged. "Not that I believe in all that stuff, but I'm Gemini."

Violet frowned. "How old are you?"

"Twenty-eight."

"Hmm. The Saturn return might explain it, but . . . No. It's no use. I can't get anything. It's like you're not really there or something."

Ian addressed Poppy. "She's a regular little sorcerer, isn't she? Give her a few years to practice and you could put her on the stage."

"Is everything mockery with you?" Daisy snapped.

Allie cleared her throat and shot a glance at Poppy.

"Why take life too seriously?" Ian countered.

"Because," Violet said, "it doesn't last very long. Because it's precious and once life here on Earth is gone, it's gone forever."

"Live fast 'cause it don't last. Right? Die young and leave a pretty corpse."

Poppy cringed. She glanced at Daisy and then at Violet, both of whom seemed in a momentary state of shock.

"You should be ashamed of yourself," Allie said, her tone icy.

Ian turned to Allie and laughed. "What? It's from that old Blondie song. Die young and stay pretty. Live fast 'cause it don't last."

"Don't you think," Allie said, "that it's a tad inappropriate given the circumstances?"

"Obviously not," Violet replied, "or he wouldn't have said it."

"Really? I'm not so sure. I think he's a—"

"Daisy," Poppy began, but realized she couldn't scold her sister for voicing what was probably also her own opinion. "Let's change the subject, please, everyone."

"So, what's your story?" Ian asked Evie, who until now had been a spectator of the conversational chaos rather than a participant.

"Why does she have to have a story?" Daisy snapped.

"Everyone's got a story," Ian replied. "At least, a beginning and a middle. We won't talk about the end because Poppy wants us to change the subject."

"But why does she have to tell you?" Daisy persisted. "You're a stranger. You don't matter to her."

Daisy, Poppy thought, could be fiercely loyal. She was like their father in that way. She could also be rude, and that was something of which Oliver Higgins had never been guilty.

"It's all right, Daisy," Evie said. Then she addressed Ian. "My story is simple. After I graduated from high school last year I decided to take some time off before college."

"That's it?" he asked.

"That's it."

"Fair enough," Ian said. "Is there any more risotto?"

"No," Daisy said flatly. "You had three servings, more than any of us got."

Ian shrugged and tossed his napkin onto his empty plate. "So be it."

Poppy realized something then. Daisy was itching for a fight, but she was never going to get one from Ian. He just didn't care enough about what people thought about him to take offense. And that, Poppy thought, must be an . . . interesting . . . way to get through your life. It certainly was not how she and her sisters had been raised. They had been raised to care about their conduct and the reputation that would result. And that, Poppy thought, was a pretty wonderful thing. To care.

Chapter 74

Yes, Violet thought, as she, Evie, and Daisy were clearing the table after dinner. Evie Jones was keeping a very dark secret. She was hiding an almost unbearable sadness. Violet knew it as clearly and as certainly as she knew her own name and that Grimace preferred turkey to chicken. What she didn't know at all clearly or certainly was if Evie's secret, whatever it was, might bring harm to the Higgins family. And that must not happen, not after all her family had been through. What she also didn't know was just how much of her secret Evie had shared with Daisy. Daisy definitely knew something—enough to make her leap to defend Evie against Ian's questioning at dinner.

While the food had been really good—a mushroom risotto and one of Allie's special salads—Violet had felt uneasy and unbalanced throughout the meal. When she got upstairs to her room she would meditate with a piece of aquamarine. But first, she would try to learn a little bit more about Evie Jones, the newest resident in the house on Willow Way.

"When's your birthday, Evie?" Violet asked her, as she gathered the dirty napkins from around the table.

"March twenty-second." Evie laughed and touched her hair as if the question made her nervous. "Oh my God, what made me say that? That's my . . . That was my aunt's birthday. How weird. My birthday was, I mean is, November eleventh."

Daisy laughed a bit too loudly for the occasion, Violet thought. "I'm always forgetting things like that—dates, what day of the week it is. Do you know the other day I couldn't remember my own phone number?"

Forgetting the day of the week was hardly the same as forgetting your own birthday, Violet thought. But she didn't argue that. "That makes you a Scorpio," Violet said to Evie. "Funny. I don't see you as a Water Sign."

Evie picked up a fork and dropped it back onto the table. "Oh?" she said, grabbing for the fork again. "I was never really into astrology, so . . ."

"Yes, you don't seem like a Scorpio to me. You seem more like a Fire Sign. A Sagittarius or an Aries. Yes, an Aries, I think."

Daisy frowned at her sister. "But it's not like you're an expert, Violet, right?"

"Obviously. It takes years and years of study to become a good astrologer. And you also have to have a gift. Do you have a special gift, Evie?"

Daisy looked at Evie and Evie looked down at the table. "No," she said. "What sort of gift would I possibly have?"

Violet shrugged. "Any sort. Musical. Athletic. Maybe you're really good with animals. Or with languages."

"No," Evie said, grabbing a stack of dishes from the table. "I have no gifts." She left the dining room with Daisy following her closely.

Yes, Violet thought. *Daisy's friend is hiding something big.* And she hurried to her room where Grimace—and a big chunk of calming aquamarine—would be waiting for her.

Chapter 75

Evie had taken a shower before crawling into bed, her second of the day. It had been her habit since arriving in Yorktide, first at Nico's house and now here at the house on Willow Way. It was as if she were making up for having been without a guaranteed source of running water those weeks she had been on the road. The grubbiness. The fear of being found repulsive and thrown out of a gas station convenience store. The thought of getting so dirty that it felt like bugs were crawling all over you.

Now, still warm from the hot water and smelling of coconut (there were three different types of hair conditioner in the shower caddy; Daisy had told her she could use whatever one she wanted), Evie held Ben to her chest and thought back to earlier in the evening. Poppy was seriously beautiful and it was so nice of her to allow Evie to stay with them for a while. Ian was kind of weird. She had never met anyone like him, so . . . So obnoxious. He was supposedly Poppy's friend, but even she didn't seem to like him all that much. Allie seemed very nice but a bit intimidating somehow. Maybe it was just because she was the most adult of the bunch, the one with the most experience, the one most likely to detect a lie.

Then again, Violet, who was only thirteen, seemed scarily able to hit on the truth. Evie *was* an Aries; her birthday really *was* March twenty-second. And how had Violet possibly guessed that Evie was good with languages? No doubt about it, she would have to be on her guard around Violet. She seemed very nice, not at all a vindictive type or someone out to make trouble, but you could never be sure. If only, Evie thought, she could lock this bedroom door when she left it. But she had noted that none of the interior doors in the house had locks. She would just have to be one hundred percent sure that she had any bit of evidence as to her true identity with her at all times. And that meant those old ID cards and the photo Daisy and Joel had found. About her friends' promise to keep her identity a secret she felt reasonably sure. The real problem was that there were so many deceptions to keep straight. Why had she further complicated things by telling Daisy she was expecting a check from her mother's estate? That was another lie. She would just have to be extra vigilant from now on, living amid the others in the house, and not allow a false sense of safety to dull her wits to the point where she made too many mistakes and was found out.

In spite of her agitation, the quietness of the night—there was no other house for almost a mile, Daisy had told her— the presence of other people just next door and down the hall, and the fact that there was an alarm system, lulled Evie into the first good, deep sleep she had had in what felt like years.

Chapter 76

Evie was at The Clamshell and the other women were in the kitchen. Poppy had suggested—rather strongly—that they give the inside of the drawers, fridge, and cupboards a good cleaning and reorganizing. That morning she had found an empty box of cereal put neatly away in the cupboard, a moldy lime in one of the vegetable bins, and the night before she had discovered that the good corkscrew her father had preferred had gone missing from the silverware drawer, where it usually lived.

"Where's Ian?" Allie asked, removing the contents of the junk drawer in search of the missing corkscrew. "Not that he would be of any help to us."

"Definitely not communing with nature." Daisy laughed. "You should have seen him running away from a bee yesterday. It was hilarious."

"Bee stings can be fatal," Poppy pointed out, as she combined into one box two half-empty boxes of pasta shells. "Maybe he's allergic."

Daisy shrugged. "It doesn't matter. He didn't get stung."

"But he's given me hives. Look." Violet pushed up the right sleeve of her dress and held out her arm.

"What?" Poppy cried. "Has he touched you?"

Violet sighed and lowered her sleeve over the red and white lumps. "You don't get hives from touching someone, Poppy. It's just—*him*. I'm having an allergic reaction to him. My body is displaying my discomfort at his being in my home. Our home."

Oh, Poppy thought. *Is that all?*

"He is kind of an idiot," Daisy added. "No offense."

"Of course not! Just that the guy I—"

Allie frowned. "Don't say the guy you're in love with, because you're not, are you?"

"No," Poppy said adamantly. "I was never in love with him."

"The guy you used to have casual, meaningless sex with."

"Violet!" Poppy cried. "How do you know . . . how do you know that we were romantically involved?"

Violet shrugged and looked up from the forks she was examining for water stains. "It's not a secret, is it?"

"Is he even a friend, Poppy?" Daisy asked. "Seriously, he doesn't treat you like a friend. He treats you like . . . like a lucky convenience. I can't imagine Joel treating me that badly. And if he ever did, that's the end of the friendship."

"Thank you all," Poppy said, hoping no one would miss the note of sarcasm in her voice, "for pointing out my poor judgment in character!"

"We're not saying he's bad or dangerous," Allie said. "He's no Lord Byron. He's just a waste of your time. And it's not the first time I've said it. Hey, I found the corkscrew!"

"I'm dying to shave his beard off some night when he's asleep," Daisy admitted. "Do you think we could drug him and then when he wakes up and finds his beard gone we could act all innocent and deny we had anything to do with it?"

Allie laughed. "Probably not a good idea."

"It would violate the laws of hospitality," Violet said. "Plus it would be like bullying and that's always wrong."

Daisy shrugged. "I know. Hey, Poppy? Why did you hang out with Ian in the first place? Really, I'm not trying to be challenging or obnoxious. I just want to know. Oh, ick, this milk has turned."

"I don't know," Poppy admitted as Daisy poured the offending milk down the sink. "He knew—he knows—a lot of people. Musicians, mostly. And artists. Well, not professional artists. People who worked in interesting shops. We went to a lot of parties. He took me to these hip clubs and cafés. He . . ."

Poppy couldn't go on. She was acutely aware of how pathetic that all must have sounded and the identical look on her sisters' faces confirmed it. Allie, she knew, had probably long since figured out the nature of her relationship with Ian—that she had been using Ian (however unconsciously) for his connections, such as they were—and repaying him by being the gorgeous girl on his arm. The relationship had been an exchange of goods and services, not a real emotional exchange. How careless and wasteful she had been with her precious time!

"We all form bad relationships in this life," Allie said briskly. "We all regret some of the friends we've made. The point is to learn a lesson from our mistakes and to move on."

Yes, Poppy thought. It was time to move on. So much was becoming clear to her about what she wanted, at least in her personal life. She thought then about Jon. She hadn't seen or heard from him since she and Ian had run into him on Main Street. And she thought of how lucky Julie and Mack were to have found each other before time gave either the chance to make terrible mistakes. Once upon a time Poppy used to think that all experience was for the good, but now she wasn't so sure. . . .

Daisy poked her arm. "Earth to Poppy."

"Sorry," Poppy said. "I was just thinking."

"I know." Daisy grinned. "I could smell the wood burning."

Poppy swatted Daisy. "Ha, ha! Very funny little sister. Very funny."

Chapter 77

"Bertie and I missed you."

"I'm sorry. I missed you, too." Daisy was way too embarrassed to admit to Mrs. Wilkin that she had quit her volunteer position in a fit of pique. They were alone in the Wilkins' apartment. Daisy had brought Muriella a box of scones Allie had made that morning. It was the least she could do, she thought, after having abandoned her friends.

Mrs. Wilkin looked closely at Daisy. "I hope all is right at home," she said. "With your sisters."

"Everything's fine," Daisy assured her. "I just didn't have a ride for a while, so . . . Tell me what's been going on here? Is that guy Tom still cheating at checkers?"

"Tom is dead," Mrs. Wilkin stated flatly. "He passed about ten days ago. I'm afraid Bertie's yet to find another lying checkers partner."

"I'm sorry," Daisy said, and she was sorry.

"There's already someone new in Tom's room," Mrs. Wilkin told her. "People keep dying and people keep replacing the dead."

Daisy thought Muriella sounded sad, even angry. It *had to*

make you angry at times, when your mature self-composure and sense of resignation slipped and you knew that you didn't have very long left in this world. It must make you furious, Daisy thought. And there was nothing you could do about it.

"Where is Mr. Wilkin now?" she asked.

Muriella sighed. "He went for a walk on the grounds."

"You didn't want to go with him? We could go and find him if you like."

Muriella shook her head. "I think he needed to be alone. Funny, isn't it, that even near the end, when you'd think all that people would want to do is to cling to whoever is left, they sometimes need to be alone."

Daisy felt a terrible urge to make up an excuse for having to leave—she had never witnessed Mrs. Wilkin in such a mood and it depressed her—but she fought the urge with all her might. She was going to be a doctor someday. And that meant she was going to have to deal with all sorts of people in all stages of life, young and old, healthy and ill. It was important and it was what she was meant to do.

"Tell me again about the trip you and Mr. Wilkin took to China when he retired," she said, moving her chair a bit closer to Mrs. Wilkin so that she could take her hand. "You have such wonderful stories."

Chapter 78

The Higgins sisters and Allie were in the sunroom, which was anything but sunny. Rain had been coming down in sheets all afternoon and every lamp in the room was lit against the gloom.

Violet was reading a book on astrology and drinking yet another cup of that decaf green tea she had become so fond of. Daisy was working on a crossword puzzle, her pen flying. Allie was once again attempting to get through one of Oliver Higgins's books, a deep frown of concentration on her face. Poppy was thinking about Daisy's friend Evie. She liked Evie. She had no problem doing small favors for her, like driving her to The Clamshell, even in a rainstorm. Evie was an excellent houseguest and more than repaid any kindness Poppy showed to her. Still, over the past week Poppy had caught a few inconsistencies in Evie's brief tale of herself and was beginning to suspect that something was not quite right. For example, she could have sworn that Evie had said she grew up in Winter Lake, which was a town in Vermont, but then, just that morning, she had heard Evie tell Ian that she had grown up in Crookville, which was a town in

New Hampshire. Both couldn't be true. Unless of course at some point Evie and her parents had moved from Vermont to New Hampshire. And there was another thing. Poppy had been in the study a few days earlier, leafing through one of her mother's coffee table art books, when Evie had come in.

"I'm sorry," she had said. "Am I disturbing you?"

"Of course not," Poppy assured her. "Hey, do you know French? I took Spanish in school. I don't know what this phrase means." She turned the book toward Evie and pointed to the words.

Evie shook her head. "No," she said. "I have no idea. Sorry."

And then she had left. The odd thing was that yesterday Poppy had gone into the study in search of her phone only to find Evie settled in an armchair, reading a hardbound book. She hurriedly thrust the book between her leg and the arm of the chair but not before Poppy had seen the title. *Le Colonel Chabert,* by Honoré de Balzac. And she recognized the volume as one of her parents' collection of novels in the original French. She hadn't commented on this to Evie, only glanced around for her phone and gone away. But the incident had been bothering her. . . .

"Penny for your thoughts?" Allie asked.

Poppy looked up to see that Allie had addressed the question to her. "Actually," she said, "I was thinking about Evie."

Daisy dropped her pen. "What about her?" she said, snatching it from the floor.

"Well, she hardly ever talks about her home or her family or her friends. And when she does tell us something it doesn't always match what she's told us before. Do you think she's hiding something?"

"Yes," Violet said promptly.

Poppy nodded. "So it's not only me. I wonder if she is who she says she is."

Daisy leaned forward in her chair. "Of course she's who she says she is," she said emphatically. "Why would she be lying?"

"To confuse anyone who was trying to find the truth about her," Violet said matter-of-factly. "Like when her birthday is."

"No," Daisy said. "I don't believe it."

"I think," Allie said, "that Poppy is probably right. Evie is hiding something. But then again, do you know anyone who isn't? Secrecy isn't necessarily a bad thing."

Poppy sighed. "Well, I guess it doesn't matter what went before. Evie's a nice person and she's a good houseguest. Unlike Ian."

"Right," Daisy said. "And that's all that should matter. By the way, when is The Bearded Wonder leaving?"

"Soon," Poppy promised, and she meant it. "Very, very soon."

Chapter 79

"Ian," Poppy said, "you need to leave."

Ian looked up from the pile of pancakes he was rapidly consuming. "Why?" he asked, his mouth full.

"Because I told you to," Poppy said, wiping up a bit of spilled maple syrup from the countertop. "Honestly, I don't know why I invited you to come here." *Because I was weak. A pushover. But not anymore.*

Ian swallowed, took a slug of coffee, and smiled. "Because we're friends."

Did he really believe that, Poppy wondered. Could he? "No, Ian," Poppy said. "We're not. I don't think we ever were."

Ian said nothing for a moment as he wiped his mouth and beard of pancake crumbs. "You know," he said, putting his crumpled napkin next to his plate, "now that we're on the subject, you kind of asked me here under false pretenses."

"What do you mean?"

Ian laughed unpleasantly. "You know exactly what I mean. I thought we'd be sleeping together, but then you stick me on the couch in the study. What's that about?"

Poppy knew she shouldn't be surprised by this caveman-ish attitude, but she was. Surprised and somewhat sickened. "Ian," she said, her voice higher than it needed to be, "we haven't been—involved—for almost a year! Why would you ever think I was going to sleep with you?"

"Since when did you get all Puritan?" he shot back.

Suddenly, Poppy was overcome by an anger so intense it frightened her. "You never even sent me or my family a card!" she cried.

"What?"

Poppy took a deep breath. It wouldn't do to have a stroke over Ian's emotional negligence. "When my father died," she said more calmly. "You never even sent us a sympathy card. What sort of friend is that?" *The sort of friend I never should have allowed in my life—or in my home.*

Ian laughed again. "You've got to be kidding. Those things don't matter. Greeting cards, all those made-up holidays, they're all just moneymaking scams."

"Those things *do* matter," Poppy argued. "They matter to *me* and if you really knew me even a little you would have understood that. Allie knew that. She came to the funeral. She's a real friend."

"The way you go on about Allie." Ian squinted at her. "Are you two doing it or something? Is that why you banished me to the study?"

"You make me sick, Ian."

Ian pushed away from the counter, the legs of the stool scraping on the tile floor. "Fine," he said. "I'll pack my bags and leave tomorrow morning. I made a date with this girl I met last night."

"I want you to leave this afternoon," Poppy said firmly.

Ian shrugged and stalked off toward the study, presumably to pack, and Poppy made a vow not to lay eyes on him again. And she would apologize profoundly to her sisters and to Allie for bringing him into their home.

Poppy scraped the remains of Ian's breakfast into the trash and put the dish, cup, and silverware into the dishwasher. When she turned back toward the counter she spotted the letter from the scholarship committee at Adams College. Really, she thought, what was the harm in accepting the offer? If after some time she did feel she was in over her head or too uncomfortable among the scholarly types she could always quit, having at least the satisfaction that she had made the effort. She pulled her cell phone from her pocket and made the call.

Chapter 80

Evie stopped short at the door of the sunroom. Allie was standing in front of a wooden easel, her back to the door, gesticulating wildly with a paintbrush.

"Come on!" she cried. "Seriously? Allie, use your . . . Use whatever it is you're supposed to use! It's just a freakin' picture!"

"What are you doing?" Evie asked, stepping into the room and trying to keep the amusement out of her voice.

Allie didn't turn away from the easel. "Making a massacre of this piece of expensive canvas."

Evie went over to Allie and her easel. "It doesn't look so bad to me. It's that plant over there, isn't it? The one with the yellow flowers?"

"Nice try. It's that lamp over *there,* the one with the Tiffany-style shade."

"Well, it's still . . . pretty."

"No need to be nice. I know I suck." Allie sighed and put her palette and brush on the easel's shelf. "The thing is I've really tried, but I just can't seem to make what I see in front of me appear on the paper. There's this huge disconnect somewhere. I am profoundly untalented when it comes to painting and drawing and that's that."

"Maybe you should take some lessons," Evie suggested.

"I have. And I've only succeeded in embarrassing myself in front of the others in the class. I give up. Why don't you take my paints and see what you can do with them?"

"Thanks," Evie says, "but I don't know how much longer I'll be around. I mean . . ."

"Well, use them while you're here."

"I used to like . . ." *Careful,* Evie told herself. *Be careful with what you reveal, especially to an adult.*

"What?"

"Nothing. Just that I used to paint a bit when I was a kid."

Allie tilted her head and eyed the canvas. "Well, pretty much anyone has to be better at painting than I am, even a kid."

"You have paint on your nose."

"Do I?" Allie attempted to cross her eyes to get a view of her nose.

"Don't do that!" Evie laughed. "Trust me, it's there."

Allie sank into a chair and Evie took the one across from her.

"What's it like working at The Clamshell?" Allie asked.

"It's okay. Billy—Mr. Woolrich—is really nice. I wish he would get married again. He seems so lonely."

Allie smiled. "Marriage isn't always the answer to loneliness, believe me. But it's nice of you to want him to be happy."

Evie smiled. Her father, she thought, just like Billy, hadn't asked to be abandoned. An odd thought crossed her mind. Maybe someday her father would find someone new to love and to love him in return, in spite of what had happened to him, in spite of what he had done and failed to do. She wondered how she would feel about that. Would she want to destroy the new relationship in retaliation for what had happened to her mother? No. It was a sickening thought, she realized, to want to hurt someone so badly, to deprive them of simple happiness. Even her father. Especially her father. Someone she . . .

"I worked as a short-order cook once," Allie said, breaking through Evie's troubling thoughts. "Just for the hell of it. I didn't need the money. I just thought, there's a slice of life I know nothing about."

Evie laughed. "And? What happened?"

"I quit after a week. I kept burning myself on the grill or the griddle—that's a cute word—or whatever it was called. All that grease flying through the air. Ugh."

"The fry cook at work," Evie said, "his name is Al, told me he's been doing it for thirty-two years. I don't know how he can stand the smell of grease day after day. I've only been at The Clamshell for a little over a month and already I'm sick of it."

Allie shrugged. "Maybe he can't smell it anymore. People do get so used to things they stop even noticing them. Things and people. That's why so many marriages—well, any long-term relationships—fade away into oblivion. One person stops really noticing the other or both people become blind to what they once found so special and interesting in each other." Suddenly, Allie laughed. "Listen to me, going on about relationships! I had one ridiculous marriage when I was practically still a kid and nothing serious since."

"Do you want to get married again?" Evie asked.

"Only if I'm in love with him and he's in love with me," Allie replied promptly. "I mean, really in love, with the good, the bad, and the ugly. Otherwise, no thanks. I've plenty of money—I'm lucky, did I tell you that?—to have myself taken care of in old age. I'll install myself in some swanky spa-like residence and be waited on hand and foot by people hoping to get what's left of my millions when I die."

Evie thought it sounded like a cold and sad existence (though not as bad as being homeless), but she didn't share her opinion with Allie. Besides, the less she said on *any* topic, the better. Already she had probably said too much, like telling Poppy she didn't know French. What had she been thinking, reading the Balzac right out in the open? She had been lulled by a false sense of security. Hopefully, Poppy hadn't noticed the title of the book.

"I'll be going back to Boston soon," Allie announced.

Evie was taken by surprise. "Why?" she asked. "I mean, do you have to leave?"

Allie laughed. "There's only so long I can freeload on Poppy! Not that she sees me as a freeloader. Not that I *am* a freeloader. We're friends. I came here in hopes of doing her a service and I guess I'm thinking maybe my time is up. I've done what little I can. And Poppy does seem happier, less worried than she was when I showed up on her doorstep."

When, Evie wondered, would her own time be up? "It's fun that you're here," she said. "I mean . . . You're interesting."

"Thanks. Better than being boring. So, what about you? Are you planning to make Yorktide your home? I mean, after the summer, when The Clamshell closes for the season, will you be moving on?"

Evie fought a black moment of despair. Why couldn't everything just freeze at this moment in time, with them all together at this wonderful house on Willow Way! Now that Ian was gone it was even more of an idyllic spot than it had been . . .

"Evie?"

"Sorry," she said. "I haven't given it much thought." *My future.*

"Well, if you find yourself in Boston this fall, give me a call. I'll give you all my contact information before I go."

Evie managed to smile. "Thank you," she said. "Thanks." Another safe haven, however temporary. She was grateful.

Chapter 81

"I'm glad you were free this evening."

Poppy smiled. "How could I say no to a sunset picnic, and on the beach no less." *And,* Poppy added silently, *I didn't want to say no to you.*

Jon had shown up at the house with a big wicker basket in the bed of his truck. "It belonged to my grandmother," he told Poppy as she climbed into the passenger seat. "It's the most well-made thing I've ever seen. And it weighs about a ton even when it's empty."

When he had spread a blanket on the sand Jon began to unload the basket's contents. A bottle of chilled white wine, a large bottle of a specialty ale with one of those metal locking mechanisms, a wedge of Brie, a baguette, a bunch of grapes, and a giant chocolate chip cookie. "Nothing very original," he said. "I'm not very good with menu planning."

"Neither was I until recently," Poppy admitted. "And it's lovely, thank you."

They had the beach to themselves except for a very tall man walking slowly behind his metal detector down by the water's edge, and a few hopeful seagulls who stationed themselves within distance of catching any food that might be tossed their way.

Jon handed her a glass of wine (well, a plastic cup of wine) and poured some of the beer in his own cup. "Cheers," he said.

"Cheers."

"So, what's been going on since we last talked?" he asked.

Poppy wondered where to begin—with the scholarship committee, with Ian's departure, or with Evie's arrival? She decided to start with the committee. "Well," she said, "there is something kind of big. At least, it's big to me. A few weeks ago I was asked to take my father's place on the committee that awards the scholarship in my mother's name."

"Really? Did you accept?"

"Not at first," Poppy admitted. "Honestly, I found the idea pretty terrifying, me in a room with a bunch of professors! I felt they'd all consider me a fraud. I'm sure I was only asked as a courtesy. But I finally worked up the nerve and said yes. I went to my first meeting last night."

Jon raised his cup. "Good for you. So, how did it go?"

Poppy laughed. "I was a nervous wreck. But pretty much everyone was nice and the head of the committee, Dr. Dolman, explained very clearly the criteria the committee has set for the awarding of the scholarship. He gave me a file of information on the past two winners so I'd have a good idea of the sort of student they're looking for."

"*Pretty* much everyone was nice?" Jon asked.

"Yeah. There was this one guy, a professor of philosophy, who clearly thought I was a seriously poor replacement for my father. Which I am, of course, but . . . Let's just say he seemed more interested in sneaking a look at my legs than in listening to what I had to say. Not that what I had to say was all that interesting."

"Poppy," Jon said almost sternly. "Stop cutting yourself down! You're just as smart as any academic. And a so-called professional shouldn't have been trying to get a look at your legs."

"He was wearing a wedding ring, too."

Jon frowned. "You're sticking with the committee though?"

"Yes. Now that I've taken the first step some snobby creep isn't going to scare me off!"

Jon busied himself slicing a few pieces of the Brie with a white plastic knife, and then offered the paper plate to Poppy. Brie was her all-time favorite cheese.

"Is that friend of yours still staying with you?" Jon asked suddenly. "The guy, I mean, not Allie."

"Ian. No." Poppy laughed a bit embarrassedly. "I sent him back to Boston. He was getting on everybody's nerves. Especially mine. And I finally realized he never really was a friend, not a true one."

"Good." Jon looked down at his cup. "I mean, good that you—"

"That I what? Came to my senses?" Poppy laughed more freely now. "Too bad it took so long!" *Be brave, Poppy . . .* "Jon, there was nothing between us, you know. There was once, but that was a long time ago and it was never serious. It was back before I began to grow up. I just wanted you to know that."

Jon looked up at her and smiled. "Thanks. I appreciate your honesty. And I can't say I'm sorry to hear he's history."

"He made Violet break out in hives. Really. She was allergic to him!"

Jon laughed. "Poor Violet."

"And I really thought Daisy was going to pop him one. She's not a violent person at all, but something in Ian brought out the thug in her."

"I suspect that Daisy's one of those fiercely loyal people.

Joel's told me enough about her to make me think that if she even suspects someone she loves is being ill-used she'll come out fighting."

"Joel's absolutely right. And there's something else to tell." Poppy explained that Evie, one of the girls who worked at The Clamshell, was staying with them. "She's an excellent houseguest and I really have no problem with her being there."

"But . . ."

"But, well, I don't know. At some point she has to move on. I mean, she can't stay with us forever. Daisy says she's trying to save enough money to pay a first and last month's rent somewhere in town, but that could be a very long time. The Clamshell isn't open all year round and she might have trouble finding a job for the winter months. The town really empties out." Poppy sighed. "The problem is I can't see myself being heartless enough to ask her to leave. I get the feeling she might be all alone in the world."

"Except for you and your sisters."

"And your cousin. Daisy said Joel considers Evie almost a sister."

Jon was silent for a moment. And then he said: "I hope you'll keep me up to date on how things are getting on with Evie. I mean, if she can't seem to get on her feet. I'd like to help if I can. With all the people my family knows in this area there's bound to be someone with a room to let or a job to get her through until spring. Dad shuts the restaurant down for most of January and after that there's a skeleton staff until April, but if we put our minds to it we could probably come up with a job for Evie, at least something part-time."

"I promise to keep you posted," Poppy said. "And thanks."

Jon shifted on the blanket so that he was facing Poppy,

rather than sitting at her side. "I've been wanting to say this for some time now," he began, "but I wasn't sure I had the right."

Poppy felt her heart speed up, just a bit. "Oh?"

"Well, I'm still not sure I have the right, but here goes. I think there's enormous value in what you're doing, Poppy. Being there for your sisters. I hope you see that."

"I do," Poppy said. "Sort of. But remember, I didn't choose to come home and play parent. I was told to. Sometimes I feel like I'm just following orders, being the dutiful daughter. I don't feel like I'm doing anything particularly noble or selfless." Poppy laughed. "Mostly all I do is complain about my responsibilities!"

"Complaining," Jon said with a smile, "can be underrated. But seriously, Poppy, sometimes it's good enough just to play the part. The results can still be worthwhile. You might not be wholeheartedly devoted to being your sisters' guardian, but you're *there*. You're making sure the bills get paid and dinner is on the table and the house is clean. There's value in maintaining normalcy for those you love. There's value in being reliable."

"Not very glamorous, being reliable, but I suppose you're right. We all need—at least, we all want—someone on whom we can rely, at least part of the time. First, it's our parents. And then . . ."

"Yes," Jon said. "And then. It's like that great old song, 'Someone to Watch Over Me.' Total independence isn't always ideal. Well, that's just my opinion."

And suddenly, Poppy felt an unfamiliar and yet entirely welcome wave of emotion overcome her as she looked at Jon Gascoyne. She wondered if there was anyone on whom he could rely. On whom he wanted to rely. And suddenly she knew that she wanted him to want to rely on *her*.

And then Jon leaned in and she did too and he kissed her and she kissed him. It was a very good kiss, Poppy thought, sweet though hinting at passion to come. She liked it very much.

"You're very nice," she told him, taking both of his hands in hers. *What wonderful hands,* she thought. *What a wonderful man.*

"I hope you don't consider *nice* a bad word. It is for so many people."

"No," Poppy said earnestly. "I think it's a very good word. One of the best."

Chapter 82

Evie felt unutterably weary. There had been a string of nasty customers, as if someone had put out a sign at the town line inviting all rude and impatient people to come by The Clamshell that afternoon. And the guy that was supposed to relieve her on her breaks had never shown up, which meant that Evie hadn't gotten any breaks. Billy had covered for her during her lunch hour, which had been only a half hour as he had an appointment with a roofer that couldn't be put off.

Only an hour left to her shift. Surely, she could survive another hour.

The door to the restaurant swung open and a group of four teenagers, two boys and two girls, came tumbling in. They were talking and laughing loudly, and for a second Evie wondered if they were drunk. She remembered overhearing some of the conversations between the people at the party Joel had taken her to earlier that summer, how she had felt so utterly alone and alienated from their world, how she had felt so envious of their freedom from worry, of their carelessness and their mindless assumption that the world was theirs for the taking. These teens were also from that other, enviable world.

Suddenly, Evie felt tears threatening and she turned her back to the order counter to grasp hold of her self-possession. As she did so her elbow caught the china mug in which Billy drank his coffee and it fell to the floor, shattered. The teenage girls laughed uproariously and as Evie hurried aside to get a broom and dustpan she thought she heard the words *clumsy* and *bitch*.

"I'll take their order," her coworker Marcus said, patting Evie on her shoulder as he passed.

Grateful for that small act of kindness, Evie began to sweep up the shards. One large jagged piece had flown under the big freestanding shelves on which were stacked various stainless steel bowls. Evie bent down and reached for it with her left hand, cutting herself across the palm in the process. "Damn," she muttered, hastily sweeping up the remaining bits and pieces of china and dumping the lot in the trash. Then, she went to the cabinet in the kitchen where the first aid kit was kept. It was pretty depleted—there was no antiseptic or antibacterial cream—but she did find a few Band-Aids. They were all a little too narrow to cover the cut entirely so she put two side to side and used a third placed crosswise on top to hold them down. It would have to do for now, at least until she could get home that afternoon.

Home. Evie knew she shouldn't be thinking of the Higginses' house as home—it would only hurt that much worse when she had to leave—but she couldn't help it. It *felt* like home, or almost. A place where she could be safe. But for how long? Like Allie, maybe her time as a houseguest was drawing to a close.

Evie took a deep breath and walked back out to the order counter.

"What happened to you?" Marcus asked.

Evie looked at her hand. The blood was already seeping through the bandages.

"I cut myself on the broken mug," she said.

Marcus frowned. "That looks pretty ugly."

Evie shrugged, though the sight of the blood had made her feel a bit queasy. "It's okay," she said. "I just bleed a lot."

Marcus raised an eyebrow skeptically. "If you say so. Just don't drip blood onto a customer's fries. I doubt Billy can afford a lawsuit."

Chapter 83

A little before three o'clock in the afternoon, Poppy settled on the front porch in the old wicker rocking chair her father had loved to wait for her friend Julie. The chair could use a new coat of paint and she made a mental note to get to the chore her mother had so enjoyed. Since Poppy had been back home this summer with her sisters she had finally begun to understand that there was pleasure to be found in the simplest of tasks when they were done in the service of other people. Pleasure and something more. It was like Jon had said the other evening on the beach. There was value in maintaining normalcy for those you loved. There was value in being reliable.

Poppy smiled to herself. That magical evening! She hadn't told anyone, not even Allie, what had happened with Jon. At least for a while she wanted to hold the memory of that wonderful kiss all to herself. She remembered something that Allie had said not long before, when they had been talking about Evie. Secrecy, Allie believed, wasn't necessarily a bad thing, and Poppy agreed.

On the ride back to the house that evening Jon had held

her hand (when he didn't have to shift) and Poppy had found the gesture inordinately romantic. She remembered thinking that *this* was love. She had never known romantic love before and yet, somehow, she recognized it. Jon had kissed her again before she got out of his truck and he had waited until she was safely inside before driving away. Poppy had stood in the hall, watching through the windows alongside the door as he disappeared down the drive. Briefly she wondered if Allie and her sisters had witnessed Jon's kiss. But when she found them all in the living room a few minutes later, absorbed in a movie, it was clear they had not, and for that she was glad.

At exactly three o'clock, Julie drove up to the house in the ancient station wagon that Poppy remembered had once belonged to Julie's parents. Poppy went down the steps to meet her.

"Should you be driving?" she asked, watching her friend climb out of the car with some difficulty.

"You mean, how do I fit behind the steering wheel?"

"That, too."

"It's not easy. Will you help me get this monster out?"

Virginia let herself out of the back seat while Poppy helped Julie remove Michael, who was quite a sturdy boy—built like his father—from his car seat.

"Why don't you all go out back to the garden?" Poppy suggested. "I'll meet you there with lemonade and cookies."

Julie and the kids made their way to the garden and Poppy hurriedly gathered the refreshments. A few minutes later she found her friend settled in one of the Adirondack chairs and the kids chasing a yellow butterfly.

"I'm definitely going to need your help getting out of this chair," Julie said. "I kind of fell in."

Poppy laughed. "No worries. How do you feel?"

"Besides massive and lumbering? Fine. Actually, this has been the easiest of my three pregnancies."

"And the last? Sorry, I shouldn't have asked that."

Julie shrugged. "I don't know. Maybe, maybe not."

A shout of glee from Virginia caused Poppy to look over her shoulder. "I found a worm!" she cried, holding up the wriggling creature for the adults to see.

"That's nice," Julie called back. "But now put him back where you found him. He has to get home to his family."

With a frown, Virginia complied.

"How do they feel about getting a new brother or sister?" Poppy asked.

"Virginia is excited to help play mommy. Michael wants to know if the baby will be deaf like him."

"What do you tell him?"

"What *can* I tell him? That we don't know yet. But that if he—or she—is deaf, Michael can help teach him—or her—to sign."

"When did Michael learn to sign?" Poppy asked.

"Just as soon as we did! His coordination is still that of the average five-year-old, of course, but he has no trouble making his thoughts known!"

"Hey, remember when we were kids and we used to build fairy houses in the woods behind your house?"

"And you had a really cool swing set and jungle gym," Julie said. "If you weren't so generous about letting me use it I would have been jealous."

"I forgot all about that! Daisy was always falling off the jungle gym, that's why my parents got rid of it."

"Fun times. Except for Daisy's bumps and bruises."

"They *were* fun." *And so innocent,* Poppy thought. *So fleeting.*

"Have you seen Jon lately?"

Poppy was glad she was wearing sunglasses; she had felt her eyes widen at Julie's question. "Yes," she said casually. "I saw him on Tuesday."

Julie finished her glass of lemonade before she said, "He kissed you, didn't he?"

Poppy choked on a sip of her own drink. "What!" she exclaimed.

"Well?" Julie asked, grinning.

"I have no idea how you knew that, but yes. He did. And I kissed him back." Poppy leaned forward and lowered her voice though there was no one but Virginia to hear and she was too young to care about the adults' conversation. "Julie, I . . . I've never felt this way before. And I have no idea what, if anything, will happen next. . . ."

"Time will tell. Remember, Jon's not going anywhere."

Maybe I'm not, either, Poppy thought. *Maybe Yorktide is where I'll stay. . . .* The possibility didn't at all frighten her the way it had at the beginning of the summer.

"You know," she said, "I don't have a very good track record romantically speaking. I'm so afraid that I'll do or say the wrong thing and ruin things with Jon before they've even begun."

Julie sighed. "Poppy, I've told you this before. You think— and worry—too much! And really, you've got to work on your self-esteem! Do you know how odd it is, plain ol' Julie Mayer, farm wife and cheese maker, having to tell tall, gorgeous, college grad Poppy Higgins, whose famous parents left her this beautiful quirky home and an amazing legacy, to have some faith in herself?"

The children made an appearance at just that moment. Both, Poppy noted, had grass stains on their shorts.

"You're pretty," Virginia announced.

"Thank you. You're pretty, too. And fast."

"I'm the fastest-est person in my class."

Poppy smiled. "Wow."

"Want to know how to sign? Michael will show you."

Poppy shot a look at Julie, who shrugged. "Uh, sure."

Virginia signed to her brother and then looked back to Poppy. "I told him to show you how to say 'you are pretty and nice.'"

Michael did. Poppy tried to mimic his hands, but he was simply too fast for her. "Could he do it more slowly?" Poppy asked. So Michael did, but still Poppy found her hands not doing what she wanted them to do. Suddenly, both Julie and the children burst out laughing.

"You just said, 'I'm a bubble,'" her friend told her.

Poppy put her hands to her face. "Yikes! A bubble? Signing is a lot harder than I thought it would be."

Michael signed to his sister, who then turned to Poppy. "He says, practice makes perfect."

"He's a smart guy!"

"Well, we have to be going," Julie announced. "Mack's going to be home for dinner tonight, which has been a pretty rare thing lately what with his taking on some overtime. We're going to make a celebration of it. There's only one problem standing in the way. . . ."

"What's that?" Poppy asked.

"Getting me out of this chair."

Chapter 84

"When did this happen?" Daisy asked. She had accidentally walked in on Evie in the upstairs bathroom a few minutes before. Evie had been standing at the sink, letting warm water dribble along her left palm, and wincing.

Now back in Poppy's old bedroom, Evie shrugged and dabbed at the wound with a dry towel. "A day or two ago. I don't remember exactly."

"I really think you should get that checked out," Daisy said, frowning. "I mean, I saw that you were wearing a bandage, of course, but I had no idea the cut was so bad."

"What do you mean checked out?" Evie said, holding the towel over her hand. "By a doctor?"

"Of course by a doctor." Daisy swiftly pulled the towel from Evie's hand. "A wound that deep could easily get infected. In fact, it looks to me like it *is* infected. See how it's all red and puffy around the edges."

Evie sank onto the edge of the bed. "No," she said. "No doctors."

"Why not?"

"You *know* why, Daisy! What if I get found out?"

Daisy shook her head. "You mean, what if the doctor finds out you're using a fake ID? So what? It's not a crime." Or was it? Daisy realized she wasn't at all sure of Evie's legal situation. If she weren't sworn to secrecy she would ask Freddie. . . .

"There's no record anywhere of Evie Jones. Not the Evie Jones I'm pretending to be. I made her up. She isn't real."

"But . . . But why would anyone check to see you're who you say you are? And anyway, you're eighteen. You can't be sent back to live with your father's disgusting friends." *But could she be charged with a crime?* Daisy wondered.

Evie put her uninjured right hand to her forehead. "I know, I know. It's just that I want to leave my past behind me. I want none of it to exist anymore. I want to forget my life before now ever happened. I don't want anyone of them to know where I am."

Daisy was beginning to feel as if she was missing something in Evie's arguments, but she couldn't put her finger on what, exactly, it was. "But—"

"Besides," Evie interrupted, "I have no health insurance and I have no money to pay a doctor."

"I'll pay for you," Daisy said promptly. "I have about fifty dollars stashed in my room and more in the bank." Money was nothing when a friend's health was concerned, of that Daisy was one hundred percent sure.

Evie shook her head. "I can't take money from you. You're already being so generous, letting me stay here."

"Then what about Joel? We could ask if he has any money he could lend you."

"I know, but please, Daisy, please! Don't say anything to anyone, not even to Joel. The cut really isn't as bad as you think. I'm sure that in a day or two it'll be completely healed."

Daisy looked down at her friend's hand and wasn't at all

sure of that, but she knew that to further press Evie at this point was not the way to make her change her mind.

"All right," she said reluctantly. "I promise I won't say anything to anyone. You look exhausted. You should probably get to bed. Do you want me to put a new bandage on for you?"

"No, thanks," Evie said, and Daisy thought she looked about to cry. "I can do it myself."

> *He needs but look about, and there*
> *Thou art!—a friend at hand . . .*

Daisy lay on her bed. Her mind was in a whirl. It was what she wanted to be, a friend at hand for Evie. But things had gotten complicated. Well, more complicated. Keeping someone's secrets was a tricky business. It could make you feel as if you were doing something very wrong. As if you were hurting that person, and not helping at all.

There's got to be a solution, Daisy thought. Yes. Antibiotics. She would get her hands on some antibiotics—but how did you do that without a prescription? You borrowed them from someone, with her permission. Or you stole them from someone, without her permission. The trouble was, as far as Daisy knew, no one at the house was taking antibiotics, but they *might* be. Allie might keep any medication she was taking in her room. But it would be such a terrible violation of the laws of hospitality, to essentially break into Allie's bedroom and steal from her.

Daisy sighed. No, it was a desperate, ridiculous idea. She was horrified that she had contemplated committing a crime, even if it was for a good cause. There had to be another way to help! Maybe Violet knew of a natural, herbal cure for infection. . . . But going to Violet would involve breaking the promise of secrecy she had made to Evie.

What else, what else! All right, Daisy thought, if Evie wouldn't see a doctor in private practice, maybe she could be persuaded to go to the emergency room, although Daisy wasn't at all sure how it actually worked when you went to the ER. The only time she had been there was when she had broken her ankle falling off her tricycle and her parents had taken care of everything. Would Evie be asked to show identification? That was what she was so afraid of, being found a fraud. . . .

Daisy rubbed her eyes and realized she felt more desperate for help than she had felt in a very, very long time. What would her father suggest she do? Suddenly, Daisy remembered something he used to say about having the courage to make an unpopular decision when your conscience told you it was the right thing to do. And what was her conscience telling her to do now?

"Thanks, Dad," Daisy whispered. There was nothing for it. She was going to have to break her promise to Evie—one of them, anyway—and turn to one of the adults in her life for help. It might mean the end of her friendship with Evie and that would be so, so sad, but Evie's life could be at stake and to save her was worth any sacrifice.

Now—to whom would she go for help? Allie. Allie was the oldest adult close to hand and she was definitely smart, but she had gone to bed early with a bad headache. Daisy supposed she could wait until morning to talk with Allie, but . . . No. She thought of the wound, so raw and puffy and hot, and knew that she had to act now. Poppy. She would have to trust in Poppy. There was a reason Oliver Higgins had chosen Poppy to be legal guardians of her two sisters. He had had faith in her.

Daisy very quietly opened the door to her room and peered down the hall. Evie's door was closed. Quickly she walked to what had once been her parents' room and knocked.

"Come in," Poppy called.

Daisy opened the door and quietly closed it behind her.

"What's up?" Poppy asked. "You look worried."

"I am worried," Daisy said. And she told Poppy that Evie was on her own and in dire need of their help. "She's got a really bad cut on the palm of her hand. It's infected Poppy, I'm sure of it."

"Wait a minute, what do you mean she's on her own?" Poppy asked, her hand over her heart. "Is she a runaway?"

"No." *Be careful, Daisy!* "Well, she *was* a runaway. After her mother died of cancer her father sent her to live with some old friend of his. The man treated her badly so she left. But she's an adult now. She's eighteen. She just doesn't have anyone to turn to but us."

"What about her father? Where's he now?"

"I don't know," Daisy admitted. "I don't know if Evie knows. He's an alcoholic. I don't think he'd be of much help even if we knew where to find him."

Evie. Good. She hadn't slipped and called her Sophie. At least she wasn't breaking every promise she had made to her friend.

Poppy frowned. "I wish you had told me this before."

"Why? Would you have refused to let Evie stay here?"

"Of course not. It's just that I would like to have known the truth. I mean, she's living under my roof, she's my guest, and that means I'm at least partly responsible for what happens to her. Never mind. What's done is done. All that matters is that we convince Evie to get medical attention."

"Well, that's kind of the problem," Daisy said. "She absolutely refuses to see a doctor. She told me once she's afraid of needles so maybe that's why. I really tried to persuade her, but I got nowhere. Do you think you could convince her to go to the ER?"

"I can try."

"Thank you, Poppy."

"Don't thank me until I succeed. If I manage to succeed."

"You will." Daisy so hoped that she was right. But she knew that by not telling Poppy about Evie's real identity, by not telling her the whole truth, she might be setting her sister up to fail. And that wouldn't solve the problem that was Evie.

Chapter 85

This was one of those parental-type challenges, Poppy thought, that she didn't feel very positive about meeting. But while she wasn't Evie's legal guardian, she was the nominal head of the house and she believed she had no choice but to intervene on Evie's behalf.

Here goes, she thought, knocking on the door of her old bedroom. Evie let her in without first asking who it was. Poppy wondered if she had guessed that Daisy would not let things drop.

"Evie," she said, "can we talk?" Ominous words, she thought. Maybe she should have started differently.

Evie nodded and sat on the edge of the bed. Poppy thought she looked very tired, even more so than she had looked at dinner an hour or two earlier. She noted that the bandage on the palm of her left hand looked fresh.

"Evie, Daisy told me that you had to leave a bad situation a while ago."

Evie wouldn't meet Poppy's eye. "She promised she wouldn't say anything."

Poppy sat next to Evie now. "Don't be angry with Daisy,

okay? She's just really worried about you. She said the cut on your hand is pretty bad. She said it's infected." Poppy smiled. "You know she wants to be a doctor someday."

Evie shrugged. "She's exaggerating how bad it is."

"Maybe. But it can't hurt to get it looked at, right? I'll take you to the ER. And I'll stay with you while they clean the wound and do whatever else it is they need to do. We'll be back home in a few hours." *Home. Not Evie's home . . .*

Evie finally looked up and gave Poppy a weak smile. "Thanks," she said. "But can it wait until morning? I'm really tired. The Clamshell was super busy and really, the cut isn't all that bad. I promise."

Poppy considered. Evie had acquiesced without any protest at all. She wondered if she should find that suspect. After all, Daisy had said Evie had flat-out refused medical attention. But maybe Evie had agreed to go to the ER because Poppy was the authority figure in the house and she respected that. And maybe her motive for agreeing to Poppy's suggestion didn't really matter. "All right," Poppy said. "I can't force you to go tonight. But first thing after breakfast tomorrow, okay?"

"Okay."

Poppy got up from the bed. "Goodnight, Evie," she said. "Sleep well."

Daisy was waiting for Poppy in the master suite. "Well?" she asked in a whisper the moment Poppy came through the door. "What did she tell you?"

"She didn't tell me anything," Poppy said, "other than she thinks you're exaggerating how badly she's hurt. But she did agree to go to the ER first thing in the morning. She says she's exhausted from work today and just wants to go to bed."

"I am so relieved, though I wish she'd agreed to go tonight. Do you think she's mad at me for telling you . . ."

"I honestly can't say," Poppy admitted. "She just seemed very tired. Anyway, you did the right thing, Daisy. Frankly, I feel awful I didn't ask her about the cut before now. I mean, I saw the bandage, but . . ."

"Don't feel bad," Daisy said quickly. "Evie doesn't call attention to herself, that's all. Look, can I go with you guys in the morning?"

"Of course. Though you'd better bring a book to read. No one gets out of the ER quickly."

"Right." Daisy moved a few steps toward the door and then turned back. "Poppy? I'm glad you sent Ian away."

"I don't want to talk about it," Poppy said. "But, I'm glad, too." That part of her life was well and truly over.

"I bet Jon's also glad."

Poppy felt herself blush. "He is."

Chapter 86

Evie peered into the dark upstairs hall. No one in either direction. She listened. No sound from the bedrooms. Now was the time. Evie left her bedroom—no, not hers, never hers—and quietly closed the door behind her. She had a headache and the wound to her left hand was throbbing. Daisy was probably right. The wound was infected.

In the hall she stopped in front of the keypad that armed and disarmed the alarm system. Poppy had given her the code without reservation, and now Evie entered it. She had no choice. The system would go off if it detected movement around any of the first floor windows or doors. She felt bad about leaving her friends unprotected for what hours remained of the night, but if she were to succeed in making her escape . . .

Evie made her way down the stairs, careful to avoid the spot on two steps she knew to be creaky, and went into the kitchen. The first thing she noticed in the pale glow of the nightlight was Grimace, perched atop the fridge, his unblinking eyes trained upon her. She wondered why he wasn't with Violet, in her room. She wondered if he had sensed her intention to run away and had been waiting here so that he could . . . What? Convince her to go back upstairs? But that was silly, Evie thought, looking away from the cat. Still, she hoped that Grimace wouldn't give her away.

Evie tore a piece of paper from the notepad by the telephone. *Thank you for everything,* she wrote with a stubby pencil by the pad's side. *Please don't try to find me. You were nicer to me than I probably deserved. It's better that I just go.* She did not sign her name. What name could she sign? Sophie was gone into the past. And Evie . . . It might be time to send her away as well.

Evie stared down at her note, her final words to the Higgins sisters. Was it *really* better that she go? A part of her wanted to stay until morning and tell Poppy and her sisters and Allie everything, the whole truth. To come clean would be such a relief! But if she did unburden her secrets, including the fact that she was only sixteen, then she would be sent back to live with her cousins, if they would have her. If only her father could help her, but she didn't even know where he was—or even if he was alive. No, Evie determined. It was no good wishing and hoping for miracles. She would go.

"Good-bye, Grimace," she whispered, looking back to where he still sat atop the fridge, staring and keeping watch. "Take care of Violet."

With careful steps Evie walked to the sunroom. She would leave the note on a table there, where it might not be found first thing in the morning. She needed as big a head start as she could get if she were to reach Portland undetected. Hopefully it would be easy to get lost in the city, to blend in with some of the other young people she had seen milling around in the parks and on the busy downtown sidewalks the day she had been there with Daisy and Joel. Hopefully it would be easy to avoid getting emotionally attached to anyone the way she had in Yorktide.

Still, the decision to start over in Portland wasn't without its worries. Where would she stay? Finding shelter in York-tide had been ridiculously easy, a real stroke of luck, and she couldn't expect to be so lucky again. If she absolutely had to she supposed she could stay in a shelter at nights for a while, though the idea frightened her. It was a good thing they existed, but she couldn't forget the television report she had seen earlier in the summer. She couldn't forget what the sixty-three-year-old woman had said, how she had woken up one night to find a man groping her. . . .

And there was the matter of getting a job. Again, she had been so lucky the day she had wandered into The Clamshell. That sort of luck wouldn't happen again, definitely not in a big city where the competition for work was more fierce, where everyone had to be more savvy and cautious than they needed to be in a small town. And like it had been with Billy, she might need to prove she had a permanent or semi-permanent address in order to be hired. And what if she couldn't get paid in cash, like Billy paid her? How could she cash a check without a bank account? And if a miracle did occur and somehow she found a decent job and a safe place to stay, what then? Well, she would scrimp and save until . . . Until what? Until trouble found her again? Until once again she was forced to flee?

Before Evie lost the last of her nerve, she opened the front door and stepped into the night.

Chapter 87

"Were you up before me this morning?" Poppy asked when Daisy came into the kitchen around eight.

Daisy shook her head. "No. Why?"

"I could have sworn I manned the alarm last night just before I went to bed. But when I got up this morning it was turned off."

"You probably just forgot."

"Maybe." Poppy poured more coffee into her favorite mug. "Have you seen Evie this morning?"

"No," Daisy said. "She's usually up by now."

"I was hoping to get to the ER before nine. Would you check on her, Daisy? She was so tired last night she's probably still asleep."

"Sure." Daisy dashed upstairs and knocked on Evie's bedroom door. When there was no answer she quietly opened the door and peered inside, hoping not to wake Evie if she was getting some much-needed rest. But Evie was not in the bed; the covers were thrown back and the pillows were crumpled. Daisy figured Evie might be in the bathroom or . . . A tiny niggling thought followed her down the hall to the bathroom. It, too, was empty.

Now the tiny niggling thought began to swell and Daisy ran back to the kitchen. "She's not in her room," she said, trying to keep the panic that was rapidly rising in her out of her voice.

"Maybe she's in the garden. It's so lovely out there in the morning."

Allie came into the kitchen then and Poppy asked her if she was feeling any better than she had the night before.

"Yes, thanks. Got my period this morning so that explains the headache. I'll have some of that coffee if you don't mind."

"Poppy—" Daisy began, but she was cut off by the appearance of Violet, whose expression was both grim and fearful. "What's wrong?" Daisy demanded.

Violet held out a folded bit of paper. "I found this in the sunroom," she said, her voice shaking. "It's a note."

Daisy's heart thudded painfully. She knew, she just knew what the note would say!

Violet handed the paper to Poppy. She read what was on it and then passed it to Daisy.

"Evie's gone," Daisy said, handing the note to Allie with a trembling hand. *And I should have known that this would happen!*

Allie shook her head. "I don't understand. Why would she have gone? She seemed so happy here. What does she mean by we treated her better than she deserved?"

Poppy hurriedly told Allie and Violet that Evie had been on her own after having run away from an abusive situation. And then, she explained about the wound. "She agreed to let me take her to the ER this morning. Why didn't I insist on going last night!"

"You couldn't have forced her," Violet said. "It's not your fault."

"If only she had come to me. . . ." Allie put her hand to her head, as if the ache had returned. "The other day . . . I thought we were establishing a bond. I might have been able to stop her from running away again. I might have gotten her to listen to reason."

Daisy clasped her hands together, in a futile effort to steady herself for what she had to do next. "There's something else," she said. "Something I haven't told you."

"Damn it, Daisy," Poppy said, "what now?"

"Evie's real name is Sophie Steuben. She's been using a false ID. That's another reason she wouldn't go to see a doctor. She was afraid of being found out somehow. I guess she was afraid of someone from her past finding her. Her father or the man who tried to hurt her."

"Who else knows this?" Allie demanded. "Does Billy Woolrich know?"

"No," Daisy said. "Only Joel. She swore us both to secrecy."

Poppy put her mug on the counter with a bang. "You should have told me about the fake ID last night, when you told me she was on her own."

"Would it have helped?" Daisy cried. "Would it really have made a difference?"

Poppy sighed. "I don't know. But I would have turned to someone for advice. Maybe Freddie. She would know more about Evie's—Sophie's—legal situation."

Allie shook her head. "If she was lying about her name, she might have been lying about other things, too."

"Her age."

Daisy turned to Violet. "What?"

"She was lying about her age," Violet explained. "She's not eighteen."

"How do you know that?" Poppy asked.

"I just do," Violet insisted. "Did anyone really *look* at her? She can't be older than Daisy."

Daisy shook her head. "But she swore to Joel and me over and over that she was legally an adult!"

"This is no time for guesswork," Poppy said. "We've got to call the police and report Evie missing."

Allie pulled her cell phone from her pocket. "I'm on it."

Daisy and her sisters listened to the call on speakerphone.

"I'd like to report a missing person," Allie said, her voice remarkably calm. "A teenage girl."

The dispatcher, a woman, asked when the girl had gone missing.

"Some time last night," Allie explained. "We found a note this morning. She left on her own, she wasn't kidnapped."

"I'm sorry," the dispatcher said, "but in Yorktide, a person is not officially considered missing until he or she has been gone for twenty-four hours."

"What!" Daisy cried.

"But we think she might be ill," Allie went on, her voice not so calm now. "And she . . . she might have a false identification with her."

"I suggest you call the area hospitals, maybe ask around the neighborhood if anyone has seen her. She might have changed her mind and be coming back. It's not unheard of. If after twenty-four hours she hasn't returned then call us again and we'll get right on it."

Daisy felt tears threaten when she heard the dispatcher's words. She looked at Violet and saw that her sister's face was ashen.

"All right," Allie said shortly. "Thanks."

"A hospital is the last place Evie would go," Daisy said when Allie had ended the call.

"Daisy, where do you think she might be headed?" Allie asked.

Daisy considered. For a long and frustrating moment her mind was a blank. And then she recalled Evie's behavior when she and Joel and Evie were in Portland that day, how she had gotten so upset about the notion of getting a tattoo. But maybe the tattoo wasn't really what had upset her. Maybe it was seeing all those sad people, kids and adults, who looked tired and hungry and knowing that someday she, too, might be in their situation. Someday soon. Forced to gather where there were services to help them find food and a place to sleep at night. Forced to form a community of sorts. And then it all clicked into place.

"Portland," Daisy said. "I think she might be heading for Portland."

"Why?" Poppy asked.

"It was just something I remembered from when Joel, Evie, and I were there."

"We'll search for her ourselves," Allie said.

"We need more people to help," Poppy said. "Daisy, you call Joel. I'll call Jon."

"Mr. Woolrich, too," Violet said. "He'll want to help. And Freddie and Sheila."

Poppy shook her head. "God, I hope she's not doing something stupid like trying to hitch a ride."

"How else can she make it north to Portland?" Daisy asked. "Assuming that's where she's headed."

"A bike?" Allie asked Daisy. "Does she have a bike?"

"No."

"Could she have taken one from the garage?"

"Doubtful," Poppy said. "Violet's would be too small for her, and both mine and hers are locked up. Combination locks, nothing that can be picked."

Allie sighed. "How far could she have gone on foot?"

"Depends on when she started out," Poppy replied. "And on if she knows exactly how to get wherever it is she's going. And if she's running a fever, which she might be if she has a bad enough infection."

"Does she have any money?" Violet asked.

"I don't know," Daisy said. "If she has any it can't be much."

"Wait a minute. There's a bus out of Yorktide isn't there? To Portland? I'll go to the bus stop, see if she shows up. I'll ask if anyone's seen her," Allie said.

"Good," Poppy said. "Daisy and Violet, start calling everyone. Don't forget Julie and Mack. I'm going to the garage. Maybe she *was* able to take one of the bikes. Maybe I'll find footsteps leading . . ."

Poppy hurried off to the garage. Violet picked up the landline and began to dial. And Daisy stood frozen. Do no harm. That was the promise a doctor made when she swore the Hippocratic Oath, that she would do no harm. What pathetic sort of doctor would Daisy Higgins make? All she had ever wanted to do was help, but in the end it looked like she had done an awful lot of harm indeed.

Chapter 88

"You never should have told anyone about her using a phony name," Joel said angrily. "You promised her!"

Joel and Jon Gascoyne had gotten to the house on Willow Way within twenty minutes of the sisters' plea. Poppy had made another pot of coffee—stronger, this time—and had offered both men something to eat. They had refused.

Daisy's eyes were red from crying. "But I—" she began.

"Neither of you should ever have made such a promise," Poppy said forcefully. "It was irresponsible."

"It didn't seem irresponsible," Daisy argued. "We thought we were helping."

"And how could we have known she was going to run off again?" Joel protested.

"Well," Jon said, "that's in the past. Now we have to find her. Look, we can't be absolutely sure Evie is heading north, can we? Poppy, you take your car and head down toward Bermondsey. Use the back roads. Drive along the beach. She's not going to be walking out on the highway. At least, I hope she isn't, the way summer people drive."

Daisy burst into tears again. "She could be anywhere,"

she cried. "She wouldn't want to be seen. She could be lost in the woods . . . Oh, God, this is all my fault!"

"Daisy," Allie said firmly, putting her arm around her shoulders, "try to stay calm. We believe you. You thought you were acting for the best."

Poppy turned to Violet, who was holding Grimace tightly to her chest, as if he were a shield. "Violet, you stay here and wait for Freddie and Sheila to arrive. Julie said that Mack will get out on the road as soon as his shift is over, and he's spread the news about Evie among the other drivers. And Mr. Woolrich said he'd delay opening The Clamshell today so he and the staff can be available if we need them. And Daisy?" Poppy looked at her sister, feeling a wave of great sympathy for her. "You'll be on foot through the fields and the wooded areas out back. Anyone who doesn't know the woods might easily get lost. Evie might still be wandering in circles."

Daisy nodded.

"I called my brother and father right before I picked up Joel," Jon told them. "They're waiting for instructions. Allie, you'll be checking the bus station and the town. Someone out early might have seen her, a farmer making deliveries to a market, someone at one of the breakfast places. With all of us mobilized . . ."

"I'm off," Allie said, hurrying out of the kitchen. Jon gave Poppy a reassuring nod and he and Joel followed Allie out to their car.

Poppy went over to Violet and kissed her forehead. "She'll be okay," she told her sister. Violet managed a small smile. Grimace managed a purr. Poppy then turned to Daisy. "Keep a clear head, all right?" And then she kissed her cheek. "This is not your fault, Daisy. It's not. This all started long before any of us met Evie. Sophie."

Daisy nodded and wiped again at her eyes.

When Poppy got out to her car the others had already gone. She slid behind the wheel and suddenly remembered the conversation she had had with Jon at The Friendly Lobsterman, the conversation about the young hitchhiker he had seen in Wells. About how it was difficult to know how to help people who were homeless. About how dangerous it could be to offer one's home to someone who needed shelter. And here, for the past weeks, Poppy had unknowingly been doing just that, sharing her family's home and resources with a homeless and possibly underage teen. *Would* she have welcomed Evie if she had known more of the truth? Would she have taken the risk? Certainly not if she had known for sure that Evie was still a child. That much was clear. She would have turned to Freddie for answers about what to do for the girl. How to get her home, if there was a home for her to go to. And if there wasn't . . .

Poppy pulled onto Shore Road and headed south toward Bermondsey.

Chapter 89

Freddie sat at the kitchen table and opened her laptop. "I'm too old to go searching for a missing child on foot," she told Violet, "but I'm not too old to go searching online or to call in some favors. And armed with the girl's real name, and the fact that she'd talked about coming from Vermont and New Hampshire, I should have some luck before long."

Violet wasn't sure she believed that, but she said nothing. Grimace, clutched in her arms, wiggled to a more comfortable position. She had been holding him tightly for almost a half hour; she didn't know how much longer his patience would last.

"And I'm not too feeble to make some phone calls," Sheila said, taking a seat across from Freddie. "There's your buddy Jim Gannon, Freddie. Didn't he use to work for the District Attorney's office in New Hampshire? Maybe he knows someone who can help us."

"Good. Call him. He knows everyone."

"I wish we knew *exactly* where Evie—Sophie—came from," Violet said suddenly, aware of the note of anxiety in her voice. "It would save us a lot of time. We can't afford to waste any time."

"Now, don't go worrying, Violet," Freddie said briskly.

Violet watched as both women began their work on Evie's—Sophie's—behalf, Freddie typing away on the keyboard and Sheila talking to Freddie's old friend. She knew that everyone would do their best to find Evie, but the thought of her out there somewhere all on her own, at the mercy of unscrupulous people, badly frightened her. And because Evie was a friend, whatever happened to her would in some way also happen to Daisy and to Poppy and even to Violet. To *everyone* in Yorktide who had formed a connection to Evie!

Suddenly, Violet realized that she felt very young and very helpless. She realized that she wanted her mother and her father more in that moment than she had at any other time since their passing. She *needed* them.

That's when it happened.

Her arms went rigid, forcing Grimace to yowl and leap to the floor. Her vision swirled as her heart rate ramped up. She felt sweat pour from her skin and at the same time she felt terribly cold. Her knees began to wobble. . . .

When Violet came to she was seated at the kitchen table, her head resting on its surface, Grimace in her lap. Sheila was kneeling by her side, her arm around Violet's shoulders. A hand—Freddie's—put a glass of water close by. "Drink this," she said. "When you're able."

"Is this the first time?" Sheila asked gently.

Slowly, Violet sat up in her seat and put her hands on Grimace's back. "No," she said in a weak voice. "It's not the first time."

"You poor child. Have you told anyone?"

"No. I thought I could handle it by myself."

"If you're all right, Violet," Freddie said, not unkindly,

"I'm going to get back to my search. Like you said, we can't afford to waste time."

"I'm fine," Violet said.

With a loud groan Sheila got to her feet and sat next to Violet at the table. "Kneeling," she said, "is not advisable after the age of fifty."

Violet managed a smile. "I'm sorry I've been so much trouble."

Sheila pushed the glass of water toward Violet. "No trouble at all. *I'm* sorry I didn't realize you were experiencing . . . What is it, exactly, that you've been experiencing, Violet?"

"Fear," she said promptly.

"Of what?"

"Of losing the rest of my family. Of losing Grimace and my home."

Sheila sighed. "You poor, poor girl. I do see why you would be afraid after all you've been through. But I do wish you had come to me or gone to Poppy. Will you promise that from now on you'll be open about your feelings with those of us who love you?"

As if urging Violet to say yes to Sheila's request, Grimace got to his feet on Violet's lap and tapped her face with one massive paw. "I promise," Violet said. "I'll really try."

"Bingo. Maybe."

"What is it?" Sheila asked.

"Looks like I might have found something," Freddie reported. "An e-mail back from someone I know—don't ask how—in the Vermont state police. A Joanne and Ron Shettleworth filed a missing persons report when their niece—one Sophie Steuben, age sixteen—ran off a few months ago."

"How exactly are these people related?" Sheila asked. "Are they really blood relatives?"

"Yes. The uncle, Ron, was brother to Sophie's mother, Evelyn. At least, that's what they told the police."

Before they could absorb this latest information, Sheila's cell phone rang.

Violet listened to Sheila's side of the conversation, which consisted only of remarks on the nature of "oh," and "I see." Finally, she thanked the caller. "That was Jim Gannon," she told Freddie and Violet when the call was ended.

"That was fast. You called him less than an hour ago."

"Be that as it may, he informed me that a man named Daniel Steuben was taken in for vagrancy about six or seven months ago, but was never charged. Seems the decision maker at the police station recognized him—there had been some crossing of professional paths at one time—and knew his story—a car accident that killed his wife—"

"A car accident?" Freddie frowned. "That's news to me."

"And then a slide into an addiction to painkillers, which resulted in him losing his job, his house, and his daughter."

"Poor man," Violet murmured.

"Yes. Good man, bad luck. Anyway," Sheila went on, "he was let go with a warning and some kind advice. Since then Mr. Steuben seems to have gotten his life somewhat back on track. He's living in a furnished room in a town just outside of Portsmouth and has a job. Jim will e-mail you the address, Freddie, and the phone number of the landlady."

Freddie nodded. "I think," she said, "that we found Sophie's family."

"Now," Sheila said quietly, "all we need to do is find Sophie."

Violet leaned down and rested her head against Grimace's.

Chapter 90

"Evie! Can you hear me? It's Daisy! Evie!"

She was getting hoarse from shouting but shout on she would. Since Daisy had left the house in search of her friend almost two hours earlier she had replayed every conversation she had ever had with Evie—well, those she could remember—searching her memory for something she had missed, some clue that might have told her that Evie was not really eighteen, that maybe the story Evie had told about her mother's death from cancer and her father's alcoholism wasn't entirely true. But she kept coming up blank. She *should* have realized that something was wrong, that Evie was hiding something more about her past, but she hadn't, though Poppy, Allie, and Violet had all been smart enough to suspect.

Daisy had already walked the fields surrounding the house, scanning the horizon for a telltale pink spot that might be a hoodie, even peering through the dirty windows of the old, unused storage shed that had been there forever and that no one claimed or bothered to tear down. But Evie was nowhere to be found. Now she turned her attention to searching the heavily wooded area that extended for about three miles south and west. She was thankful it wasn't hunting season as she was wearing an old olive-colored shirt and dark jeans, nothing to distinguish her from the natural world of tree trunks and crumbling stone walls and moss-covered boulders. And here under the thick canopy of leaves the light was never really bright and often played tricks with your eyes.

"Evie!" Daisy listened as carefully as she ever had listened in her life. But she heard nothing but the chirping of birds and the noise her own feet made as she stepped on broken twigs.

It was true that Daisy felt plagued by self-recrimination, but if she were honest with herself—and why wouldn't she be now?—she also felt a bit angry with Evie. Evie hadn't trusted in their friendship; she had chosen to turn her back on the relationship they had been building. Evie might have needed Daisy in all sorts of ways, but Daisy had needed Evie, too. *I still need her,* she thought now. *And she's gone.*

Eyes darting from side to side, Daisy walked on, hoping for some evidence that Evie had come this way. She was deep in the woods now where the leaves were still wet with dew and the rain that had fallen for a while the night before. Daisy brushed away a low-hanging branch and was showered with water, cold without the influence of the sun. She was sure she looked every bit as bedraggled as she felt inside.

"Evie! Don't be afraid! Everything's going to be okay! Evie, are you there?"

Nothing.

About that self-recrimination . . . Daisy couldn't help but wonder what her sisters, and Allie and Joel and Jon, would think of her if Evie was found hurt—or worse. She didn't see how she would be able to go on with her life while facing the condemnation of the people she loved. She knew that she shouldn't be focused on her own selfish concerns, not when Evie's survival was at stake, but she was only human, only a stupid, misguided kid! She had a good excuse for being weak and scared and . . .

"Ooof!" Daisy landed heavily on her knees and the palms of her hands. "Stupid tree root!" she muttered, climbing awkwardly to her feet. Tears of frustration spilled from her eyes and hastily she wiped them away, realizing only after that she had probably smeared her face with soil and bits of last year's fallen leaves.

Focus, Daisy, she told herself. Again she called out Evie's name as loud as she could and then waited, still and silent, for a response. Again, nothing.

And she walked on, hoping beyond hope that she would come across her friend, while absolutely dreading what she might find. There was a stream a few hundred yards ahead. If Evie had tried to cross it in the dark, she might have slipped on the wet rocks, fallen and twisted an ankle or hit her head and been knocked unconscious. She might have drowned. And if she *had* been able to cry out for help before losing consciousness, who would have heard her? Only the bears. There were bears in these parts.

"Aaaaahhh!"

Daisy jumped and whirled in the direction from which she thought the terrifying sound had come. "Evie!" she called. No reply. And then, as if hearing the noise in retrospect, she realized that it had been the voice of a fox, a vixen's scream, not the cry of a desperately wounded woman seeking help. She had heard the sound many times before. She should have known.

Daisy's frustration was mounting. She hoped that Allie was having better luck at the bus station or in town, or that Jon and Joel, who were heading north, had come across Evie along the road, or that Poppy, going south toward Bermondsey, would stumble across someone who had seen a brown-haired teenage girl with a backpack and a pink hoodie. And Freddie was super smart and she knew so many people in high places. . . . Daisy hoped that Freddie, at least, had located Evie's father or someone who might know more about her. . . .

But hope alone wasn't going to get results. With grim determination Daisy walked on in the direction of the stream.

Chapter 91

Poppy pulled into the parking lot of a strip mall to gather her thoughts and review her progress—rather, the lack thereof—she had made so far. She had taken Route 1 as far as Bermondsey and then farther south to the next town of Foreston. She had tried to get a look in every car she passed or that passed her, wondering if she might see Evie in the passenger seat. She had gone into every gas station she came upon and asked if anyone had seen a girl about sixteen to eighteen years old, alone and on foot. She wished she had a picture to show, but a verbal description was all she could provide and not an entirely accurate one at that. Daisy had told her that Evie's wardrobe was severely limited but that didn't mean they knew exactly what she had been wearing when she left the house in the middle of the night. All they knew for sure was that she had taken her backpack.

At one point Poppy had parked in a ridiculously expensive lot and gone down to the beach on foot. Evie might have gone there to rest, assuming she had made it this far. Assuming she was heading south. Assuming she hadn't already gotten into bad trouble.

But she had seen no one even remotely fitting Evie's description. And she was beginning to despair, and not just about the runaway girl. For the past few hours, since the search party had mobilized, Poppy had been worried about her sisters almost as much as she had been worried about Evie. She had seen the look on Violet's face, the way she was clutching poor Grimace as if he were a lifeline.

And Daisy. If anything bad happened to Evie, Daisy would further blame herself. Poppy looked at her watch— her father's watch—and thought about taking a minute to call her sisters. But time was wasting and she didn't want to tie up the lines of communication. Besides, Freddie and Sheila were at the house and would be of some comfort to the girls. *I am a lioness with her cubs,* she thought. She had never dreamed she would come to feel so fiercely protective over Daisy and Violet in such a short period of time.

But what to do next for Evie . . . Suddenly, Poppy's cell phone rang. She reached for it on the passenger seat, but in her agitation she dropped the phone on the floor of the car where it slid half under the seat. "Damn!" she cried, scrabbling for it as it continued to ring. "Sorry, hello?" she said, finally bringing the phone to her ear.

"We got her," Jon said without preamble. "Daisy was right, she was heading north. We called 911 immediately and I'm pulling up to the hospital now behind the ambulance."

"Is she . . ."

"She's alive, Poppy. She's got a fever though. I'm no doctor, but I think it's pretty bad."

"I'm on my way."

Poppy ended the call and rested her head on the steering wheel. The sense of relief made her feel slightly dizzy. And then she remembered how she had been too late for her mother's final moment. She lifted her head, took a deep breath, and started the engine.

"Please, God, let her be all right," she prayed aloud as she drove out of the parking lot. And though Poppy didn't make it a practice to talk on her cell phone while driving, in this moment she made an exception.

Daisy answered on the first ring.

"They found her, Jon and Joel," Poppy said. "Tell everyone there. I'm going to the hospital."

"I'll get someone to take me there."

"No. Go home and stay there. Violet might need you."

"But—"

"No buts, Daisy. I need you to go home."

"Okay. But call me from the hospital. Please?"

Poppy heard the strain in her sister's voice. "I promise," she said. "The moment I learn anything you'll be the first to know."

Chapter 92

She wondered where she was. A room of some sort, she thought. She was definitely indoors. She wondered if she were dead. But dead people didn't think, did they? Because she was pretty sure she was thinking. Sort of. Or dreaming. Or maybe you could think and dream when you were dead. Who would know the answer to that?

There was a girl. She was closing the front door of a big house behind her. It was dark.

Was it a memory?

She became aware that two large round yellow eyes were staring at her. She tried to look away from the penetrating gaze of those eyes—unattached to a face of any sort—but she couldn't seem to turn her head. She thought that her own eyes must be open because she saw those other eyes so she tried now to close them, but they seemed to already be closed. The large round yellow eyes began to fade and then they were gone.

Now there was a sound . . . A tinkling sort of melody. It stopped abruptly. And then there was a voice.

"Where do they live? Okay. And her father? Good. Let

me know how the search goes. Yes. She looks so frail. . . . It's breaking my heart to see her like this."

Her father. Was someone searching for her father? Or was it someone else's father who had gone missing?

"Daddy?" She wasn't sure she had said the word or had only thought it.

Someone came close to her. She couldn't see the person clearly, but she felt the person take her hand.

"Evie, it's Poppy, Daisy's sister. Did you say something?"

"Daddy? Are you there? Are you there!" She was sure now that she had spoken those words aloud. But no one was answering her! No one . . .

Chapter 93

"I just talked to Freddie," Allie announced, coming into the kitchen where Daisy and Poppy were picking away at a crumb cake from their favorite bakery. Some people couldn't eat when they were upset. Not the Higgins sisters.

"And?" Poppy asked.

"And she's been in touch with Sophie's father. Dan Steuben. He's been living and working in New Hampshire for the past few months."

"What a relief," Poppy said.

Maybe, Daisy thought.

"I'll be going down to pick him up. Billy offered to come with me. He pointed out that Sophie's dad might be a fine man, but with all he's been through he might not be entirely stable."

"And you said?" Poppy asked, wiping powdered sugar from her hands.

"I said I'd appreciate the company. We'll leave tomorrow morning and bring him back with us by afternoon."

"Assuming he wants to see his daughter," Daisy pointed out.

"According to Freddie," Allie said, "he does, very much. Ever since Sophie went missing he's been calling his brother and sister-in-law daily, hoping for word."

"Good," Daisy said. A father should be concerned about the daughter he had effectively abandoned. "Still, I wonder how Evie—Sophie—will feel about seeing her father again. I've never heard her say a nice word about him."

"Well, she asked for him when I was with her in the hospital yesterday," Poppy said. "At least, she called for him. She said, 'Daddy, are you there?'"

"You said she was in and out of consciousness. She probably doesn't even remember calling for him."

"Why are you so opposed to this reunion, Daisy?" Poppy asked.

"Because of everything Evie—sorry, Sophie—told me about her father."

"Daisy," Allie said gently. "Sophie was lying to us about a lot of things."

That was true. "Still," she said, "maybe we should wait until Mr. Steuben's actually in Yorktide before we tell her. What if Allie shows up at his door and he's run off? Evie—Sophie—will be devastated all over again. She's already been through so much."

"I totally understand your feelings on this, Daisy," Allie said, "I do, but I think we have to trust in what Dan's brother and sister-in-law told Freddie. According to Joanne Shettleworth Dan rarely drank and was most certainly never an alcoholic, either before or after the accident. And according to Ron, Dan was a wonderful husband and father. They both suspect that Sophie needed to blame Dan for everything bad that happened because she couldn't accept that her life had been so dramatically disrupted. By the way, she was never sent to live with one of Dan's old friends. That was another lie."

Daisy sighed. "Okay, fine. We'll believe in the Shettleworths' version of Evie's father and hope for the best. Darn! I mean, Sophie. When am I going to get that straight!"

"And maybe you, Daisy, being her friend, should be the one to tell her that he's coming to see her. If it wouldn't make you too uncomfortable," Poppy added.

I deserve to be made uncomfortable, Daisy thought. By keeping Sophie's secrets she had endangered her friend's life. "No, I'll tell her," she said. "When we visit her this afternoon."

"Where will Dan stay when he's in Yorktide?" Poppy asked Allie.

"Billy's taken care of that, too. Dan will stay with him." Allie smiled. "He didn't think it was the best idea for a strange man to be staying in a house full of women."

"Billy should have known about Ian . . ." Daisy muttered.

The doorbell rang then and Poppy went to answer it. A moment later she returned with the infamous Nico.

Speaking of strange men, Daisy thought, hiding a smile.

But Nico was all humility. "Sorry for just stopping by like this," he said. "But I had to apologize in person. Well, sort of in person; I don't think I'd be allowed to see Evie in the hospital, but you can apologize to her for me. Anyway, I feel like a certified heel. I never would have told Evie to leave if I'd known she had no money and nowhere to go. The idea that she was essentially homeless never even occurred to me!"

In spite of her prejudiced opinion of Nico as a heartless poseur, Daisy believed he was telling the truth.

"Well, it's over now," Poppy said. "She's safe."

"What can I do to help?" Nico asked.

"Befriend Sophie—that's her real name—and her father if they decide to stay in Yorktide," Allie said. "Maybe help them to find jobs or a place to live."

Nico nodded. "All right. I'll see what I can come up with. Call me when you know more." With that he was gone.

"So that was Nico." Allie shook her head. "Somehow I pictured him with a swirling mustache and a black cape. A cartoon villain."

"By the way," Daisy said, "I asked Billy how he had arranged for Evie to stay at Nico's. He told me that back when Nico was just starting out as a working artist, Billy's wife loaned him money for food and rent. They both knew he was on his way to some fame. And they agreed that they'd give him two years to repay them back. Long story short, it's been ten years and Billy hasn't seen a penny of the money. He figured Nico owed him."

"Reciprocity makes the world go round," Poppy said. "That's something Mom used to say. We really do owe each other kindness in return for kindness."

"For some reason that makes me think of Violet. Probably because she's so kind. How is she today?" Allie asked.

"All right," Daisy said. "She's in her room with the ever-vigilant Grimace."

Poppy shook her head. "I feel as bad about my neglect of Violet as Nico feels about throwing Sophie out of his house. It simply never occurred to me that Violet was in trouble. She always seemed so self-possessed. The poor thing. Having panic attacks and hiding the fact from me."

"From all of us," Allie pointed out. "None of us saw what was going on."

"I hope she forgives us for not helping her sooner." Daisy frowned. "I was so wrapped up in myself and then with Sophie. Hey, I got it right."

"I'm the one who's really responsible," Poppy pointed out. "I'm her legal guardian. I'm her surrogate parent."

"Don't beat yourself up, Poppy," Allie said. "It's hard to help someone who isn't crying out for help, either directly or indirectly. Violet didn't want us to see her fears so we didn't. She's got a powerful will, our Violet."

"You're talking about me."

Daisy, Poppy, and Allie turned to see Violet standing in the doorway, Grimace draped across her arms.

"We were saying how much we love you," Daisy told her younger sister.

Violet smiled. "Thanks. I love you guys, too. Can I have a piece of that cake?"

Chapter 94

It was Daisy who had told Sophie that her father was coming to see her. Her first reaction had been to reject the notion of his visit. Daisy hadn't asked why; she had held tightly to her hand and waited. And then, almost immediately, Sophie had found herself saying, "All right. I'm glad he's coming." Daisy still had said nothing, but had sat with her for a while until a nurse had come in and suggested Sophie be left alone to get some rest.

That morning Sophie had woken with a strong sense of urgency. She couldn't bear for her father to see her looking sick or unkempt, no matter how low he himself might have fallen. She realized that she still wanted him to feel proud of her. So she had asked the nurse on duty if she could take a shower and wash her hair. The nurse had stood just outside the shower stall in case Sophie began to feel weak or dizzy, or in case she needed help as her left hand, bandaged and protected by a plastic bag, was pretty much useless. Unfortunately, she wasn't allowed to wear her own clothes, but the nurse had given her a fresh johnny and had somehow come up with a pretty blue cardigan for her to wear over her shoul-

ders for the length of Dan Steuben's visit. Seeing that Sophie was exhausted by her efforts, the nurse had also offered
to dry and comb her hair. Her kindly attentions brought tears
of gratitude to Sophie's eyes.

Now she sat up against the pillows of her hospital bed,
Ben at her side, and waited for the arrival of the man she had
tried for so long to utterly reject.

At exactly two forty-five there was a knock on the door
of her room. Sophie opened her mouth, but for a moment no
words came out. And then she was able, in a small voice, to
say, "Come in."

The door opened slowly and there was her father. Dan
Steuben. He closed the door behind him and stood, hands at
his side. He was wearing a plaid shirt Sophie vaguely remembered. He looked thin but better—healthier—than he
had when she had last seen him all those months ago. Or
was that wishful thinking?

"Hi," Sophie said.

Her father smiled. "Hi, Sophie."

His voice. So well remembered! And the way his hair
curled a bit around his ears. And his eyes, so like hers. *This
is my father,* Sophie thought. *Mine.*

"How did you get here?" she asked. "To Maine." Daisy
might have told her this, but her short-term memory didn't
seem to be working so well these past few days.

"Your friends Allie and Billy drove to New Hampshire to
pick me up," her father explained. "I've been living just outside of Portsmouth. I got a job at a dry cleaners a few months
back. It's not much, but it's helping me get back to . . . To
life."

"Oh," Sophie said. "I mean, that's good. Allie and Billy . . .
They're really nice. I like them."

"And they like you. Billy said you're the granddaughter
he never had."

"Where's your cane?" she asked.

"I don't need it all the time now."

"Still, maybe you should sit down."

With a slight limp, Dan walked over to the large gray guest chair by his daughter's bed and sat. "How do you feel, Sophie?" he asked. "I heard you've been through quite an ordeal these last few days."

"I feel okay," she said. "Weak. A bit confused."

"I'm not surprised. But the doctor said you're going to be fine. They'll keep you on antibiotics for a while though, just to be safe."

Sophie nodded. "Dad? Are you . . ." She turned her head away. She was so scared of what his answer might be. She was so afraid that he would lie to her.

"No, Sophie," he said, his tone firm. "I'm not taking the pills anymore. I haven't been for the past five months. Some days are difficult—the pins the doctors put in hurt . . . But I'm done with the drugs for good. I promise. I'm . . . I'm in a better place, especially now that I know you're okay."

Sophie turned back to him. "Okay," she said. She believed her father. She had to believe him.

Her father reached out then and touched her right hand where it lay against the white sheets. After a moment, Sophie took his hand in hers.

"Your wedding ring," she said, feeling the smooth metal beneath her fingers. Billy Woolrich, she remembered, still wore his, too.

"I've never taken it off."

Sophie thought of what her cousin, Alexa, had told her about her father. That he was at times homeless. She would ask him about that, but not yet. "But you could have sold the ring," she said. "It could have bought you food or . . ." Or a hotel room where he could have stayed for a few nights.

"No," her father said firmly. "I couldn't have. Better to

go hungry than let this bit of her go. This bit of *us*. I loved her, Sophie. I'd give anything to trade places with her. If only it had been me who had died. Then you'd still have your mother. She was so strong. Stronger than me." Dan smiled. "She used to say that I was the romantic in the family and that she was the one with the practical head."

Sophie felt tears come to her eyes. Her poor father. And to think she had been so angry at him for being sick and depressed that she had thrown out the photo from her mother's locket! She would never tell him what she had done and she would replace the photo as soon as she could.

"Oh, Dad," she said. "I wish you wouldn't feel that way. It wasn't your fault, any of it. I'm sorry I couldn't—no, I'm sorry that I *wouldn't* believe that."

Her father leaned in toward her and looked intently into her eyes. "You were hurt, Sophie. Devastated. No one could expect you to just accept what had happened. It was perfectly normal for you to need to affix blame somewhere. And I was the obvious choice."

"But I shouldn't have tried to *punish* you. I should have seen that you were hurting and helped you. I'm so sorry that I let you down."

"It's me who let you down, Sophie. I did try, honestly I did, but . . . I failed." Dan Steuben put his other hand over Sophie's. "But now," he said, "it's all right. Everything is going to be all right. Even Ben thinks so. Right, Ben?"

Sophie smiled. "I know I have to apologize to Aunt Joanne and Uncle Ron. When I . . . When I left, I guess I really wasn't able to understand the trouble I was causing them. I was just so miserable. I wasn't thinking right. I hope they can forgive me."

"I'm sure they can," her father assured her. "I'm sure they already have. They've been beside themselves worrying about you. They thought that maybe it was something they said or did that made you run away."

"No. They were nice to me. It wasn't that."

"Well, that's all in the past now, Sophie. We have our entire future ahead of us."

"That's kind of scary."

"Yes," her father said. He leaned closer and gently kissed his daughter's cheek. "But it's also kind of wonderful."

Chapter 95

"So she was never in foster care, like she first told you," Joel said. "And she wasn't almost raped by some friend of her father's she was staying with. And thank God for that! There was no friend in the first place. And she's not eighteen. She's only sixteen. Violet was right about that."

Daisy and Joel were in the sunroom at the house on Willow Way, trying to make sense of all that had happened since they had befriended a girl named Evie Jones.

"And her father isn't an alcoholic," Daisy added. "He got addicted to pain meds after the accident and all the operations on his legs. And her mother never had cancer."

"How did she keep it all straight? All the different stories."

"I don't know. I keep thinking that if I had paid closer attention to what she was telling us I might have seen the truth under all the lies."

"But how? No, don't blame yourself, Daisy. Look, I'm sorry I was so angry with you for telling Poppy that Evie—I mean, Sophie—was using a phony ID. I realize now it was the right thing to do."

"It's okay," Daisy assured him. "I was angry with myself, too, for a whole lot of things. I still kind of am."

"You know," Joel said after a moment. "She really did put us in a bad position. I know she didn't mean to, but when you lie to someone like she did you make that other person complicit. Responsible somehow. I'd never tell Evie—Sophie—but I have kind of a bad feeling about it all. I'm not mad at her, exactly. But . . . I feel like I was used, even though I know she meant no harm."

"I know," Daisy said. "I feel exactly the same way. I still want to be her friend, but I think we might have to start, well, not from the beginning, but almost."

"The thing is we have to give her time to learn how to be honest again. She's been so in the habit of lying to protect herself. Behavioral change usually doesn't happen overnight."

Daisy laughed. "And I'm not the most patient person, I know. But I'll give her all the time she needs."

Joel shook his head. "You should have seen her when we found her, Daisy. I swear I thought she was dying right then. She was raving, literally raving. I was terrified. It was like something out of a gloomy old Victorian novel. You forget sometimes that life is so fragile. That even now, even in the twenty-first century, people can die of something as simple as an infection."

"Infections are never simple, Joel. But I know what you mean. We take so much for granted. I guess I learned that from Evie. I mean, Sophie. She has so little and I have so much. Even a stupid pair of hand-me-down sunglasses was a big deal for her."

"Do you think she'll be all right?" Joel said. "I mean, you met Mr. Steuben at the hospital. Do you think he'll ever be healthy enough to—well, to be a father again for Sophie?"

"I don't know," Daisy said honestly. "He seems nice. And

it's clear he loves his daughter. But if for some reason he can't be there for Sophie, now that she's got us all in her life I don't think she'll ever be alone again the way she was. We won't let her be."

"I hope you're right." Joel scooted forward in his chair and rested his elbows on his knees. "Daisy, can I tell you something that has nothing to do with Evie? I mean, Sophie. Wow, that's driving me nuts."

"Of course," Daisy said, thinking she had never seen Joel look—look sheepish before. "You can tell me anything."

"Well, the thing is, I kind of met someone."

Curiosity struggled with heartbreak, but curiosity won for the moment. "Where?" she demanded. "Who is he? Do I know him?"

"I don't think you know him. His name is Kevin and he's eighteen and he lives in Wells and he works in the kitchen at that new French bistro in Ogunquit. He's saving up to go to culinary school next year."

"But how did you meet him?" Daisy pressed.

"It was his one afternoon off a week and he was heading to the beach along the path at The Starfish and I was just coming off a shift and . . . And I said hi. And he said hi back. And then, I don't know, we just started to talk."

"And who asked who out?"

Joel laughed. "I can't even remember. I was so beyond nervous. But we're getting together on his next afternoon off."

Curiosity sated, heartache took over and Daisy had to sternly remind herself that her love for Joel would give her the strength to be happy for him even if they were to grow apart. "When do I get to meet him?" she asked. "Kevin."

"We haven't even gone out yet!" Joel protested.

"Well, if it turns out you two really like each other I want to meet him immediately. I want to make sure he's worthy of you. Just . . ."

"Just what?"

Daisy bit her lip, an old habit she thought she had completely abandoned. "It's silly, but . . . Just promise me you won't totally forget me."

Joel jumped up from his chair and captured Daisy in a tight hug. "It *is* silly because you're my best friend. But I promise. And you had better not totally forget me when some Romeo comes along!"

Chapter 96

"It's hard for me to remember to call you Sophie," Daisy admitted. "I still say Evie sometimes when I talk about you with my sisters or with Joel."

Sophie smiled. "That's okay. Evie—Evelyn—was my mom's name. But I do think I should go back to being me."

"That sounds like a very good idea."

Sophie had been released from the hospital a few days earlier and after having collected her things from the Higgins house, she had moved in to Billy Woolrich's house, where she had what had once been Susan Woolrich's sewing room all to herself. It was what she wanted, she told Daisy and the others. To be under the same roof as her father. At the moment, however, she and Daisy were sitting at the table by what Sophie had come to think of "Violet's Secret Garden."

"I'm sorry I lied to you, Daisy," she said, reaching for her glass of iced tea. "I hated doing it, really, but especially after you found out about my real name I didn't know what else I could do. I was so afraid. I was always so afraid."

"It must have been horrible, feeling so alone."

"It was. And it was my own fault. It was stupid of me to run away from my aunt and uncle's home. So many terrible things could have happened to me. They almost did."

"You weren't thinking clearly," Daisy said soothingly. "That's all."

Sophie smiled a bit. "Am I thinking clearly now?"

"I don't know. What do you want to happen next?"

"I want to be with my dad. Not just at Billy's house but after, in our own home someday."

"Are you sure?"

"Yes," Sophie said firmly. "And not because if I say that I don't want to be with him I'll have to go back to my aunt and uncle's house. I want to be with my dad because . . ." The words caught in her throat. "Because I love him."

"I know," Daisy said. "I can tell."

Sophie wiped tears from her eyes. "I missed him so much. Even when I was telling myself I hated him for what had happened to my family, deep down I knew that I didn't hate him. I *couldn't* hate him, though I tried awfully hard to. Remember that picture of my family you and Joel found? Well, I still have it. I know I said I'd throw it out, but it's the only picture of my father I have and in the end I just couldn't bear to let it go."

"I'm glad you kept the picture. Look, maybe I shouldn't ask this, but . . . does your dad have any money at all?"

"I didn't think so," Sophie admitted, "but Dad told me that back when he got in trouble—back when he was suspended—the other partners in his law firm were really supportive—I mean, they'd all been together for years—so when they bought him out they offered to hold his share in the firm in trust for the day when he would be back on his feet. They believed in him, Daisy. Even when I had no faith in him at all they knew he would recover. And Dad accepted their offer. He also must have had some hope for the future. A future with me."

"Wow. That's amazing. So now what happens?"

"Dad and Freddie have been in touch with his former partners. Someday soon, maybe six months or so from now, if Dad continues to stay off the drugs and prove that he's responsible and all, he can be reinstated to the bar and he'll get control of his money."

"You're lucky to have this second chance with him."

"Oh, Daisy. I'm so sorry that you can't have a second chance with your father."

"Yeah. Me, too." Daisy sighed. "But you know what? It was really great when he was here, and that's what I have to focus on."

"It's not easy though, is it?" Sophie thought of her mother. Memories were *not* enough of a person to possess, but if they were all that you were allowed, well, you just had to make do.

"No," Daisy agreed. "It's not easy. So, do you think you and your dad will stick around in Yorktide for long?"

Sophie laughed. "I'm not sure we have a choice! Freddie's already offered my dad a job in her office and Allie contacted the high school for information about how I can register and Billy's acting like he really *is* my grandfather! Last night he asked if I wanted a cup of warm milk to help me sleep!"

"That's fantastic! Not the warm milk part, that sounds kind of gross. But about your staying on in Yorktide. Hey, maybe we'll be in some of the same classes. And Joel and I can introduce you around."

"That would be great. When I started over at my cousins' school, well, neither of them really wanted me around so . . . I can't really blame them. We were pretty much strangers all of our lives and then suddenly, there I was, living just down the hall."

"Well, you're not a stranger *here*," Daisy said firmly. "And guess what? I can't believe I haven't told you this yet. Joel met someone!"

"No! What's he like? Is he as fabulous as Joel?"

"I have no idea. I haven't met him yet. But I keep telling myself that Joel has good taste in people—I mean, he's my friend and yours!—so how bad could this guy be?"

"You'll miss him," Sophie said gently. "I mean, when he's spending time with this guy."

"Yeah. But everything changes. And sometimes things work out okay in the end."

Sophie reached across the table and put her hand on Daisy's arm. "A lot of times."

Chapter 97

Poppy had been in bed for almost two hours, but no matter how tired she felt—and she felt very tired—sleep would not come. The fact was she was too keyed up. So much had happened in the past week or so and there was so much to process, from Evie's transformation to Sophie and the uncovering of what had really happened to the Steuben family, to Poppy's new relationship with Jon Gascoyne.

But at that moment, the Steuben family and their predicament was uppermost in Poppy's mind. She was deeply touched by how so many members of the community, including Jon's parents, Albert and Matilda Gascoyne, and Nico (whose real name, Poppy had learned from Freddie, was Thomas Nicholas Brown), had come forward to help Dan and Sophie Steuben, virtual strangers, get their lives back on track. It seemed that putting a face to the *fact* of homelessness galvanized people into action. *Not in my backyard. . . .* That awful mindset! Well, sometimes unpleasant or frightening things *were* in your backyard and you had no choice but to acknowledge them and if at all possible, to eradicate them or, at the very least, to render them neutral.

And poor Violet, Poppy thought, shifting under the light-weight blanket. She had gotten the first panic attack after reading an article about homelessness and fearing that it might happen to her, too. As they all had learned over the past days, losing one's home was something that happened not only to lazy or criminal people but also to good, hard-working families. Anyone could meet with a tragedy. Anyone could experience a run of bad luck. Anyone.

And then it came to Poppy, like the proverbial lightbulb switching on in her head. Why not create a charity to raise money for homeless families in Maine? True, she had no idea where to begin such a venture, but there were people who *did* know and she would find them and go to them for guidance.

Why not?

This is my life, she thought, her excitement building. She had found her path and her purpose and who knew where it would lead? Poppy smiled into the dark and remembered that earlier in the summer she had told her sisters and Allie that the catalyst for a significant change in her life hadn't yet made itself known. Allie had then suggested that maybe the catalyst was already there and Poppy just hadn't recognized it for what it was. And in fact, Evie—rather, Sophie Steuben—had been that catalyst all along. Sophie and her father and what so tragically had happened to their family.

Poppy sat up, turned on the lamp on the bedside table, and reached for the pad and pen she kept in the drawer. There was so much to do! Step one: She would have to educate herself on the existing situation of the homeless in Maine, learn what laws and agencies and services were already in place. She would have to get to know the various Maine communities—her own town of Yorktide for starters (she remembered Freddie mentioning a food bank in Yorktide and one in nearby Oceanside; she would visit both), the community of the state, the community of homeless families—before she could take her proper place and make a change for the better. She would volunteer at a shelter. She would talk to people, listen to their stories. She would start to make a difference.

Poppy felt elated and realized that she had never experienced quite the sensation of—of *rightness*—she was experiencing at that moment.

The life-changing decision needed to be shared. And first thing in the morning, she would share it with Jon.

"Where is everyone?" Jon asked, running a finger along a shelf of books in the sunroom.

"Allie took Daisy and Violet and Sophie to the outlets in Kittery," Poppy told him. "Sophie needs a lot of essentials for school, clothes and the like."

"Ah. Brave woman. Three teenage girls let loose in a mall!"

Poppy laughed. "You know, it's rare I'm ever alone in this house. It's . . . It's far too big for just one or two people. It's meant to be filled with voices."

"So, what did you want to tell me?" Jon asked, going to sit in one of the comfortable armchairs. "You sounded pretty excited when you called."

"I am excited!" And Poppy, taking the chair next to his, told Jon about the decision she had made late the night before. "Well," she said when she had finished, "what do you think? Am I crazy? Am I getting in over my head?"

Jon smiled. "I think that no, you're not crazy and that if you go about things in an organized way you won't get in over your head. And I think that setting up a charity to help homeless families is a wonderful thing to be doing and I'll help in any way I can. Honestly, Poppy, I can't get the image of that young hitchhiker out of my head. The boy I told you about that day we had lunch at my dad's. Maybe my helping with your organization will allow me in some way to atone for not trying to help him. For just letting him stand there on the side of the road, all alone."

"Thank you, Jon. But you're already so busy with your family's businesses . . ."

"Not too busy to be there for the woman I love."

"The woman . . ." Poppy couldn't go on.

Jon got up, took Poppy's hands, and raised her to her feet. "I love you, Poppy. I wanted to say it long before now, but maybe even now is too soon. Is it?"

"No," Poppy said. "No, it's not too soon. It's perfect timing. Before now, I wouldn't have been able to . . . to appreciate those words. I wouldn't have felt worthy of them. But now . . . I think that maybe I can be."

Jon drew her toward him. "It's I who have to be worthy of you." And then he kissed her. This time, in the privacy of the sunroom, the kiss was both sweet and passionate, both gentle and urgent.

When it was over, Poppy rested her head on Jon's shoulder and he held her tightly. "It's true," she whispered, "life in Maine really *is* the way it should be."

Chapter 98

Poppy was in the kitchen making a big pot of ratatouille for dinner. Not only was it an easy dish, it made good use of local, seasonal ingredients, and somehow, it tasted even better on the second and third day. In the past weeks she had come to really enjoy cooking, not that she was under any illusions about her skill level. But so far she hadn't poisoned anyone and lately she had been getting more compliments than complaints. The zucchini and tomatoes from her favorite farm stand were washed. She would serve corn on the cob as well, another summer no-brainer. And of course there would have to be bread. Poppy smiled to herself. She and her sisters were fiends for carbs.

Why the thought of bread should make her think of Sophie, Poppy didn't know, unless it was the fact that while Sophie had been staying with them she had tucked into each meal Poppy and Allie served as if it were her last. Well, Poppy thought, the poor thing was probably afraid that the meal might indeed be her last, at least, the last eaten in a clean and secure place.

A few weeks had passed now since Sophie and her father

had been reunited under Billy Woolrich's roof. Poppy and her sisters had helped furnish Sophie's room there with a few items from the house on Willow Way, including a desk, chair, and table lamp. Freddie and Sheila had bought Sophie a laptop, essential for schoolwork. Allie had contributed a fancifully framed wall mirror Sophie had picked out at Home Goods as well as a beautiful handcrafted wooden jewelry box where Sophie could keep the precious items she would certainly accumulate over time. There were instances, Poppy well knew, when decorations and trimmings could be considered essentials for comfort and happiness, and this was one of them. Sophie had been without her own possessions for too long.

Others had helped get the Steubens settled, too. Freddie had arranged for the Shettleworths to ship Sophie's clothing to Maine. The few household items of the Steubens' that had not been sold off or repossessed would remain in the Shettleworths' basement until father and daughter were more permanently established. Julie had offered Sophie a job helping out with Virginia and Michael two afternoons a week once the baby was born. And Nico, keeping good on his promise to do something good for the Steubens, had given Dan a hefty gift certificate to Macy's so that he could replenish his wardrobe with all of the basics. If he were to work in Freddie's office, he needed to look the part. Freddie had a strict no-flannel-or-jeans rule. She believed that sloppy clothing fostered sloppy thinking.

"Hey."

Poppy looked up and smiled. "Hey to you, too."

Allie came into the kitchen and perched on a stool at the counter. "Ratatouille," she noted. "One of my favorites."

"Mine, too." Poppy looked more closely at her friend. "You look like you have something on your mind," she said. "You know you have the worst poker face ever."

"I do have something on my mind. I'll be heading back to Boston at the end of the week."

"Pressing business?"

Allie laughed. "Some, but even so, I can't be a house-guest forever!"

"Don't be silly," Poppy scolded. "It's been so good having you here. You were a real help to me, to us all."

"I don't know about that, but I certainly enjoyed the summer."

"So, when will we see you again?"

"I'll be back before long," Allie promised.

"Good. You're welcome to stay here any time, you know that."

"Thanks, but actually, what I meant was that I've decided to buy a small place in Yorktide. Well, maybe a big place. I'll see what strikes my fancy."

Poppy put down the knife she had been using to cut up the vegetables. "Why Yorktide?" she asked. "Not that I won't be thrilled to have you as a neighbor. We all will be. But why leave your life in Boston?"

"I'll keep the house, it's such a gem. I've decided to move some of my belongings up to your old apartment on the third floor and rent out the lower floors. And I'll visit back and forth. You can't keep me away from the museums! Okay, and the stores. But . . ."

"Yes?" Poppy prompted.

"Well," Allie said, "I like it here in Yorktide. I like the peace and the quiet and the beauty. I like that in five minutes I can be picking apples or having a gourmet dinner dock-side. And I also like being close to you and your sisters and Freddie and Sheila and Jon and his family. I like Julie, the little I know of her. And Billy and Sophie and—"

"And Dan?" Poppy asked. "Why, Allie, I do believe you're blushing!"

Allie put her palms against her cheeks. "At my age? Ugh. Anyway, I know it sounds—unexpected—and it is quick, too, but . . . Honestly, I'm not trying to be a selfless savior type. It's just that Dan and I have spent a fair amount of time together in the past few weeks and I really like him. Who knows, maybe my friendship can help make him strong again. I really believe Dan wants to regain his independence and be present for his daughter."

"And for you, as well?" Poppy asked gently.

"I hope for me, too," Allie admitted. "But I'm willing to take a chance. I have no expectations. If he doesn't feel the same way about me in the end . . . Well, at least I'll know my heart isn't dead after all. And that I'll have done a good thing by being a friend in need."

"You're a brave woman, Allie."

Allie laughed. "Brave or crazy, which is pretty much the same thing."

"When it comes to love, I think you're right!"

"So, you're totally committed to setting up the charity? You know it's going to be an awful lot of hard work, not to mention the steep learning curve involved."

"I know, but I'm one hundred percent for the idea. It's odd. Being an advocate for the homeless is the last thing I ever dreamed I'd become, and yet, it feels right. I've been so lucky in my life, Allie, in spite of losing Mom and Dad. It's time I started to give back. And who knows where it will lead me? I feel excited about the future for the first time in my life, not intimidated by it."

"That's the spirit! Now, you've solved the problem of the meaningful career . . ."

"Back to the subject of love?" Poppy couldn't restrain a big smile, nor did she want to. "Well, I don't mean to brag, but I've solved that, too."

"Jon Gascoyne?"

Poppy laughed. "Who else? We're in love and I feel ridiculously happy. You know, I came back to Yorktide after my father died sort of dreading everything. And yet, this summer—this summer with my sisters—has turned out to be the most important few months of my life."

"So far," Allie pointed out.

"Yes," Poppy agreed. "So far!"

Epilogue

***FROM THE JOURNAL OF
FREDDIE ROSS***

I have to admit that back when Annabelle died after her cruel battle with cancer, I had my doubts about the survival of Oliver and the girls. I didn't think for a minute that they would succumb to something as ridiculous as a suicide pact or go completely off the rails and join a cult dedicated to the cultivation of—I don't know, of magic beans that sprouted dollar bills. But I did worry. Not that I let Oliver and the girls know my concern. Only Sheila was privy to my troubled thoughts. It was just that the Higgins family was so tight. So—well, it's not a word I like to use very often, but they were so perfect, or damn near to it.

But in typical Higgins fashion they pulled through. Of course father and daughters grieved. But they went on and you could even say that in some sense they flourished. At least, neither Sheila nor I were able to detect any seriously suspicious or worrisome behaviors. If Oliver curtailed his travels and stuck closer to home, it was, I believe, more about his desire to spend time with his children than the result of a debilitating depression. Poppy took herself back to Boston, did her job, and paid her rent. Daisy and Violet continued with school and favorite activities, if in a somewhat more subdued fashion than usual.

And then, three years on, Oliver died and the world shook again. I was the one to find him, thank God, as it would have been dreadful for one of the girls to come across their father in such a state. Dead. His heart had never been good. Neither had his father's before him. It was only a matter of time and Oliver had known that. His will and wishes had been firmly and legally in place for years. Still, and I would never admit this to Daisy, who in spite of her razor-sharp mind is quite the romantic, but for a while I, too, wondered if Oliver had died of a broken heart. Sentimental nonsense, of course.

Anyway, when the girls were left orphaned, when Poppy was summoned back from Boston to be the de facto head of the Higgins family, I girded my loins (so to speak) and anticipated—what? Chaos? Emotional breakdowns? Bad behaviors? Sheila, who has a lot more faith in the basic strength and goodness of human nature than I do, told me that I was being unfair to the children of my old friend. Have faith, she said. Have hope.

So I did. To the best of my ability. And look what happened. Yes, there was some moaning and groaning. Yes, there was some testiness and even minor, sporadic chaos. And yes, there was the upsetting fact that none of us, not even Sheila, saw just how badly Violet was handling the loss of both parents. But in the end—by which I mean the present time, a full year after Oliver's death—all has come right. Poppy has found her purpose in life, and what a good and meaningful one it is, to be devoted to relieving the plight of homeless families. Equally as important, she's found love with a person of substance who loves her unreservedly. Jon

Gascoyne proposed to Poppy last Christmas (with his grand-mother's engagement ring) and they are set to be married this October, after which Jon will move into the house on Willow Way and I daresay that all will be well. Already Violet has benefited from her monthly visits (supervised by Poppy, still a skeptic) to a certified psychic; she hasn't had an anxiety attack since February and has become friends with a girl her own age, new to Yorktide and a fellow other-world enthusiast. (Interesting note: Violet saw this girl from a distance last summer, when she and Sheila attended one of those ghastly craft fairs. The friendship, Violet says, was in the stars.)

As for Daisy, she seems happier than she has been since before the death of her beloved father. Having Sophie as a friend and classmate is certainly part of it, and let's be frank—once Joel is off to college in the fall, Daisy will need a friend to hand. (By the way, Joel won that prestigious scholarship to study with the pros at the Berklee College of Music. I foresee big things for that young man.) And Sophie has proved a good friend to Daisy. She and her father (and more on him in a moment) are still bunking down with Billy Woolrich but are planning to move into their own rental by summer's end. They see a family counselor once a week (I help with that expense; the way I see it, it's an investment) and in my humble opinion (backed by Sheila's less humble opinion) they are well on the road to healing the damage done to their relationship by that tragic car accident and its dreadful aftermath. In fact, it's fair to say that I feel very proud of all four girls—young women—though I have no right to take pride in them, not being in the least responsible for their remarkable survival of the almost unbearable loss of family and, in Sophie's case, home.

As for the restoration of Dan Steuben's career, well, his suspension from the practice of the law should be reversed later this year if he continues clean and sober, which I have no doubt that he will. It means too much to him—being a father for his only child—to fail again now. He works for me as a clerk and over the months I've been introducing him to my clients in the hopes that before too long I can finally retire (something Sheila has been pestering me to do for years now) and hand over the practice to Dan.

Maybe the most interesting personal development to have come out of this past, turbulent year has been the nascent romance between Dan and Poppy's friend Allie. I must admit that when Allie decided to buy a house in Yorktide last fall I had my suspicions about her motives. Well, actually, it was Sheila who suggested to me the idea that Allie was a wee bit smitten with Sophie's father. It seemed to the both of us the height of foolishness to pin one's hopes on a relationship with someone who had been so badly damaged and who was still in such a precarious emotional and financial state. But we said nothing and watched and hoped and I am now prepared to say that our concerns, while to be expected, seem to have been unnecessary. As I said, the romance is nascent, but it's definitely there and Sophie seems to find in Allie a true friend so . . . Well, who knows? One can only hope.

And get dressed. Poppy is hosting a party at the house on Willow Way this evening to celebrate Dan's forty-fifth birthday. The usual suspects will be present, including, if you can believe it, Nico, and a few other locals with whom Dan and Sophie have become friendly. Sheila says I'm to wear something "special," but I've never been sure what exactly that means, so I'll perform my usual helpless act and in the end she'll pick out my outfit. Works every time.

Set in a picturesque Maine beach town, bestselling author Holly Chamberlin's heartwarming and insightful novel delves into the choices and changes faced by two families over the course of one eventful summer . . .

Everyone in Yorktide, Maine, knows sixteen-year-old Sarah Bauer. She's a good student and a dutiful daughter, as well as a beloved best friend to Cordelia Kane. So it's a surprise to all when sensible Sarah reveals that she is pregnant.

Though shocked, Sarah's family is supportive. But while Sarah reconciles herself to a new and different future, the consequences ripple in all directions. Her father—a proud, old-time Mainer—tries to find more work to defray expenses. Her younger sister grapples with a secret she can't share. Cordelia feels abandoned, and Cordelia's mother faces the repercussions of a long-ago decision. As Sarah's mother, Cindy, frets about how she'll juggle child-care with her job at the local quilting store, she seizes on an idea: to band together and make a baby quilt. Piece by piece, a beautiful design emerges. And as it progresses, reflecting the hopes and cares of the women who create it, each will find strength in the friendship and love that sustains them, in hardship and in joy . . .

Please turn the page for an exciting sneak peek of Holly Chamberlin's newest novel A WEDDING ON THE BEACH coming soon wherever print and e-books are sold!

Chapter One

Bess Culpepper steered her white Subaru wagon past the First Congregational Church at the crossroads of North Street and Log Cabin Road, noting with pleasure the pristine whiteness of the stately old building. Just beyond the church was the serenely charming Arundel Cemetery with its well-tended stone grave markers. Not many moments later Bess turned left onto Main Street, making a right onto Western Avenue at The Village Baptist Church.

She didn't need to drive through Kennebunkport in order to reach her destination but she so loved the quaint town with its charming boutiques, beautiful homes, and the famous though unassuming bridge over the Kennebunk River that she chose to do so, patiently inching her way through the heavy summer traffic. Founded in 1653, Kennebunkport's year-round community was small—only a few thousand people made their homes there through winter—but in summer the population swelled to much larger numbers.

As Bess drove through Dock Square—at an even slower pace; cars vied with heavy foot traffic—she recalled the many delicious dinners she had eaten at Hurricane Restaurant, and the excellent local musicians she had heard there as well. She vowed to stop into Abacus Gallery before long; there was always something special and absolutely essential to be found there. Bess loved to shop.

Once out of the center of town, she made a left and began the final leg of her journey to Elliott Beach along roads that were shady with the dark green leaves of trees and bordered by charming Colonial style homes, their lawns colorful with blooming rhododendrons, their gardens bright with peonies and roses.

Summer had always been Bess's favorite time of the year. Winters in Maine were long and more often than not, brutal. Fall was gorgeous but too short and many years spring came almost too late to be properly appreciated. But summer! Now there was a season to be cherished. The sun in the sky until nearly eight o'clock; temperatures that didn't call for layers of fleece and wool; the sound of local bands playing rock and blues at the restaurants with decks and patios. Summer provided an excuse (as if there needed to be one) to eat ice cream whenever the mood struck and to wear bright and happy colors with pretty names like Mint Froth and Petunia Pink and to visit the beach without the risk of frostbite.

And this summer would be the most special of them all because this summer forty-two-year old Bess would be getting married. Like many women, she had dreamed of her wedding day since she was a little girl, long before she had any conception of the real meaning behind the pomp and ceremony. She had poured over magazines and websites and had spent just as many hours imagining scenarios based on the classic fairytales she had read and the movies she had watched throughout her childhood and adolescence. The magnificent wedding scene in *The Sound of Music*. Audrey

Hepburn wearing Givenchy in *Funny Face*. Queen Victoria marrying her beloved Albert. Sigh.

Of course, the details of a wedding—from the dress to the veil, from the ring to the bouquet—had been easy to conjure, even as she progressed through varying moods and fancies. At twelve Bess had thought Princess Diana's frothy confection by David and Elizabeth Emanuel was the model for the perfect wedding gown. At twenty, she had seriously considered the possibility of getting married at the top of Cadillac Mountain, a location that seemed to call for a lacy, prairie-style dress, like something a bohemian bride might have worn back in the nineteen-sixties. At thirty, a sleek frock like the one by Narciso Rodriguez that Carolyn Bessett had worn on her wedding day had seemed just the thing.

What had been more difficult to imagine through the years was the groom, that necessary figure who would make a wedding possible. But Bess hadn't been worried. Prince Charming would make an appearance at the right time as all romantic heroes did. He might come in an initially off-putting packaging like The Beast or in an all-around glossy form like—well, like Prince Charming—or somewhere in between the two, a Mr. Darcy complete with a bit too much pride or prejudice but an otherwise stellar character and on sound financial footing to boot. (Bess had dated enough deadbeat guys to appreciate the value of financial health.)

But as she approached her fortieth birthday Bess had begun, just a little, to doubt that her very own Knight in Shining Armor would ever show up to walk side by side with her through life. She needn't have worried. Less than a year later, Nathan Creek had spotted her across a crowd of partygoers, introduced himself, and asked if he might take her to dinner one evening. Bess had said yes; six months later Nathan had proposed; in about two weeks' time they would be married.

For the past eleven years, Bess had owned a party and event planning company called Joie de Vivre. The business continued to flourish even in years when the economy was not as robust as anyone would like it to be. People needed to honor loved ones and to acknowledge milestones no matter how much or how little money they had. Bess strove tirelessly to create special occasions tailored for each client; she loved what she did and could think of no career for which she was better suited.

So, when it came time to plan her own wedding, Bess was in the perfect position to make her dream a reality. A wedding on the beach. That was what she wanted and that was what she was going to have. And an essential component of that wedding was a charming vacation house from which Bess could hold court prior to the big day.

Her amazing assistant, Kara, had found just such a place. Driftwood House had cost Bess a fortune as the owners quite wisely preferred to rent for a four-week minimum, Maine's short summer being prime time for discriminating vacationers. But nothing was too good for her wedding or, perhaps even more importantly, for her friends. And not just any friends. The friends she had made in college and had kept and cherished all the years since. Marta Kennedy, long married to Mike MacIntosh, another of the old gang. Chuck Fortunato, now husband to Dean Williams. And Allison and Chris Montague.

There was only one dark spot in the sunny scenario. Two of those dear friends, a couple since freshman year of college, were nearing the finalization of a divorce. Bess and the others were deeply puzzled. No explanation or excuse had been offered. Questions had been deflected or met with silence. Endless hours had been spent guessing at reasons why the seemingly golden marriage of two such perfectly matched people as Allison and Chris was about to be so decidedly broken.

The upsetting fact of the impending divorce hadn't put Bess off from wanting—indeed, from needing—both Allison and Chris at her wedding. Even the fact, recently uncovered by Mike through an unprofessionally chatty colleague in the law, that Chris had been the leader in the divorce proceedings hadn't put Bess off inviting him.

Marta, however, had strongly suggested that before extending Chris an invitation Bess ask Allison how she felt about her soon to be former husband attending the wedding. So, Bess had called Allison one evening and after a few minutes of small talk had broached the delicate subject. "I'm thinking of asking Chris to the wedding," she said. "But I wanted to check with you, first. It's totally fine if you say you'd rather I didn't. The decision is yours."

After a long moment of silence Allison had given her permission if not exactly her blessing. "Of course, you should ask him if that's what you really want. It's your day, Bess. It's all about the bride."

For a split-second Bess had wondered if Allison had meant something snide by that last remark but dismissed her suspicion as ridiculous. Allison was never snide. Still, Bess had gone on to extract a promise from her old friend that she was one hundred percent sure that she was okay with Chris attending the wedding. "It's just that it would be a shame for him not to be there," she said. "Even knowing . . . Even knowing that it was Chris who initiated the divorce."

Allison had laughed then, an unhappy, almost manic laugh. "I suppose I should have known it would come out sooner or later," she said.

But she had offered no further information and ended the call quickly after that. Bess sent the wedding invitations the very next morning. Before a full week had passed Chris had returned the reply card with the *Will Not Attend* box firmly checked off and a brief note scrawled on the back of the card. "I wish you and Nathan the best," it read.

"I'm sure he'd like to come to the wedding," Bess told Marta on the phone that night. "He probably just thinks that it would be awkward seeing Allison. I'll tell him that Allison is fine with his being there. He'll change his mind. You'll see." Marta had not been so sure.

Bess had gone on to pursue Chris with a vengeance, first with texts and emails and when they went unanswered, with a handwritten letter. When after two weeks Bess had received no reply to this missive, she had called his cell phone; the call had gone to voicemail and Bess had left a carefully rehearsed message in a determinedly chipper voice.

Still, Chris did not respond and finally, with both Marta and Nathan urging she back off, Bess agreed to leave the matter alone. But in spite of Marta's telling her that she was being dangerously naïve in thinking that by bringing Allison and Chris under the same roof she would work a miracle of reconciliation—and that was indeed Bess's fond hope—Bess wasn't sure she had done the right thing by ending her campaign to get Chris to join his old friends at her wedding this summer.

Driftwood House! There it was just ahead. Bess turned into the drive and parked outside the three-car garage. The house really was lovely. Built about ten year earlier, the cedar shingles had softened to silver. Gables, a traditional aspect of the Shingle Style home, gave a soaring aspect to the two-story structure. A back porch looked out over a lawn that rolled gently down to a set of wooden stairs that led directly onto Elliot Beach. There could be no more perfect setting for Bess's perfect wedding.

Bess got out of her car and smiled up at the house. It was

certainly large enough to accommodate her friends comfortably. Mike and Marta were due to arrive first, followed by Allison, and then by Chuck, Dean, and baby Thomas. He would be the only child in Driftwood House until the day of the wedding when Bess's nieces and nephews, all seven of them, would make their boisterous appearance. Bess had included Marta's three kids in her invitation to the wedding but Marta had told Bess that she could use a vacation from her brood. It was the first time Bess had heard Marta say such a thing. In fact, imagining Marta without her children gathered around her was almost impossible to do. But everyone needed a bit of a break from responsibility, even a Super Mom like Marta.

The car unloaded, Bess brought her travel bags inside and stowed them in the largest of the three bedrooms on the second floor. Then she returned to the car and began hauling the boxes she had packed at her office into the den, the room she had designated as her command center. A laptop and printer; charges for both of her cell phones; notebooks and pens; a framed photo of Nathan taken on the first long weekend they had spent together. In this pleasant room, the wedding of the year would take its final form.

Bess was no stranger to the fact that an outdoor wedding was a fairly big risk—even in the summer bad weather could be an issue—but she was prepared for all eventualities. Her back-up plans had back-up plans and she had taken out insurance against every imaginable disaster that might disturb the perfection of her big day. She had even hired a children's performer to help keep her sisters' offspring occupied before and after the ceremony. Bored children could mean trouble.

Bess opened one of the boxes she had brought to the den and removed a handcrafted leather folio, a gift from an admiring colleague who would be out of the country at the time of the wedding. Indeed, many of the vendors and clients with whom Bess worked had sent her incredible gifts. The owner of a high-end boutique in Ogunquit had given her a gorgeous John Hardy bracelet. A new corporate client in Portland had sent a large cut crystal dish from Tiffany's. There seemed no end to the arrival of baskets filled with caviar, pates and cheeses, or those crammed with cookies, candies and jams. One vendor who had been working with Bess for years had given her two tickets to the Boston symphony orchestra; Bess had passed them on to Kara, who loved classical music. She had, however, kept the gift certificate for dinner at The White Barn Inn right here in Kennebunkport; Nathan had never been to the venerable Maine institution and was sure to love it. Everyone did.

Bess's phone alerted her to a call from her fiancé. She smiled as she heard Nathan's familiar voice greet her. The proverbial "everyone" said that the initial excitement of a romantic relationship wore off but Bess didn't believe that it had to. Ten, twenty, even thirty years from now she fully expected to find a smile on her face when she heard Nathan's voice on the other end of the line. Romance didn't have to fade and die. It just didn't.

"So, does the house measure up to your impossible standards?" he asked when Bess got through telling him how much she loved him and he had returned the sentiment.

"Pretty much," Bess admitted. "Though I haven't made a full inspection yet."

"You know your friends will love it, flaws and all."

"I know but . . ."

Nathan laughed. "But you won't be happy unless every tiny detail is perfect. Well, just be careful not to lift anything too heavy. I'll be there before you know it."

"And you're Mr. Universe!"

Nathan, while fit, was in fact fifty-three years old. He

laughed. "No, but I do own a monster of a hand-truck and a pretty heavy duty dolly."

"Good. And be sure to bring Bungee cords, too. And a screwdriver. Never go anywhere without a screwdriver. My father told me that once and he was right."

Nathan promised to bring a screwdriver and with another protestation of love he signed off.

Bess sighed in contentment. She felt so very lucky to have finally found The One. Even her family liked Nathan and they had never liked anyone she had dated, not that they had ever said as much. They were far too reticent a bunch to speak freely about tricky things like emotions. Bess had grown up in rural Green Lakes, Maine, as had generations of Culpeppers before her. Introducing the cosmopolitan Nathan to Owen Culpepper, a man who had never traveled further north than the paper mill town of Madawaska on the Canadian border or further south than the amusement park in Old Orchard Beach, and to Emily (nee Wade) Culpepper, a woman who had dropped out of high school in her junior year to help care for an elderly relative, was bound to be tricky. But Nathan had very quickly won over Bess's parents with his sincerity and good humor. Even Bess's sisters and their husbands had given him the thumbs up.

The raucous caws of a seagull caused Bess to frown. She went out to the back porch and eyed with suspicion the giant bird staring at her from the lawn. Hmm. How to keep seagulls from swooping in on the food at the reception? It was a problem she hadn't considered. Maybe she could enlist her brothers-in-law to be on seagull patrol. They could shout and wave their arms when one of the birds came too close for comfort. But that could prove dangerous. What if the bird was made angry by loud noise and vigorous movement?

Still, the image of Gus and Walt shouting and waving

made Bess smile as she turned back into the house. Both were good men though decidedly lacking in anything remotely akin to glamour. Like Bess's sisters, Ann and Mae, neither had gone to college. Neither earned much money in spite of working long and arduous hours. Gus could not afford to replace two front teeth he had lost in a hockey accident back when he was in his early twenties. Walt suffered from a degenerative disc issue that caused almost constant pain. But as far as Bess knew, neither man had ever expressed dissatisfaction with his life; neither man allowed personal hardship to get in the way of his being a dutiful husband and father. And not once had either Ann or Mae complained to their big sister about her husband; both women seemed full of genuine affection for their spouses. But would Bess's sisters ever confide in her about anything vital? That was a question that possibly muddied the waters when looking for a clear vision of Mae and Ann's married lives. Even assuming that neither of Bess's sisters were lying about their happiness, and taking into consideration all of the stellar qualities Bess's brothers-in-law exhibited, Bess still had never been able to identify the passion or romance in her sisters' marriages. Unlike the passion and romance at the heart of what was going to be *her* special marriage.

But Mae and Ann's domestic bliss or lack thereof was of little concern at the moment. No doubt about it, there was a layer of dust on the living room's baseboards. Kara had ensured that the house was stocked with the cleaning supplies; Bess located a duster and briskly went about the task of chasing dust. Not one little thing was allowed to mar what Bess was sure would be the best wedding ever.

Connect with  Us

Visit us online at
KensingtonBooks.com
to read more from your favorite authors, see books
by series, view reading group guides, and more.

 Join us on social media

for sneak peeks, chances to win books and prize packs,
and to share your thoughts with other readers.

facebook.com/kensingtonpublishing
twitter.com/kensingtonbooks

Tell us what you think!

To share your thoughts, submit a review,
or sign up for our eNewsletters, please visit:
KensingtonBooks.com/TellUs.